Praise for
IN EVERY MIRROR
SHE'S BLACK

'A thought-provoking read.'
Prima Magazine

'A rich narrative, weaving together each woman's
perspective to unpack nuances around foreignness and
belonging... Åkerström shows that for all the protagonists'
differences, being a Black woman in a white-dominated society
will inevitably lead them to the same fate.'
Vulture

'An engaging novel that presents the nuanced
experiences of Black women from all walks of life. The
author takes on misogynoir masterfully in this book
that's never quite what you think it is.'
Essence

'A beautiful novel [that] highlights what it's really like to be a
Black woman today... Contemporary and vivid,
this story will captivate and educate.'
Good Morning America

'Åkerström sustains an undercurrent of darkness,
a pulse of anxiety, so you as the reader never quite know
where you will be from page to page.'
Bad Form

IN EVERY
MIRROR
SHE'S
BLACK

LOLÁ ÁKÍNMÁDÉ ÅKERSTRÖM

HEAD
of
ZEUS

An Apollo Book

Please be advised, this novel discusses issues of
sexual assault and suicide. For helpful resources,
please refer to the back matter of the book.

First published in the UK in 2021 by Head of Zeus Ltd
This paperback edition first published in 2022 by Head of Zeus Ltd,
part of Bloomsbury Publishing Plc

975312468

A catalogue record for this book is available from
the British Library.

ISBN (PB): 9781801108607
ISBN (E): 9781801108614

Printed and bound in Great Britain by
CPI Group (UK) Ltd, Croydon CR0 4YY

Head of Zeus Ltd
5–8 Hardwick Street
London EC1R 4RG
WWW.HEADOFZEUS.COM

To anyone who has ever felt unappreciated,
uninvited, or invisible...
Your voice is more powerful than you think.
You are allowed to exist without explanation.
Never let the world convince you that your struggles are invalid.

PART ONE

ONE

America had decimated Kemi's love life.

It had shredded her dignity and tossed its slivers into the air, cackling like a hyena. Relegated to picking up questionable prospects, Kemi was tired of wearing her invisible armor. A two-ton defense system that screamed to the world she didn't need a man.

She couldn't carry that weight anymore.

Lately, her dating life read like a dossier of shame. First, there was that one memorable dinner with Deepak.

"I think I told you I'm a software developer, right?" Deepak began to overdose on his own voice twenty minutes in. Kemi simply glared at him. She figured his name-dropping his career the sixth time wasn't worth a verbal response. The rest of the evening, Deepak intermittently punctuated his monologues with his love for "Black booty."

Then there was the silent date with Earl, a white accountant from Ohio, who summoned visions of a serial killer. Earl kept staring into nothingness past her face. Each time he tried glancing her way, his hawk eyes floated down her cleavage then darted back to the intriguing void beyond her.

She wasn't sure if he was shy or scheming.

And how could she forget the Jamaican real estate agent, Devan, whose gaze kept trailing every white woman who sauntered past their table while professing unflinching love for the sisters?

America had stretched Kemi's limits and run her resolve through an involuntary boot camp. According to every dating survey she had ever read, she—a Black African woman—was the least desirable relationship prospect, alongside Asian men.

Those surveys said first choice was someone else.

This verdict chipped away at Kemi, carving and presenting a weaker version of herself that received every suitor through a skeptical lens of paranoia. Yet, like a glutton for punishment, she kept going back to the app that faithfully failed her with precision.

"Don't worry, my dear." Her mother's drawl would float abruptly into her stream of consciousness whenever she found herself swiping faces left or right on her iPhone.

Then it would taper off into a miniature sermon, followed by a reprimand. "God's time is the best. Go to church! Stop wasting your time! Don't let the devil tempt you unnecessarily, sọ gbọ? Are you listening?"

Her mother's tenderness was always delivered with a healthy backhand of realism. Kemi would automatically nod at each passing statement, knowing full well her mother was on the phone and couldn't see her.

Frankly, she was tired of nodding during family discussions, in executive boardrooms, and on boring dates. She was tired of being the archetypical Strong Black Woman, impervious to vulnerability. Pretending she didn't need a man's touch for years had lost its luster.

She was lonely.

"Seriously? How do you do it, *guurl*?" Connor's Boston Irish accent cut through her concentration like a grating radio frequency. "You are one remarkable woman!"

She didn't look up at him. Whenever Connor launched into faux urban speak, Kemi averted her eyes to spare his dignity. She had been reviewing the latest brand layouts an advertising agency had sent over. With eyebrows furrowed and forehead resting on her fingers, she scanned the copy, cringing at language that showed a single point of view had been responsible for the global campaign meant to cut across diverse views.

She was still mad at Connor for insisting she review it once more, even though she'd been adamant it was a waste of time. He'd simply waved her out of his office, saying if anyone could bake brownies out of shit, it was Kemi.

"What?" Kemi half asked, still reading the crap copy.

"I said," he dragged on, "you are one remarkable woman, Kemi. Congratulations!" He fully stepped into her corner office with its panoramic glass windows that mentally separated her from cubicle life. It physically didn't, but Kemi needed it to.

She wanted him to leave her space. He pressed on. "You won National Marketing Executive of the Year! Again! Congratulations!" A grin spread across his lightly freckled face. He folded his muscular arms across his chest, shirt sleeves rolled up to the elbows.

She responded with a deep breath and then, "Thanks, Connor," tapering off into a smile.

"Well, thank the awards committee! We can't go public yet with the news because it is embargoed until early May, but we should celebrate early. I'll get Rita to fix a cake and some champagne," he added.

"Thanks, but really, I don't want to make a fuss about it. It's a huge honor but—"

He cut her off. "Well, we're gonna make a fuss about it, about you, so on Friday, Rita will get the cake and champagne, okay?"

She smiled again, deeply this time, revealing equally deep dimples. That was when she caught it. Again. The naked look in his eyes. That split-second linger that revealed her boss wanted her.

She turned sharply away from him and back to the copy she was struggling to fix. "Thanks again, Connor," she said, hurrying him along so he would leave. She felt his looming presence before Connor turned to go with pounding feet. Kemi glanced up in time to catch that familiar gait she'd been seeing almost every week for the last four years. The swagger that screamed to everyone it met that he ran the place, even if he didn't actually own the company.

She couldn't stay at Andersen & Associates any longer.

Thoughts of resigning swam in her head daily. They swan-dived in on Mondays whenever Connor rounded the team up for meetings. They did laps on Tuesdays whenever he circled her, walking a tightrope between flirting and bossing. They surfaced for air on Wednesdays whenever he was out of the office on client runs. And they continued with butterfly strokes into the weekend when she tried to bury them.

Though she had finally settled into her executive role and had turned a few key client portfolios from red ink into black, Connor McDonough's look reminded her that she was still a specimen to be sampled and tested. Or rather, tasted. He was already married to his first choice, yet he wanted to try her like cheese on toothpicks handed out to passersby at a farmers market.

He had no intention of making a purchase. He was one of those men who wanted to steal into the fridge at night to binge while everyone was asleep, only to return to their diets—*their wives*—come morning.

Connor had tried to hide his leering over the years unsuccessfully. He classed everything Kemi did as "remarkable" even though she was just doing her job, his mediocre way of worming himself closer to her through empty flattery.

She picked up loose sheets of horrendous copy from her desk and started ripping them, one after the other. Shredding and shredding and letting the pieces float like confetti about her desk and office with a view of Capitol Hill far away, framed by light-pink cherry blossoms.

Like cold water to the face of a drunk, the high-pitched buzz of her desk phone interrupted her paper-ripping parade, followed by the high-pitched voice of her personal assistant, Nicole.

"Ms. Adeyemi?"

"Yes?"

"There's an Ingrid John Hansen on line one from Sweden. Should I put her through?"

She'd never heard the name before, but Kemi was also used to Nicole butchering names. She received the transfer from her assistant.

"Kemi Adeyemi," she introduced herself.

"Kemi, I am Ingrid Johansson from von Lundin Marketing based in Stockholm," came a distinct melodic lilt that seemed on the verge of bursting into show tunes.

Recognition rushed in at the mention of "von Lundin," the international firm currently mired in a global scandal that probably started with lazy, poorly researched copy similar to the one she'd just ripped into confetti.

Ingrid continued before Kemi could respond.

"I am honored to get this opportunity to speak directly to you. I am head of global talent management, and we have just created a brand-new top management position that will report directly to our CEO, Johan von Lundin. Although he prefers to be called *Jonny*," she poured out in a single breath. Rather, "Yonny" in Ingrid's accent. "We have created the position of global diversity and inclusion director, and we think you are perfect for the job."

Kemi let Ingrid's words sink in. She was being headhunted directly by one of the largest marketing agencies in the world.

The words *"How did you find me?"* stumbled out inelegantly. She couldn't take them back. Of course she was easy to find.

"We follow the National Marketing Awards closely, and we know you won Marketing Executive of the Year last year. You have worked with major brands, and we know you have been involved in some of their most diverse campaigns. We need your talent and expertise."

"After the IKON fiasco, right?" Kemi didn't want to bring it up, but she had to. IKON was an international Swedish clothing brand marketed by von Lundin, and one of their advertising campaigns would, no doubt, be used as a case study in future advertising curriculums across universities worldwide as a prime example of what not to do.

It was something along the lines of using "Leave your color at the door, we don't need it" while promoting a series of blouses and dresses fashioned in delicate, bone-white lace. It riled Swedish society, all the way from minorities in its upper echelons to newly arrived immigrants, and had caught the attention of international press quick to jump on the country's integration issues. That copy should never have left von Lundin's pitching stage. Unless that team was indeed lacking in diversity and the reason why Ingrid was currently quiet on the other line. The phone call reeked of damage control.

"Y-Yes," Ingrid continued after a two-second silence. "It was an unfortunate incident, but it also showed us how much we need to diversify our top management. We need strong voices at the table, and we want you, Kemi," she continued. "We need you here in Sweden."

"Thank you for the offer, Ms. Johansson, but my life is here in the States." Kemi looked down at her watch. Ten fifteen on Monday morning and her week was already off to an intriguing start.

"I understand, and I'm sure Andersen is lucky to have such a remarkable talent, but I would love you to please consider a meeting with us."

Remarkable. There was that word again.

"I can't fly to Stockholm."

"Oh, no," Ingrid sang. "Jonny will come to you."

BRITTANY-RAE

Brittany-Rae Johnson was born to first-generation immigrants who fled Jamaica and settled in the muggy warmth of Atlanta, Georgia, for no clear reasons explained to her. While she was growing up as their sole child, reminders of her Jamaican roots were found at

Uncle Dajuan's house three streets away whenever they visited him on weekends for curried goat and her parents switched into patois.

"Jamaica boring!" she'd often hear him joke as they dug into reminders of home off their Sunday plates.

"Boring?" she'd start her futile argument. "People go there for their honeymoon."

"Mi point exactly," he'd reply while cracking into bones. "Dem go for lovey-dovey, make babies, smoke ganja, and come back to dem real life. Boring!" He'd finish off by licking his fingers one by one. One man's paradise...

Her parents had struggled financially up until both their retirements. That wasn't going to be her own destiny, if she could help it.

So, when Samuel Beaufount had floated into her life riding on his wings of fame and wealth, Brittany clung to him like a backhoe digging her out of Patois, goat, and ganja.

She had dreamed of going to fashion school to become a designer, envisioning sketching outlines, poring over fabrics, and launching her own line on catwalks in Paris and London. But Beaufount had derailed her and thrust her down the path of modeling.

Fifteen years ago, his air of self-importance had walked into Brittany's textile design class way before the man himself did. As the legendary designer behind Beaufount—upscale men's brand and go-to choice for metrosexuals who enjoyed pink shirts and turquoise trousers—he was going to be their guest lecturer for the term. This was his way of giving back to the next generation of designers, per the press release put out by his company.

His presence therefore demanded their rapt attention. He stood much taller and broader than they'd all seen on TV. Mindless bantering among the students died down the second Beaufount strolled into their class. He glided in wearing a pink pin-striped shirt encased in a green tartan suit, topped off with a green polka-dotted bow tie, his platinum hairdo slicked off his face.

His brown gaze swept over each student, wordlessly accepting or rejecting them. It landed on Brittany, and he followed its pull, planting himself in front of her desk, the class waiting with bated breath. He peered down at her for seconds, which stretched on for an eternity in Brittany's mind, as he singled her out. Once she'd peeled off her initial feeling of dread, another emotion had bubbled up within Brittany. Beaufount had made her feel like the most exquisite creature he'd ever seen.

"You shouldn't be in here," he finally said with a deep baritone that belied his flamboyant exterior. "You should be modeling."

Barely a week later, Beaufount became her manager. The first time he backed her into a corner had only been two weeks after that initial standoff in her textile class.

Beaufount remained the unrelenting weight bearing down on her slender, five-foot-eleven-inch frame. She still hadn't talked to anyone about it besides a therapist she saw maybe once a month whenever she slunk into self-shaming.

Even her best friend, Tanesha, hadn't been privy to any of it, and Tanesha had been sitting right next to her when she had become Beaufount's pet project.

"Do you want to see something special?" Beaufount had asked Brittany when he'd invited her to his sprawling estate on the outskirts of downtown Atlanta. She had responded with a smile then a nod before setting down her porcelain teacup lined with golden vines on an equally delicate center table.

He led her through an intricate maze of grandiose rooms until he settled in front of gilded double doors. He glanced over his shoulder at Brittany, a coy smile on his lips, before opening both doors at once in a dramatic fashion.

His works in progress. A shrine to designs that were slowly materializing from creative ghosts in his mind to full-bodied apparitions worth thousands of dollars.

The walk-in closet swallowed up an awe-stricken Brittany, and Beaufount quietly shut the doors behind them.

Six months after he became her manager, Brittany dropped out of fashion school. Fifteen years later, thirty-eight-year-old Brittany stood in the galley as a flight attendant, serving water and champagne in small glasses to rich people.

Brittany had witnessed how the affluent floated into her cabins. They had an untouchable aura. She could sniff them out like a bloodhound. They often came dressed in understated ways, wearing very little bling, maybe one piece of jewelry—but worth a year's salary. It was the difference between affording one Michelin-starred course versus buying the whole damn restaurant on a whim.

She'd often wondered how that cloak of impenetrable privilege would feel around her shoulders.

For a few months in her early twenties, she had tasted privilege with Samuel Beaufount, but as seasons changed into decades, Brittany had seen levels well beyond his stature.

The first few passengers in British Airways business class were settling in, shoving hand luggage into overhead bins, and handing suit jackets to her colleagues who were roaming through the cabin ensuring comfort.

Brittany took a quick look in the sliver of a mirror above the parked food carts to check her makeup and push loose strands of her bone-straight weave back before picking up the tray and heading down the aisle. Her cherry-red lips widened into a smile as she started her routine, handing out glasses and asking the passengers if they wanted champagne or water. She never broke stride, moving from one uninterested passenger to the next, occasionally pausing as a hand reached onto her tray.

The cabin was rather empty today. She was manning the last flight to Washington out of London that Thursday evening. Most of the business travelers had caught earlier flights to make it in time for corporate meetings or to close deals over lavish dinners.

"Welcome on board," she said, stopping by seat 6A where a man with blond hair brushed back from his face sat gazing out the window. He was wearing a sky-blue shirt, and his left hand, which tapped restlessly on his knee, bore a titanium watch. "Would you like something to drink? Some wine maybe?" He turned, pinning her with an intense gray-blue glare. She shifted her weight uncomfortably as he kept staring at her.

"Would you like something to drink, sir?" she repeated.

"Yes, yes, of course," he answered, in an accent tinged with something Nordic. He reached for a glass of water, making eye contact over the rim as he downed its contents in one go. She smiled and was about to turn when he reached out again.

"One more...please." He grabbed another glass and repeated the same over-the-rim scrutiny of her, making her uneasy. If that was his way of flirting, she wasn't into it.

"Thank you." He handed both glasses over just as a tall, lean woman with similar blond coloring came rushing up the aisle, panting. She was wearing a masculine-cut shirt buttoned up to her chin.

"*Oj! Förlåt att jag är sen!*" She was breathless, cheeks flushed pink, as she dropped her bag onto the empty seat next to the blond man.

The tall woman seemed frazzled, and Brittany offered to help her settle in—grabbing her bag, pushing it overhead—while feeling the man's eyes all over her. They had to be Scandinavian from the way the woman was fretting, Brittany noted. The flight was still boarding economy class. Technically, the woman wasn't late.

"*Ingen fara, Ingrid.*" The man held up a splayed hand, gently rocking it back and forth, seemingly trying to calm her down.

"Would you like some water, ma'am?"

The woman nodded, and Brittany took her leave to fetch Ingrid's water.

With Ingrid's thirst quenched and the man on his unnecessary fourth glass of water, Brittany decided to switch aisles to do the safety demonstrations and to avoid his intense gaze. Inappropriate businessmen came with the job. But this one disconcerted her, and she could feel his striking looks slowly chip away at her composure.

A few moments later, the plane lifted off into the sky. Once the pilot turned off the seat belt sign, passengers started pulling out laptops across the cabin. A few kicked off their shoes and reclined their seats, ready to sleep away nearly eight hours on expensive tickets. The woman the blond man had called Ingrid was already on her laptop.

Brittany was tired of serving others—a task she had never

wanted to do in a career she had never desired. She was tired of rushing off to fulfill their every whim and desire. Tired of pretending to care when they asked her opinion of which tray of overly processed airline food she would recommend. As if they were dining in a fancy restaurant, not currently sitting in a narrow metal tube over the Atlantic.

Now a seasoned flight attendant, Brittany was jaded enough to know that pursuing a career in fashion this late in life required a miracle. So, she stood patiently as the blond man stole precious minutes deciding over beef or fish.

"Hmmm," he pondered, brows dipping as he studied the menu.

"The braised beef comes with pan-fried root vegetables and broccoli rabe," she said, trying to prod a decision out of him.

"It looks really good," he said, smiling. "But..."

"But?"

"The sea bass looks good too."

He finally decided on the fish, which he ended up barely touching. When Brittany came to pick up his tray, she found his fingers rapping on top of it as if in a trance. Ingrid didn't seem to mind this gesture. His fingers stopped their furious dance as he peered up at Brittany.

She stole back to the privacy of the galley once the cabin lights were dimmed for the evening flight. She pulled off her navy-blue apron, straightened her skirt, and was about to turn around when a full frame swallowed up the tight space between them.

"*Jesus!*" Brittany was startled but quickly composed herself. She hated tight spaces. Especially when blocked by large men. "May I help you with something?"

The man from 6A was a few inches taller than she was, and his pupils widened, adjusting to the low light.

"I never got your name," he said, reaching out for a handshake. She gave him a weak smile and took his hand.

"Brittany."

His gray-blue eyes swiftly scanned her face in response. He then fumbled inside his pants pocket, pulling out a crisp business card on quality stock. "This is my card."

She took it, flipping it around to read. "Von Lundin Marketing... Sounds interesting. What do you do?"

"I sell people stuff they don't need."

She chuckled at his response. He laughed in an unexpectedly boyish way until his mouth morphed back into a serious line.

"I'd like to take you out to dinner." He sounded unsure of his own voice, but he held his intensity.

"Mr. von Lundin."

"Jonny. Please call me Jonny."

"I appreciate the offer, Mr. von Lundin," she started, "but I have a boyfriend."

MUNA

"*Hamama.*" Turtledove.

The word, which Ahmed had said in Arabic, startled Muna. She'd been sitting next to him out on the spacious verandah on small wicker chairs. A meager metal table with peeling white paint creaked between them. Beyond them was a still lake shimmering in the morning light, while leaves on nearby oak trees rustled softly in the wind and birdsong filled the air. Poppies and daisies had started springing up all around Solsidan, the sprawling property that was a former monastery turned asylum holding center, tucked deep within the lush countryside three hours north of Stockholm.

The monks were long gone, and their abandoned monastery had been purchased by a Swedish philanthropist who had chosen to remain anonymous. Within months, the mystery person had refurbished its weathered grounds, which held living quarters and a large cathedral turned into a dining hall, and had opened its doors for refugees and asylum seekers fleeing wars in various countries, including Somalia, Iraq, Libya, and Syria.

"*Hamama*," Ahmed repeated before turning back to look at her with honey-amber eyes sparkling under the morning light.

Muna had woken up early and started her daily task of sweeping around the main welcome building, pushing wind-blown leaves and flower petals into heaps to discard later. Wandering onto the verandah, she'd spotted Ahmed cradling a mug filled with coffee, a crack racing down its side. He'd been staring into nothingness again, and she wondered what ran through his mind. She wondered if he also had dreams of despair like she often had. Most of their fellow refugees here did. She still knew little about him besides the fact that he was a Kurd, and he seemed to have a venomous relationship with a few other men from Syria at their center.

While his mother tongue was Kurdish and hers Somali, Arabic bridged their worlds. She'd been sweeping past him when he gestured wordlessly for her to stop and take a seat.

It had been five minutes since Muna had adjusted her ocher-orange jilbab and settled into a wicker chair next to him. Five minutes of silence.

"I can tell the sounds of so many birds." Ahmed took a sip of cold coffee. "Doves, robins, nightingales, sandpipers, thrush." She quietly watched him take another taste. "I know them all."

"How do you know all these bird sounds?"

"I used to be the most popular gardener—no, landscape artist—in all of Aleppo," he continued. "I was called a magician because I could create garden oases out of desert sand." He was fixated on the lake, watching small ripples across its surface. "Princes flew me on their private jets to create masterpieces," Ahmed said breathlessly. "I knew exactly which flower to plant, which colors to combine, how to create beauty out of ugliness. Eden out of hell. They wanted me. Needed me."

She watched him lift that mug of comfort to his handsome profile the same way she'd observed him do so for the last nine months. She'd watched that face slowly cover up with a dark-brown beard he refused to shave. Watched his eyebrows arch in pain while his honey eyes tried to focus in the distance.

He'd been rejected again. She knew. They all knew. He had been denied residency by Migrationsverket—the Swedish Migration Agency—and was back on his final appeal. He couldn't do it anymore. The emotional drain had begun to take its toll, dragging him further down into a place where he rarely smiled anymore.

And all the girls at the center wanted a glimpse of Ahmed's disarming smile.

She remembered that night when a large bus had brought her, Ahmed, and fifty other refugees from southern Sweden all the way to this sanctuary in the middle of the Swedish woods. Darkness had coated the landscape, and a new type of fear had crept into her. One of isolation in a foreign place.

Her journey had started in Somalia in a company of three. But she'd gotten off the bus at Solsidan alone. Her mother, Caaliyah, and younger brother, Aaden, were buried somewhere deep at the bottom of the Mediterranean Sea. Aaden had toppled off the rubber dinghy first, and she'd seen her mother reach for him before going overboard herself, her blue jilbab floating like a jellyfish until it had slipped from view. The strong arms of a man from Algeria wrapped tightly around Muna's waist had stopped her from resembling a jellyfish too. That day, Muna learned just how loud she could scream.

When she arrived in Sweden weeks later, her voice was still hoarse. She'd stood rooted by the side of the bus, her small sack in hand, wearing the same ocher-orange jilbab she donned today.

Ahmed had turned around and seen her. He noticed her trepidation and reached back to help carry her sack, which weighed nothing. She looked at him and nodded a thank-you. And that was the first time she'd basked in Ahmed's smile.

SOLSIDANS ASYLCENTER: the words on a metal plaque perched by wooden double doors read as they filed into a large hall that night, flanked by two short rows of staff—three on each side.

"*Välkomna till Sverige!*" a thickly bespectacled white man, who introduced himself as Mattias, Solsidan's manager, greeted them, and then followed his Swedish welcome with "*As-salāmu ʿalaykum!*" Mattias looked sturdy and in his fifties.

To Muna, Mattias was suspiciously cheerful for the late hour. The crowd responded weakly. They were hungry and tired. Most hadn't showered in weeks.

Mattias led them next door to a cathedral where fresh sourdough bread and bowls of root vegetable soup were waiting for his new batch of residents. It had been close to eleven p.m. when they'd gathered in that ornate cathedral to sit around oval tables, slurping soup and dipping bread.

She'd quietly sat with a group of Eritrean and Somali women who had been balancing multiple children on knees and hips. A baby started wailing with guttural sounds of discomfort, and she suspected that baby was crying its last tears. It must have journeyed over mountainous terrain, abysses called oceans, and in conditions that would have killed a grown man. She had witnessed babies of similar age cry their last along the way. She recognized that deep wallow of pain no mother's breast milk could soothe. A bastion of despair no doctor could fix. That baby had a few days left on earth, she estimated.

She had noticed the shift as tables started filling up with similar languages and dialects. Arabs, Afghanis, Somalis, and Eritreans congregating and convening, and Ahmed, sitting away at his own table. She had studied the handsome stranger who had helped her with her sack and wondered about his story.

Two years later and their sanctuary had morphed into an unwitting prison with Mattias their judge, warden, banker, and omnipresent guardian. Over the last nine months, Ahmed's disposition had slowly chipped away with a resignation that scared her.

"Look!" Ahmed pointed to a modest garden a mere twenty yards from where he and Muna now sat. "My yellow roses are blooming." Mattias had finally allowed him to start digging his fingers into dirt again. He'd given Ahmed that small patch of land for him to play with. After all, how smart of Ahmed that he was a gardener, Mattias had always said.

"They are beautiful."

"Yes. Like you, Muna."

She lowered her eyes shyly at his compliment. She'd never heard of a Kurd having a relationship with a Somali, so his compliments remained just that—flattery with no prospects of romance. In Muna's world, courtship led to marriage, or it was all performance done in vain.

"What will you do now?" she asked, redirecting his thoughts.

"I don't know, dear Muna, but I am tired."

"Please don't talk like that. *Insha Allah khair.* Have hope."

He let out a grating laugh. "Hope?"

"Yes, Ahmed. Hope."

She couldn't tell him that she had finally been approved. She'd been allowed to stay in this country. But Muna didn't want to leave Solsidan. She didn't know anyone or anywhere else. She couldn't leave her friend behind. But he already knew.

"Congratulations," he said, looking at her smooth face framed oval by her jilbab. "I heard."

"I am sorry."

"Don't be. Allah doesn't will it for me yet. He is trying to teach me something."

"Haven't you learned enough?"

He winced and drank once more from his near-empty mug. She continued studying his profile, the long scar that raced down his left cheek, the new bruise under his left eye he'd gotten from a scuffle with a fellow resident who had spat in his face and blamed him as a proxy for the Kurds trying to carve their own country out of Syria and break it apart.

Like Muna, he had no one here. So they often sat together in silence for long stretches of time. Taking solace in the fact that as long as both of them were there, they weren't fully alone. Two years later, she still knew very little about him.

She watched his lips purse into hard lines, his arms folded across his chest, his look forlorn. And she knew there was no way Mattias or anyone else was going to make Ahmed love this land. He had never wanted to come in the first place.

Ahmed interrupted Muna's thoughts by reaching for her hand, and she recoiled sharply. He knew better than to touch her that way, but the sparkle in his gaze told her all she needed to know.

"I wish I could marry you, Muna."

"I think you like to look for trouble, Ahmed. I can see it in your eyes."

He smiled. "Trouble always seems to find me."

"But not anymore. Look where you are. Look where we are." Muna swept a hand across her chest in unnecessary exaggeration.

Spring had brought the monastery back to life after a long, harsh winter that found them cursing their decision to flee for their lives in the first place. If this had been an exclusive retreat out in the countryside, people would pay big money for this getaway, she speculated. There were narrow hiking paths all around the lake, winding past oak forests and wildflowers. Soon it would be time to pick blueberries like Mattias had shown them last year. Soon they would make blueberry jam and juice out of the tart berries and make lemonade out of life's lemons.

The birds chirped louder as the sun rose higher. It was bright now, and everyone and everything was springing back to life. Muna was sitting with a man who knew each birdsong in their current symphony, and she ached for him to open up to her. To tell her more about why he'd run. To explain the long scar that ran down his face, whether he got his amber glare from his mother or his father, and if they were still alive.

Because she wanted to open up to him as well. To tell him about her brother, Aaden, who had loved football with an obsessive passion, and her mother, Caaliyah, who had gathered them immediately to run for their lives after her father, Mohammed, was killed. She wanted to tell him in painstaking detail how she had lost them all.

But Ahmed didn't want to grow roots, Muna was realizing. Not emotionally. Uprooting one's life was always too hard and like torturously pulling out teeth; she sensed he'd been unwillingly yanked out too many times in life.

So, she remained patient with him.

"At least it is peaceful here. It is only a matter of time before we are free, but it is quiet and lovely living by the lake." Her voice finally failed her because she realized she didn't believe her own words.

She watched his jaw clench. Ahmed turned to her.

"My dear Muna," he started. "I love your spirit. But I would rather go back home and die fighting for something than die here in paradise doing nothing and listening to birdsong."

TWO

"Sweden?" Kehinde repeated over the phone. The cacophony behind her showed it was close to dinnertime, and Kemi's twin sister, Kehinde, was trying to wrangle Kemi's nieces and nephew. She should have known not to call now.

"Yes, Sweden," Kemi continued as she strolled down Pennsylvania Avenue, leaving work late as usual. After Ingrid's call, she'd mulled over the notes she'd scribbled down.

Ms. Johansson and Mr. von Lundin were flying to Washington, DC, to meet with her on Friday over lunch. Later that afternoon, Connor was planning to celebrate her achievements with cake at the office, since she was now the "hottest chick" on the market—his words.

Connor had anticipated competitors trying to poach her, oblivious to the fact that Jonny had already moved in. A&A was plankton compared to von Lundin, a shark.

Kemi felt flattered. If only her dating prospects mirrored her work life. Then she could fully revel in the intoxicating power she currently wielded being chased by two powerful men.

"What about Sweden again?" Kehinde's lack of concentration cut in like bad phone reception before she yelled at someone in the background and dropped something metallic-sounding.

"One of the largest marketing companies in the world wants me to move to Sweden and be their director of global diversity!" Kemi half screamed into the receiver.

"Congratulations! Take it and go. God knows you need to shake up your life in many ways."

"Just like that?"

"Yes, just like that. Look, I'm burning my sauce. Come down to Virginia for the weekend, and we can talk more. The kids are asking about their cool auntie." Kehinde hung up.

Kemi put her phone away and continued trekking down Pennsylvania Avenue on that warm, spring evening, little petals of cherry blossoms floating around. Whenever she was in doubt or paralyzed by indecision, Kemi let her twin sister make decisions for her to help lift the load. Mostly because they seemed to work on a telepathic awareness and instinctively knew what was best for the other. Especially when the other fought against it.

As was customary for all Yoruba twins, they were named Taiwo and Kehinde upon birth. *Taiwo* means "to taste the world first," and *Kehinde* means "to come afterward." But once she was old enough to decide, which meant after her father paid her last college tuition bill, Kemi chose to go with the shortened form of her middle name *Oluwakemi*—"God takes care of me"—mostly as a way of metaphorically cutting the umbilical cord from Kehinde so they could be their own people and not be defined by being identical twins.

Still, their parents and everyone else within their extended family called her Taiwo, her choice be damned.

At eighteen, the twins had moved from Lagos to the U.S. to start college at the University of Richmond. Kehinde had sunk into a parent-pleasing computer science major while Kemi had dallied around studying marketing. With both parents in Nigeria, the twins became even closer, also getting advanced degrees together at Richmond, never daring to separate in America.

Fifteen years after their arrival, Kemi had ventured to DC, while Kehinde was still living in Richmond suburbia.

Kehinde told her to take the job. To "shake up" her life—a loaded statement Kemi knew meant to stop swimming in the cesspool of desperation she was currently in.

"*You deserve an equal in every sense of the word.*" Kehinde's oft-repeated words floated into her mind as a notification pinged on her iPhone. A potential suitor looking for a date.

"*You've worked so hard to reach where you are in your life and your career,*" Kehinde's voice droned on in her head. Kemi put her sister at the back of her mind as she read the notification. A young good-looking African American electrician was interested in her.

"*Look, I know love has nothing to do with your background or career, but seriously, when a director of marketing starts consider-ing dates from janitors, something is wrong.*" An electrician who works out regularly, loves to read, and enjoys Thai food—her favorite.

"*I mean, what would Daddy and Mommy say if you brought home someone unworthy of your stature?*" She flipped through photos of the electrician in different stages of undress, showing off washboard abs that looked painted on.

"*Anyway, I know you are lonely and tired of searching, but God's time is always the best. See how He brought Lanre into my life when I was least expecting a husband, ehn?*" She wondered if she could bounce a quarter off those abs.

And then she clicked "accept" to find out.

A few days later, Kemi stared at the nervous, blond pretty boy in front of her. She had noticed heads turn when Jonny strolled in behind Ingrid, some surely wondering if he was a model, others trying to place which movie they might have seen him in.

Jonny was now twirling his butter knife, rapping manicured fingers on the table, and fidgeting with anything that wasn't screwed into place. Ingrid seemed unfazed by his jitteriness and was leading the entire conversation as they dined on steaks too heavy for lunch. Jonny had insisted on taking them to the most expensive steakhouse in Washington, DC. He apparently wanted to show Kemi he could afford any demands she had.

If Jonny thought his lunch choice would impress her, Kemi decided at that moment he was a rather blunt tool of a man.

"Kemi, we would be honored if you'd seriously consider our proposal." Ingrid beamed.

"I hope my presence here doesn't suggest otherwise," Kemi replied before taking a bite of tender filet mignon that melted when it hit her tongue.

"Of course. We don't doubt that, and we appreciate your making time to meet us this lovely Friday," Ingrid continued, forking a few leaves from her bowl of salad. Kemi became overly self-conscious after a glance around the table revealed she was the only one tucking into her decadent meal.

Jonny buttered and downed two freshly baked brioche buns but hadn't touched his steak. His mind seemed to be roaming and fluttering, filled with thoughts Kemi wasn't sure had to do with their recruitment efforts. To Kemi, his fidgeting seemed to spell out a man uncomfortable in his own skin. Eyes from other diners were still trained on their table, and Kemi wondered if he was tired of strangers' stares coming in from every direction.

Was this how utterly attractive people suffered? Kemi wondered. Locked up in a cage of their own as the world floated around them, parting like the Red Sea as they walked past, gawking at them, seemingly transfixed?

The world wasn't there yet. The world wasn't ready to listen to gorgeous people decry their beauty as a disadvantage. They would get no sympathy from Kemi in that struggle. Instead, Jonny's fidgeting was irritating Kemi to no end.

"How much do you want?" Jonny jumped in again, his eyes settling on her, daring her to deny him one more time. This was the side of him that easily used his privilege to bully, Kemi thought. "Whatever it is, we will double it."

"You're asking me to give up my life here. It's not a decision I can make lightly between mouthfuls of food," Kemi said, "no matter how nice the steak." She held his gaze.

"Of course not," Jonny said. "But I will make that transition easy for you. Besides doubling your current pay, I will take care of everything else. Moving your stuff over, including your car. Getting you signed up for Swedish classes. I will make your move to Stockholm as painless as possible. I guarantee you, Kemi."

She stopped chewing and stared back at him. She could help him the way he needed to be helped. There he was, one of the most powerful men in marketing and advertising, offering his company up on a platter. A tiny part of her reveled in his desperation. All because he knew he had to "diversify" and didn't understand how to take it from a buzzword into tangible actions beyond hiring brown faces. He was ready to throw as much money as he could at the problem he knew he had to fix in order to save his bottom line.

"So, this new position," Kemi started, "is it for show?" The possibility of being added simply to satisfy a diversity quota in a foreign country was more than she could emotionally bear. The last thing she needed was to become a prop in another man's country. Her heart couldn't take any more struggles.

Her direct question caught him off guard.

"For show?" he repeated, eyes narrowing. "Of course not. I would never disrespect you that way. I'm creating this new position of global diversity and inclusion director because we are lacking without it. I see that. We need to be more inclusive."

"What does inclusivity mean to von Lundin Marketing?" Kemi challenged him. "Because buzzwords are thrown around these days with no true intention behind them."

Jonny glared at Kemi while Ingrid stopped picking at leaves to look at Jonny, waiting for his answer.

"Well..." Jonny began, piecing together a rebuttal. "Inclusion means—"

"Let me cut to the chase," she cut him off. "How diverse is your top management?"

That was when she saw his jaw tense, eyes blazing. He didn't like to be interrupted. Her cutting in when he hadn't finished had somehow physically derailed him because he started unfurling his fingers and furling them back into fists, continuing the motion as he stared her down. Kemi furrowed her brows, studying him. There were quirks about Jonny von Lundin she couldn't quite work out. She wasn't sure if he was used to getting his way every single time, if he was born with a nervous twitch, or if it was something else.

Ingrid jumped in to prod their conversation along because Jonny seemed frozen.

"As head of human resources, I assure you this is an issue Jonny and I are actively working on. Starting with hiring you, Kemi."

They—rather, Kemi—finished lunch, and Jonny escorted both women to the door, where the valet pulled his rented sedan over and opened the doors for Ingrid and Kemi.

"Jonny likes to drive himself," Ingrid said, as if reading Kemi's thoughts. "Except in London. He uses a driver there."

Jonny drove her back to Andersen & Associates, where she knew that Connor, Rita, Nicole, and her other colleagues were waiting with cake and champagne. She felt like an adulteress slinking out of her lover's bed and heading home without showering. She knew her skittish disposition was going to give her away.

"It was a pleasure, Ingrid and Jonny," she thanked them before stepping out of the car.

"The pleasure is ours, Kemi," Ingrid said.

"You'll have my decision next week. Safe travels back to Stockholm." With a short wave, she walked back into her building.

"There she is!" Connor's voice met Kemi as she neared her office, two champagne flutes in hand. He strode up and gave her one. She smiled weakly and turned to look at the crowd of about twenty colleagues who had already started cutting into a square-shaped cake, pulling out slices of crimson sponge. Red velvet, her favorite.

Connor followed her gaze to the confection. "You seem like a red velvet kinda *gal* to me, so I had Rita pick one up." His eyes swept back to her and over her chest. Kemi reached up to readjust the neckline of her blouse. He bit his lower lip suggestively.

She accepted a piece of cake and took a sip of champagne, which turned into fire as it hit the back of her throat. Someone started clinking glasses, and soon, it was a cacophony of silverware hitting glass.

"A toast to the amazing Ms. Adeyemi," Nicole, her assistant, started. "I am so honored to call you my boss."

"Hear, hear!" Colleagues lifted half-drunk glasses in salute. Someone else clinked for a toast.

"Kemi, you are such an asset to this company. A&A would be lost without you," Bill, a salesman from Nebraska, said.

"Hear, hear!" More sipping of champagne.

She stiffened when she felt Connor's palm on the small of her back as he slid in close to say a few words.

"You guys already know I think Kemi is a rock star." He grinned boyishly. Light freckles over his nose and his ginger coloring made him seem years younger than his late forties. "Winning National Marketing Executive one year is amazing..."

He turned to look at her, his hazel eyes locking hers in place, naked once more. Heat from Connor's palm resting on the base of her spine shot up her back. The sensation mirrored burning her tongue on hot soup.

"But two years in a row? That is fucking unbelievable, please excuse my French," Connor finished before tapping Kemi's flute with his. With that caress, Connor finally crossed the line and solidified her decision. She was moving to Sweden.

Amid cheers from colleagues celebrating her award, Kemi leaned in close to Connor.

"I need to talk to you," she whispered. He nodded, chugging the last few sips from his glass before leading her toward his office, eyes of curious colleagues trailing them.

"Is everything okay?" His brows creased in concern as he closed the door behind them. She gathered her breath.

Truth be told, she enjoyed her work at A&A. Her career had blossomed as far as Connor would let it. But that was her crux. Connor was her ceiling. He said he trusted her work, yet he overrode her decisions to show his status too many times. It was Connor's way of saying, *Give me what I desire, and I'll give you what you want.* She was never going to be able to dethrone him.

Meanwhile, Jonny was crafting her very own bespoke throne with full control. How could she refuse?

Kemi was ready to leave. She hadn't accepted von Lundin's offer yet, but hanging around Connor for the foreseeable future was a much worse fate. She would take her chances.

Connor inched closer, and she took a step back in response, which stopped him dead in his tracks.

"What's wrong?"

"I'm leaving."

"Wait, what?"

"I'm leaving Andersen."

The news appeared to physically stun him. His eyes widened, his nostrils flared, and his strong freckled arms—always exposed by sleeves rolled to his elbows—flexed.

"Leaving? Why?"

"I got an offer from another company that I'd be a fool to refuse, Connor. It's strictly business."

"Strictly business?"

"Don't take it personally."

"Who is it?"

"It's not important. I had hoped you'd be happy for me."

"So, I never made you happy?"

He was interrogating her like she was dumping him for one of his friends. His concern transformed into a quiet anger simmering beneath the surface.

"Connor, I need this new job."

"Well..." He bit his lower lip. "What can I say except congratulations."

"I didn't want to tell you like this."

"It's okay. We'll figure it out." She didn't believe him, but they had to move on.

"Thanks for understanding."

He chuckled, clearly pained. "It wasn't my choice, but I hope whoever you've chosen over me, over us, is damn well worth it. I hope they groveled on their knees for you because you're worth every penny."

She nodded in response. He walked up to her and gathered her into his strong arms for a hug. She felt his head turn toward her neck and take in a deep breath of her citrus scent, his hands on her back roaming a few inches and stopping before reaching an inappropriate place. She knew he'd never fully cross that line. He'd been tiptoeing along it for the last four years.

"Give us one more month before you leave," he demanded against her neck, his breath hot against her skin.

She forcefully pushed him out of their embrace. She watched him compose himself, a smirk of embarrassment on his face. Then she took a deep, anchoring breath before offering a terse reply, frustrated that he was forcing her to nod in submission one last time.

"I'm sure it can be arranged."

He nodded, acknowledging his consolation prize, before turning to go.

"Connor," she called out. He spun to face her again. "Please don't tell them yet."

He pursed his lips, giving her another quick nod in quiet solidarity before striding out.

BRITTANY-RAE

"Johan von Lundin." Jamal's words drawled over the business card he found on their bedside table. Lifting the card to his nostrils, he took a whiff. "Hmm...smells like White Savior. What is this? Cracker of the week?"

"Stop!" Brittany scolded as she worked to refasten her bra. She was sitting on the edge of the bed, cozy within the town house they shared in Alexandria, Virginia, a ten-minute drive from Washington, DC.

"Here, let me help you." Jamal let the sheets slip off his taut, naked body and inched over to help her. He undid her work instead and pulled her back down for a hungry kiss while she yelped in startled jest.

"I just wanted some more," he purred against her lips, and she deepened the kiss before pulling back again.

"I've got to go, baby," she said, trying to get up again. "I gotta work my next shift."

He wrestled her gently back down for another kiss, begging her to stay. She was always halfway around the world somewhere, and he was left waiting to wrap her in his arms for a few days before she was off again. They'd done this for too many years.

They'd met at a rooftop terrace bar in the Dupont Circle neighborhood of the nation's capital. Jamal had seen the svelte model, wearing a red catsuit, saunter in with a friend. She'd glanced around, looking to settle somewhere until she paused in his direction. He'd lifted his glass in a toast toward her, and she'd returned that gesture with a coy smile, one that suggested she also liked what she'd seen. Jamal navigated through the crowd toward her, but he was pulled here and tugged there by acquaintances along the way. By the time he planted himself squarely in front of her, they burst out laughing in tandem.

"That was quite the obstacle course," Brittany said before clinking her cocktail glass with his. "Well done."

"At least I got here." He laughed.

"Brittany." She extended a neatly manicured hand in greeting, which he eagerly grabbed as if it were a prize for completing the course.

"Jamal," he introduced himself. "Do you come here often?"

"Whenever I'm in town, yes."

"You're not from around here?"

"Not really. I pop in and out of Dulles for work. I'm a flight attendant," she continued. For some odd reason, she felt comfortable enough to tell this stranger her routine.

"I see. Which airline? If I may ask, of course."

She sidestepped his question. She wanted to know more about this tall, dark, and handsome brother who exuded confidence and class.

"My turn," she flirted. "Are you from around here?"

"DC born and bred. I'm an attorney. Business attorney. I chase bad guys in suits."

"How valiant," she teased him. "Do you enjoy your work?"

"Maybe I can tell you if I do over dinner?" he said. She smiled, and they clinked glasses once more.

That had been four years ago, and their relationship had grown stronger with each passing year. Everyone they knew said they made the perfect couple. Good-looking, statuesque beings. The former model and former basketballer.

"How long are we gonna do this?" Jamal broke off to stroke her back, running a finger down its smooth groove, momentarily lost in the task at hand.

"What do you mean?"

"You know what I mean."

"Look, we've got time. I need to figure out my next move," she started.

"Can't we figure it out together?" His caressing hand had stopped moving.

She took a deep breath and bit her lower lip. They'd been existing in this comfortable space for the last twelve months of their relationship. Not moving forward, but not taking any steps backward either. They'd both talked about starting a family, but Brittany's work schedule made it impossible. He often reminded her that she hated her work anyway, but still, that wasn't enough for her to quit. There had to be another reason why she wasn't rushing to leave it behind.

"Babe, you hate your job. You're tired of creeps pestering you all day long. Why don't you just leave?" he said. "You know I'll always take care of you, right?"

"Same way you took care of Denise, right?" she said.

"*Jesus*, Brit. We're four years in, and you still bring her up?"

"Because you lied about her when I met you. And it's been bothering me ever since."

"I've explained and apologized a thousand times that I was afraid of losing you. Denise and I were long over when I met you!"

"You were engaged to her. For three years!"

"And I was the one who broke it off, okay? She was cheating on me!"

Brittany remained silent. This she already knew. Yet, he'd lied with a straight face about just how serious his previous relationship had been. He hadn't wanted to go into much detail besides the fact that his ex had broken his trust. It had been a sore spot he didn't want to talk about back then, so he'd lied.

Brittany detested lying men because Beaufount had lied to her with conviction too.

"If anything, that episode of my life shows I can commit and that I'm a long-haul kinda guy. I'll take care of you if you want to quit your job."

"I know, but I need something of my own too. I can't be some trophy girlfriend with nothing to do. I gotta work."

"Find something on solid ground. Get something in DC. Heck, you could go back to modeling again."

"Seriously?!" Brittany rolled her eyes. He was picking at her old scab.

"Babe, you shut down traffic when you cross the street. You can pick it up again."

"I'm not going back to modeling."

"Why not?"

"Drop it!"

He let out an exaggerated sigh and stared into her cocoa-brown eyes, his arms wrapping tightly around her once more. Brittany knew he loved her deeply. Desperately, even. She wasn't sure she was equally as desperate about him though.

"Look, I don't want to lose you to some rich white boy, okay?"

"But a loaded brother is alright?"

He laughed, and she joined him. He was insecure. Brittany understood. She'd been working both first- and business-class cabins for a while now and had batted off advances of every nature from wealthy men and women.

"Is this what this is all about? That darn card?" She pointed at the business card lying on their bedside table. "Look, baby, I love you. It would take a lot to shake me off you, and money is the least of that. You ain't so bad yourself." She kissed his cheek.

Brittany reached for Jonny's card and made a grand show of ripping it apart in front of Jamal. A difficult task, because his card wasn't made from cheap stock paper, so she crumpled it in her palm instead and threw it across the room.

"See?" She looked to him for validation.

Jamal grabbed the back of her neck and pulled her down for another deep kiss before rolling her onto her back and making love to her once more.

"We meet again." Jonny broke their stare-off as he stepped onto the plane heading to London from DC the next day. She quickly collected herself after faltering upon seeing him.

"Welcome aboard, Mr. von Lundin," she greeted him, pulling out of her momentary daze.

"Jonny," he whispered as he squeezed past. He found his seat and settled in while Brittany calmed her breathing, shocked and disappointed by her own reaction upon seeing him.

Yes, he was an arresting man, but he meant nothing to her. She had waited on equally stunning passengers over the years. She was obviously shocked that he had strolled back onto her flight a few days later. The disappointment she felt in herself, though, was a heady mix of guilt and shame because Jonny was now sparking heat within her. The kind she had reserved for Jamal.

She came around with a tray of welcome drinks, and he flashed her a grin, seemingly in good spirits. He grabbed some orange juice in an unhurried fashion.

"Not as thirsty as the last time?" she joked. "Where is your business partner?"

"She had to get home to her family, so she took an earlier flight."

Jonny himself had spent the day roaming around DC, playing tourist for the umpteenth time, hiding behind his sunglasses, he told Brittany. A pitiful attempt that hadn't deterred fellow tourists from accosting him for photos.

"They keep thinking I'm *that* Swedish actor who became famous playing a vampire." He grinned.

"Yeah, I can see it." Brittany laughed, nodding in agreement. "And you? No family?"

"No one to rush home to right now." His clear gaze held hers, the humor falling off his face.

"You will someday." She smiled at him.

"You seem so sure." Jonny didn't return her smile.

Once airborne, he wasn't as indecisive about his meal choice this time around, and he ate with an appetite that couldn't be sated. Brittany brought him extra pillows, extra drinks, extra snacks, extra attention. The next time she strolled down the aisle, he grabbed her hand lightly. She jerked at first, frightened. His grasp tightened softly, pulling her toward him. She squatted down next to his seat.

"Please have dinner with me in London," he whispered out of earshot of other passengers. She was about to shake her head in refusal when he solicited again.

"I know you have a boyfriend. It's a harmless dinner. I would love to get to know you."

"Mr. von Lundin..." she started.

"Please call me Jonny." He pulled out another card and a pen and scribbled Canary Wharf—Yamamoto 20:00 with his left hand.

"Please," he said one more time before pressing the card into her palm and letting go of her hand. He leaned back into his seat and pulled down his sleeping mask.

Brittany got up and straightened her skirt while slipping his card into her breast pocket. She headed back to the galley feeling flushed and warm. Her stomach churned, throwing off her appetite. She couldn't stop the fire bubbling within her, making her sweat in the cool cabin.

Jonny, on the other hand, slept through breakfast and awoke when she asked him to adjust his seat for landing. At first, he seemed disoriented, his hair wild from sleep. His fingers seemed to switch into some finicky autopilot as he started fidgeting instantaneously. His gaze finally settled on her in recognition, and he relaxed.

"Can I get you something to drink? Unfortunately, it's too late for breakfast, as we've started our descent."

"No worries. Thank you."

"Of course," she said before continuing down the aisle, feeling his eyes on her as she walked away.

MUNA

"Muna! Muna!" Caaliyah's cries cut through a thick, opaque cloud of smoke.

"*Hooyo!*" Muna screamed back, trying to make her way toward her mother's voice like a beacon from a lighthouse.

They collided, and Caaliyah's large arms pulled her tight into her grasp. "Oh, Muna!" was all she managed as her grip around Muna tightened.

Something terrible had happened. Enough to have flattened half of the small stack of apartments they lived in. The room that once held her father had crumbled into rubble, and as they turned to try to make their way toward it, a loud roar filled the air. Half of their apartment block fell down, giving way to four floors of daylight. With eyes widened and cries snuffed out in shock, Caaliyah and Muna stared out into the sky from their wall-less fourth-floor apartment in the only section still standing of the collapsed building.

Muna wasn't sure what possessed her to pull out those photos that afternoon at Solsidan, but the repercussions were immediate. A tear snaked its way down her cheek and landed on her brother's face in the small, matte photo she was holding. She frantically rubbed it away, worried the tear and its salty sting would wash away all she had of her family. Overwhelmed, she put the photo back in its little envelope, browned from use, and stuffed it into a small pouch that held whatever documents were left to prove her existence. She wrapped the pouch in a scarf, placed it in the bottom of her sack, and then locked that sack in a tiny locker at the far side of the room she shared with eleven other women, who were all in the cathedral eating lunch at the moment.

Her chest heaved as she tried suppressing tears. She needed fresh air, and she needed it fast. So she ran and ran, her jilbab billowing in the light spring breeze like the ghost she was, as she made her way toward Solsidan's beautiful lake and the lovely trail that meandered about a mile and a half around it. She pushed past two old, Iraqi men with walking canes taking a leisurely stroll. The men mumbled in high-pitched Arabic in response to her startling them as she breezed past. Muna overtook four Eritrean women dragging toddlers along the path. One toddler, a girl no more than three years old, burst into tears, and her mother lifted her in one fluid motion and settled her on her right hip. Muna ran past a family of ducks, which scattered in every direction, flapping angrily, as she cut through them.

She ran until she found Ahmed under that old oak tree. This was one of many spots where they often sat together in silence, looking out at shimmers dancing off the lake. He sat on the damp ground under the tree, throwing small rocks into the lake, looking tired. He'd skipped lunch again, and with each passing day, his handsome face was chipping away into a gauntness she barely recognized.

Ahmed saw her frantically approach him, and he rushed to his feet, concerned.

"Muna? What is wrong?" He kept his distance but was now squarely on his feet. She continued to hiccup her cries, overwhelmed and afraid that she was going to suffocate. She kept gasping, short of breath, willing her lungs to open up. Her right hand clawed at her neck.

"I can't breathe." She pushed the words out in Arabic.

His brows furrowed in pain as he watched her cry, tears streaming down her face. Her milk-chocolate face, he'd often said fondly.

He took a few steps forward and grabbed her as Muna crumbled toward the damp earth. They stood in that embrace for a few more minutes until she could feel her breath evening out against his chest.

"I miss them too," he finally said in Arabic. Those words were enough to pull her head from his chest. She watched as his face started to contort, making way for tears. "I miss them every day."

Before she could console him too, his mouth found hers in a forceful gesture that jerked her head back. His breath was stale from not having eaten in over a week, but she let him kiss her anyway because she sensed Ahmed loved her, and she loved him, and they were all they had in this seeming paradise of a place, where they were safe from bombings and beheadings.

His beard tickled her face. She was unsure of what she was supposed to do with her mouth because she had never kissed before. He pulled her closer to him, but he seemed tired, with no energy to fumble with her layers of clothing. Instead, he fell to his knees in front of Muna and hugged her legs, staying in that position and crying against her gown. All she could do was run her fingers through his thick, brown hair, which felt like the finest silk. She didn't want to stop touching it.

"How can a man have such baby-soft hair?" Muna's whispered words cut through their moment. It was the most amazing thing she had felt in a long time, she told him. She kept stroking it, feeling its strands glide over her palm and through her fingers.

Muna felt her heart swelling for the broken man on his knees at her feet.

That night, as they all dined in the cathedral on boiled potatoes and baked salmon in desperate need of salt, Ahmed stormed in with a wild look, a full bottle in one hand and a sack in the other. Muna had seen sadness cloud his golden gaze before. She had seen jovial mischief play across those eyes once in a while too. But this expression? She had never seen it before.

Ahmed's presence was enough to silence all the voices in that grand hall as everyone turned to look at him. Most hadn't seen him in days, and some knew he'd been starving himself out. They weren't sure if it was in protest or if he had simply given up. No one was going to notice him. No one cared about him. Muna had witnessed them frequently laugh in his face. "*Who are you starving yourself for, you crazy man?*"

He walked over to where Muna was sitting with two other Somali women and her Eritrean bunkmate, Fatimah, who was cradling her baby boy. Ahmed held his hawklike intensity as he approached Muna in silence. When he got to her, he handed over his worn-out sack, carefully placing it on her lap. Muna observed him quietly. He gave her a weak smile before saying in Arabic, "This was my family. I couldn't save them."

"What's going on, Ahmed?" she asked him as quietly as she could amid all the eyes on them.

Ahmed turned without responding and headed over to a corner of the cathedral where a few Syrian men were gathered. "*The crazy man,*" they cackled upon his approach. As he got closer to their table, they got to their feet defensively. Ahmed assessed each man wordlessly.

Without warning, he jumped onto their table, doused himself with liquid from the bottle, and pulled a cigarette lighter from his pocket. Before the men could register what was happening and reach for him, he set himself ablaze.

The cathedral went up in flames, and people rushed frantically out of harm's way. Everyone was screaming, all except the man with the eagle eyes who stood as quietly as he could while fire opened tracks of raw flesh across his skin and face. He stood silently until the flames engulfed him so completely that he growled in agony.

Muna's face contorted in confusion at what was unfolding. Ahmed? On fire? She sprang to her feet and ran toward the burning pillar while everyone else ran out of the building into the late April evening.

"*No. No. No. No. NOOOO!*" The words roared out of her in rapid succession.

Before Muna could reach him, Ahmed tumbled off the table and onto the polished floor like a charred obelisk.

THREE

Kemi had promised Kehinde she would drive down to Virginia that very weekend. She hopped into her Lexus SUV on Saturday and arrived in Richmond two hours later, just in time for lunch. Her six-year-old twin nieces, Shola and Sade, and their nine-year-old brother, Bolu, came rushing to the door to welcome their cool auntie. As usual, she came bearing gifts. Her brother-in-law, Lanre, bellowed in short fits, which made him even more endearing.

"You're going to spoil these children, *o*," he reprimanded before giving her a hug.

"*Ahn, ahn*, someone has to spoil them, *nau*, and I am their only auntie." She stepped into their five-bedroom villa on the outskirts of Richmond, a symbol of immigrants who had done well for themselves, carving out a satisfying chunk of American Dream pie.

Kemi walked into the waft of *dodo*—plantains—frying on the stove, and the sight of Kehinde sweating over them. Though they were identical twins, Kehinde matched Kemi's curves with a leaner, more angular frame. Unlike Kemi's, her face was dotted with stubborn pimples and weathered by stress.

"Welcome, Auntie-DC-Too-Cool-for-Us," Kehinde belted out while flipping slices of plantain. Kemi hugged her from behind before settling her oversize purse on the kitchen island. Lanre followed her in. The kids had already grabbed their gifts and scattered off in different directions.

"Smells good. Jollof rice, *abi*?" Kemi asked, trying to confirm her wish. Kehinde nodded in response.

"So," Kemi jumped right in. "I'm thinking of taking it."

"Good for you!" Kehinde seemed elated.

"Taking what?" Lanre asked.

"The job in Sweden," Kemi said.

"Sweden, *ke*? What is taking you all the way there?"

"One of the largest marketing firms in the world."

"And how do you feel about it?" Kehinde chimed in, scooping out perfectly fried plantain.

"Nervous. A whole new country with a language I would have to learn. But they want to double my pay and promised me they will take care of everything—moving, car, apartment—everything."

"You see how God works, *ehn*?" Kehinde launched into an impromptu sermon. "He has prepared greener pastures for you."

"Made sweeter by double pay," Lanre cackled, and they all laughed.

As she tucked into Kehinde's always-on-point jollof rice with grilled chicken and *dodo*, her heart started pounding anew. Kemi felt embraced by their comfort. One she knew she could always retreat into whenever self-doubt grabbed her.

It scared Kemi sometimes, this odd shift where she could strut into boardrooms and walk out with million-dollar deals then crumble into herself if a guy she fancied responded lukewarmly. Kemi's confidence was fragile despite appearances. One minute, she could feel like the most powerful woman in the world bringing in important clients to Andersen. The next minute, she could feel like shit when doors were held open for svelte women with bone-straight hair while being slammed in her face.

When it came to one-on-one flirtatious talk free of business speak, she cowered and became increasingly self-conscious, folding into herself like origami. That razor-sharp confidence that always looked great in dresses wrapping her curves became blunt and anemic. This dichotomy living within her—a killer at work, killed by romance—jumbled her emotions daily.

She didn't have a problem *attracting* men. On the contrary, a day couldn't pass by without someone pushing boundaries with her. An inappropriate squeeze here masked as an innocent bump, verbal innuendos there, and the slow walk of eyes from her face down to her ample cleavage and curvy hips before making the same violating trek back up to her plump lips.

She was tired of these visual assaults. She oozed something that attracted men the way a famished person stared down a Crock-Pot of beef stew. Comfort food that made you feel satisfied when home alone, yet one you'd never dish out to impress guests.

Once everyone scattered into different crevices around Kehinde's house to lounge off lunch, Kemi locked herself in her regular guest room. The one with a Midwestern-sourced quilt thrown pretentiously over a rocking chair and floral prints that drowned its occupants in a mad world of peonies. Kemi often wondered what Kehinde was trying to prove, if she was physically wrapping herself in quintessential Americana and hiding away her Ankara prints in order to feel more American.

Kemi reached into her oversize handbag for her laptop, booted it up, and continued her investigation into Jonny von Lundin. The one she'd already started the second she'd gotten off that initial phone call with Ingrid Johansson. She had created a folder on her laptop marked "Sweden," and in went photos and notes and anything else she could dig up about her new boss.

Getting past superficial content on Google had been difficult because the juicier bits of his life were written in Swedish. There were articles in English talking about this jet-setting entrepreneur who bucked tradition with refreshing nonchalance. The person who had eaten bread and butter while Kemi had eaten filet mignon for lunch was a man of few words and had an unnerving intensity about him.

Apparently, he never gave any interviews, but sources described him as both obsessively focused and unflatteringly dismissive. No one could really get a bead on Jonny von Lundin, the man who had inherited an empire but couldn't seem to make it through a simple lunch without getting flustered.

She still wasn't sure what to think, except she remembered him wriggling in his skin, tapping and fidgeting frantically. Gestures Ingrid had seemed accustomed to. Kemi sorted through hundreds of photos online. Standard business shots in crisp suits. A few more casual ones in dress shirts.

Business newspapers and journals covered von Lundin's IKON marketing debacle in painstaking detail. She watched CNN panelists dissect problems at his company. One panelist in particular, an African American female professor from Howard University, had delivered a zinger: "*Imagine you're sitting in a soundproof room with your wife on the other side, making decisions on her behalf. We all know that never ends well.*"

Then there were the assorted lists of most eligible bachelors, which also flashed across her screen multiple times. As Kemi dug deeper, she pulled out roots that shook her. Tabloids made intimations about his range of relationships over the years and suggested underlying fetishes or a teenage rebellion that never loosened its grip on him. Girlfriends from everywhere but Sweden. Red carpet appearances with his "spice of the week," one tabloid described. A possessive arm around an impossibly proportioned waist here. A proud pose next to ridiculously long legs there. A man who clearly rolled in different circles with women spanning different shades of brown.

Kemi had been bowled over at what she'd stumbled across about his love life. What she'd witnessed in her two hours with him and Ingrid and what she'd been reading about him online seemed at odds. The dour-faced, albeit attractive, man who'd sat across from her hadn't seemed capable of this level of "obsession" the press kept speculating about.

Based on his dating track record, Kemi decided she would not excuse him for making such glaring diversity blunders within his company.

Kemi dug deeper, unraveling articles in Swedish, using Google Translate to decipher them. Siblings. Two older sisters. They all shared the same look and coloring. One sister, Svea, was rumored to be having on and off flings with a member of the Swedish monarchy over the last ten years. Both sisters were well plugged into high-profile positions within the von Lundin empire. Jonny ran marketing, Svea ran the family's publishing company, and the eldest, Antonia, ran their charity foundation.

When she'd searched for the job opening at von Lundin Marketing on its career page, nothing had come up. No public announcements for the director of global diversity and inclusion, and she wasn't sure if Sweden ran human resources differently, or if this entrepreneur with his "refreshing nonchalance"—as one article said—had rules regularly waived for his insouciance.

Jonny had promised her full control when it came to diversity and inclusion on all their marketing campaigns and projects. Something she'd never quite had at Andersen. Not with Connor so close and always hovering. Jonny trusted her to bring his company into a space worthy of its global position when it came to voices, views, and vantage points. He'd flown all the way across an ocean to petition her for two hours.

By the time she was done digging into Jonny's past, the sun was well below the horizon.

———————

Kemi rang Ingrid on Wednesday.

"*Det är Ingrid.*"

"Ingrid! It's me, Kemi," Kemi said, her pitch inching one level higher than normal.

"Kemi!" Ingrid surpassed her pitch. "How are you today?"

"A lot on my mind that involves Sweden," Kemi said. "Is this a good time to chat?"

"Yes, of course. I was just reading an article about a fire," Ingrid said.

"Oh no! Hope no one was hurt."

"Well, it says it was at an asylum center and someone died."

"Oh, I'm sorry to hear that."

"Between you and me," Ingrid's voice dipped into an exaggerated whisper, "it's a center that Jonny donates to anonymously, so obviously we're invested in making sure everyone is okay there."

"Really?" Kemi was surprised. She hadn't pegged him as the philanthropic type.

"So?" Ingrid transitioned. "Any good news for us?"

"*Um*, yes, good news for you. Hopefully a beneficial relationship for me too," Kemi added.

After a long pause, Kemi accepted Ingrid's offer, which was received with a squealed "*Yes!*" That squeal fueled Kemi's ego and fed it every good sensation that meant she was sought after and wanted.

Ingrid launched into a breathless series of next steps. She would be sending contracts, relocation packages, global shipping assistance, and steps for expediting Kemi's work visa and residency. Ingrid's exact words were, "*Just send us a copy of your passport, and we'll start the process for you!*"

No one had ever said "just send me your passport." Especially if that passport had been forest-green and bearing Nigeria's golden emblem. It had taken Kemi and Kehinde fifteen years to transition from student visas to work visas to green cards and—finally—naturalization in the U.S.

Her new navy-blue passport, slipped into a metaphoric von Lundin envelope with the outline of Jonny's puckered lips as its seal, was going to ease her transition into Sweden.

Kemi was expected to officially start the first week of August. She'd promised Andersen & Associates the month of May to tie up loose accounts and hand over duties to a temporary replacement. Von Lundin Marketing would fly her business class to Stockholm for a few days at the end of May to meet relevant colleagues and get an abridged tour of her new workplace.

This gave Kemi June and July to move her entire life and start afresh under a glorious Swedish summer. Kemi imagined all she could do in those months to make herself ready for her new life: a diet, new clothes, something that would help tame her curves.

"You were built for cuddling," her friend Ngozi—Zizi—once teased, a joke she later recited whenever Kemi fell into her occasional funks and launched a campaign to lose a few more pounds despite having curves in all the right places.

"Stop it with diets, okay? You think that will change anything?" Ngozi pressed on, puzzling Kemi.

"Is that supposed to make me feel better?"

"Look, you're beautiful. You know this. Don't let doubt crawl into your head. I've seen you at work, I know how you command a room. Heck, that creepy boss of yours wants your ass!" Ngozi continued, trying to lift her friend up from a place she ought not to be wallowing in.

"That's the point, Zizi! I don't want leering. He's not going to go home and leave his wife for me," Kemi burst out in frustration. Zizi stared at her, confused.

"Do you want him to?"

"No! Of course not."

Zizi studied her friend. "Your standards are impossible, Kemi."

Kemi laughed at the irony in her words. Her twin sister felt her standards were bottom-of-the-barrel low.

"No man will save you. For such a smart woman, you're still swimming in fairy tales that make us feminists weep in shame," Zizi continued. "He doesn't exist, and he's not coming to save you from your self-pity. The sooner you realize this, the sooner you'll let a sane man into your life."

Kemi regarded her friend of four years, angry that she always seemed to cut her with truth she wasn't ready for. She had a handful of coddling friends who tap-danced around her feelings, while Zizi used direct words to bitch-slap her back into reality.

They had met when Kemi had just started at A&A. Ngozi was working for one of a few design firms Kemi's company hired for marketing campaigns. Kemi had been enamored by her fellow Nigerian, who had strutted in with an unapologetic, larger-than-life Afro and no makeup. Ngozi had been calm and measured in her responses, pinning each person with an all-encompassing stare that momentarily shut everyone else out of the room as she gave each interrogator her undivided attention.

All Kemi knew was that she wanted to be like Ngozi when she "grew up," even though they were the same age. She immediately scheduled a lunch date with Ngozi after that meeting, and for weeks to follow, they met for lunch every Thursday. Those lunch dates turned into inviting each other out to parties. Those parties became getaways to Paris, Aruba, and Brazil. And those getaways led to Kemi ugly-crying as Ngozi's maid of honor in Jamaica. After her destination wedding, they resumed their Thursday lunch dates.

Zizi was often impatient with Kemi's indecisiveness. "*Do something or go home,*" she'd always breathe down Kemi's neck. She was tired of listening to Kemi complain about Connor. "*Fuck him, or report him—just make a decision!*" Zizi would snap. When Kemi mulled over whether or not to return a guy's call for fear of coming off as desperate, Zizi would snap again, "*Call him, or die single. Your call!*"

For all their closeness, she hadn't initially told Zizi about the von Lundin offer. Mostly because she wanted to come to Zizi ready with her decision. She wanted to show her friend she could be decisive without her prodding—even if she did still need input from Kehinde.

Kemi wasn't sure she wanted to work for Jonny von Lundin. In fact, she suspected she really didn't want to work for him because he had freaked her out with his random fidgeting. Besides, she feared he needed her so he could tick off the diversity checkbox on his top management team.

But Kemi *was* sure she wanted to leave the U.S. because she was tired of being beef stew. Or, according to Zizi, *"built for warming a man's bed and nothing more."*

A few days after accepting Jonny's offer, Kemi finally shared her news with Ngozi, spilling all of the details of her pending move with elation over their Thursday lunch tradition. Zizi quietly observed and listened while rolling a fork through overpriced spaghetti Bolognese at a restaurant lined with men in business suits.

When Kemi stopped to collect her breath, looking for signs of acknowledgment from her confidante, all Zizi did was shrug and say, "I'm happy for you," in a flat voice before lifting a fork heavy with spaghetti to her mouth, avoiding Kemi's eyes.

Serving Kemi that lie sealed this lunch date as their last.

BRITTANY-RAE

Brittany decided not to google him. Not yet. Though temptation dug claws into her, she chose not to dig back. Because googling Jonny meant guilt scraping at her relationship with Jamal.

A war of betrayal had already begun waging within her, tearing at the crusade she had started fifteen years earlier against the likes of Samuel Beaufount. Every pale face since then was his. Black muscle, preferably solid from sport, became her rock and dwelling place. Therapy over the years had held her hand and pulled her off the ledge of blame. None of it had been her fault, her therapist had tried convincing her. Beaufount, who had promised her the world, was the sole owner of his deeds.

Now she was allowing this white stranger to entice her out on her one night off before she had to grab the first shift out of town the next day.

She pulled out her phone. Eight thirteen p.m. Lights sparkled all around Canary Wharf, one of London's newer posh districts filled with skyscrapers, where lavish apartments battled for space with financial powerhouses. It was also her least favorite part of town. Emotionless towers of glass and metal, as she often described it.

She'd been standing at an intersection near the restaurant for the last five minutes, pressed up against a wall, pondering if she should or shouldn't go in as she saw him choose a table by the window. He clasped his hands together, wringing them continuously as if lost in thought. She couldn't make out his attire, but his hair was brushed back off his face. Now he seemed to be blowing into those clasped hands, as if warming himself from an invisible draft. He occasionally craned his neck out the window, clearly looking for her, waiting for her to show up and share his table.

But some force kept her firmly pressed against that wall, and she couldn't get herself to inch closer to Yamamoto, the Japanese restaurant he had chosen, where she was supposed to have met him—she glanced down at her phone again—fifteen minutes ago.

She brushed a nervous palm down her buttercup-colored spring dress and adjusted the light-brown leather jacket she was wearing before turning to the man at the window once more. She stood rooted because she had no excuse to take one more step toward a man guaranteed to upend the consummate life she'd built with Jamal.

Unless Jonny was the excuse she needed.

In spite of her vacillation, she propelled herself toward the restaurant, pulling her bag closer. A valet rushed to open the door for her, and the maître d' led her to Jonny's table.

As they approached, Jonny shot to his feet, fists bunched at his sides.

"Mr. von Lundin, your guest, Ms. Johnson." The maître d' handed her off to Jonny before half twirling and vanishing into the background once more.

Jonny took her in, eyes never leaving her face, never roaming as she stood in front of him. She broke their wordless standoff with a weak "Hello" and realized right then she shouldn't have come.

"I was worried you wouldn't come," he said. "Please join me." She half expected him to run around the table to pull out her chair in a chivalrous fashion, but he didn't. Jonny waited until she'd seated herself before reclaiming his seat. He'd chosen the most visible table in the house, perching them like boutique-store mannequins in the window for all to see. They probably looked the part too: Brittany's statuesque frame balancing his suave look. This time, he dressed in a navy-blue shirt over darker blue jeans and sand-colored suede oxfords, watch on his wrist like a trusty sidekick. The less he wore, the more he reeked of privilege to Brittany. He didn't need to physically scream to the world he was wealthy.

"I probably shouldn't have," she responded, a nervous laugh following.

"I'm glad you did." He smiled awkwardly, revealing small teeth, too many for his mouth. That grin made him a smirking teenager one second, and then he went back into an austere-looking man when he dropped the grin.

"This is where I hide out every time I'm in London," he continued before pulling the drink list closer.

"Behind soulless glass and metal in Canary Wharf?" The words rambled out before she could stop them.

"Yes, my cozy place." He laughed. She relaxed.

They ordered sake while Jonny asked the chef to surprise them on her behalf. He toasted her presence and downed his sake, eyes locking with hers over its rim.

Jonny set his glass down. "You're the most exquisite woman I've ever met," he said, unblinking. She giggled at his proclamation. He didn't share her amusement and simply gawked at her. Was he joking? When he didn't break into a smile, Brittany's chortle died down, and she cleared her throat.

"Thank you."

"I mean it."

She soon realized Jonny was a man she had to pry words out of. Their conversation was a continuous stream of one-liners. He'd been running von Lundin Marketing since his twenties and had grown it from a small studio space with two employees in Stockholm into a multinational firm with offices in Stockholm, London, New York, and Hong Kong.

Yes, he'd been to Jamaica several times. "So relaxing" was all he divulged about his time on the island. He'd passed through her hometown of Atlanta once.

Yes, he was in his thirties. She was three years older.

Yes, he had siblings. *How many?* Two. *Brothers or sisters?* Sisters. *Older or younger?* Older.

By their fourth course, Brittany was exhausted.

"You don't talk much, do you?"

"What do you mean?"

"It seems like you enjoy one-word answers." She grabbed a piece of eel sashimi with her chopsticks.

"I'm answering your questions."

"I'm not interrogating you. And you haven't asked me one thing about myself all night."

"What would you like me to say? I'll say it."

He shifted in his seat, his left fingers starting a small tap dance on the table.

She popped the sashimi into her mouth. That was when she caught him watching her mouth, his slightly open, observing her chew, seemingly in a trance. She stopped chewing, and his eyes darted back to hers.

His rapping fingers curled back into his palm, as if he were begging his fingers to stop moving.

For Brittany, the look on Jonny's face was more ravenous than she had anticipated. One she hadn't expected so early on in their date. Their *date*. Those words turned into poison. She was on a date with a strange man while her boyfriend waited for her across the Atlantic.

She jumped to her feet. Jonny was immediately on his feet too.

"I'm sorry, I shouldn't have come," she said, gathering her bag, getting ready to flee.

"Wait," he pleaded. "Please." She scurried out of the restaurant, not expecting him to give chase, but he was hot on her heels. She barely made it a few steps down the sidewalk when he caught up with her.

"What did I do? What did I say?" He was in her face, asking her breathlessly. The air around him suggested rejection was new territory.

"I have a boyfriend. I don't know what I was thinking." She grasped for some semblance of dignity.

"I'm sorry," Jonny started. "I'm so sorry I upset you."

"You didn't upset me. I wasn't thinking." She pushed loose strands of hair behind her ear. "I wasn't…"

Brittany never finished her sentence because Jonny swiftly pulled her toward him and covered her mouth with his. In an equally fluid motion, she pushed him back and swept a hand across his face in a piercing slap. A slap hard enough to startle and reroute a couple about to walk past them on the sidewalk.

"Don't ever do that again." Her words delivered as a whisper. "Ever."

Jonny's hands remained balled into fists at his sides. She hugged her bag tightly once more. Self-conscious, she peered over her shoulder in time to catch a small group disband. The valet ran off while the maître d'hôtel and a waiter darted back into the restaurant.

She turned back to Jonny.

"Good night."

Before he could answer, she spun around and scurried down toward the Thames River and a footbridge that would take her across to West India Quay, leaving Jonny staring after her.

———————

Brittany arrived back home in Alexandria, Virginia, the following day to an elegant bouquet of yellow tulips and purple lilies that covered her dining table.

"What's the occasion?" She smiled as she walked up to the spread and dipped down for a whiff. She spun toward Jamal, who was leaning against the kitchen's doorframe.

"Baby, these are gorgeous!" She swallowed up the distance between them. "What are we celebrating?"

"You tell me." His terse words halted her advance. Jamal stretched out a hand and gave her a card.

Opening it, the words "Please forgive me. Jonny" flew at her like a verdict.

MUNA

Herregud. My God.

The Swedish officer muttered it under his breath. Taking off his navy-blue cap, he ran large, smooth fingers through his tawny hair. Fingers that suggested desk work. He glanced wordlessly at Mattias, who was standing behind Suleiman, a native-speaking Somali interpreter the officer had brought along. Mattias shrugged. He hadn't been there when Ahmed had turned himself into ash, he reiterated once again to the officer. But many people had seen Ahmed hand something to Muna.

Now Muna wasn't cooperating.

While the Swedes pondered next moves, the interpreter Suleiman studied her, trying to detect evasion.

The officer turned to Suleiman, his face flushed red with frustration. "Ask her if she was fucking him," he demanded in Swedish.

"That is inappropriate. I cannot ask her that type of question." Suleiman turned sharply toward him.

"I don't care. Ask her now," the officer grumbled back. "The man burned himself alive last night."

Muna listened to their conversation. She'd been living in Sweden for two years and took abridged Swedish for Immigrants (SFI) language classes weekly at the asylum center. As the asylees didn't have personal identification numbers yet, lessons were taught by volunteer teachers from the local municipality. They needed those ID numbers to officially register for free language classes subsidized by the government.

The municipality had also volunteered a handful of advisors to help Solsidan's dozens of asylum seekers expedite submitting their applications. Strategic saints, Mattias often joked about them to Muna. The sooner they could get everyone uprooted and out of Solsidan, the quicker the locals would have their lake back. Despite having nothing else to do for two years besides sweeping Solsidan's front verandah and ridding it of dead leaves during autumn, snow during winter, and loose flower petals during spring, Muna's Swedish was competent enough to understand him.

Still, the police officer had insisted on bringing along his interpreter despite Mattias assuring him that Muna spoke Swedish. "*Så hon fattar.*" So she understands, the officer had stressed.

Mattias's office doubled as a makeshift interrogation room. Several police officers were already checking buildings and property grounds. Ahmed's locker had been emptied of its sparse contents. Someone had tipped them off that Ahmed had given Muna a small sack before killing himself.

Now they wanted to know what and why and if Ahmed was just the tip of a radicalized iceberg gliding beneath the surface of Solsidan.

"What did he give her?" the officer asked Suleiman.

Even though she'd known Ahmed since their arrival, they'd become closer over the last nine months when they often sat silently with each other's company as comfort. That sack he'd given her was what she'd waited patiently for him to share. There was no way she was letting this crimson-faced man destroy his memories. Ahmed had placed what was left of his heart in her palms. She hadn't even had time to mourn Ahmed.

Suleiman gave an audible sigh and proceeded to ask her if she had indeed been fucking Ahmed. Muna remained tight-lipped. Suleiman knew their relationship never reached that depth, because she glared unwaveringly at him.

"I need you to respond," Suleiman said in Somali. "Do something. Say something. So they leave you alone." His pitch lowered to a whisper. The officer eyed Suleiman suspiciously. Those were too many words for a direct question.

She peered at him for a few seconds before shaking her head. "*Nej*," she answered in Swedish. *No*.

The officer leaned in closer. "Then what did he give you?" He was getting more impatient, yet not once did he scream at her. They must teach them this self-restraint, Muna thought to herself as memories of Somali police officers surfaced. She remembered hearing them screaming randomly at jaywalkers as they lollygagged around Mogadishu. This Swedish officer didn't need to yell. His clear eyes were screaming loudly at her.

Suleiman translated, and Muna shook her head once more.

"She's obviously lying because we have several witnesses who saw Ahmed walk up to her and hand her a bag or something!" the officer asserted. Mattias—who'd been standing with his arms crossed over his chest, rocking on the back of his heels, and taking in the conversation—decided to step in.

"Who are the witnesses?" Mattias asked.

"Several."

"Well...are they Somali? Arab?"

"Does that matter?" The officer seemed perplexed.

"Yes, it matters. Here, the Arabs don't like the Africans, and the Africans don't like them either," Mattias started. "And the Syrians don't like the Kurds and vice versa." Suleiman glanced at Mattias, a wry look that seemed to question his audacity. Mattias had just summarized complex cultures spanning centuries into a melodic rhyme delivered in Swedish.

"I'm tired of this tribal nonsense," the officer muttered under his breath. "Get to the point."

"What I'm saying is that you may not have credible witnesses," Mattias explained. "Everyone is trying to get everyone else kicked out of the center. I know for a fact that there are a group of Ahmed's own countrymen who would have loved to have seen him kill himself months ago."

The officer flew to his feet, towering to just under the door's top frame. "This is getting us nowhere," he proclaimed before telling Suleiman to warn Muna that if she didn't produce what she was hiding by the end of the day, she would be sent back to Mogadishu on the next flight. He stormed out of the room.

Muna pursed her lips at his empty threat. He knew nothing about asylum and how his own system worked. Suleiman got to his feet to follow his boss out.

"*Macasalaamo,*" he said softly to Muna. *Goodbye.* He lingered on her oval face an extra second before picking up his black folder from the table, nodding at Mattias, and striding out.

Mattias watched him go and then turned back to Muna, who was still sitting and staring at him. He studied the eighteen-year-old quietly.

"Was Ahmed your boyfriend?"

"*Nej!*" Muna screeched in Swedish. She seemed to have caught him off guard, as his shoulders bunched up at her scream, and he adjusted his glasses. "*Nej!* Ahmed is dead! Let him rest in peace!"

"I didn't mean to upset you, but the police want him to rest in peace too. They want us all to live in peace. They want to know if Ahmed had, you know, radical thoughts or leanings."

"Ahmed wasn't a terrorist!"

"I am not saying so. Just that he was on a hunger strike. He stopped shaving for many months and..."

"What are you saying?"

"I don't know, Muna. You knew Ahmed better than anyone here. Does he have other friends we should know about?" Mattias asked. He ran the place, was responsible for divvying up chores among the refugees, and Muna knew he'd seen her and Ahmed frequently spend time together on his verandah. "Ahmed the gardener," Mattias had often called him fondly. Ahmed's roses were now in bloom.

Muna glared at him, biting hard on the inside of her cheek to stop her tears. She would not cry in front of him.

"Please help us help him rest in peace," Mattias continued, walking closer to her. "Muna, be reasonable. If you're lying, you will get into a lot of trouble."

She sprang to her feet in defense of Ahmed. "Leave me alone, and leave Ahmed alone!" she wailed before dashing out of his office, her gown billowing behind her. She ran down the hall and into the open courtyard now sprouting with Ahmed's flowers.

The officers were trickling back from their various tasks around the property, adjusting caps and hopping into white vans etched with fluorescent yellow and blue blocks of color. They would continue another day.

When Muna got to her room, Fatimah from Eritrea was sitting on the bunk bed beneath hers, breastfeeding her baby. Both mother and son turned in Muna's direction when she flung the room door open so widely, it hit the wall. Muna's chest was heaving. Fatimah eyed her as Muna started gathering folds of fabric between her thighs, ready to climb up to her top bunk.

"Muna…" she started, but Muna wasn't having it.

"Did you tell them?" she railed at Fatimah. The baby didn't seem startled and just clamped down harder on his mother's overstretched nipple.

"Why are you screaming?"

"You were sitting next to me."

"Everybody was there. Everyone saw that crazy man give you a bag. Don't accuse me!" She clicked her tongue in annoyance and readjusted the boy as he slurped greedily. Muna's nostrils flared.

"If you told them about Ahmed's bag, may Allah punish you!" Muna spat, not waiting for Fatimah's reaction before climbing up the ladder to her backup safe space.

The tree by the lake where she had often met Ahmed was now off-limits because she'd buried his memories there last night after he'd killed himself, to be retrieved under similar cover of darkness once she left Solsidan for good.

———

Since its opening, Solsidan had received batches of asylum seekers quarterly, holding them while Migrationsverket decided if they could take an inch forward or a triple jump backward. When she'd asked Mattias about their benefactor, he'd told her he was a rich man named Johan von Lundin who preferred to remain anonymous in the media. Mr. von Lundin had visited once in its five years of operation. It was on Solsidan's opening day when he had cut the blue-and-yellow ribbon patterned after Sweden's flag to welcome them. After that glorious day, he had never visited again, though the center did receive its monthly allowance through his assistant.

Now Muna had been granted residency before Ahmed's death and was being relocated from Solsidan to temporary housing in Tensta, a suburb northwest of central Stockholm. The last time she spoke to her Migrationsverket case handler—Mr. Björn, she called him by his first name—he'd delivered the news in person. She was being placed in a three-room apartment with two other Somali women who would be joining her from different centers—one in Dalarna and another south of Stockholm.

She didn't know the ages of the other Somali women, but if Mr. Björn was also finding them a home as Muna's roommates, then maybe they were very young and had come alone too. She held on to that knowledge like a lifeline. It meant she could look forward to isolation loosening its grip soon.

A few weeks prior, when Mr. Björn had granted her asylum, they'd been sitting in a sparse conference room with muffled voices outside its walls as the only noise, joined by the occasional swooshing of paper being flipped as he studied documents in front of him. Muna sat, hands clasped and resting in a makeshift cloth valley between her thighs as she waited for him to speak. Mattias no longer had to be there as her guardian. She was eighteen now.

"Congratulations—you can stay here forever," Mr. Björn said in a tone that had flatlined decades ago. The grandfather figure with thinning hair and a moustache he never bothered to prune hadn't looked up at her when he uttered those words. Muna had remained silent, waiting for his next words, which he delivered at sonar frequency.

He glanced up from his manila folder of papers resting on the small conference room desk. "If you're a bad girl," he said, "we can take it back. *Fattar du?*" He slid Muna's proof of residency certificate toward her. Muna nodded.

"If you're good, you can get citizenship in five years," he said. He then stressed the low probability of her becoming fully Swedish, since she came from a "strong" culture that was hard to shake. He spoke this to her without reservation.

"Good," he said, closing his folder and shuffling to his feet. Tucking the folder under his left armpit, he flicked his right palm upward, summoning her like a magician to stand. He walked her down the gray-washed corridor into an open hall where varying shades of brown bodies, interspersed with the occasional white of Russian and Polish descent, were slid halfway down seats waiting for their numbers to be called.

Mr. Björn had wished her well.

FOUR

The end of May rolled around, and it was soon her last Friday at Andersen. Kemi sat on the edge of their communal table at the office, wrapped in a bubble where the voices of colleagues floated inaudibly around her. Rapturous muffled laughter at a joke offered. Humming and slow-motion bobbing of heads in agreement with a shared anecdote. Everyone coming to the same conclusion: she was going to be terribly missed. "Irreplaceable" was the word her assistant, Nicole, shared. Connor was leaning against a wall across the room, arms folded, observing her with eyes hooded in a sadness she'd never seen in him before.

A month had flown by in a flurry of handovers, wrapping projects, and tying up loose ends. The last of Kemi's boxes had been delivered to her house the evening before, so she came into an office with an empty desk and a workday dedicated to reminiscing and saying goodbyes.

They were all going to miss her, but Connor... He was going to mourn her, this she knew.

He never made it to the fridge in time for his midnight snack. Her leaving was unfinished business for him. His disposition told her this from across the room, and something familiar bubbled up within her along the lines of pity, not the relief she had anticipated.

She made her way through the line waiting for farewell hugs, and in her final act of acquiescence, she headed toward him. When she reached him, his arms fell to his sides in resignation. He didn't touch her.

All Connor could do was let out a small, forlorn sigh and wish her well.

Then he turned and left.

———

Later that evening, she silently watched Andre—the electrician from her dating app—tuck into jasmine rice at one of her favorite restaurants in Arlington just outside Washington, DC. They weren't officially dating, but over the last couple of weeks, they'd been occasionally trying out different Thai restaurants around town. He'd been giving her workout tips on the best way to tone up without losing her curves. She'd been warming his bed in return and had finally bounced a quarter off his washboard abs.

He stopped chewing. "Rough day at work, huh?" Andre asked, reaching for his glass of Singha beer.

"Don't worry about it." She shrugged.

"I wish I could, but I'm not a robot," Andre said.

She was unsure of how to process his words. Was he admitting he'd developed feelings for her?

"I...I don't know what to say."

"You don't have to say anything. Look, I know I can't take care of you the way you deserve, so I'm happy with what you've given me so far."

"Don't talk like that. Of course you take care of me. Life isn't all about money," Kemi retorted. "Besides, electricians make good money."

"You really believe introducing me as an electrician versus an electrical engineer doesn't make a difference to you?" he challenged her with a smirk. She remained silent.

"You're ambitious and driven," he continued. "You're fierce and a freak in those sheets. You deserve more than I can give you."

"What is this, Andre?"

"I care about you. A lot. But I know I could never please you because I've got imaginary shoes to fill. You're always looking over your shoulder like you're gonna miss something or someone better."

Kemi couldn't believe what she was hearing.

"Are you joking?"

"I mean, it's not like we're exclusive or anything. You're not my girlfriend."

Humiliation pulled her eyelids shut like window blinds. Andre was dumping her despite getting sex with no strings attached. Even that wasn't enough to keep him around, and her ego scattered into a million pieces, spilling over their plates of spicy chili basil pork. When she opened her eyes, it was to his face contorted in anticipation of a backlash.

"You're ending this because you care about me," Kemi stated.

"Yes."

Lately, the way people were showing they cared about her was to act like assholes. Zizi with her indifference, Connor with his aloofness, and now Andre with his insecurities. Sweden was the right decision, and she couldn't wait to board her flight on Saturday evening for her whirlwind introduction.

That night, their goodbye sex was demure and comatose. The freak, as Andre often called her, died a quick death.

BRITTANY-RAE

A week after the statement bouquet arrived, another one was delivered. Brittany explained the second bouquet away by telling Jamal that Jonny was obsessed with her.

Then radio silence from Jonny for three weeks until a dozen light-pink roses were delivered to their town home with a note that read, "I'm coming to see you. Jonny." That was Jamal's breaking point.

That evening, Brittany sat on the edge of their bed, next to crumpled pieces of damp tissue. She'd blown her nose, wiped her tears, rinsed, and repeated that action as Jamal started pulling clothes off hangers and shoving them into two large suitcases he'd flung onto the floor.

Every time she tried calling his name, she was silenced with a hand held up to her face. Stop, his hand said. Just stop.

"This is too much," Jamal mumbled to himself as he moved from closet to suitcase and back.

"Jamal," she called out.

"That one business card you just couldn't throw away, huh?" He stopped in front of her.

"I don't know him."

"I googled the bastard." Jamal caught his breath. "He collects Black women like trophies. Did you know that? Huh, Brit?"

"I swear to you," she cried out. "I don't know him like that."

"Then why does he keep sending you goddamn flowers? What the fuck is he apologizing for?"

"For being an asshole!" Brittany wanted to scream, but she couldn't tell Jamal. She had agreed to that dinner. She had been complicit in the derailment of their relationship, and she had no one else to blame. Jamal hadn't deserved any of this.

"I'm so sorry."

"Why him?"

"What?"

"Why him, huh?" Jamal was furious as he stormed around the bed and planted himself in front of her.

"Baby, don't be like that," she cried, but he cut her off.

"Is it because he's white?"

"What?"

"So he can protect you?" he continued. "Can he open doors I can't?"

Jamal's stunning words propelled Brittany onto her feet as she tried to reach for him, but he grabbed her by the wrists to hold her back.

"Brittany," he started, his voice beginning to give way, "I deserve the truth."

"I swear to you. I don't know this man. I don't care about him."

"Why did you keep his card?"

"Because I was curious, baby. That's all."

"Why were you curious?"

Brittany had no words for him, so Jamal let go of her wrists, and fresh tears filled her eyes.

"Please, baby. Let's talk about this. We can get through this."

"We have nothing if I can't trust you," he said before resuming his packing. The shrill buzz of the doorbell interrupted their fight, and Jamal turned to her.

"I swear to you, if that son of a bitch is behind that door, I'm going to kill him," he said with an unnerving calmness.

Brittany took a deep breath. Jonny wouldn't dare. He'd already upended her life from a distance. As Jamal strode toward the front door of their town house, Brittany quickly grabbed a bathrobe, slung it around her purple night slip, and dashed after him.

Jamal peered through the peephole, dropped his head, and stared at the ground for a second or two before glancing back at her.

Brittany knew.

He opened the door to Jonny standing on their steps wearing a white polo shirt over form-fitting jeans, a single sunflower in his left hand. Jamal breathed out through flared nostrils. It must have been a maddening sight. A strange white man standing quietly at their door, staring at him, not blinking.

Jonny's gaze moved over to caress Brittany, who was now standing next to her boyfriend. At this provocation, Jamal stepped forward and headbutted Jonny, sending him flying backward down the stairs and knocking him unconscious the second he hit concrete.

Brittany screamed and rushed down to help him. She checked for a pulse. He was limp, blood gushing from his left nostril and from a gash on his forehead. She pulled his polo shirt up to his face and used the cloth to keep pressure on his nose as Jamal watched.

That his girlfriend would swoop down to this stranger instead of calling the cops about a stalker must have confirmed Jamal's worst fears. She had to have been having an affair with him. Jamal strode back in to finish loading his suitcases, while Brittany was left outside in her bathrobe, hooking her arms under Jonny's armpits and dragging him up the stairs.

By the time she hoisted the unconscious man onto their couch,

Jamal was heading back to the door, two suitcases in hand. His laptop satchel was slung across his chest. He didn't turn around to acknowledge her or say goodbye. He simply left with a hard slam of the door. Brittany continued sobbing as she sat next to the stranger who was unconscious and breathing slowly.

Then she called her best friend, Tanesha, in Atlanta. Tanesha listened quietly as Brittany unloaded everything. The encounter. The date. The flowers. The breakup. The headbutt.

"Listen, boo," Tanesha started. "I better be hearing sirens right now!" Brittany hadn't called the cops, and Jamal's words had come back to her. "*Is it because he's white?*"

Tanesha tried comforting her over the phone. "No, he's the freak. No, you're not racist. No, Jamal doesn't hate you. Sounds like you want Jonny. Wait, where is Jonny from again? No, you're not crazy. Yes, chase his ass out with your... What are you holding again?!"

––––––––––

Brittany had attacked a man once in self-defense. Samuel Beaufount had backed her up into a corner and assaulted her in his massive Atlanta villa.

"I have a gift for you." Beaufount had smiled before motioning for her to follow him toward that grand closet of masterpieces he was still designing. Once inside, he pulled a sheer frock off a hanger and held it up in front of her. "Go on. I want to see how it fits."

She assessed the featherlight outfit bound to cover nothing and shook her head. "Samuel, I can't wear this," she said.

"I'm thinking of branching into women's fashion and want you as my muse." He smiled at her. "I want it draped over that body of yours." His eyes trailed those words over her body. She nodded shyly and pulled her dress over her head, standing in front of him in her bra and panties. When she reached for the gossamer gown in his hands, he charged at her instead, hands circling her neck, his mouth coming down hard on hers as he pushed her onto the floor.

For several minutes, with one hand trying to pry off Beaufount's chokehold, Brittany's other hand flailed in search of a makeshift weapon. His strength consumed her, his girth excruciating, his breath hot on her face as he choked her. Brittany's free hand landed on a metal hanger lying barely within reach. Her fingers worked furiously to grab it, those delicate limbs inching as far as possible. When she finally did, she swiped its sharp hook across his face as hard as she could. He growled, releasing her, and she fled, not daring to look back or bothering to gather her clothes.

In response to the scar that it had left, the legendary designer's team sent out a press release blaming the attack on a crazed fan.

She enrolled in flight attendant training the next week.

That Jonny, in his delusion, could sweep into her life, destroy it, and somehow justify it blew her mind. She'd met him three times, and those encounters had been brief.

She watched Jonny slowly regain consciousness on the sofa she'd hoisted him onto. He tried lifting himself up but then looked down at his bare chest. She had stripped off his bloody top, which was now soaking in her sink.

As he tried sitting up taller, she switched on the table lamp next to her. He turned sharply toward her.

"I'm sorry." He winced as if seized by pain. Something didn't feel right to Brittany, and she knew he probably needed to see a doctor.

"*Sorry?* Why did you come to my house?"

"I needed to see you. I...I can't stop thinking about you."

"Am I supposed to be flattered? You're stalking me! You've been sending unwanted flowers, and then you disrespectfully show up at our house...at my boyfriend's..." Her lips began to quiver. Growling in frustration, she sprang to her feet and stormed up to him.

In the span of a week, Jonny had destroyed everything she'd been building for years. Now, he was staring at her like a confused puppy, wondering what he'd done wrong, as she held a metal clothes hanger inches from his face.

"I'm so sorry." He put his hands up to stop her and winced again. "I swear I didn't mean to make you sad."

"Stop talking!" she cried.

He reached for the arm holding the hanger, slowly running his palm up her elbow. Then his eyes followed his exploring hand as it slid up and down her arm, mesmerized by the repetitive motion.

Brittany was taken aback. Had she attracted a psycho?

She yanked free from his grasp and slapped his face. He received her blow, pupils growing wider in the low light. She tried hitting him again, but he grabbed her wrist and got to his feet, crushing her to his bare chest.

He seemed to be replicating the rhythm of her heaving chest. Breathing at the same tempo, he inadvertently calmed her racing heart, slowing her down until her anger fizzled out. Though he was still holding her wrist, he didn't try to take the hanger away. Instead, he traced his free fingers along the length of her neck, his attention locked on the movement of his fingers.

Brittany looked away, half expecting his lips to cool down the scorching trail his fingers left along her neck. When moisture from his mouth never came, she turned back to find him drinking her in intensely with a look that shook her core. And when his kiss came, it wasn't a maddening possession but rather a slow pressure that plied her mouth open. As he deepened their kiss, he slowly spun them around so she was now positioned in front of the sofa. He released his hold on her forearm and moved both hands up to cup her face, his mouth claiming hers completely.

With the hanger still in hand, she reached behind him to feel his bare back, splaying her fingers over the muscles working as he kissed her with renewed fervor. She could still do it. Drag the hook across his bare skin and send him the message that he couldn't always get his way. But she let him pry it from her fingers.

Her surrender was apparently the shot of adrenaline he needed to fully possess her. She gasped at his revved-up passion, lips parting. He reclaimed them once again. His hands moved down to wrap tightly around Brittany's waist, gently lowering her to sit. Breaking off their kiss, he fell to his knees in front of her.

Jonny never joined her on that couch. Instead, his eyes, dark and brooding, hooked hers as he slowly pried her legs apart before dipping down.

MUNA

When Muna left Solsidan on a minibus with nine other asylum seekers who had been granted residency, there was no fanfare. Those leaving shared goodbye hugs with residents they cared about.

Mattias stood at the entrance as they loaded themselves and their sparse belongings onto the bus, which was arranged for free by the municipality's "strategic saints," as Mattias often joked.

Though she'd arrived with a small, rather lightweight sack, she was now leaving with a modest duffel bag filled with secondhand clothes, a winter coat, a few toiletries, and other bits and pieces she'd squirreled away over the years. Her secondhand smartphone was tucked in a pocket. Ahmed's sack was tied to a belt under her garment.

The crimson-faced officer had stopped harassing her for it. He no longer cared, he'd said. They had more important work to do. It seemed her "boyfriend" had been unpopular, the officer had underscored calmly. His eyes did all the screaming for him, and Muna feared the thoughts that lived comfortably in that man's heart.

"Muna Saheed." Mattias met her with a smile when it was her turn to say goodbye. "Don't forget us when you become *statsminister.*" *Prime minister.* He hugged her, gave her three small pats on the back, and whispered that she would go far.

Because she was *duktig. Smart.*

As the minibus hurtled down Solsidan's driveway before turning onto smoother, backcountry, single-lane roads, Muna didn't turn to look over her shoulder. There was no need to give one last glorious look of gratitude. Or marvel at the sprawling property that had camouflaged her for two years in the middle of nowhere. She didn't want to see the spires of that cathedral turned dining hall for Muslims. She didn't want to see Mattias standing there, looking on and waving to those who'd turned around with frenzied waves for him.

She wasn't ungrateful. She simply couldn't justify looking back longingly at a place that had claimed her heart as penance just for being there. She, Ahmed, and fifty others had raised Sweden's modest population of roughly ten million by fifty-two more bodies—well, fifty-one, since Ahmed was now dead—the night they arrived. She knew deep down, Sweden was never going to forgive her for coming.

At least you're alive, those aging walls seemed to scold her. Through long, deep winters, bouts of isolation, and the type of boredom that bred insanity. *Du borde vara tacksam. You should be grateful.* That was society's mantra for the likes of her. Because only ingrates went up in flames, burning themselves alive.

Three and a half hours later, after meeting mild traffic along the E4 highway, the minibus deposited the group in front of Stockholm's Central Station. Various accented versions of *"Tack!"—Thanks!*— floated from the seats. *"Det var så lite." You're welcome.* The driver's first words since he'd picked them up at Solsidan. He climbed out of the van and opened the double doors of the trunk so they could grab their bags.

Muna could count on one hand how many times she'd been to the photogenic capital. Solsidan was just too far away to casually hitch a ride to Stockholm. Most trips had been for meetings at Migrationsverket with a legal counsel provided by the agency from their local municipality.

Newly minted Swedish residents, fresh from Solsidan's treasury, all strolled into the train station, merging with crowds of people quietly bustling about. They headed underground toward the metro—*tunnelbanan.* They shared hugs once more, promising to keep in touch, before spreading off in varying directions, immediately discarding those promises at the station. With Stockholm's tentacles of trains leading them off, they were heading into new lives buried at different margins.

Muna was now alone. She moved with languid steps, each step

trying to give her hope in a world quickly becoming pointless to her. In his final act of guardianship, Mattias was guiding her again through words scribbled in Swedish on a yellow Post-it note.

Take the blue line toward Hjulsta. Get off at Tensta station and wait outside.

She was to meet a "Gunhild" right outside Tensta metro station, an administrative officer from Spånga-Tensta municipality. She was now going to be Muna's point of contact.

She sat silently on the train as it bobbed and weaved, moving her away from Stockholm's beating heart to its resting toes. Tensta metro flooded her with Technicolor bulbous artwork etched across its stone walls. Stylized leaves and flowers, vivid animals, symbols celebrating unity and diversity. The richness of those colors fascinated her, and she wished she could transport some of that underground vibrancy into life aboveground.

When Muna breached the surface, she didn't have to wait for Gunhild. If there was one thing she'd learned in her few years here, Swedes were married to punctuality.

The minute she walked out those doors, an older woman in her late fifties or early sixties padded toward Muna. She wore her graying blond hair in a bob, sporting oversize glasses with thin rims resting on the tip of her nose. She was lean with no extra fat, a build that suggested long walks every morning—or days spent escorting a steady stream of immigrants to various apartments all over Tensta.

"You must be Muna," Gunhild said in Swedish, her kind, turquoise eyes twinkling, ringed with wrinkles and crow's-feet. "Welcome home! Mattias's description of you was perfect!" She reached out a slender hand, which Muna took gently, lest she crush the woman's fragile fingers.

"I'm Gunhild from the municipality, and I will be showing you your new apartment," she said before turning on her heels. Muna followed. "It's close by, and the other girls, Khadiija and Yasmiin, are already waiting for you. They arrived earlier this week." Muna couldn't keep up with the lady's seasoned steps.

"Mattias mentioned you're *duktig* and your Swedish is good." Muna nodded silently. "You don't have to worry, Muna. I will help you get settled in."

The apartment was four long streets away. It was one of hundreds of evenly sized apartments spread across a cluster of identical four-story buildings reminiscent of honeycombs. Unlike the glistening gold of honey though, these buildings were designed with modest grays and beige brick to blend in with their surroundings.

Gunhild opted to take the stairs up to the fourth floor where Muna's new apartment was wedged into a corner with views of a nearby park and wooded area. Gunhild rapped thrice on the door before digging for her spare keys, Muna's new keys, to unlock it.

"*Hej, tjejer!*" *Hi, girls!* Gunhild called into the room as they both kicked off shoes by the door and pushed them into place with sock-clad feet. Muna and Gunhild rounded the tight entryway into a living space. Two women were seated, one on a smoky-gray canvas sofa and the other on its matching loveseat, fingers scrolling over smartphone screens. A quick scan around the living room revealed sparseness—an empty canvas Muna hoped they could make their own together.

Khadiija and Yasmiin turned to take in their new roommate, smiles spreading across varying shades of brown. Khadiija had impossibly sharp cheekbones and wore a pink hijab, which stopped just over the bust of her long, floral-patterned summer dress with splashes of fuchsia, lime green, and butter yellow. Yasmiin's shoulder-length tresses were uncovered and flowed down in waves, framing an apple-shaped face with chubby cheeks.

Both rose to their feet to pull Muna, the youngest of the lot, into a three-way embrace while Gunhild looked on. "*Soo dhowow.*" *Welcome.*

But they didn't pull apart. Not right away because both Khadiija and Yasmiin felt Muna trembling, shaking in their arms.

Then the sobs came. Violently. Eyes shut tightly, mouth arched in a grimace, heart beating wildly. The way a toddler reacted when something frighteningly unexpected happened.

Silently, they cradled Muna as she hiccupped out the hurt, cried despair away, and slowly let isolation ease its grip on her.

FIVE

KẸMI

"Taiwo? Taiwo? Are you there?" her mother, *Iya ibeji*, crowed over the phone sitting on Kemi's mahogany nightstand.

It was the last Saturday of May, and Kemi was packing for her initial trip to Stockholm to meet her future von Lundin Marketing colleagues and get a glimpse of her new life. Ingrid and Jonny had planned this introduction to Stockholm.

"Taiwo?" No response from Kemi. Her mom still refused to call her Kemi.

"Okay *o*..." she continued. "Maybe there's something wrong with your phone. Call me back *sha*." *Click*. Her mother disconnected the call.

Seven minutes. It had taken *Iya ibeji* seven whole minutes to realize Kemi hadn't been paying attention to words she'd been firing in rapid succession like bullets. The trigger of that barrage was Kemi's mention of her new job offer and impending move to Europe. It had taken Kemi weeks to divulge this information to her mother.

Usually, a pang of guilt ate at Kemi whenever her mother's prepaid minutes dwindled away, making calls from Lagos on one of her three cell phones, each tied to a different telecom provider. *Iya ibeji* needed a backup of the backup in case she ran out of minutes with idle talk.

"Sweden, *ke*?" Her mother had launched into a tirade. Sweden? What was dragging her there? Who was forcing her? She should be careful. They didn't know anyone there o!

Kemi's thirty-four years on earth weren't enough to warrant common sense. There had to be a sinister force beyond Kemi's control that *Iya ibeji* was certain was luring her daughter to that cold place Africans weren't supposed to willingly venture to.

"Isn't it minus thirty degrees in that place? *God o!*" her mother's voice had half cried into the citrus-scented air of Kemi's spacious bedroom as she continued packing a small Samsonite hard case.

She made the trek from her walk-in closet to the navy-blue suitcase splayed open on her bed multiple times. Reducing her choices down to six statement pieces had been challenging. Two V-neck blouses that flattered her bust. Two wrap dresses that followed her curves. A pair of tailored black trousers that complemented her rear. Her prized indigo-blue Prada spring jacket. A striped navy-blue-and-white nautical blazer. Items that she hoped would communicate confidence with a sprinkle of cachet. She packed them with unease because "skintight" and "elegance" always seemed to be at odds. She carried the same struggle inside. Was she ever going to be enough without accentuating herself?

The possibility of potential suitors crossed her mind too, so she raced over to her antique chest and pulled open a drawer of lingerie, fishing out favorites. After all, she could switch country of choice to "Sweden" in her dating app once on the ground.

As she stuffed black lace underwear into the bulging case, her phone rang once more, shimmying across the nightstand. She didn't bother. She knew a quick glance was going to reveal "Mommy." It shrilled defiantly as she pressed her case shut. The phone rang until it lost its voice. Silence filled her room once more.

She moved her suitcase, along with her oversize handbag, to the living room of her Penn Quarter condominium. Indecision had made her crappy at packing, and now she had to check in a suitcase as opposed to her initial plans for carry-on only.

Indecision had also choked her right before she made the wallet-denting condominium purchase two years prior. Kehinde had exhaled sharply at the price before finishing off with: "If God wants you to have it, then it's yours." Her mother had danced and sung at the news on the other end of the receiver. *Praising the Looooord always...* Kemi was certain her mother had mentally omitted a zero from the price, hence her jubilation.

Zizi had egged her on. "Buy a place worthy of your career," she had said during one of their lunches. "You deserve it. Or are you waiting for some sugar daddy to come buy it for you?"

Zizi.

Kemi was surprised by how quickly thoughts of her friend had drifted out of her daily existence since their wordless fight. That emotional space for a sounding board was now slowly being filled by a deep conviction and nagging belief that Zizi had always been jealous of her. After all, they did work in the same industry and Kemi had won National Marketing Executive two years in a row.

She rewound several heart-to-hearts they'd had over the years. Zizi's impatience with her each time she'd needed help in making a crucial decision. Zizi rallying around her, flying in on the wings of body positivity and twirling back out, sprinkling shade like confetti upon her exit.

Kemi saw it now. Zizi was never going to be happy about this big move. It meant a role reversal for Zizi. That Kemi had decided to break free, expand her options beyond the States, and had chosen not to settle quite yet. After all, she always imagined Zizi to be the free bird that had clipped its wings too quickly with marriage.

Her phone convulsed once again, and she contemplated silencing it until she remembered she was waiting for her taxi to Dulles Airport.

Sure enough, the driver's voice, tinged with a West African accent, greeted her. "I'm downstairs," he casually informed her before cutting the call, as if he paid for phone usage by the second. After a quick check around the condo to make sure anything that could potentially explode in her absence was switched off, she locked up and took the elevator twelve floors down to F Street where the unmarked black Chrysler sedan was waiting. Upon giving her a short wave, the driver pushed himself out and regarded her with a wide smile.

"Good afternoon, madam." He reached for her bag, making a grand show of courtesy, leering suggestively with a toothy smile never leaving his face.

"Where are you going?" His first question came before they'd even left her block in the district. She pretended not to hear him and busied herself with her phone. He wasn't easily deterred.

"Hello? Hello o?"

"Yes?" she answered curtly. He smiled at her through the rearview mirror.

"Where are you going?"

"To the airport." He burst out laughing, a booming bellow that vibrated throughout the car. One she suspected many women had heard in the back of his taxi.

"You're a funny woman," he said. "I know you're going to the airport. I am the one taking you there." He looked back at her again. She gave him a half smile and bowed back to face her phone.

"Are you going abroad? It says Scandinavian Airlines on your reservation."

"Yes, I am."

"Are you going to Switzerland?" He studied her through his mirror. She hoped he didn't plan on killing her with mindless conversation, because he was distracted from the road.

"No. Sweden."

An unexpected silence hung between them, one she quickly wrapped herself in. They were barely five minutes into her ride when he promptly broke it.

"Are you married?"

She cut him a stern look.

"I'm just joking. Me, I'm happily married with four small children," he continued. "I was wondering if you're meeting your husband in Sweden."

"Thank you for your concern."

He cackled once more. "My name is Kweku."

"Nice to meet you, Mr. Kweku."

"Please call me Kweku. What is your name?"

"You already know."

He guffawed. Kemi wasn't sure if Kweku was laughing at her uptightness or chuckling to mask his own embarrassment. He continued laughing, scanning traffic as he merged onto the expressway.

"I know your kind."

"Excuse me?"

His shining eyes laughed at her through his mirror again. He certainly had her attention now.

"I know your kind. You and your white boyfriends. Always acting jumpy when your brother tries to talk to you."

Kemi didn't know how to parse through the layers of his insult. Besides the fact that her last few dates had all been "brothers" and her Thai-eating, gym-hitting, friends-with-benefits electrician Andre was also African American, she was incensed.

"You're dangerously crossing the line, Mr. Kweku," she threatened.

"I'm not trying to offend you, madam."

"You've done a fantastic job so far!"

He cackled once more, but this time, it was a weaker, less confident gargle. Like he'd realized that he had indeed crossed a line and tossed his tip away. His apology was silence the rest of the way to the airport.

When he deposited her on the sidewalk at Terminal 1 to catch the first leg of her trip via Copenhagen, his face had assumed a resting flatness in anticipation of no gratuity. He got out, pulled her case from his trunk, and mumbled something along the lines of *thank you* and *goodbye*.

She kept his tip.

———

After her dinner of Arctic char and dill potatoes, Mr. Kweku cackled his way back into her mind. Good riddance, she thought as the cabin lights were dimmed for the night flight.

I know your kind.

His words dug into her. They felt unfair. Unnecessary. Uncalled for. She had tried. Had opened her arms wide, seeking love and companionship where she could. Yet, Kweku had sniffed the air around her and assumed she was prejudiced. She had really liked Andre, but he dumped her before they were officially dating. It didn't matter now anyway. She was leaving town.

She thought of Connor. If she were being completely honest with herself, she had basked in his attention despite his occasional cringe-worthy gestures and that nasal Boston-Irish lick. Otherwise, she wouldn't have hurt so badly when he gave her a terse goodbye without so much as a hug after all their professional years together. They had been a great team at A&A. They had worked on many successful projects together. Instead, Connor had decided to end it selfishly by cowering in the face of his desire.

By the time she arrived in Copenhagen, she had breezed through three movies with no sleep and was still wide awake.

Late Sunday morning, her connecting flight landed smoothly in Stockholm to glorious spring weather. The descent into the city of islands had given her an impressive view of its landscape. The people milling around baggage claim were a lot more subdued than those at Dulles. Besides the clanking of heels and jiggling of luggage carts, the air was devoid of loud, boisterous chatter.

As she waited for her Samsonite case to roll out, she felt a presence position itself next to her, and she glanced toward it. Her eyes met a shoulder clad in a baby-blue dress shirt before working their way up to its wearer. Lush waves of brown hair settled around his neck. The same coloring matched a neatly trimmed, full beard. The white man easily cleared six feet, and when he sensed he was being observed, he flashed her an icy glare. She quickly averted her gaze in response.

When her bag rolled out, she struggled to pull it off the belt. In an exhibition of the antithesis of chivalry, the man hopped out of the way to give Kemi better access to her bag as she traveled with it down the belt. She pulled it off on his other side. She hadn't been anticipating that chill.

Ingrid had arranged transportation for her with a few recommendations on where to have brunch, lunch, and dinner within walking distance of her waterfront hotel on Blasieholmen. She would have joined her, Ingrid quipped, but it was Sunday—she had to be with her family and prepare her two young kids for *dagis* on Monday. *Daycare*.

They planned to meet each other at the offices of von Lundin Marketing Birger Jarlsgatan early the next day.

MS. ADEYEMI, the digital tablet read in block letters as double doors parted, and she was thrust into a low-key arrival hall of waiting families, friends, and chauffeurs. The driver, a middle-aged white man with thinning curls and glasses on his nose, waited until she walked up to him.

"I'm Ms. Adeyemi," Kemi said. He smiled at her, introduced himself as Kalle, shook her hand, and grabbed her suitcase, which he wheeled quietly into his taxi. The next words Kalle spoke to her were forty minutes later when he dropped her off in front of the avant-garde, cream-colored Lydmar Hotel with waterfront views of the Royal Palace.

This time around, Mr. Kweku's intrusion would have been appreciated in lieu of Mr. Kalle's silence. She didn't realize how comfortable she'd become with superficial chauffeur banter asking her who she was, where she was going, and welcoming her to town.

Her mind raced back to the rude man at baggage claim and Mr. Kalle's detachment, and she began slinking back into that dark space paranoia had carved out within her.

BRITTANY-RAE

Brittany awoke at four thirteen a.m. to muffled sounds coming from the guest toilet. She'd woken up on her couch in her purple silk night slip, her bathrobe heaped onto the hardwood floor next to the sofa. The single light source was a sliver coming from the partially cracked door to the toilet. She slowly got to her feet.

The muffling continued as she tiptoed closer. Through the gap, she could see a topless Jonny on his knees, wiping tiles aggressively with one hand while holding a phone to his ear with the other. His Swedish sounded berserk. Frantic. When she pushed open the door to inspect closer, he sprang to his feet with wild eyes. A blue-black bruise had spread across the bridge of his nose, and the small cut above his left eyebrow had started bleeding again, flowing down in a thin red line.

He'd found his blood-drenched white polo shirt soaking in the sink. From his fingers dyed crimson to drops of light red trailing down the sink and covering her tiles, she was staring at a man who couldn't even wring out his own laundry based on the mess he seemed to be making.

Jonny stopped yammering in Swedish and froze, staring at her. "*Hallå? Hallå?*" a female voice screeched on the other end. He disconnected the call with a quick tap.

Their mute stare-off stretched on until Jonny broke it with a step forward, and Brittany reciprocated with a step backward. He inched forward again, and she took another step backward.

"Please, I need your help," Jonny pleaded, continuing his advance. "I don't feel well in my head."

She stared at him as he stumbled out of the bathroom on unsteady feet. Without warning, Jonny fell to his knees, his phone flying out of his grasp. He gripped his head tightly and winced in agony. Like he was being assaulted by a frequency he alone could hear.

When she bent closer to examine his head, she smelled herself on his breath and bolted to her feet. "I-I-I'll take you to a clinic."

Fifteen minutes later, they were sitting at the twenty-four-hour urgent care clinic a few blocks from her town house in Alexandria. Jonny had reluctantly donned one of Jamal's T-shirts while Brittany had tidied herself up, replacing the slip with jeans and a long-sleeve cotton shirt.

She sat across from Jonny on a blue plastic chair. The waiting room was sparse at this hour—an older man was in a corner sitting with a younger man who appeared to be his son. The night nurse, a Black lady well into her fifties, was escorting a geriatric woman with a walker out of the doctor's office. She seated the woman in the waiting room and repeated several times that a taxi was on its way to take her home.

Then she turned toward them—Brittany sitting with arms crossed, and Jonny with a forlorn look on his face that screamed domestic dispute. With pursed lips, the nurse waved them up to the reception desk. Brittany didn't get to her feet. There was only so much humiliation she could take. Jonny would have to explain his way out of this one by himself.

With fingers rapping maniacally on the countertop, he impatiently answered the nurse's questions.

No, he didn't have insurance. Yes, he was European. Yes, he didn't mind paying everything up front. No, he hadn't been mugged.

Yes, he'd been in a fender bender...

Brittany saw Jonny's eyes dart left and right at the lie. He couldn't hold the nurse's gaze anymore. The nurse could probably deduce he was falsifying details. But she let him carry on.

No, the other driver sped off. Yes, it was a rental car.

No, he wasn't on any drugs. He hadn't been drinking either.

"Looks like you got banged up pretty good," the nurse said, her focus on the screen as her fingers typed at freakish speed. His own fingers continued their tap dance. Loud enough to draw an irritated glance from the nurse once again.

MUNA

"Muna... Muna..." A voice softly tried to wake her. Muna responded with a purr and a feline stretch, slowly fluttering her eyelids open. Khadiija's face peered down at her on the couch.

Muna eased into a sitting position. Darkness streamed in through open blinds on curtainless windows. She felt a cool draft around her face and noticed the top half of her jilbab was missing, leaving her abaya beneath. Her lean fingers rushed into her hair, feeling freedom around two foam-soft, woven cornrows, and she glanced at Khadiija. The one with the high cheekbones.

"How long have I..." she started in Swedish then switched to Somali. "How long have I been sleeping?"

"It's past midnight. Yasmiin is already asleep. I wanted to move you to your room." Khadiija fought a yawn before shuffling to her feet and handing Muna a familiar ocher-orange ball of cloth. She pointed in the direction of their shared bathroom. "Shower and toilet." Then she twirled a one-eighty and pointed. "Your room. See you in the morning. *Habeen wanaagsan.*" Good night.

Collecting herself after a few seconds, Muna got to her feet and immediately closed the blinds. They couldn't be careless with such things. Her duffel bag was still sitting close to the front door. Her memory was jolted at the sight of it. Panicked, she ran searching palms over her midsection until they settled on that familiar bulge. Ahmed.

Her room was a narrow wedge with a single bed decked in clean white sheets, two pillows, and a throw for warmth. A smoky-gray towel, matching their sofa, was folded neatly and resting on its edge. In the corner was a small, bleached wood desk with a chair stowed beneath it and a magnet board on the wall above it. Rounding out its sparseness was a freestanding wardrobe with double doors.

This was hers. A place with lock and key where she could steal away to whenever she wanted. She covered her mouth to squelch a giggle. *Hers. Hers. Hers.* In her modest home back in Mogadishu, she's had her own room—a similar sliver of a space—because sharing one with her preteen brother would have been inappropriate.

Her nighttime routine was hurried. A tiptoe to the bathroom to brush her teeth and splash warm water on her face. She would shower in the morning. Back in her room, she switched her abaya for a loose-fitting, cotton nightgown and carefully placed Ahmed's worn-out sack on her bed, its roughness in stark contrast to the smooth bedding. She pulled her own sack of valuables out of her duffel bag and set it next to his.

She had never seen herself capable of such discipline. Weeks had gone by without her so much as peeking at its contents. Temptation had gnawed at her, but she'd been wiser. Whatever was in there was worth more than a careless look.

"This was my family." Ahmed's Arabic words had sounded weak to her before he killed himself. Whatever it held, she had to protect.

When her apartment crumbled in Mogadishu, her father—Mohammed—had been in bed for over a week up to that moment, battling a chronic cough that never eased. Caaliyah was worried that her husband's work as a laborer, inhaling cement day after day since Muna's birth, had caused his sickness. Muna pictured the dust coalescing within his lungs, forming concrete blocks that slowly suffocated him.

"Don't worry about me, *habibti*," he'd reassured his wife, wheezing before being seized by another whooping fit. "As long as your stomach is filled, this is a small sacrifice."

Caaliyah had often lifted his hand to her cheek, quietly transferring her warmth to him, showing—in her own small way—that he meant the world to her. "*InshAllah.*" Caaliyah had always ended that intimate gesture with this phrase, rubbing his hand between hers. *God willing.*

Mohammed was a poor man when her mother had met him and an even poorer man when he died under slabs of his own roof as Mogadishu went up in flames. Now there was no one to turn to. Her maternal family, flush with wealth from trading cattle, had promptly disowned her mother the day she brought home a cement carrier—a man old enough to be her own father—as the person she wanted to marry.

Muna was born and brought home from the hospital into a destitute cocoon of poverty filled with nothing, save the love her parents shared, and her father doted on her.

Pulling in a deep breath, Muna emptied the contents of Ahmed's sack onto her bed. Out came crumpled photos, silver chains, a stack of passport photos in varying sizes held together by a slack rubber band, several misbaha prayer beads, pewter rings, burnished pieces of jewelry, a palmful of sheared sheep wool.

A small, folded cloth striped red, white, and green with a flaming yellow sun in its middle caught her attention. She assumed it was the flag of Ahmed's land as she unfolded the cloth to assess its bold design. Then came brown, cinnamon-colored sand. Lots of sand she hadn't anticipated on her pristine, white sheets. It had trickled out of a clear plastic bag he'd wound tightly. Sand from his country.

She started straightening out the rumpled photos. A picture of five young men positioned stiffly around an older man who sat in the middle, their eyes regarding her with a golden intensity even Ahmed's amber stare hadn't been able to match. All born of the lean-faced man with a long, gray beard and a black-and-white *jamana* scarf tied into an elegant turban on his head.

Five handsome men with varying lengths of luscious, chestnut-brown hair. She remembered that soft feel when she'd taken strands of Ahmed's hair through her fingers. She studied his face, much fuller, and clearly much younger than the rest.

She continued smoothening out more family photos. A woman with arms around a young teenage girl; she assumed they were his mother and sister. Subsets of the brothers together. She giggled at one with Ahmed carrying a black-faced sheep with matted wool around his shoulders mid-laugh, his hair wild, picked up by the wind. Then a close-up photo of him staring intently at his viewer. The smile that made his eyes sparkle was gone on purpose this time, and she fawned over her beautiful Ahmed in his photo.

A few minutes later, she pushed Ahmed and his family away and grabbed the stack of passport photos. The rubber band snapped out of its misery before she could untwine it. She started laying each photo out side by side. Faces tanned by the sun, some austere, some jolly. Some caught in stark surprise by the flash. They all seemed to be official-looking photos—it looked like Ahmed had found all their identification cards and painstakingly ripped these photos out of them.

As she was laying them out, one accidentally flipped over, and she saw a full name scribbled behind it. She started reexamining the photos. They had all been labeled with names. Full names. Varying last names.

Why hadn't Ahmed just gathered their Syrian ID cards instead? Then she would have had their full details. The complete cards would have been more useful than cutouts of the passport photos. Unless he wanted them to rest in peace this way, Muna thought.

She laid out 104 passport photos of different people with different family names. Then she looked behind Ahmed's own family photos. Names. Full names. Of his brothers, his father, his mother, his sister. He'd immortalized every single one of them in ink.

Including himself. Ahmed Tofiq Rahim.

Muna fell to her knees by the side of her bed and wept. Her tears streamed silently as she muffled each sound, not wanting to wake Khadiija and Yasmiin at this hour. He'd given her everything, his entire life, in that small sack.

"I think you like to look for trouble, Ahmed. I can see it in your eyes." She remembered her words to him one morning as they sat on their verandah. He'd smiled at her mischievously as he often did whenever he moved into his jovial space.

"Trouble always seems to find me."

She wasn't sure how long she sobbed into her bed, but when she felt those tears start to dry up, she lifted her head and assessed the forensic evidence spread out in front of her. He had left her chunky breadcrumbs to his past. As she reached for the sack once again, she heard a crumpling sound and reached back in to pull out a browned piece of paper with sloppily scribbled Arabic.

Al Zawr village, 2013,

Kurdistan. North Syria.

His scribbling included his name too. Ahmed Tofiq Rahim. Nothing more. As if the pen had run out of ink or his fingers had simply given up.

"Ahmed Tofiq Rahim," she said out loud, breathing life back into his memory. "Ahmed Tofiq Rahim." Realization flooded in.

"Why?" she mouthed. Why hadn't Ahmed given Migrationsverket all this? They would have allowed him to stay instead of denying his application. They would have understood that he was the victim. That his entire village had been destroyed. He wouldn't have had to kill himself out of hopelessness.

Yet, she hadn't relinquished Ahmed's sack to that crimson-faced officer whose eyes spat what his mouth couldn't. The same reason, she deduced, Ahmed hadn't offered his life to the migration agency to secure freedom.

The only person he had trusted was Muna Saheed.

SIX

KẸMI

"Kemi!" Ingrid cooed, ready with a hug, as Kemi approached the reception lobby of von Lundin Marketing from the elevators.

Kemi was waiting in a white V-neck shirt paired with black pants, her striped blue-and-white nautical blazer resting over the ensemble. She wore simple pearl studs, and her crocheted braids were packed neatly off her face.

Wearing baggy pants and a boxy top with a high collar, Ingrid leaned in for their embrace. Kemi instantly felt overdressed.

"*Hej*, Ingrid!" Kemi greeted. "I'm so excited to finally be here."

"And you brought excellent weather with you!" Ingrid said, hooking an arm through Kemi's. "The team is thrilled to have you here. They can't wait to meet our new director of diversity."

Arm in arm, they marched down gray-blue halls decked out in Scandi-chic lines. Simple curves interspersed with sharp angles. Chairs looking deceptively impractical but ergonomically designed. Meeting cubes like space pods. Low-hanging bulbous lamps. Splashes of greenery to break up the futuristic vibes. Large, narrow windows looking down onto wealthy district Östermalm's busiest street.

When Ingrid ushered her into a conference room with views of lush, green Humlegården Park from spotlessly buffed windows, there was an immediate lull in the low-key conversations being held in Swedish. Eight colleagues sat around a modest table fashioned from recycled plywood. A quick scan revealed an even split between men and women, all white, all fair-haired.

"Kemi, meet your fellow directors. Welcome to your team!" Ingrid declared, and they all got to their feet, in varying states of casual attire. Kemi took a deep breath upon realizing she was the sole person of color at the meeting. For all of the faults within Andersen & Associates, their rooms had color and range. She was reminded again of what had caused the IKON fiasco at von Lundin and why she was here.

She went around the table, exchanging firm handshakes, repeating first names and mentally associating them with their physical features—different shades of blue eyes and fair hair—so she could quickly fish them back out later.

Björn Fältström, head of business development. *Bearded.*

Patrik Mölander, head of finance. *Plump.*

Greta Ljungström, head of operations, or COO, she casually reframed for Kemi. *Golden.*

Espen Wiklund, head of client services. *Elfin.*

Rikard Sundström, head of investor relations. *Ruddy.*

Ann Childers, head of communications. *British.*

Pernilla Dahlgren, head of IT, chief information officer. *Petite.*

Maria Larsson, head of media relations. *Tall.*

"And, of course me, Ingrid Johansson, head of global talent management, or as you know, human resources," she wrapped up before pulling out a chair for Kemi. "And you, our global diversity and inclusion director."

Before everyone settled back in, Ingrid pointed to pots of coffee, freshly baked cinnamon buns, red grapes, and honeycrisp apples that had been set out on a table. The directors made their way over to the stash, pouring fragrant black coffee into mugs, its nutty aroma permeating the room.

Espen Wiklund picked out a nicely shaped bun, placed it on a recycled cardboard plate and brought it to Kemi as an offering. He bore a smile, which wrinkled the corners of his peridot eyes. Freckles dotted his beguiling face, and low-cropped reddish hair crowned his head. "These are from the Green Turtle and are the best buns in town." Espen's English was tinged with a British accent.

Espen, charming in an understated way, was the first director Kemi was going to remember—images of Connor's ginger coloring flashed before her. Kemi thanked him, accepting his gesture.

There was one person missing from the room. She inquired after Jonny as she raised the pastry crowned with sugar pearls to her mouth.

"I'm so sorry I didn't tell you." Ingrid's face took on an uncharacteristic seriousness. "Jonny has been involved in an accident in the U.S."

"Oh my God, what happened?" Shock washed over Kemi.

Ingrid started fidgeting with the projector. "He's going to be okay," she replied. "He had a mild concussion after a minor car accident. No one knew he was even back in the U.S."

As Ingrid punched buttons, their other colleagues settled back into their seats with a nonchalance that suggested Jonny disappeared often.

BRITTANY-RAE

Brittany sat in a corner of the examination room a wretched mess. Jonny had begged her to come to the back room with him, in case the doctor used medical terms in English he didn't quite understand.

"Yup." Dr. Patel pulled away, switching off his small flashlight. "I suspect a concussion."

At that proximity, Brittany was certain Dr. Patel could smell sex on Jonny's rank breath. The good doctor turned to her with a knowing look. He probably knew the signs of domestic abuse. One second, enemies, the next moment, lovers. A bruised face with a mouth that was once filled with her.

"Fender bender, huh?" the doctor questioned, skimming his chart. Jonny dropped his gaze. Brittany bit her lower lip and nodded. There was nothing she could say to convince him that they weren't together or hadn't been sparring violently.

Dr. Patel scheduled Jonny for an MRI so he could further assess if there was any cerebral damage or internal bleeding. Jonny thanked him, averting his eyes, and Brittany knew full well he was hightailing it back to Sweden on the next flight home.

This is ridiculous, Brittany thought to herself as she stormed out of the clinic and toward her Honda, Jonny trailing her in a slow gait, running fingers through his hair repetitiously. She didn't even know how to dissect what had happened.

What was happening between them? This stranger had made her come again and again while never leaving his knees, rendering her senseless on her couch until sleep had claimed her.

She needed to hear Tanesha's voice now more than ever. Jonny's droning voice weaseled into her thoughts instead. "I am so sorry I've hurt you. I want to fix it. I want to make this right. I-I-I'm not good at this."

They stopped in front of her car.

She turned to look at him, arms wrapped around herself in protection. His hooded stare fixed on her in desperation.

"You came to my house uninvited," she started. "You kept sending flowers I didn't want. You won't take no for an answer!"

"You never told me to stop sending flowers. You never said no."

Her eyebrows contorted, confused. Was the bastard turning this all on her?

"Are you kidding me?" Rage gathered steam within her. "Are you freaking serious right now?"

"You never said no," Jonny continued. "You never said you wanted me to stop contacting you. I need people to be direct with me. I need to know."

She took deep breaths to calm herself down. She'd already hit him twice before, and she wasn't that "angry" Black woman he seemed to be conjuring up with ease from within her. Brittany was breathing heavily now, her eyes searching his face.

Her mind kept giving off alarms about this man, but her body kept failing her.

The same way it had when he sought her attention from his seat in 6A. The same way it responded when he swallowed up the space in the galley when he handed her his card. The same way it prickled when he assessed her over the rim of his sake-filled glass in London. Not to mention last night, when he claimed her so dutifully, studying her face, trying to memorize what she liked with each moan.

She contemplated either letting him back in her car or leaving him in that empty parking lot to find his way back into whatever hole he crawled out of.

The alarms got louder and louder until she finally asked, "What is wrong with you?"

After their failed date in London, Brittany had googled him the second she burst into her hotel room in West India Quay. She spent the rest of the night scrolling through photos of him. Reading articles and gossip spreads about him, though there were no one-on-one interviews with him. Finding him more intriguing with each click. Wallowing deeper in guilt each time she looked at Jamal, his face glistening with hope of their future together.

And here was Jonny, looking like shit with bruises and a new bandage over the cut on his eyebrow, gaping at her, trying to convince her he wasn't a stalker.

You never said no.

Those words floated back at her, and she shut her eyes, remembering specific rumors she'd read. Links to articles that were purely speculative about his unwillingness to engage with the press, his strange intensity. Social awkwardness. Boundary issues. Nothing that anyone could prove or point to in a real way, but something Brittany saw in him too. He seemed to live in an explicit world of black and white.

Jonny stared intently, unrelentingly. The look exacerbated by his crush on her, because he couldn't seem to lie. Every inch of him wanted her, and he didn't know how to hide it.

When her eyelids fluttered open, he was inches from her face, studying her. He shook his head one more time.

"Nothing is wrong with me. You didn't tell me to stop," he whispered. "I would have if you'd told me to. If you had said no."

Tears pooled in Brittany's eyes, and she watched his brows dip in concern, watching her cry.

"Are you okay?"

She kept shaking her head. No, she was not okay. She was confused.

Flustered. Falling apart. Unraveling faster than she could compose herself. Jonny traced his fingers up her cheeks to soothe her.

"Ssshhh. Please don't cry," he pleaded. His lips covered hers softly, his tongue sweeping in between them gently. She sobbed against his kiss, receiving his remedy for her rapidly beating heart.

"Is it because he's white?"

"So he can protect you?"

"Can he open doors I can't?"

Jamal's words slowly lost their sting as Jonny wrapped his arms around her, pulling her closer. He deepened their kiss, and she relished this new intimacy.

Wealth and power weren't the only reasons she was letting him devour her at the crack of dawn in that parking lot. Protection through privilege wasn't why she wasn't pushing him off her and swiping a palm across his face for the third time.

Of all his peculiarities, the one that bubbled up to wrap itself around her with comfort was this:

Brittany had finally found a man who couldn't lie to her face.

PART TWO

SEVEN

BRITTANY-RAE

Jonny came from old money. The von Lundin name was entrenched in Sweden. It spanned centuries of patriarchs who had been Hanseatic merchants on Gotland, an island off Sweden's eastern coast. Once dropped, the name fluidly unlocked doors and removed barricades. It seeped into various arts and culture committees, sat on the board of different philanthropic initiatives, and had an easy audience with the Swedish monarchy. Wealth so calcified, it hadn't expected Brittany in its future.

Brittany never wanted this thing with Jonny she couldn't quite define exposed. A foreboding sense of shame took root within her. It came skipping along, holding hands with guilt over the way she had easily hurt Jamal. Guilt wore a veil of judgment. Had she held Jonny to different standards?

After their raw kiss in the parking lot of the twenty-four-hour clinic as daylight fully broke, fissures had snapped open within her. From their sulfuric cracks oozed the malaise-inducing trinity—shame, guilt, and judgment. She drove Jonny home in silence. He fiddled with his hair nervously all the way. She quietly scrambled eggs while he sat on the barstool by the kitchen's center island, his focus following her movements.

He seemed to be silently studying her. The way she pushed away stubborn strands of hair as she bowed over the sizzling frying pan. The way she simultaneously scrunched her brows and pursed her lips when pondering her next moves.

Brittany dished out a large scoop of golden mush atop a slice of buttered toast and slid the plate over to Jonny. He caught it with both hands, looked at the hastily presented breakfast on his plate, and then glanced back up at her.

"What's the problem?" she asked.

Jonny lowered his gaze and said nothing. She passed him a fork, settled in next to him with her own plate, and dug in. Jonny didn't eat but continued scanning her as she chewed, her jaw working, not savoring. He watched her a few moments longer.

"If we're going to do this, you're going to have to stop doing that." She broke his leering midbite without glancing at him then continued shoveling eggs into her mouth.

"Doing what?"

Brittany shot him an icy glare, and in return, Jonny shone that grin of a thousand teeth.

That toothy grin sealed Jonny as Brittany's secret. Something—rather, someone—she could indulge in because he was so besotted and couldn't hide it. With her, he lacked emotional restraint and laid himself bare for all to see. With each touch, he meticulously crawled closer into her sphere. He seemed to be learning her like a textbook, scanning her features like topography on a map. Sooner or later, he'd be ready to take his test, this she knew.

Jonny left for Sweden the next day with the details he'd been craving from her for weeks: her phone number and email address.

Later that day, Jamal came by for the rest of his stuff. This time around, there was no pleading for him to stay. The unholy trinity had settled within her, so she busied herself with nothing in the kitchen as Jamal pulled books and vinyl records off shelves in the living room. If anyone else had walked into that space, the palpable tension would have suffocated them.

Once two more suitcases had been loaded and rolled toward the front door, Jamal did a curious thing. He went in search of her and found Brittany sitting on a barstool with a mug in hand, flipping through coupon booklets—daily junk mail she often trashed right away. He chuckled, and she knew it was at her pretense of being busy. He walked up to her, slipped a hand around her waist, and bent low to kiss her cheek.

"Goodbye, Brit," Jamal delivered. Relief escaped her as a low sigh. They would remain cordial. She'd feared a complete shutout. She spun to look at him. As if propelled by a crazed spirit, she flew into his arms.

"I'll help out for three months until you decide what to do with it," he said, referring to the town house they shared. He paid their monthly rent, his attorney's salary being more than enough to afford it. She covered their utility expenses on her meager cabin crew salary, despite her experience and seniority at the airline.

"I'm so sorry," she apologized. "I didn't want us to end like this." Jamal's grip tightened on her back in wordless loss.

All he offered her was a pained smile before turning to leave.

Her June work schedule arrived early Monday morning. A jam-packed 120 hours of scheduled airtime shuttling between DC and London as well as having New York, Miami, Austin, and Los Angeles roundtrips. Plus, she was currently bidding for her July schedule. As a member of the senior crew who worked first class and business cabins, she still had some flexibility. Her phone danced on the table next to her laptop.

"I need to see you." Jonny's words were rushed.

"Are you back in Stockholm?"

"Yes, I just landed. I need to see you." A long pause hung between them. She hadn't thought this far ahead.

"I need to sort out my schedule for June. It arrived today, and I need to plan out the month."

"Send it to me," he demanded, before adding, "please."

She did.

A week later, Brittany landed at Heathrow Terminal 5. As she walked amid a gaggle of navy-blue-clad colleagues click-clacking and dragging carry-ons down the arrivals hall, Jonny startled her by calling out her name. Her secret was trying to burst out of its cage when she wasn't ready to show it to the world.

Caught midlaugh in response to an inside joke from another crew member, her smile slid off her face as she caught sight of him. Collecting herself, she turned to wave off her curious colleagues who craned their necks backward to fill up on gossip as they continued their trip down polished halls. When she turned back to him, he'd transported himself within inches of her face.

He tried leaning in for a kiss, but a firm hand to his chest halted his advance.

"Not here. I'm at work," Brittany deterred him, her eyes sweeping over her shoulder in search of an invisible snitch.

"I needed to see you," he said. She looked around them. "I want to get to know you. I know you have to work the flight tomorrow at two in the afternoon, so I wanted to spend the day with you," he divulged. She shouldn't have given him her schedule.

"At your command? Regardless of my own plans?" she countered, touching her hat and patting it a half inch in place. She noticed Jonny's gaze following her movements.

"If you want to," he corrected himself, fists balled at his sides again. Brittany tugged at her lower lip as she scrutinized the man frozen in front of her. A man who turned heads as people in the arrivals hall rubbernecked past him. His piercing focus blotted out Heathrow, turning it into a deserted ghost town, his eyes only for the lady in front of him.

She could never let him out of her secret box. Her parents wouldn't understand. Right now, they were placing bets on if Jamal would get on one knee before year's end. She couldn't face Tanesha either.

She would ride this thing out. Indulge his steadfastness until they both tired of the relationship. His track record according to Google estimated about one month after catching his flavor of the week—er, month. By her calculation, they had about two and a half weeks left.

She finally answered him. Yes, he could spend the day with her.

Jonny walked them to the outdoor pickup area, where a burly white man in a dark suit and a petite blond wearing a shirtdress, cinched at the waist with a belt, came rushing to the couple.

"Good day, ma'am." The chauffeur reached for her carry-on luggage before she could protest. She thanked him after receiving his name. Frank. The petite blond with a bob cut and precision bangs seemed mesmerized.

"You're even more beautiful in person, Ms. Johnson," she said in a tone tinged with a Swedish accent. "Can I call you Brittany?"

"Thank you. Yes, of course. And you are?" Brittany stretched out a hand to greet her.

"Eva!" she squealed. "Jonny's assistant here in London...and sender of flowers," she finished in a whisper. From Brittany's brief encounters with him, witnessing him failing to properly wring out his own shirt and his need not to upset her, it made perfect sense that he would delegate romantic gestures to his assistant.

"Great to meet you, Eva."

The pixie smiled in response before turning to Jonny and releasing a barrage of Swedish. He nodded as words streamed out of Eva, occasionally interjecting with a halting air-sucking sound, which intrigued Brittany. She realized she loved listening to him speak in Swedish. His inflections. Those soft sounds—like catching one's breath—that weren't actual words but seemed to be moving his conversation with Eva forward. After watching him listen to Eva intently, she realized not only did she want to know why he was making those odd Swedish sounds, she also wanted to know him better.

Frank helped Brittany into a shiny, charcoal-colored Range Rover then placed her bag in its trunk. Jonny strode around to the other side. Eva rode shotgun, and soon the foursome shuttled toward Jonny's eighteenth-floor penthouse made of glass and steel in Canary Wharf.

En route, Eva rattled off the day's plan.

"First, you'll get a chance to clean up. Then, you'll enjoy a catered lunch, followed by VIP tickets to a late-afternoon play. Finally, a boat will pick you two up from Victoria Embankment and take you back to Canary Wharf for a redo dinner at Yamamoto."

"A redo?" Brittany asked.

"Yes," Eva said. "Your last dinner was abruptly interrupted."

"Interrupted?"

"Yes," Eva continued. "Jonny doesn't like loose ends."

Eva turned back to her phone and continued furiously swiping up and down.

Brittany turned to Jonny, who was sitting skin-close to her, gorging on her presence. "You assumed I would spend my one free day with you?" Low-grade irritation broiled within her.

"I knew you would spend the day with me," he said.

"But..."

He caught her words in a kiss that instantly derailed any further sentences. One hand moved up to cradle her right cheek as he kissed her. He'd missed her desperately, his lips showed her. Flashes of Beaufount floated across his face, and Brittany fought them off as Jonny deepened their kiss.

His phone beeped with a text message, which suddenly tore him away from her.

Brittany caught the message when he checked it. Klart!

A grin stretched across his face.

"Good news?" Brittany was curious. Their Range Rover became a desert once again as he peered at her.

"Yes."

———

Floor-to-ceiling windows wrapped around Jonny's Canary Wharf flat in East London's Docklands. Brittany stepped in and took a deep breath as she soaked up the sparsely furnished space that screamed wealth. She was ordered to take her heels off and park them by the door.

"It's a Swedish thing." Eva beamed before running loose inside while Jonny stood by the mahogany shoe rack.

The caterers delivered lunch right on time and laid out the essentials: freshly baked bread, whipped butter, spring mix salad, a dressed-up dining table, and wine glasses. Their meal—Cornish hens, sweet potato mash, roasted vegetables—was warming on low heat in the oven. Eva walked up to a man standing next to the table and wearing a white jacket, a tattoo peeking out just above his collar. After a few hushed words, she dismissed him. Then Eva hurried around the place, adjusting, patting, and inspecting before running back to Brittany.

"Your room's this way, so you can freshen up." She trotted off with Brittany's carry-on, which burly Frank had insisted on bringing up for her despite the fact it weighed nothing. Eva flipped on lights to an en suite room torn out of the pages of an upscale home decor catalog. Large, plush, light-gray duvets. Pillows stuffed with feathers, easily responsible for the death of a hundred geese. Fresh flowers. Lots of them. A mix of yellow and lilac tulips. More of those floor-to-ceiling windows. A full-length mirror on the remaining real wall, which was also painted light gray.

So much gray, Brittany thought. The car, the decor, the walls—everything was so gray. It was probably Jonny's favorite color.

Brittany stepped into the room on unsteady feet. A room this strange woman was now calling hers. She'd been around affluence and had experienced many things, but she'd never seen such exquisite views of the Thames before. As the gravity of the situation slowly dawned on her, she felt herself fading away, unable to recognize the woman staring back at her through the glass window reflecting clouds and sky.

She stood there, surveying the city of London—which seemed to stretch out in every direction—when Eva took her leave. She was still standing there when Jonny leaned against the jamb of the door, observing her. The slight sound of a sniff, and he was instantly behind her, hands on her waist, asking what was wrong in a hushed voice. Why was she upset? Did she hate it?

Brittany shook her head, words long gone, swallowed up by the unholy trinity—shame, guilt, and judgment. They had firmly lodged themselves now, and there was no going back.

"Are you okay?" he whispered against her neck before trailing it with his tongue. No, she was not okay. "Are you?" His hands wrapped around her and started unbuttoning her crisp, white shirt. She slowly whirled around before he could get the last button unclasped. She hadn't let him finish that task, and he let out air, as if frustrated. Then he grabbed at the last button, quickly unhooking it while she faced him.

Brittany ran her palm up his cheek to look at him, feel him. On cue, his eyes turned toward the motion, but she moved his face back to look at him. He regarded her quietly. She assumed he was search-ing for clues on her face so she didn't have to say yes or no. She was beginning to learn Jonny's mannerisms too.

She stroked his cheek silently, heating it up beneath her palm. "Show me what you've learned." As if unleashed from a cage, he tightened his hands around her waist and crushed her against him. His tongue swept into her mouth with slow, calculating strokes. Just the way she liked it. Just like he did back in Alexandria the first time they got together.

High in his watchtower, they wrestled for air, the world outside locked away. They started shedding clothes. First, her white shirt and pencil skirt. Then his T-shirt, which she helped him out of, leaving his hair in disarray. His mouth covered hers once more then traveled to her bare shoulder, his teeth lightly grazing its length. She murmured in response. His mouth continued along her collarbone.

"Show me what you want," he said softly.

The words overwhelmed her like an anvil on her chest. She pulled back, forcing his head up to engage with eyes darkened by pupils twice their size. He was panting, and he searched her face, confused. Brittany twisted her lips, trying to hold back tears. Constant crying wasn't going to make him go away.

"I'm sorry..." he began to say, but she reached her fingers up to his mouth to stop him.

"No," she began. "You've done nothing wrong."

"You keep crying," he pointed out, a finger reaching up to wipe those droplets that kept sending him off course.

"No, I'm not sad. I really am not."

"So, you're happy?"

Those words had never crossed her mind with him, and she rebuked them immediately. This wasn't how she'd imagined happiness could look. She made a mental note to call up her therapist once she was back in the U.S. Maybe she could help Brittany exorcise the hold Jonny had over her.

She never answered him. Instead, she pulled his head down for a kiss, which he hungrily accepted, fusing her lithe frame to his once more. Brittany gave him one more lesson to file away. She didn't like to be talked to while in the moment, because it could cause tears.

Two hours later, Brittany announced she was starving.

"Oh shit!" Jonny popped out of bed, pulled on his boxer briefs, and padded out on tiptoe, trying not to wake any ghosts floating around. Brittany chuckled from beneath cotton-candy-soft sheets. She could wear this life comfortably. If only she and Jonny could lock themselves up in this watchtower forever while she taught, tested, and graded him.

A few minutes later, he came back carrying a tray loaded with their chicken and sides. He rushed back out to get plates and cutlery, and for the next few hours, Brittany told him about her life. Her family, her travels, her brief stint as a model, her dreams of becoming a fashion designer. He listened, smiling occasionally. For Jonny, it seemed, each smile was his brain hitting the "save" button. Jonny shared about his family. His parents had retired early. They buried themselves in charities and concerts, socializing with the rest of society's upper echelon.

"You will like Svea," he said, mentioning one of his sisters while sketching up and down her thigh with his fingers. "I think you two have a lot in common." He dipped low to kiss the trail while she twirled his wheat-colored hair around her fingers.

"Really?"

He hummed positively against her thigh.

"And Antonia?"

"She scares me." He laughed. "She's the oldest. Fifty years old. Svea is forty-six. I was the mistake." Right; Brittany remembered she was three years older than him—he was thirty-five.

"God, you make me feel like a cougar." She snickered. He grazed her thigh with his teeth in response.

"I like this cougar." His mouth worked its way up from her right thigh. Once it took a left turn inward, Eva's plans for them that afternoon went to hell.

But dinner at Yamamoto, he would not compromise on. He wanted her to experience his favorite place properly, he said. She got up to shower, and he joined her. She taught him a few more things she liked under powerful sprays, and soon, they were dressed for dinner. He donned a black shirt and slicked wet hair off his face. Brittany pulled out a black wrap dress she always carried and threw on colorful beads. Once in the elevator, Jonny turned to her and pressed a close-lipped kiss to her mouth.

"You're beautiful," he murmured against them, his forehead resting on hers. She received his kiss then cleaned red stain off his lips with her thumb, not wanting to leave a trace of her on him.

One week later, Brittany clasped her hands in front of her, cherry-red lips spread wide, boat hat perched, ready to welcome passengers onto her flight to Miami, Florida. Her jaw dropped when Jonny strode on board.

"I never should have given you my schedule," she whispered between clenched teeth, giving his chest a light, playful punch. Jonny kissed her in front of her colleagues and the line he was holding up, enveloping them in *awwws*.

Brittany's summer became a heady blur filled with Jonny in every sense. He had made it past his one-month infatuation period and now trailed Brittany all over throughout the month of June. Hopping on with her in London or flying to DC to meet her there if he couldn't sneak a ticket on board her cabin. Besides his London inner circle of Eva and Frank, Brittany had begged him to keep their trysts under wraps. She wasn't ready to go public, and he told her he would wait. He didn't want anyone else but her.

He aced his tests, drawing on ways she liked to be pleased. In Alexandria, he'd learned how to taste her just right. In London, he'd learned how she wanted foreplay. In Miami, he'd perfected his rhythm against her. In New York, he'd learned how to scrub her back in a bathtub to make her purr like his cougar. Their joke. In Los Angeles, she'd demanded he show her what he liked, and he'd died a painful death from pleasure.

July brought more of the same, with longer stretches of listening. He told her about his childhood and how his quirks had caged him. His parents had assured him he was fine and that he should ignore them. His mannerisms and the other children's mockery had threatened to eat him from the inside out until he learned his strengths and how to use them. He still couldn't read people perfectly, but he learned Brittany. How to please her, pleasure her, and make her cry those happy tears again.

That was why he stared at her in confusion as she moved languidly atop him one Friday night in early August in London. Canary Wharf had turned into a blanket of glowworms in the dark night. She'd been sitting astride him, his hands locked on her waist, and he'd been moving against her just the way she liked. Slow thrusts with a small rise and back down again. This time, she seemed distracted, and he stopped, his mouth open, trying to catch his breath.

"What's wrong?" His voice was labored. She sensed he was so close. She shook her head.

"Nothing." The words barely came out. Brittany made a retching motion, sprang off him, and bolted toward the toilet.

She was cowering over the toilet bowl when she heard him softly push open the door. Her body convulsed in sobs as she held on to the lid for oxygen. They'd eaten the same sea bass for dinner, so she couldn't have become sick so quickly. She wasn't drunk either.

That was when she heard Jonny take in a deep gulp of air before softly muttering the words, "Oh, fuck..."

MUNA

The first night Muna slept in her own bed in that Tensta apartment, she'd woken up the next afternoon. Morning was long gone, along with both Khadiija and Yasmiin. Shock had initially swallowed her when she'd glanced at her phone. One twenty-three p.m. She had slept an entire morning away.

She heard a whizzing sound, quickly dressed herself, and dashed to the front door. Two white envelopes were lying on the floor in front of it. Picking them up, she read her name out loud.

"Muna Saheed." Her mail. She was getting letters sent to her own place. And it felt so good. Both letters had been from Skatteverket, the tax authority, sending confirmation of her personal identification number and registration in her new district, Spånga-Tensta. They might as well have been handwritten love notes. She held them to her nose, closed her eyes, and savored their sweet paper smell.

Over the next month, Muna floated in a state of nesting. Her room became her cocoon, and she filled it with colorful knick-knacks. She rarely ventured downtown. Downtown sucked money. She scraped decor together from secondhand stores, African shops, and Middle Eastern kiosks dotting Tensta.

Her first deposit from the social insurance agency—Försäkringskassan—had made her feel like a millionaire. About 6,800 kronor as her monthly benefit and 4,700 kronor for maintenance. Their apartment was already subsidized. The numbers—11,500 kronor—blazed from the page like neon lights. Wealth beyond her dreams.

When she received that first confirmation slip of the deposit, she rushed to her room and pressed her lips to the photo of a laughing Ahmed carrying the black-faced sheep on his shoulders. The picture was fastened onto the board hanging above her desk with a magnet. Next to it were photos of Caaliyah, Aaden, and Mohammed. Her desk now had textbooks for her Swedish class neatly stacked on it.

When she pulled back from the kiss to assess the magnetic board, her smile died. Everyone she had ever loved was dead, their smiles frozen in time. As she stepped back to assess it in its entirety, she realized her magnetic board of photos was a virtual graveyard.

Khadiija and Yasmiin became sisters to Muna more quickly than she had anticipated. As the youngest of the lot, Muna never wanted to be alone. She clung to Khadiija, the oldest at twenty-five, whenever she went shopping or went to the community center to relax and meet new Somali friends. She even hung around the Lebanese restaurant where Khadiija worked washing dishes and wiping up after customers.

Muna would follow Yasmiin, twenty-one, to the Ethiopian hair salon in the square where she worked as a hairdresser and did makeup. Their talk always revolved around men. This fine man. That hot man. Muna thought Yasmiin was obsessed with men. Then while massaging leave-in conditioner into Muna's spongy Afro, Yasmiin confessed she'd met someone.

"I can't share too much yet." Yasmiin beamed at her sister-friend through the salon's finger-greased mirror. "You will meet him one day...if I still like him."

Khadiija and Yasmiin hadn't gone into that space of complete trust with her. The space where pain flowed freely and despair suffocated them. They didn't ask one another either. Their bedrooms felt like individual safe houses to Muna, off-limits to one another, and the living room stayed their communal place. Sisters when sitting in open spaces, strangers once locked behind each bedroom door.

Muna knew she would have to be patient with them. Dredging up memories and facing reasons people fled demanded time. The same way she'd waited months for Ahmed to hand her his life.

Khadiija and Yasmiin would do the same in due time, she hoped.

Once in a while, Gunhild with the kind eyes from the district checked in on her. Sometimes, they met up for lunch at the café at Tensta konsthall or took in an exhibition at the gallery. Other times, the woman dragged Muna on long walks, the younger woman struggling to keep up.

On one occasion, they met up for *fika*—a coffee break. Muna took a bite of her *kanelbulle*. Cinnamon bun. It tasted stale, but she continued chewing softly as she listened to Gunhild.

"I worry about you," Gunhild said, abandoning her own bun after the first dry bite. Beyond getting an update on her weekly Swedish classes, Muna still hadn't found a job. But it had barely been a month since she left Solsidan. She wondered why Gunhild was hurrying her up. After all, she was still basking in the fact that she had a home.

"You don't need to worry about me," Muna replied, her eyes not quite meeting Gunhild's.

"Of course I worry about you. You have no family here in Sweden."

"I have been running for so long," Muna said. "I just want to enjoy the feeling of standing still."

July rolled around, and Muna slipped into a long funk. She missed sweeping around the verandah at Solsidan, a place now radio-silenced and parked in her memory, almost as if she'd dreamt it all along. As menial as the work had been, she'd had purpose. Holed up here in Tensta, she began to wonder if it would all end with her going up in flames too. Boredom was certainly rubbing at her, trying to spark a fire. She still moved in a daze. The trauma she had endured often manifested itself as quiet tears once she was locked in her room, staring at her graveyard of photos.

One day, while at Yasmiin's salon, Muna let out a sigh before ranting about her boredom. She was sitting in the corner of the salon, resting her cheek on a palm.

"Don't worry," Yasmiin said. "I will help you."

Two months later, she was sitting in Kungshallen, the underground food court opposite Hötorget in the center of Stockholm, where the family of a Turk named Yagiz ran a doner kebab stall.

"Hmm," Yagiz mumbled as his dark eyes roamed over Muna. He had pulled himself from shearing thin slices of kebab. "Do you have to wear that gown? Is a hijab not enough now?" he questioned her in heavily accented Swedish. He was a handsome man with jet-black hair worn like a rooster and shaved at the sides. He also sported a handlebar moustache. "We're in Sweden, for God's sake. The freest place on earth!"

Muna wasn't sure how to respond to him.

"Look." Yagiz gave his moustache a quick stroke. "I want to help you, but this is an issue. The offices we clean are for rich business-people. You can't be roaming around in your jilbab during the day when they're having important meetings."

Muna wondered if her brother in Islam had lost his faith.

"If you wear that gown, you have to work at night to clean the offices," he explained. "This means going home at midnight. Do you understand?"

She nodded.

"Do you want to be walking alone at night? Hmm?" Yagiz asked.

She shook her head. No, she didn't want to be going home at night if she had other options.

"Good. Only the scarf, okay? I don't want Allah's wrath on me," Yagiz said, attempting a joke. Muna didn't smile. He pushed himself to his feet, wiped his hands on the apron around his waist, and summoned Muna to follow him. They walked back to his stall, where he ordered one of his workers in rapid Turkish to wrap up a doner kebab to go for Muna.

"Here." He handed the warm paper bag to her. She thanked him.

"So, I will give you the day shift on Monday, Wednesday, Friday," he said, pulling out his smartphone as well as a cigarette, which he hung between his lips in anticipation. He tapped, slid, and scrolled until he found his timetables.

"Tomorrow, go to this address at six a.m. sharp." He rattled off an address. "You will meet the others at the front door. They'll bring a shirt for you."

She nodded. "How will I know them?" she asked.

Yagiz responded with a deep roar that vibrated between them, his laughter telling her all she needed to know.

"Remember, only scarf!" he stressed before turning to leave for a smoke outside.

KẸMI

When Kemi arrived back in DC after her May visit, she immediately looked for a property management company. She planned to hold on to her condominium as an investment and rent it out until she fell out of love with Sweden and fled back. She also decided she would leave her car behind. Stockholm's public transport had been impeccable when she'd been there. Plus, riding around on buses, trains, and ferries would give her an opportunity to explore and integrate quicker.

"That's all!" David, a property manager she'd retained, grabbed the form Kemi had just signed and glanced over it one last time. "You don't have to worry about a thing 'cause you're in good hands." The cliché slid off his tongue.

They had been sitting around her glass-top dining table in her condominium. Earlier, David had roamed around, clearly impressed. She wasn't sure if he was floored by its size and decor or if he was confounded that she owned it. She suspected the latter, because he had double-checked the year she was born.

"This place will go like hotcakes with renters," he continued, picking from his stash of boilerplate one-liners. "I mean, the location, the ridiculous size, the view, fully furnished..." His eyes swept the dining room before settling back on Kemi.

"So, what is it you do for a living again?" he asked. Anger brewed deep within her.

"You can read it on the form I just signed," Kemi said tersely. David sniggered before getting to his feet.

"And it's Sweden, right?" he asked, once on his feet.

"Yep." She also got on hers and led him toward the front door.

Her whirlwind trip to Stockholm had been packed with activities and meetings. After her initial introduction to her new working team, Ingrid had pulled up a PowerPoint presentation and spent the next hour and a half detailing how they worked, their communications strategy, current projects, and where Kemi would fit in nicely to tie it all up with a rainbow-colored bow tie.

After which, Ingrid added, "Oh, you'll be reporting to me, by the way."

At first, Kemi was shocked. That wasn't what Ingrid had sold her over the phone. She was supposed to be Jonny's direct report. Somehow, Ingrid explained it all away.

"Well, he's never here. Greta does his job for him anyway. You and I already have good chemistry. Jonny really doesn't know what is going on."

Kemi had glanced around the room as the other functional heads nodded in agreement with Ingrid. It was more efficient this way, their dispositions seemed to say. Her gaze settled on Espen, and he shrugged at her.

"It's not a big deal," the voice in her head—the one that had primed her into a nodding people-pleaser—pleaded. "You're still getting twice your former pay and a senior-level position in one of the most powerful marketing firms in the world." It seemed the world was currently going crazy over the Scandinavian touch—style, decor, lifestyle, fashion—so von Lundin Marketing was a solid investment. If she could pull them back from the ledge of a diversity faux pas, she would be lauded within the industry.

But still. Her gut said run. Her ego said stay.

After an unnecessarily meticulous presentation, they all piled out of the office and strolled three blocks down to a high-end sushi restaurant where all its waitstaff were white, and its chefs were Japanese people who didn't speak a lick of Swedish.

Kemi felt exposed in her skin. She was used to being the sole Black woman in many rooms, but this place, this air floating around her, felt different. It was blown-up bubble gum, slowly shrinking in on her. Lunch was a mishmash of Swedish interspersed with silence as chopsticks were lifted to mouths. Occasionally, someone would remember she was there and ask her something in English.

"Really? You have two master's degrees?" Greta asked as she gripped salmon sashimi with her chopsticks.

"Yes, I do." Hadn't Greta read her resume? Especially if they were going to be working closely?

Kemi launched into a more personal presentation of herself and her accomplishments while the group simply listened and nodded. Once she was done, it was to heavy silence and looks being thrown around. Espen dove in to end her misery.

"We're lucky to have you," he started. "We need smart women around here."

The bleached-blond Brit, Ann Childers, flashed him a look. "Hey! Careful now," she joked.

Kemi wasn't sure Ann was being jovial. Kemi laughed uncomfortably. Ann muttered something quickly to Espen in Swedish, and Espen shook his head, hands clasped in some form of resignation. Kemi observed. She needed to learn Swedish—fast.

She tried making small talk. While polite, the group divulged only enough to answer her questions. Yes, some of them had two master's degrees too. One even had a PhD. Kemi sank deeper into the angular chair she was sitting in, willing it to swallow her up. She'd bragged about her conversational Spanish, only to find out that Patrik Mölander was married to a Chilean woman and was fluent in Spanish and Portuguese. Everyone else around the table, even Ann, could speak another language fluently.

For the first time in her professional life, Kemi felt lacking. She had to pull out mental pom-poms to remind herself that she had been personally headhunted. They had flown across the Atlantic to poach her. She was excellent at her job. America had elevated her. Now she felt Sweden was trying to deflate her in some way.

After a long lunch, the group strolled languidly back to the office as if they'd dined on heavy steaks instead of light raw fish and rice. Espen hung back to keep Kemi company as they walked.

"So, how was your first day in Stockholm? Yesterday, right?" he prodded, hands in pocket, kicking his long legs slowly to match her pace.

"The weather was lovely, and I got to sleep in a bit." She was looking down at the pavement as they walked. "I needed to after a long sleepless flight. At least I caught up on movies."

His laugh in response was strained. "And did you explore the city?"

"I took a walk across the bridge over to the old town, Gamla stan, right?" Kemi half asked. He nodded. "It's such a beautiful city. I feel like Stockholm put its best foot forward for my arrival," she said. Espen gave her a crooked smile.

"Well, I hope you keep that wonder," he said. "My wife is from Cape Verde, and she's still struggling."

Kemi's interest was piqued. "Why?"

"Well…" Espen cleared his throat. An unsure gesture that let Kemi know maybe he was getting too personal with a colleague. After all, today was their first meeting. "Oh, I don't know. She feels like Stockholm tricked her. Seduced her with its beauty and then turned into an ugly monster in front of her."

Kemi's gut elbowed her. *"Listen!"* it said.

"What do you mean? Does she hate living here?"

"I won't say hate," he tried to explain. "She just finds it challenging. She still hasn't found a job since we got married, and she moved here to be with me. It's killing me to see her so frustrated."

"How did you two meet? If I may ask, of course."

"Umm, we met online. I thought it would be easy for her. I have many friends who have met their partners online, but they've mostly been Swedes or already based here."

"What did she study? Can't you help her find a job?"

"Yeah...I'm now finding that harder than I thought." Espen was suddenly quiet, and Kemi sensed he was closing up. That was all he was ready to give her. He had painted Stockholm as a seducer. She could clearly see why. Long, narrow, fingerlike buildings colored in soft melon yellows, pale peaches, and pastel reds. Labyrinths of waterways and ferries gliding along. Flowers in full bloom, transitioning from spring to summer. The city was sexy, and if Stockholm was a man and she'd met him in a nightclub, she would have propelled herself right away to ask him to dance.

She had gotten recommendations for cool places to hang out for drinks and music from the childless ones on her team—Espen and Maria.

They steered her to some clubs around Stureplan, the heart of their chic work district, and to Gamla stan for some jazz and blues in case she wanted some soul to "feel at home" instead. The same cringe she often felt around Connor's faux urban banter surfaced. Was she supposed to feel like a fraud for preferring alternative rock? Being Black apparently required liking specific music choices.

And that night, she did meet "Stockholm" in a nightclub in the form of a tall man built like a professional hockey player hanging in a corner with his friends. He didn't take his eyes off her that evening as she sat quietly by the bar, soaking in the club's electro-funk vibe, watching human eye candy, and sipping on a green cocktail. He cradled a whiskey glass, which was continually topped off by an unseen entity, as he stole glances her way. Whenever their eyes met, he held hers and prolonged it. His gaze never roamed her curves suggestively. He leered at her from across the room packed with bodies, yet he never approached her or asked her to dance. By the time Kemi left, she felt dejected.

Was this Stockholm? Something that lured her, but she could never quite have? Because if it was, Washington, DC, wasn't looking too bad. At least men in DC moved their feet and came over.

As she dragged herself back to her hotel that evening, Kemi passed two Black women, and she was happy to see unfamiliar yet familiar faces. She gave them a smile, which was returned with a blank stare like she was a specimen in a laboratory—bacteria that had broken out of its petri dish. It had to be what she was wearing, because the ladies were simply dressed in baggy pants, loose tops, barely any makeup, and braids that needed to have come out weeks ago. They had to be around her age, early to midthirties. As she walked past, all three simultaneously turned to take one another in. The two ladies poring over Kemi's expensive outfit—the dress, the heels, the Prada jacket—Kemi taking in their lackadaisical outfits, a sneak peek of herself after a few years in Sweden.

The next day at work was spent getting her set up in the system and configuring her work laptop. Over lunch, Louise, Jonny's assistant in Stockholm, ran her over to an apartment in Karlaplan, where she would stay for her first six to nine months until she got settled and moved into her own apartment. The apartment was one of a handful scattered around Stockholm that Jonny's family owned. It was housed in a twentieth-century stone building with narrow elevators, which had metal mesh curtains one had to manually pull closed before the actual doors sealed you in like a crypt.

As if reading her thoughts, Louise assured her it was a lovely place. She opened old, refurbished doors into a minimally clad but exquisite space. A two-bedroom loft with nice park views and polished wooden floors, it was fully furnished in grays with a few striped nautical tones.

"We usually reserve this space for important consultants who have to work with us for a few months," Louise said, pushing brunette strands behind both ears. "It has everything you need, and of course, you can call me for anything you can't find. I will be here once the movers arrive with your things from the U.S."

Kemi stood quietly, soaking it all in. She had never gotten anything this easily in life. This was too effortless, and her instincts to run were jolted once more. What did von Lundin really want from her? There had to be more.

She wandered around the spacious loft. She walked up to a window and looked out onto a park in the distance, watching as cars circled it in a wide loop.

"Thank you, Louise," Kemi said, observing the looping cars. "It's lovely."

On her last day visiting the office on her whirlwind tour, Jonny finally made an appearance. His whipped-butter face now boasted a large, blue-black bruise over his nose and a scab above an eyebrow. He roamed the hallways wearing sunglasses so no one could look him in the eye. She'd been given an office similar to the one she had at Andersen: half wall, half glass—sealed in, yet visible to everyone.

"How are you feeling?" Kemi asked him. "I heard about the accident." Jonny nodded, lips pressed together.

"All is well. No need to worry," he answered. "Hope Ingrid and everyone has taken good care of you."

"Yes, of course."

"Good. Looking forward to working with you," he said before turning around, grabbing his gym bag, and telling his assistant Louise, who had been trailing him around the office, that he was taking the rest of the week off to go hide out on Sandhamn, the island in Stockholm's archipelago where his family owned property. Louise shared this nugget of intel with Kemi once Jonny had padded out of the office.

That flighty encounter with Jonny had unsettled Kemi. Were they ever going to actually work together? Or had he brought her over here to park her in the office for show while he jetted off to fulfill his whims?

That night, she'd ended up in a lounge in Gamla stan, found herself a barstool, and prepared to perch there alone for the night, when she was approached by a more courageous man than the one from her previous outing. He was much older than she was, with teeth that suggested decades of smoking, crow's-feet around beady, pale eyes, leathery sun-beaten skin, and greasy, light-brown curls, all crammed into an expensive three-piece suit. She tried swiveling in another direction upon his approach, but he was already by her side. She lifted her glass to her lips, gearing up for his intrusion.

He didn't say anything at first and instead leered at her with a grin. She ignored him, which prodded uninvited words out of him.

"Can I get you a drink?" he said in heavily accented English. She shook her head.

"Do you live here?" he continued, leaning on the counter next to her. She turned to look at him, watching beads of sweat collect around his forehead and upper lip.

"I'm here on business," she said. What she really wanted to say was "Fuck off," but years of metaphorically nodding had softened her into an overpolite mess.

"Are you American?" His voice lit up. "I hear an accent." Technically, she was. Her newly minted American passport was her badge. But she was African, and she let him know this. There was a shift in the air around them. As if forgoing the lottery for an instant jackpot. *Oooh. African.*

He inched closer.

"You're African? Where? Ghana? Nigeria?" He rested a hand on her arm, which she quickly jerked out of his touch. He seemed unfazed. "I lived in Africa for many years. Working with the UN," he shared. He was stealing into her space, and she wanted him gone.

"I know a couple of African girls." His eyes roamed down to her hips before he swallowed up more inches between them. "You girls are something else." He mimicked a West African accent, a smile carving into his tan, leathery face.

"Excuse me!" Kemi slid off the stool and onto her feet, but he blocked her exit.

"Wait, wait," the greasy man pleaded. "Don't go yet. What's your name, *ehn*?" She pushed past him and out of his reach when he tried to grab her arm. She burst into the warm spring night, taking deep breaths, trying to calm her racing heart. She should have slapped him. A nice, strong backhand slap. She should have showed him one more thing African girls were good at.

That voice came back again. Her gut screamed while holding her ego in a headlock. *Run home to DC!*

No, she was too far along. She couldn't let self-doubt climb in now. This move to Sweden had been handed to her on a platter, and she'd be a fool to go back to the status quo. Sweden was coming with its own dating rules, and she knew she'd have to work hard to decipher them.

After all, in addition to a new career opportunity, wasn't she looking for love? To be enough for someone?

She wrapped her arms around herself, hugging her chest, and stepping lightly down Gamla stan's cobblestones toward the waterfront for a relaxing stroll back to her hotel. The city shimmered, and its golden reflections bounced off unusually calm waters that evening.

What a tease of a city.

June and July were a flurry of preparations. Closing accounts. Canceling memberships. Clearing out her closet and driving some boxes down to Kehinde in Richmond for storage. Andre the electrician had texted a couple times in between, looking to get laid. She ignored his messages. Andersen & Associates seemed like the last chapter in a book she was eager to close. Besides a few LinkedIn notifications indicating that Connor was occasionally viewing her profile, he'd extracted himself from her life.

Before her move, Kemi spent her last few days in Richmond with Kehinde, Lanre, and their kids.

"How are you feeling?" Lanre asked as the three adults settled in the living room, carrying after-dinner mugs of tea.

"I don't know yet." Kemi lifted the mug to her lips.

"Haaa," Kehinde interjected. "And you're leaving in a few days? You're not serious at all."

"I mean, I'm excited. I need this change. I need this reminder that I'm worth it, that there's something else out there for me," Kemi continued. "I would love what you guys have."

Lanre pursed his lips and nodded. "It is hard work but fulfilling."

"I know," Kemi said. "My sister is happy. That's all the evidence I need."

Indeed, Kehinde had reached contentment. Or was it resignation from dreams unachieved? Kemi wasn't sure of anything these days, so she settled on contentment.

"If it doesn't work out, you know we'll always be here, right?" Kehinde said softly.

Kemi met her eyes, tears pooling. She twisted her lips to hold them back and nodded swiftly, not trusting herself to speak.

EIGHT

BRITTANY-RAE

Back in Alexandria, Brittany must have sounded like a blubber-ing mess to Tanesha, who listened quietly on the other end. Trying to speak between sobs and gulping for air was challenging. Brittany punctuated each unintelligible stream with, "*Oh God!*"

"Babe... Babe..." Tanesha tried calming her down. "Deep breaths, breathe, breathe." Brittany finally stopped trying to talk and completely gave herself over to despair. She knew her friend was slowly letting it all sink in. Brittany was pregnant. From that man she had sworn to Tanesha that she hardly knew. She'd kept him a secret because sharing him would have brought judgment from her parents. And Tanesha.

Brittany had sworn to her friend she would never date a white man. She always said that the ones she met represented oppression and violation and kept the circle jerk going because they were all in on it together.

"You've been working first class too long," Tanesha would say whenever Brittany's strokes over white men felt too broad.

"You don't understand, Tee," Brittany cried into her phone. "This wasn't supposed to happen! I use birth control!" She had become the 2 percent. While 98 percent of people were safely covered and continued on with their lives, hers had just come crashing down.

"Wait! Back up... When did you start seeing this guy?"

If she wanted Tanesha in her corner, she needed to fully come clean. She started from the beginning. Told her everything about Jonny. How he'd gotten under her skin and made her feel things in a way she'd never felt before.

"He kept flying to meet me at my stopovers," Brittany said. "Talk about being loaded! You should see his London pad. He also has a London assistant and chauffeur."

She told Tanesha about his quirks that made him feel like a drug to her. A quick study who unwittingly held her in his palm.

"God, I feel like I've lost my damn mind," Brittany said. "He's so intense, Tee. I mean, this guy has memorized my body and what I like."

"Okay, too much information, *guurl*!" Tanesha said. "But, just so we're on the same page... How so?"

Jonny had mined his strength—his meticulous fervor—to utterly seduce her, Brittany explained. He'd sealed it with his secret weapon: an inability to lie.

"He can't even look me in the eye and lie," Brittany continued. "Isn't that what women want? A man who treats them like a queen? Down to anticipating her every want?"

"Hmm. Sounds like a man who worships and adores you. And freaking owns everything," Tanesha said. "So, how did he take the baby news?"

Brittany sniffed back tears. How had Jonny reacted when she'd barfed her brains out during sex? He'd found her on her knees in the bathroom, puking her guts out. He had clearly been scared, unsure of how to make her feel better.

When she turned to look at him, his eyes were wide. He had deduced it all on sight.

"You're pregnant?" He seemed frozen by the bathroom door. She left his question hanging, got to her feet, and flushed the toilet. She squeezed past him to her room. He followed her. After grabbing a towel, she popped into the shower. Still stark, he sat on her bed while she washed off, waiting for her.

When Brittany stepped out in a towel, he got to his feet, hands balled into fists by his sides, a naked statue frozen in her room.

"Jonny..."

"I want it."

"You don't know what you want. This was going to end sooner or later." Brittany brushed wet hair off her face. Jonny's eyes followed her hand before returning to her face. "You knew that."

"I know what I want." He held his intensity. "I want you... I want it... I want us." She shook her head, suppressing tears with hard bites on her lower lip.

"I can't keep it." She started to cry. "I can't. It's selfish to ask me to."

"Please," he pleaded.

"Jonny, this is insane. We both knew it wasn't going to last." She sniffed. "Your track record..."

"I love you."

The words from Jonny landed before they were both ready. Gravity sunk them straight to the floor.

"What?" The barely audible word slid out of Brittany. Jonny closed the space between them, settling into his favorite spot inches from her face.

"I love you." He said those words again, louder.

"You don't know me."

"I do."

Brittany cried. "I don't know what to do with a baby right now.

My life in Alexandria..." He watched as she gasped for air. Jonny instantly reached out to stroke her cheek, trying to calm her breathing, before pressing closer to her.

"I swear to you," he whispered against her cheek. "I'll take care of you. I'll take care of our baby."

Those words from Jonny's mouth had been too real for Brittany to process. *Our baby*. He had gathered her into his arms as she sobbed the rest of that night.

She relayed a condensed version of the events to Tanesha over the phone.

"That's a good thing," Tanesha said. "He's stepping up to the plate. He promised to take care of you and his child. Heck, the dude said he loves you!"

"He's not in love. He's infatuated. There's a difference."

"How does he make you feel?" Tanesha asked.

"Everything else falls away when we're together. When he looks at me..." Brittany felt her heart beating anew.

"Brit?"

Brittany hummed back. She knew what Tanesha was going to say. They'd been friends for nearly two decades.

"I think you love this Jonny guy, but it's killing you to admit it because you're stubborn."

"Tanesha, you don't know what you're talking about."

"You're stubborn, Brit. You don't want to accept that you've fallen for this man," Tanesha said. "Girl, I hear it in your voice. Do you love him?"

A long stretch of silence, and then a soft "maybe" escaped Brittany. She muttered the word so weakly that she wasn't convinced herself. Jonny seemed to need her desperately. The wealthiest man she had ever met had given her such complete power over him. And that feeling was intoxicatingly headier than love.

She wasn't sure she loved him yet, but it was only a matter of time. Right?

"It doesn't make you weaker, Brit. He's showing you he loves you," Tanesha said. "Let him take care of you."

Jonny came to Alexandria a few days later during Brittany's break between her work schedule for August. Distance had given them both time to think. Jonny came back stronger, telling her he wanted this baby more than anything in the world because he wanted Brittany.

Her time was up. Jamal had stopped paying for their town home. With her tail between her legs, Brittany mentioned this to Jonny while they were in bed. He proceeded to immediately call Eva in London. A few melodic words of Swedish later, he hung up.

"It's sorted," he said, pushing the phone away. She thanked him, cocooning herself in the fact that he cared. That was why he was helping her out. Not because she was so desperate, she was now fully dependent on his charity. The chorus of the unholy trinity began singing within her, sounding like, *Desperation! Desperation!* to the tune of "Hallelujah."

"Come to Stockholm with me," Jonny said, planting a kiss on her belly. "Come meet my family."

"It's too soon," Brittany protested.

"If they meet you now, they won't be surprised when our baby comes later." His logic made sense. He was already trying to protect her. She pulled his head up for a kiss, but he stopped her and peered at her instead.

"Do you love me?" Jonny asked, his eyes burrowing into her.

Brittany wasn't ready for those words.

Instead, she gently pressed her lips to his in a featherlight gesture. Jonny returned her kiss fiercely, his left hand scaling the swell of her rear to crush her to his body.

MUNA

VON LUNDIN MARKETING. Muna read the words on a small, gold plaque plastered onto the Birger Jarlsgatan address. The name "von Lundin" sounded very familiar, but she couldn't place where she had heard of it before. The large, wooden door, distressed from old age, was locked. She waited for the cleaning crew Yagiz had told her about. Beyond having to wait, she knew nothing about them or how many people she was meeting.

She scanned the street, barren this early in the morning. There were a few joggers—lithe bodies with otherworldly proportions wearing skintight Lycra with swinging ponytails. The sound of their determined, pounding feet was interrupted by men rustling around in trash bins for plastic bottles and empty soda cans to recycle for money. A taxi or two whizzed by. One of Stockholm's wealthiest streets was sparse at this hour.

She adjusted her black headscarf, feeling naked as she stared down at the blue T-shirt she was wearing over shapeless black pants she'd picked up at a secondhand store. She'd put her hair in two cornrows and wound the black scarf around them. She ran her fingers over her exposed chin and the top of her neck, cool air wrapping around her. It felt good.

At ten minutes past six a.m., two men wearing matching black polo shirts and black pants came tramping toward her, followed by a woman, all with olive skin, dark hair, and features that suggested Middle Eastern. The two men introduced themselves as Azeez and Qasim. Azeez was lean, and even though his limbs looked fragile, Muna knew they had carried him to Sweden, and with that came a certain kind of strength. The woman was short, barely reaching Muna's shoulders, and was shaped like an orange. She already had her name tag pinned to her black polo shirt—Huda.

"Okay, *yalla, let's go!*" Azeez pulled out keys, punched in codes, and waited for the sharp buzz of entry before the old door willed itself open. Lights flickered on as the crew walked down the gray halls of von Lundin Marketing. The Sunday cleaning crew had already prepped the place for Monday morning. All Team Azeez did on Monday mornings was make sure coffee machines and kitchenettes were properly cleaned and stocked, that it was tidy around desks and cubicles, and that the toilets were kept clean until four p.m. when they left.

Once they convened in the staff room, Azeez handed her an extra-large polo shirt bearing a matching logo with the initials of Yagiz's cleaning company, YSR, which Muna would later find out represented *Yagiz' Städning och Rengöring*—Yagiz's Tidying and Cleaning. Menial tasks were doled out, and Muna immediately went for a mop. She reminisced about Solsidan, where she had made sure the verandah was always spotless, as she gripped the long, wooden handle with purpose. She would pour her heart into this. She would work so hard that Yagiz would make her boss.

Employees started streaming in between nine and ten that

morning. Muna pressed into the wall as they came in and milled around the common areas. She watched groups casually stroll into the kitchen, pour themselves coffee, and chat about their weekends. Concerts, family activities, *kräftskivor*—crayfish parties. Words like Maldives, Greece, and Argentina floated in the air. Many of them had been away all July. Early August meant reconvening to brag about their luxurious holidays as much as they could as long as they were all bragging equally, Muna noted.

Envy knotted deep within her. The one thing she would pick if presented with those luxuries was family. Luckily, she had sisters now: Yasmiin and Khadiija.

She busied herself around the kitchen, rearranging, cleaning, eavesdropping. She might as well have been a phantom. They paid no attention to her moving around them. Their conversation died down when a pair of heeled footsteps came clunking into the kitchen area. Muna turned in time to see a Black sister, shaped like the number eight, come in. She had lots of hair on her head. Extensions, Muna could tell. She was wearing a black-and-white vertical-striped dress and a white jacket. Muna gawked at her, enamored by her presence in this space.

The Black sister's gaze reached Muna from the group, and she nodded at her with a smile. Muna looked away and back down at her hands, which were holding a cleaning cloth.

The group switched to English. Muna's English was weak, but she could pick out a few words. *How are you? Excited. Move. Washington, DC.* This Black woman must be American. Muna hadn't seen any other Black faces on the three floors she had cleaned. She stopped tinkering around the kitchen and watched as the group surrounded this mystery woman, who seemed to be smiling and happy. She poured herself a latte from the automatic dispenser, turned to give the group a courteous wave, and clicked away down the hall.

Muna was about to turn back to her phantom tasks when she caught it. That wordless look they were giving one another over mugs of coffee upon her departure.

One of them, a woman, chuckled. "*Alltså.. Det där var annorlunda...*" So...that was different.

Muna frowned, unsure of how to process the remark, which was followed by low giggles. This group was laughing at that woman, and Muna needed to know why. What had she done wrong?

"*Vilken vågad klänning!*" Someone commented on her "brave" choice of outfit.

"*Den där amerikanska auran... jag pallar inte!*" That American aura...I can't handle it!

"*Men hon är nigerianska...*" But she's Nigerian, a guy with short, reddish hair jumped in.

"*Strunt samma...*" Doesn't matter. All the same.

"*Jag fattar inte vad hennes jobb går ut på...*" I don't understand what her job entails.

"*Vi behöver mer bruna och svarta ansikten hos oss.*" We need more brown and Black faces here.

"*Oavsett deras kvalifikationer?*" Regardless of their qualifications? This came from an older lady exuding irritation. Muna couldn't guess her age, so she estimated higher. Early sixties?

"*Men Greta... Hon är den bästa i hela USA på det hon gör.*" She's the best at her job in the whole U.S. The redhead guy seemed to be defending her.

"*Strunt samma...*" Doesn't matter, that lady said before sipping scalding coffee from her mug once again.

Muna wanted to leave, but she was rooted on the spot, as if in invisible service as an undercover agent—a sister spy. She could gather intel for that curvy Black woman who had been smiling at them minutes ago.

That was when they spotted Muna, frozen like a statue, observing them. After clearing their throats, they quickly disbanded, leaving her to fully digest their conversation.

On the ride back to Tensta after her shift, her mind drifted back to the group and the way they were talking behind that Black woman's back. Was that how Mattias from Solsidan talked about her? About them? And Gunhild with the kind eyes? Mr. Björn at Migrationsverket with his flatlined demeanor?

Paranoia gripped her. Who could she fully trust that wouldn't see her as someone to be talked about behind closed doors?

When she walked into their apartment, it was into a waft of sesame and cardamom. Khadiija was in the kitchen cooking *cambuulo*, a rice and bean dish. Muna's stomach grumbled, and she realized she hadn't eaten all day.

Yasmiin was sitting with her feet propped atop their coffee table, painting her toenails neon turquoise. Muna shuffled in, dropped her bag by the door, and dragged herself toward the living room. She plopped her tired bones onto the sofa.

"How was it?" Yasmiin asked in Somali, examining the glittering nails in front of her. Muna pulled off her black scarf, staring past Yasmiin into space. The heavy silence was enough to drag Yasmiin's face away from her task.

"Was it that bad?"

Muna needed to think. First, that Black woman. Second, those Swedes talking about the Black woman behind her back.

"Please thank Yagiz for me," Muna said in a flat tone. At the mention of Yagiz's name, Yasmiin stopped painting her nails and looked up at Muna once more, her eyes hard.

"Trust me, I've thanked him enough."

Muna felt a fracture of vulnerability with light streaming through. She wedged her foot into the space, hoping to hold the emotional crack open. She'd been treading lightly around the two girls, afraid they'd someday fight and no longer be sisters.

"Why? Does he want something from you?" Muna asked softly. Yasmiin looked at her, laughed, then resumed her painting.

"How was your first day?"

"Okay. Not too much to do," she said. "Those Swedes...you wouldn't believe the things they talk about."

Yasmiin snickered. "I can only imagine."

"There was this beautiful sister there," Muna continued. "Dressed like she had money. I was so proud of her. But you should have heard what they said when she left."

"Like what?" Khadiija yelled from the kitchen over a sizzling pot. "What did they say?"

"I don't really know," Muna said, still processing. "They don't like her Americanness. But she's from Africa too. Nigeria. I don't know what she does, but they were complaining about more brown and Black faces...something like that."

"Hmm," Yasmiin let out. "What else? Was that it?"

Muna seemed perplexed. "Yes, but..."

Yasmiin cackled then stood, being careful not to smudge her nails.

"They could have said worse," Yasmiin said. "Like placing bets on who she fucked to get that fine job!" Yasmiin shuffled toward her room, her safe space.

"Yasmiin!" Muna called out, halting her exit. The older girl turned to her.

"What?"

"How did you meet Yagiz?"

The question threw Yasmiin off guard, and she frowned curiously at Muna.

"Why do you want to know? You like him?"

"No, no... I was just curious. He seems nice," Muna said. Yasmiin laughed at her.

"You know what they say about curiosity and the goat."

Muna hadn't heard that version, but she didn't mind being a goat to find out. "Tell me."

Yasmiin let out a sigh then padded back to where Muna was sitting.

"Well, you've seen Yagiz. Fine man," she started. "That hair, that moustache." Her hands mimed his features in the air. "I met him at that reggae dance hall club in Akalla. You know the one?"

Muna shook her head.

"Anyway, he and his Turkish boys came, stood in a corner. Looking like bosses." She chuckled. "We danced and danced. Said he loves African booty."

Muna shifted in her seat.

"We kissed and kissed—deep with tongue and everything... Have you kissed before?"

Muna remained quiet. She wasn't ready to share Ahmed. The girls had kept their own secrets from her, the pasts they were also running from. If there were a superpower she was slowly cultivating, it was patience. She could wait forever.

"We continued outside in some dark corner, and then BOOM!"

Yasmiin pounded a fist into her open palm, laughing. "Two Eritrean brothers dragged Yagiz off me, but he laughed and gave me his business card."

"Why?" Muna asked.

"Why what?" Yasmiin seemed perplexed, her laugh dying down.

"Why did you kiss a man you don't know like that?"

Silence filled the room. Muna watched Yasmiin's easy smile slide off her face. She gave Muna a smirk before turning to go. The slamming of Yasmiin's door completed the proverb about curiosity and the goat.

Yagiz was off-limits, and Muna wanted to know why.

KẸMI

"Shermmy? Shermmy?" the bespectacled teacher called out over a semicircle of students. It was Kemi's first day of Swedish class at Folkuniversitetet, an adult vocational school located a couple blocks from her office. As usual, Kemi felt overdressed. Excitement and nervousness tangoed within her. This was it. She was officially learning Swedish and making a commitment to her new home.

She looked around the group of fourteen, all sitting behind tables forming a half-moon around the teacher, a well-groomed guy in his mid- to late forties with dark hair and perfectly trimmed eyebrows.

"Shermmy's not here?" he called out again. The group flashed quick glances at one another. Everyone else had checked in, except Kemi.

"Okay then." He closed his book and was turning to walk to his desk when Kemi called out to him.

"You didn't call my name...Kemi." The man regarded her over glasses with thin frames then reopened his book.

"That's all I have," he said. "Can you spell your name?"

"K-E-M-I."

"So, how do you pronounce it?" he asked.

"Keh-me," she offered. A smile slowly crept onto his face.

"Ah, I see... Keh-me... Your name is spelled like chemistry in Swedish. *K-E-M-I*... We pronounce it 'Shermmy'!"

Once Kemi filed that trivia away for future reference, their teacher, José Lundqvist, started his lecture completely in Swedish. The students occasionally glanced at one another, trying to follow along, until someone raised a hand.

"Excuse me. I can't follow what you're saying. It's all in Swedish," a voice with an American accent spoke up.

"This is a Swedish class," José continued in Swedish. The group could make out the words *svenska* and *klass*, thus deducing his sarcasm.

"But it's our first class," the American argued. José was defiant. He walked up to the board and started scribbling in Swedish.

"If this were a free SFI class," the American continued, "I wouldn't care. But I'm actually paying for this course and would like to get my money's worth!"

The group fell silent, shocked by the man's outburst.

His words were strong enough to pivot José back to facing the class. He took a deep breath and stared at the guy, looked down into his notebook, and then back at him.

"Malcolm..." he stressed. Malcolm regarded him with questioning eyes.

"How will you learn if I keep speaking English?" José quizzed in English.

"I will learn. But you also have to understand our position," Malcolm answered. Low murmuring within the group surfaced in support. Malcolm did have a point, the murmurs whispered.

Outnumbered, José looked around the class and then settled on Malcolm, whose linebacker physique was squeezed into a tiny chair.

"Very well. If you don't follow along, just raise your hand, and I will try...in little English," he offered before going back to the board.

The class droned on for two more hours, ending at eight p.m. Kemi's brain had stopped functioning an hour earlier. She needed to rush home, get some dinner, and prep for work in the morning.

As she was stuffing a notebook and dictionary into her oversize bag, a voice floated over her shoulder. "So, what's your story?" She spun around to face the six-footer who had snuck up behind her as she packed. He had a large Afro of wispy curls, dull-gray eyes, and caramel-colored skin.

"Malcolm, right?" She extended her hand. "Kemi." His grip was strong. "I just got a job here. And you?"

"Musician," he said. "Saxophone."

"Cool!" She was overly excited and calmed herself down before continuing. "How long have you been here?" He shook his head and tsked. There was a longer story in there than she had time for tonight.

"Well, my mom's Swedish, and my dad's African American," he started. "They divorced when I was ten. She ran back to Sweden and left me with him." Kemi shifted her feet, unsure if she was ready to receive his life story as thoughts of ramen noodles swam around in her head.

"I'm sorry," she started to say, hoping to cut him off. But he continued.

"Yeah, my dad died last year, and my mom fell really ill, so I decided to move to Sweden to spend some time with her, you know."

"Oh, Malcolm, I'm so sorry," she said. He shrugged.

"That's life, you know. Now I'm here, trying to navigate all this shit and whatnot," he said, slinging his messenger bag across his broad chest. "Look, I know you gotta run. Great meeting you, Kemi. Let's chat on Wednesday." Before she could respond, he barreled out of the room like a charismatic tornado. In those two minutes, Kemi realized she'd learned more about Malcolm than she had about Ingrid or Espen so far.

Her high-heeled feet were killing her by the time she got home. She waited for the creepy elevator as it deposited its occupants—a wizened but startled couple, spooked by Kemi's presence in their building. She squeezed past them into the elevator with a smile and an oil-stained paper bag of ramen noodles in hand.

She was slowly beginning to settle into some form of routine, including finding favorite take-out joints and neighborhood grocery stores.

During her first few days at von Lundin, she sat at her desk twiddling her thumbs over her laptop. It wasn't unusual. First days were usually blurs of doing nothing useful. She simply milled around the office, meeting more colleagues, filling herself up with lattes, trying to beat the boredom. Her first lunch with Ingrid had been quick. A dash downstairs and one street over to Espresso House for salads. After tasting the coffee there, she decided she would add a pre-work stop at Espresso House to her daily morning routine.

Ingrid and Kemi returned to find their team gathered in the conference room for a "Welcome Kemi *Fika!*" party. In the middle of the table sat a neon-green *Prinsesstårta*—princess cake—topped with a pink marzipan rose. Once cut, it oozed so much whipped cream, Kemi was sure she gained five pounds just by looking at the darn thing.

Jonny, as expected, wasn't in the office, and she was told not to count on him.

After work, she'd be going to Swedish class twice a week, Mondays and Wednesdays from five to eight p.m. With the brutal first class behind her, she had to wonder if she would ever learn to hear the difference between *sjö*, *sju*, and *kö*.

Now back in her apartment, she pulled out her laptop and dug into her ramen noodles, slurping hungrily as she started pulling up browsers, prepping for her favorite pastime: scouring dating sites.

Her first week as a Swedish resident, she figured the quickest way to explore the city and find her way into its culture would be through its men. She had hope. But when she'd googled "Black in Sweden," she discovered it wasn't going to be easy. *Swedes are insular,* one site warned. *You're going to have to make the first move,* a travel article about dating around the globe suggested. *Curious guys use every reflective surface to check your body out instead of looking directly.*

She kept scrolling past profiles and faces while gobbling up her noodles. She wasn't sure what she was looking for, but she knew what her body responded to: brawn. Her electrician Andre flashed through her mind. She kept scrolling past pretty boy after pretty boy. Metrosexuals in all shades. Weathered men too. And the occasional guy who looked like he'd wandered onto the wrong website and mistakenly created a profile with a serious corporate headshot, thinking it was LinkedIn.

She paused on one bearded, brawny guy and used Google Translate to read his Swedish profile. She flipped through extra photos of Bearded Brawn, ogling various stages of undress. Wow, Bearded Brawn looked good in a suit, a dress shirt stretching suggestively over his broad chest. Bearded Brawn loved to work out too. Muay Thai boxing.

She pored through this particular profile until a pop-up notification from Bearded Brawn startled her, making her splash drops of noodle broth.

Jag ser att du kollar på min profil :) "I see you checking out my profile."

She quickly copied the text, translated it, and blushed. What the heck? This site was tracking everything. She couldn't ogle in peace without the oglee finding out? She pushed her noodles aside and typed back.

"Busted :) Sorry, my Swedish is nonexistent."

She sent it off and bit a nail. Her body was definitely reacting to this particular pick. A few seconds later, he responded.

"You're funny...and cute."

Lazy but okay, she'd play along.

"Thanks. So Muay Thai? That's pretty intense."
"Yeah I lived in Thailand for a while when I was backpacking last year, and totally got into it."

Backpacking? Last year? She quickly flipped over from the chat window to his profile to double-check his age. His photos had distracted her. She found it. Sebastian was twenty-one. *Shit*. How did he get so bearded and brawny so quickly? She had to end it now. What would she do with a twenty-one-year-old who had just returned from backpacking around the world?

"Backpacking? Wow, you seem so...young."

There was a long stretch of inactivity, and then Sebastian came back.

"I like older women."

Okurrr, Bearded Brawn.

She ended up chatting with Sebastian for over an hour, and the kid seemed like an old soul. Adventurous too, with dozens of countries under his belt. He was fluent in Spanish and totally down with the sisters.

When they met that Friday, it was to an Arctic chill that Kemi hadn't anticipated. She'd arrived early to the dinner spot he'd chosen on the island of Södermalm. She'd put on one of her flattering dresses, had done her favorite smoky eye makeup, and waited with a glass of Prosecco in hand at one of the candlelit tables for two. When Sebastian walked in, she recognized him right away. Tall, broad-shouldered, and with his beard, he had a Viking vibe about him. He looked delicious. She smiled, getting to her feet.

But he never approached her. He was still parked close to the front door, and his eyes caught hers from across the room. She frowned quizzically, trying to read his expression.

Was that...disappointment?

Caught halfway up, she quickly collected herself and sat back down, pretending she had mistaken him for someone else. She started fiddling with her cutlery. A few seconds later, she looked up to find that he had vanished, as if he'd been an apparition all along. Kemi bit her lower lip, trying to decipher what had just happened. She didn't have to think long, because her phone buzzed with a notification from her dating app. It was Sebastian.

"I'm sorry... You don't match your picture."

Those words were like salt on an open wound. She knew what she needed to do right away, but she wanted to know why he'd bolted. She knew better than to ask him only to satisfy her self-destructive sense of curiosity.

"What do you mean?"
"Uhmm... I mean... You're kind of fat."

Fat?

Kemi wasn't sure where to begin with his statement. This was the first time in her entire disaster-filled dating life that a guy had said she didn't match her photos. Photos she'd carefully curated to accentuate her best features. She was a U.S. size twelve and considered herself average. Curvaceous yes, but definitely not fat. Then again...the twelves she wore a few years ago, she couldn't fit into today. Fashion retailers were cunning creatures.

She chugged her Prosecco.

After downing its last drop, she turned back to her phone and typed:

"Fuck you."

NINE

Brittany's morning flight to Stockholm from London had been brutal. The greasy waft of scrambled eggs and pork sausages in business class had churned her stomach through the two-and-a-half-hour flight over the North Atlantic. But she kept it together by focusing on meditation exercises.

She wasn't sure if the nausea was from her growing baby or the fact that she was on her way to meet Jonny's family. Initially, she'd protested, but after the long heart-to-heart with Tanesha, she decided to give Jonny a chance to prove he was worth upending her life for. If he was worth pulling her off course into a much faster, albeit cushier, lane.

Within minutes of Brittany's agreeing to come, Eva called from the London office to plan her travel itinerary—and also get details about her monthly rent. Brittany wasn't sure how to feel about being taken care of by proxy, but she let Eva do what she did best, choosing to gloss over the fact that Eva knew how to take care of Jonny's women.

Now she was here. Her first time in Scandinavia really, even though she'd crisscrossed Europe over the years as a flight attendant. She planned to stay for five days—long enough to get a sense of what she was sinking into. Truth be told, she was terrified. Scared shitless that they would judge her on sight. Not that their opinion should matter, she consoled herself, but this rash pursuit she'd indulged in with Jonny had left her exposed and vulnerable. A state she didn't want to be in right now.

When the automatic doors of the Terminal 2 arrivals area smoothly pulled apart, Jonny was there waiting in his typical stance, fists balled at his sides. His face broke out into a grin, reeling her in.

"Jonny..."

His mouth covered hers in a fierce kiss. One that blotted out the entire hall, while strangers looked on, a bit dazed and caught off guard too. He deepened the kiss, his left hand moving to cradle her right cheek. Self-consciousness gripped Brittany, and she wiggled out of his hold. She licked her lips shyly, while he remained inches from her face.

"Jonny...good to see you too." She smiled, daring not to look around, as she already felt strange eyes scorching her skin. She was still learning how to wear their relationship with pride.

He stepped in closer and covered her lips once more with his. Brittany melted into his arms. His heat didn't seem to be waning. If anything, Brittany was beginning to wonder if he was indeed obsessed with her. But she let him kiss her the way she liked.

Until someone bumped into them. A conscious act because the following "*Förlåt, sorry!*" mumbled by the blond woman felt devoid of remorse as she shot Brittany a dirty look. The slam was hard enough to jolt Jonny back into reality, and he reached for Brittany's carry-on bag. As if on autopilot, he flattened his left palm on her stomach.

"How are you?" he asked quietly, searching her face for signs of discomfort.

"I didn't puke on the plane, so..." Her attempt at humor washed over him.

"Did you get sick again from...*you know*?"

"I'm fine. Nausea comes with it."

He gave her a weak smile and led her downstairs and out to the outdoor parking area where his silver Tesla was parked. Minutes later, they were cruising down E4 toward downtown Stockholm in a comfortable silence that wrapped around Brittany like the softest Merino wool. Moved by these feelings, she rested her left palm on his thigh as he drove. He tensed beneath her touch, and she sensed it. He seemed surprised by her show of affection. Up until this point, he'd always initiated intimacy.

"Are you okay?"

"No. Yes. I mean, of course." He seemed frazzled. "You caught me off guard, that's all." She studied his profile.

"Are you nervous too?" she asked.

"About what?"

"Revealing us to your family? To the world?"

He gently grabbed her hand from his thigh and lifted it to his lips. "I'm not nervous." He kissed the back of her palm softly, murmuring into it. "I can't wait to show you off."

Jonny started rattling off the schedule for the week, eyes firmly on the road. He had planned it all. Well, Louise—his Stockholm assistant—had planned it all.

Brittany had flown in Wednesday afternoon. Thursday was reserved for a little sightseeing. They were meeting his parents for lunch on Friday before the retirees headed out to Doha, Qatar, for a long weekend. Friday night was dinner and hitting his favorite clubs and lounges. On Saturday, they would head over to Antonia's for her traditional August *kräftskiva* in Elfvik on Lidingö, one of the many islands that made up the Stockholm archipelago. Brittany was also going to meet his other sister, Svea, as well as a few close friends there. Then she was taking the early morning flight back to London and on to Dulles by Sunday.

Brittany took a pronounced breath. This was all too much. She was going to meet the von Lundin dynasty. His parents in particular were her greatest concern.

"Well, I'm glad you're not nervous. I'm terrified." She laughed. "Your parents..."

"My parents? Oh, they're scary," he stressed. Brittany burst out laughing. Her chuckle died down when she realized he wasn't joking, his face remaining tense as he drove. The rolling countryside soon gave way to monochromatic structures as they neared Stockholm proper. Blue and red buses crisscrossed around them.

"I live in town, close to all the action," he said as he steered. Brittany gawked at the postcard-perfect setting surrounding her once they hit Strandvägen. Jonny pointed out ferries and boats lining waterfronts. Elegant, cream-colored buildings looked like cake icing piped along the waterfront. Tourists milled around, many with cameras, stopping absentmindedly in the middle of walking to take photos. They pushed on past Djurgården, which had oddly shaped buildings cresting lush, green tree lines. Jonny mentioned he was taking her there tomorrow to visit its museums.

He veered right into a quieter neighborhood, where they drove past different plaques and flags of various embassies, including the American Embassy.

"We're almost there," Jonny said before pulling into a small driveway belonging to a modest-looking villa with waterfront access. At its private pier bobbed a small speedboat, which she assumed he used to zip around Stockholm's waterways to avoid automobile traffic.

Unlike his glass watchtower in London, this villa was small, reminiscent of a hobbit cottage but still modern. Aside from a single concrete wall, the open-plan villa facing the water was floor-to-ceiling glass. It was sparsely decorated with the same gray tones as inside his tower at Canary Wharf. Railless steps, with nothing to block a drunken fall, led up to a small loft area with a vaulted ceiling, the only bedroom in the place.

"This feels more like you," Brittany said, pirouetting to take in his pad in one three-hundred-and-sixty-degree sweep.

"You think so?"

"I know so."

He grabbed her carry-on and took it up to the loft area. He jogged back down those stairs with no railings, which frightened her. Then he planted himself in his usual spot, inches from her face.

"This isn't a good place for a baby," he said. "It's unsafe. We need more space. This isn't good enough." She shushed him with a light kiss, which he took over right before an excited voice chimed in.

"*Hallå?*"

Brittany jumped when a brunette the size and build of Eva materialized from nowhere. She stared at Brittany, seemingly enamored, until Jonny introduced her.

"This is Louise, my assistant."

"Of course." Brittany reached out to shake her hand. "Nice to meet you."

"Eva told me how pretty you are." She beamed as she turned to Jonny and shot into a barrage of Swedish before Brittany could acknowledge her compliment. After about three minutes, she turned to Brittany to inform her of their arrangements.

"You must be so tired from your trip, so you just take it easy. We've ordered an early dinner. Is there anything you'd especially like?" Louise studiously inquired.

A new feeling started crawling up from within Brittany's depths. If this was what being taken care of by a man several levels wealthier than Beaufount was like, she was beginning to find it suffocating. With Jamal, she had taken the lead with everything, and he'd pulled out money as needed. He never made her feel like she wasn't independent enough to thrive without him and make her own decisions. Jonny had two pixies who were grooming her as if she were engaged to a crown prince.

She decided she didn't like them doting on her.

"Jonny thinks fish might make you sick," Louise continued. "So, a light pasta dish might work?"

"A salad is fine."

"You need to eat," Jonny whispered, wrapping his arms around her from behind. He ran his palms over her stomach and kissed her cheek. The gesture caught Louise by surprise, blood rushing to her cheeks, flushing them red. Brittany caught her change in color and disposition. This extravagant display was probably unlike Jonny when he was in boss mode in front of his staff, so Brittany tried to wiggle out of it.

"Stop," Brittany whispered back, turning toward his exploring mouth. He kissed her. "Stop doing that." Louise was smart and would figure it out if he kept running his hands over her belly. He stopped and pulled back.

A flustered Louise took her leave to go organize their dinner while Jonny pulled Brittany back into his embrace.

"Is this all we are?" Brittany asked before his mouth sought hers again.

"What do you mean?" He stopped midtask.

"I mean, this. Everything. Us..." She wasn't sure what she was trying to say. "Would we still be together if we stopped having sex?"

His brows knitted together, confused at her words. Then he crushed a kiss on her to stop her from talking.

When Louise arrived an hour later, it was to Jonny and Brittany, arms intertwined, sleeping on his couch with a thin blanket barely covering their naked bodies.

MUNA

Muna stood half-hidden by the wall, observing the Black African sister with the American accent. She was sitting in a corner, hunched over a laptop, studying something intently on the screen. On her desk was a takeaway latte cup from Espresso House. Muna studied her. She wasn't sure if she was feeling envy or pride. She banked closer to the latter. This woman seemed to be important here. Muna felt her heart swell. She had to say something to her.

Propelled by admiration, Muna fully stepped out from behind the wall and slowly walked over to the woman. She was wearing crochet braids in loose curls and beneath her smart, camel-colored blazer was a forest-green pencil dress.

"*God morgon,*" Muna greeted. She couldn't speak English, but she could pick out a few words in conversation. The woman's head shot up, and she regarded Muna with kind eyes and deep dimples. Muna guessed she was excited to see another Black face.

"*God morgon!*" she threw back before taking in Muna's uniform and the cleaning cart she had been pushing. Muna wasn't sure what came next after "Good morning." She just introduced herself.

"*Jag heter Muna.*" She patted her chest. The woman patted her chest as well.

"*Jag heter Kemi,*" she said in bastardized Swedish that Muna instantly pitied. Muna wanted to hug her. To tell her more. That she was so happy to see her sitting there. That her colleagues were backstabbers. That Kemi was beautiful and confident. That her mere presence was giving Muna hope. That she wasn't going to be resigned to a life cleaning toilets.

But all Muna could manage was "*Tack så mycket,*" *Thank you very much*, and a short wave, before running off shyly with her cleaning cart as the woman stared after her.

A few hours later, it was time for their lunch break. Her cleaning crew had already disbanded and would reconvene in an hour. Azeez and Qasim were probably off smoking outdoors somewhere, and Huda always went to the same Lebanese buffet restaurant a few blocks away.

Muna pulled her bag closer as the elevator doors slid open. She glided in and punched the button for the ground floor, slowly watching them close. Suddenly, a large, strong hand wedged itself to stop the elevator. A tall man with bright, blond hair forcefully pushed himself in, while holding a smartphone in his free hand. Muna backed up until she was pressed against the wall. The man turned his back to her, standing in front of her, his shoulders completely blocking her view. She knew almost everyone in this building but had never seen this man before.

He lifted the smartphone back to his ear. The insect-like shrilling of the person on the other end kept on and on. The man simply listened, not saying a word. The voice on the other line kept talking, and then the man disconnected the call abruptly midconversation. She watched him slide the phone into his pocket. The elevator became silent once more, and she prayed the tall man didn't hear her breathing nervously.

He must have heard her though, because he turned to look at her over his shoulder. Muna inched back into the wall, but she was already pressed up against it. The man's light eyes took her in intensely. They roamed over her face as if they were lasers scanning her. She couldn't read his expression. If he was angry or curious. She didn't know what he wanted from her. He gawked at her, pinning her with his gaze until the elevator beeped its arrival on the ground floor.

Once the doors opened, the tall man dashed out with long strides. He seemed to be in a hurry. He must be very hungry for lunch, Muna thought as she padded behind him. He pushed the front doors in haste, not bothering to hold them open for her, and poured out onto the sidewalk where a tall Black woman was waiting, leaning against a fancy-looking car.

Muna slowed down her steps as she got to the door. Wow, she thought, as she saw one of the most beautiful women she'd ever seen. A real-life model in a soft-looking, purple summer dress. The color reminded her of ripe plums.

The tall, hungry man stopped in front of the woman. She smiled at him, and then he grabbed her and kissed her, leaning her against the car. Muna had seen men kiss women like this on TV with such vigor and passion, but to witness it in person was unsettling and embarrassing.

She stayed hidden behind the front door, watching the two

beautiful human beings paw at each other in broad daylight. She wasn't the only one disturbed by it, it seemed. A few passersby kept rubbernecking as they moved along the sidewalk, including an old man with a walker who simply froze.

Who was the blond man? Muna wondered. And that Black woman? It was clear they truly loved each other, because only love would make them do this in public with no shame.

When she got back to Tensta that evening, she detoured to a small restaurant right in the square, where Gunhild was waiting for her. The older lady pushed to her feet and pulled the younger one into a tight hug.

"Muna, dear," she said in Swedish. "How are things going? If it's okay, I've already ordered us a kebab pizza. Don't worry, the meat is halal."

"It's okay," Muna thanked her. Gunhild peered at the girl through thin glasses, eyes warming.

"How is the job going?"

It had been at least four weeks since Muna had started cleaning at von Lundin. Yagiz had not rotated her to other properties because he was fully staffed. He dedicated the four resources to that office while he shuffled the rest of his staff. Muna had sunk comfortably into her routine. On the days she wasn't working, she was taking back-to-back Swedish SFI classes out in the suburbs in Tensta. If she didn't clean, she would never be in town.

"It is going well." This was her chance to confide in Gunhild about Ahmed, but she kept quiet. Telling her about him meant dredging up memories from Solsidan she wasn't ready to face. Like

Ahmed's gut-wrenching cries as he burned. She wanted her last memories of Ahmed replaced by his smiling photo, carrying a sheep, eyes twinkling. Not his face being carved open by fire and the smell of his charred flesh.

"That is good." Gunhild paused to sip hot coffee as Muna watched her. "So, have you considered going to school to study something?"

"Study?"

"Yes, study. What would you like to be when you grow up?"

Those were words she hadn't heard since Mogadishu. When her economics teacher in high school had handed her an A as her final grade and beamed at her, he'd asked her what she wanted to be when she grew up. That was barely a week before her house had crumbled into pieces, taking her bedridden father with it.

Muna bent her head low, trying to collect her emotions and prevent tears from falling. It was a simple question that didn't need tears. She sniffed, composed herself, and looked back up at Gunhild.

"I want to be an accountant."

"If you want to be an accountant, then you will be an accountant." Gunhild forged on, saying she cared about Muna too much for her to be swallowed up by Tensta and never spat back out. That she was too *duktig* to be resigned to cleaning toilets for the rest of her life. She was only eighteen, and the world needed her to blossom.

Muna gave Gunhild a weak smile, and a warm feeling spread over her chest. A feeling of importance. What if she actually did become an accountant? Being an accountant would make her an important person. Then she would be able to find a good job or open her own business. Maybe she could buy YSR from Yagiz.

She needed a little power. Just a tiny drop so she didn't have to feel so helpless every day.

KEMI

By her first few months in Sweden, Kemi realized there was one thing she could get away with that she could never attempt in the U.S. Her crochet braids could stay in three to four weeks longer and get matted beyond recognition, because no one noticed.

But by her third month there, Kemi desperately needed a professional's touch. Her hair had evolved into a wretched mess, and she was still inept at crocheting hair despite watching countless videos on YouTube. The next time she went to her Swedish class, her hair was hidden beneath a silk scarf, and the task of finding a decent African hair salon weighed heavily on her mind.

Meanwhile, Malcolm the Afro-Swede and their teacher, José, quickly became mortal enemies. They went at it for the most trivial reasons, setting out to trigger each other. If Malcolm pronounced something incorrectly, José harped on it until the rest of the class begged him to move on. Malcolm was quick to let José know that his least favorite word was "*duktig*" and its variation: "*Vad duktigt!*" *How smart!* He expressed his hatred for that phrase, essentially handing José the ammunition he needed.

"Sweden definitely doesn't reward you if you disagree with it," Malcolm said as José was discussing the country's political structure and parties compared to the fiery American system.

"How so?" José took the bait, switching to English. The guys were going at it again over random shit in Kemi's Wednesday night class, and frankly she didn't care.

The weeks after Bearded Brawn refused to sit at her table had been brutal. Right after that botched date, she strolled over to Slussen station to take the red line home. She briefly stopped by a kiosk inside the station to buy two stale cinnamon buns, which she quickly scarfed down once inside her apartment.

Licking the last few pearls of sugar off her fingers, she made herself a mug of tea to digest the guilt away. She watched a period romance movie and cried herself to sleep. The rest of that weekend, she barricaded herself in her apartment.

On Sunday night, she gave Kehinde a call to check up on the family.

"What's wrong, Kemi?" Kehinde casually inquired as soon as they exchanged pleasantries.

Kemi stayed silent on the other end.

"How is Sweden?"

More silence. Kehinde gave her sister time.

"I don't know how I feel yet," Kemi said softly, sniffing. "I mean, it's been just a few months. Autumn is here, and I'm not sure I'm looking forward to winter."

"Are you having doubts?"

"No, no...it's just that...I don't know." Kemi couldn't quite put into words what she was feeling, but her twin sister already knew.

"You're lonely."

Those words broke Kemi, and she let her cries out. No one had invited her to meet their friends and families so far. Her colleagues had firm boundaries between work and play, and she was placed squarely in the work box. She complained about making friends. Those in her Swedish class didn't seem interested in making new friends or inviting classmates home. The only person who had extended an invitation was Malcolm to come watch him play saxophone in a jazz club in Gamla stan. She had barely seen Jonny since she'd arrived, and Ingrid had switched to full-on boss mode.

Kehinde listened to her sister cry until her sniffing faded away.

"You know, you're going to have to be patient. It hasn't been that long," Kehinde tried reasoning with her.

"I know, I know," Kemi agreed. Kehinde must have realized the tears were due to the fact that she had no one else close by to confide in. Zizi was no longer in her life, and she found herself missing Zizi's voice and her faux frustration at Kemi's indecisiveness. Zizi was supposed to have celebrated this major win with her. Yet Kemi was still having a hard time unpacking what had combusted between them. A stick of dynamite buried between them that Kemi didn't know her news would inadvertently light.

Kehinde was too far away for weekend visits. Kemi hadn't lived elsewhere since she arrived in the U.S. almost two decades ago. Besides the disorienting culture shock, the gravity of the situation had started dawning on her. She had rushed in unprepared.

Kemi had tried to build routines into her day, hoping to maintain some semblance of control. Every morning, she stopped by Espresso House to pick up a tall latte. After work, she took a light stroll around Karlaplan or headed out to nearby Gärdet's green fields—only on evenings when she wasn't stuffing her face with cinnamon buns.

"Look, it's normal," Kehinde said. "You'll be fine. You'll make friends. You'll meet someone worthy. Have you been dating?"

Kemi laughed. Yes, she'd gone on a few horrible dates. Since Bearded Brawn's rejection, which she kept from Kehinde, she'd gone on four more dates. She worked hard to pry information out of two of them. At first, she'd found both Swedes mysterious and intriguing, lured by their seductive art of measured revelation and one-line answers. It wasn't until she'd reached their depths that she realized she found them both incredibly boring.

Her third date had been with a first-generation Swede whose

Chilean parents had fled Augusto Pinochet's dictatorship in the 1970s for Sweden's utopia. Their date had ended quickly because he couldn't stop staring after every blond, ugly or stunning, that walked past their table.

She did skip her fourth date in her report to Kehinde. She had been lured again by the brawny type her body craved, picking him based solely on looks. Halfway through their dinner, though, it had backfired.

"Look." The guy turned serious. "Let's just cut to the chase." He might as well have walked off the set of *Vikings* for a coffee break. "I know you want to fuck me."

Kemi had been startled by his frankness. Eventually, yes. But not on their first date. She searched for words to say while he pinned her with severe, light-colored eyes.

"Why would you think that?" Her rebuttal was weak. In response, his gaze swept down her face to her cleavage and back up, and she knew she'd picked the wrong dress for a serious pursuit.

"So..." His eyes held hers, unsmiling. "Do you?"

They had ferocious sex back in her apartment, and he was gone before she fell asleep. The rest of the week, she felt like crap, and cinnamon buns became her nonjudgmental balm.

TEN

Jonny's palm on the small of her back did nothing to calm her nerves as they strolled into the iconic restaurant, Berns, to meet his parents, Wilhelm and Astrid von Lundin, for lunch. This was the big reveal. He was going to introduce her to the rulers of their family empire.

Brittany had obsessed over what to wear. Less was more around stupendous wealth—this she observed with Jonny and her other premium passengers. She had pulled on a plum-colored chiffon dress and paired it with brown sandals. She spent a long time on her makeup to get that natural, no makeup look. Her hair was parted down the middle and brushed straight. She'd redone her weave before the trip.

The couple turned heads as they strolled hand in hand around Stockholm the previous day. People wanted to know the model Jonny von Lundin was parading around town. Louise had already fended off phone calls from several local tabloids looking for gossip.

Brittany let out a nervous sigh, which moved Jonny's hand from her back to hold her hand and give it a gentle squeeze.

"You look beautiful," was all he said as he pulled her along, not giving her enough time to take in the grand interiors holding massive crystal chandeliers with thousands of sparkling faux diamonds and deep-red velvet armchairs from the jazz era of the Roaring Twenties.

Jonny planted them in front of a modestly dressed couple seated in the corner of the large, open dining hall. Brittany was struck by his parents and their youthful exuberance despite being in their seventies. Wilhelm was lean and tall, even while seated. He was wearing a white dress shirt that complemented his full head of silvery-white hair. Astrid had low-cropped, light-blond hair interspersed with white strands, which she wore slicked back off her face. She was dressed in a light-blue business suit. No earrings, but she was fiddling with a strand of white pearls around her neck, staring as they approached, with the same piercing eyes of her son.

Jonny stood frozen in front of his parents, his hand gripping Brittany's tightly as if for life support. Wilhelm said something in Swedish and then extended his hand to his son. Jonny turned to his mother and bent low to give her a wordless peck on her cheek. A few more words in Swedish, and then he turned to Brittany.

"Meet my parents, Wilhelm and Astrid." Brittany stretched out her hand and grabbed Astrid's first. "She doesn't know Swedish yet, so please make her feel welcome," he continued in his accented English.

"So pleased to meet you, Mrs. von Lundin," Brittany said effusively.

"Good to meet you, Brittany." Astrid nodded, her smile widening only so.

Brittany turned to Jonny's father. "Mr. von Lundin." Wilhelm seemed excited to see her, and he stretched out his hand bearing a heavy titanium watch, similar to Jonny's, before she extended hers.

"Please call me Wilhelm. Nice to meet you. Jonny kept talking about an American girl," he added. "That was all he would say."

Astrid focused on her son as they settled into opposite seats. Before Jonny grabbed his napkin, Astrid said something in Swedish that made Jonny tense up immediately. The fire in his look was one Brittany had never seen in him before. He naturally came with intensity, but this glare seemed reserved for hatred. He frowned at his mother, looking like he wanted her to drop dead.

"*Är hon veckans leksak, hmm, Jonny?*" Astrid asked him.

"*Men sluta nu, Astrid!*" Wilhelm turned to his wife.

Brittany watched his father address Astrid, his face contorting. What had she said?

"*Jag vill bara veta,*" Astrid replied with a shrug.

Jonny matched his mother's stare.

"*Var hittade du henne?*" Astrid seemed persistent. "*Är det bara svarta kvinnor som gäller?!*"

Brittany shifted in her seat, clearly excluded from their exchange. Both Wilhelm and Astrid were scanning every inch of their son's face. Jonny had now lowered his head a few inches.

"*Vi ska gifta oss,*" Jonny said, no longer facing them, his eyes darting left and right.

Those words seemed to pause Astrid's fingers, which had still been toying with her pearls. Wilhelm pulled away from his wife and turned toward them once more. His gaze moved from Jonny to Brittany and back.

"*Vad sa du?*" Astrid asked firmly. From her cadence, Brittany knew it was a strong question. She noticed what looked like shock spread over his mother's face.

"*Jag älskar henne.*" Jonny's voice was stern.

"*Men...vad säger du? Hur länge har ni träffats? Är hon så bra i sängen att du har tappat huvudet?!*" Astrid sounded desperate in her response.

Brittany felt the air surrounding them rot within seconds. She knew it. They hated her. She shouldn't have come. She shouldn't have listened to him. She should have gotten rid of it.

As Astrid continued reprimanding him, Brittany watched Jonny's hands unfurl, his fingers beginning a maddening dance on the table. His feet started tapping out a rhythm. Brittany recognized this. He was slipping into that space when overstimulation consumed him. She'd learned his mannerisms the same way he'd learned her body. How to calm him down when he got agitated. How to read him because he couldn't lie convincingly. How to draw him back out whenever he slipped into some abyss. His parents should know this about him by now.

Yet, Astrid continued saying things in Swedish as her son unraveled before her. And it now made sense to Brittany. Jonny had told her his parents always said there was nothing wrong about him. Because, for Astrid von Lundin, that would mean publicly admitting that her blue-eyed, blond-haired boy wasn't perfect after all.

Brittany noticed him wince and begin to grind his teeth, so she quickly reached over and covered his distressed hands with hers.

"Sssshhh," she soothed him, leaning in closer and whispering in his ear, "Ssshhh, it's okay."

She felt his heaving breath slow down until it evened out again. His fingers stopped moving maniacally, and he threaded them with hers. The storm had passed, and he turned to Brittany. He lifted their interlocked hands to his lips and brushed a featherlight kiss over the back of her hand.

Brittany had anticipated self-consciousness from this public display in front of his parents, but all that seemed to fall away when she looked at him. A man more powerful than Samuel Beaufount;

one whose mouth slowly moved over their interlocked hands oblivious to everyone around him. Even the presence of his stoic parents, who clearly seemed disturbed by this display, couldn't pull Jonny from this raw intimacy. She was staring at a man who would give her everything she'd ever dreamed of. All she had to do was say the word, because he needed her so fully, so desperately, and could no longer control himself.

"It's all right," she whispered again, and he nodded. When he looked at his mother, it was through tears. He was drowning in them and had turned into a boy in front of Brittany.

Astrid sat rigidly with her hands clasped. Brittany noticed Astrid's eyes widen in shock as Brittany calmed her son down, making his eccentricities fade away for a few minutes. A low gasp of despair escaped Astrid. Wilhelm reached over to console his wife, rubbing her forearm. There was nothing more to be said. The air was stifling. Wilhelm slowly got to his feet. He tapped Astrid lightly, prodding her to her feet as well.

"Brittany, I am sorry about lunch," Wilhelm apologized. "Jonny and his mother need to talk about a few things, and they haven't seen each other in a while." Brittany nodded. She would accept his excuse. Right now, Jonny was crying, and her heart was breaking. She wanted to know what his mother had said to have upset him so much.

"Brittany." It was Astrid's turn. "I hope we get a chance to reschedule our lunch once we come back from Doha." Brittany nodded a second time. This had been a mistake. Once Jonny was himself again, she would convince him that they still had a chance to get rid of the pregnancy. She was still in her first trimester. They couldn't bring a child into this madness.

The older couple slowly linked arms and took their leave, while

Jonny's face remained buried in Brittany's shoulder as she caressed him. The altercation had drawn some stares, but Brittany didn't care. She was now ready to wear him with pride, because he was hers.

She pulled his head up, looked into his translucent eyes reddened by hurt, and kissed him. A few moments later, they left Berns and settled quietly on a bench in Berzelii Park a few steps from its front door.

"All my life, she has been like this." Jonny broke their comfortable silence minutes later. Brittany slowly stroked his neck, willing him to say more.

"Every single girl...woman...I've brought home, she has hated," he said. "I wanted her so much to love you. But she said so many mean things."

"What did she say?"

Jonny fell silent, and Brittany knew that was his avoidance tactic. He couldn't lie to her, so he remained quiet. He probably didn't want to freak her out by telling her what he'd discussed with his parents.

Brittany wanted to know, but she dropped it for now to be picked back up later.

"Look, you can't force people to feel what they can't feel," Brittany continued. "I saw this coming."

"How?"

"You seriously need me to spell this out?" she asked. He turned to look at her. "You're white. I'm Black. You're wealthy. I'm not. You hold the keys to their kingdom. They think I'm here to steal it."

Jonny studied her intently then leaned in. His mouth covered hers in a sensuous kiss, which elicited a moan from her. His tongue wrestled hers and won. Brittany turned into putty in his arms, receiving his slow, calculated kiss.

"My kingdom *is* yours."

He muttered those words drowsily against her lips before possessing them once more.

The next day, she and Jonny arrived at Antonia's mansion in Elfvik on Lidingö. The hilltop house looked futuristic, with impressive views of the bay at its feet. They arrived to a generous backyard lit up with firelight—candles and hanging lanterns—long tables dressed with white linen, and decorations etched with sun faces and deep-red crayfish motifs.

Jonny called out to two fair women who had been huddled together in conversation. If Astrid had been rude, then Brittany wasn't sure what to make of Svea and Antonia.

Because when they turned and saw her, their faces paled like they'd seen a ghost.

MUNA

The first time Yasmiin brought Yagiz home, Muna found him wandering around their kitchen—naked.

Muna had woken up a little past two in the morning for a pee break and had heard rustling coming from the kitchen when she opened the door to her room. The apartment was dark, save for a stream of light from the open refrigerator that illuminated the stark man rummaging around in it. Muna retreated quietly into her room but continued observing him through the crack of her door.

His muscled back was covered in tattoos. They ran from his forearms to his wrists, from the nape of his neck down to the dimple above his toned butt. When he turned around with a carton of milk in hand, they snaked across his chest down to his V-cut before disappearing into dark curls, which framed a profuse member. She'd never seen a naked man before and wasn't sure that ample size was considered average. She knew she could never look Yagiz in the eye again.

He was holding a small pouch in one hand. Yagiz pulled out a few dark items from it, which he popped into his mouth and began to chew. Muna's eyes traveled down his length again, transfixed by what she was seeing. When they moved back to his face, she noticed him squinting at her bedroom door.

She quietly shut her door, locked it, and tiptoed back to bed.

Yagiz came around many more nights after that, usually when the girls had retired to their rooms for the night. But they heard him anyway. The banging of the wooden bedframe coming from Yasmiin's room. His deep growls. Her high-pitched scream that came rapidly, climbing higher and higher.

Muna locked herself in her room, hiding from the discomfort those uneasy, otherworldly sounds brought. She tried to busy herself with her Swedish textbooks and the smiling photos on her magnetic board. Sometimes, she'd pull out Ahmed's sack and look through those photos again, counting them, studying faces, and putting them back together once Yagiz's primal grunts got louder. She needed to spare the dead that horror.

Muna had learned to sleep through their sensual violence as summer gave way to autumn and a chill enveloped their suburb outside Stockholm.

Then one night, Yagiz went too far.

Muna was jolted from sleep by a bloodcurdling scream. A deep, male voice was trying to overpower that wail coming from Yasmiin's room, but she kept shrieking as if staring down death.

Muna bolted to her feet and ran out of her door. She met Khadiija, who had also been awoken, standing by the doorjamb of her room. Muna ran over to the kitchen and picked up a dirty pot from the sink, while Khadiija grabbed a wooden serving spoon. The screams had now muffled, but they could hear sounds of a scuffle inside. The girls dashed over to Yasmiin's door and started pounding as loudly as they could.

"YASMIIN!" Muna screamed. "Are you all right?" she asked in Somali.

The muffled female voice broke back into a scream before a loud slap and a thud. Muna's pounding got frenzied until she was falling face forward into the room when Yagiz opened the door. She bolted back to her feet, spinning around to face him. His eyes were glazed as if high, and there were scratches all over his face, one that had drawn blood. She held the dirty pan high above her head by its handle with both hands. He looked possessed.

Behind him, Khadiija started hitting the back of his skull with her own weapon, the wooden spoon. When Yagiz turned to face her, Muna swept at his head with the heavy pan, felling the naked man in one swoop. While he was down, she hit his skull with the pan once more. And then again, letting out an air of resolve with each hit. When the man stopped moving, she dropped the pan and looked up to find Khadiija with her arms around a shaking Yasmiin. She was naked, her hair was disheveled, and tracks of black mascara ran down her face.

"I'm calling the police!" Muna screamed as she turned around to bolt out the door.

"MUNA! NO!" Yasmiin cried. "Please, no. Don't call them. Please... They will take me away."

"Why? That monster attacked you!" Muna was furious. Yasmiin shook her head as she tried pulling the covers over her bruised skin. Then she pointed to a white sack in the corner of the room. A room Muna had never been inside. But she didn't have time to explore it. Muna beelined for the sack, opened it, and scooped out a palmful of greenish-brown leaves. She lifted it to her nose to smell. *Khat.* A relaxing, leafy plant that turned men lethargic. Her father had chewed it often. Many of the older men she'd known growing up had chewed khat. She looked at Yasmiin, demanding an explanation.

"I help Yagiz sell" was all she offered before burying her face in the sheets, sobbing. Khadiija looked at Muna, who was breathing heavily, stunned that she'd taken out a man but also angry that she felt powerless once again. Muna peered down at Yagiz, who was breathing lightly. She saw scratches all over his back too. Yasmiin had given him those, and they weren't just from tonight. To Muna, Yasmiin had always seemed boy-crazy whenever they indulged in pointless banter at the salon where she worked. This was what happened when girls liked boys too much, Muna decided.

Muna turned back to Yasmiin and asked for his clothes. Then she solicited Khadiija's help. They dragged the naked man by his arms and feet out the door and planted him in the hallway. They heaped his clothes onto his stomach, set his bag under his head to deter thieves, and locked him out there for the rest of the night. Meanwhile, Yasmiin took a quick shower and changed into a loose, flowing boubou. She started pulling stained sheets off her bed, spotted with a few drops of blood, when both Muna and Khadiija walked back into her room, silently looking for answers.

Yasmiin stopped her task and lowered her head. Several minutes passed between them before she gathered enough strength to talk.

"I was smuggled from Italy to Sweden," she started to say. Her sisters sat on her bed, ready to listen. One of their trio was now hatching out of her past, and they sat quietly, ready to gather pieces of her broken shell. She turned to regard them with glassy eyes, and Muna became nervous.

"I did many bad things with men in Italy."

KẸMI

"L-A-G-O-M... Lagom!" José scribbled on the board to exasperation from the class. It was fifteen minutes to eight, and he seemed to be starting a brand-new lecture. "Not too little, not too much, just right," he said, pacing the room before planting himself in front of Malcolm.

"'Lagom' is a word many *Americans* struggle with." He added the emphasis for Malcolm's benefit.

"Right now, yes, when class is almost over," Malcolm muttered under his breath. Kemi giggled, and they exchanged jovial looks.

José pressed on for a few more minutes before giving them book recommendations and promising a deep dive into the love-hate relationship Swedes had with that word the following week.

As Kemi stuffed books into her large bag, Malcolm's frame hovered over her, blocking the light.

"Rushing off somewhere?"

"Not really. I was just going to grab some soup on the way home."

"Do you want to grab dinner instead?" Malcolm offered as Kemi stuffed her bag. "You haven't told me your story yet." She looked at him, twisted her lip in thought, and gave in. Sure, why not.

They strolled toward Kungsgatan that evening, wrapped in light coats. Winter was reminding them of its inevitable approach via nippy nights. They walked past two Black men who ignored Malcolm's nod in their direction as they scurried along. Malcolm laughed, hands in his pockets, a swagger to his gait.

"Brothers be losing their edge, I tell you," Malcolm casually dropped.

"You know, I had the same thing happen a few months ago." Kemi remembered the women she'd walked past who made a tongue-tied show of gawking at her and her outfit.

"I swear, this country will blunt you if you let it," he continued. Kemi recognized what Malcolm was talking about. She had felt it as people took in her different outfits. If no audible compliments were doled out, then it was the silence speaking volumes. Reprimanding her for strutting around like a peacock.

"Jesus! Where did ten months go?" Malcolm said. "I can't believe I've been here this long."

"Have you made any friends?"

"I've found some fellow expats. The American Club!" he said. "That was how I got my gig too. I play with a kick-ass band twice a week in Gamla stan."

They found a modest Thai spot where they dined on pad thai while Malcolm shared more about his family and his move to Sweden. He was struggling with the language, no doubt. But what was irking him more than anything was a certain lukewarmness, he said.

"People need to be out in these streets raising hell and protesting shit," he said as he rolled up glass noodles on his fork. "I mean, did you hear about that Blackface cake from a couple of years ago?" He lifted a loaded fork to his mouth. "Some artist dressed himself as a cake shaped like a Black sister and kept screaming as one government minister cut into it, everyone laughing like it's a unicorn birthday cake," he narrated between chews. "And no one burned Stockholm down?"

Kemi listened to his rant as several thoughts raced through her mind. In less than a year, he'd developed this carriage. She wasn't sure if he'd been building his armor of activism the day his mom left him at ten years old or if he had to expedite its construction because Sweden hated sharp edges that stuck out.

Malcolm continued until she inadvertently broke his monologue by scratching underneath her hair. He gave her a once-over, taking in her long-overdue braids she had attempted herself unsuccessfully.

"I see someone's past their due date," Malcolm chuckled.

Normally, Kemi would have rebuked a stranger for showing such audacity. Somehow with Malcolm, it was in line with his boorishness, which regularly surfaced in their Swedish class. She knew it didn't come from malice. Malcolm was reminding her she better not become blunt here.

She finally broke. "Bro, I need to get my hair done like yesterday. Any suggestions?"

"Girl, I got you." He laughed, reaching for his phone, eyes twinkling mischievously at her. She'd made her first friend in Sweden.

After that impromptu dinner with Malcolm, she felt less alone. She'd connected with someone who could, on some level, empathize with her, and she promised to come to his gig and watch him play. If he was as passionate a saxophonist as he was a debater in class, then she knew she was in for a good time.

The next morning, Kemi pushed open the door to Espresso House for her daily latte. Once at the counter, she started reaching into her purse, ready to order and pay, when someone slid a tall cup toward her.

"Your latte, Kemi. On me," the voice said in Swedish. She looked up to fully take in the barista who had spoken. She didn't recognize him. Or, maybe she did, but he wasn't the one who often served her coffee. He had mocha-colored skin with short, kinky, reddish-brown hair, a few brown freckles dusting his face, thick lips, and maple-brown eyes. She glanced at the name tag pinned atop a navy-blue apron resting over a broad swimmer's chest.

Tobias.

"Tobias..." she said, loving the way his name felt on her lips. "*Tack så mycket*, Tobias." He smiled at her, revealing a slight gap between his top front teeth.

"Have we met?" She switched to American English. She was still struggling with her tenses in Swedish.

"I make your latte every morning. Someone else just hands it to you," he said, switching to British English. Her eyes held his. Then she bit her lower lip and lowered her gaze shyly.

Tobias.

ELEVEN

Brittany saw Jonny's sisters exchange a quick word between themselves as she arrived with Jonny. The rest of the guests at Antonia's crayfish party went down to zero decibels as they watched Jonny lead her by the hand into the yard of the hilltop villa.

Antonia—Jonny whispered into Brittany's ear—was the first to walk up to the couple. She shared the same tightly cropped hair as their mother, though she wore hers a little longer. She was wearing a loose-fitting, white dashiki over wide-legged, white linen pants. There wasn't a lick of makeup on her face, which bore the same features as Jonny, down to the way they smiled and their small teeth.

"It's so great to finally meet the woman my brother is so crazy about." Antonia launched herself into Brittany's unprepared arms. Brittany caught her and reciprocated the hug.

"You must be Antonia. Nice to meet you!"

Antonia finished off her greeting with kisses on both cheeks. She ignored Jonny and linked her arm with Brittany's, leading her toward the small group of friends and family that had gathered.

"Welcome to our crayfish party!" she beamed, sweeping her left hand, which was holding a glass of wine, over the spread. As they moved closer, Brittany felt her stomach start to churn. The air was filled with a distinct salty, fishy smell. It had to be coming from the light peach-colored langoustines and deep-orange-red crayfish piled high in large, crystal glass bowls sitting on several white-linen-draped tables. She couldn't throw up right now. Not in front of his closest clique.

Antonia pointed out two tall teenage boys as hers, a sturdy-looking husband who raised his glass in a toast as they passed, and a few more friends decked out in varying expensive but casually put-together looks.

Svea came up to meet them and introduced herself. Though she shared the same hair and eye coloring as her siblings, to Brittany, Svea looked different from the others. Her lips were plumped up. Her cheekbones were more defined. Natural wrinkles for her age had been smoothed out. Her blond tresses had been straightened and she was wearing unusually high heels for a backyard party on grass. While caked on as elegantly as possible, her makeup was still several layers deep.

"You're so beautiful, Brittany" were the next words out of Svea's mouth. Since she'd been swept up into Jonny's frenzied world, Brittany felt like a fragile doll behind a glass display. The way his assistants buzzed around her like bees. The way his sisters were treating her. This was not who she was. She didn't sign up to be pampered and preened without her input. She felt like the sole concubine in Jonny's harem, pulled out for entertainment and something to be gawked at. She was getting more tired of it with each passing day. Right now, though, her singular priority was keeping lunch in her stomach as the group inched closer to the seafood-laden tables.

As they strolled hand in hand, Antonia turned to peer at Jonny, who had been trailing them.

"*Gud, vad lik henne hon är!*" Antonia said. "*Vad håller du på med, Jonny?*"

They stopped walking when Jonny suddenly rounded on them and stood inches from Antonia's face. Brittany felt excluded from their tense standoff.

"*Vad menar du?*" he asked sternly.

Brittany swallowed uncomfortably. While she didn't have any of her own, she knew sibling fights weren't pretty.

"*Du, var försiktig,*" Antonia smirked.

Jonny didn't answer, but he glared down at his sister angrily. What had Antonia said? They continued their standoff until Antonia broke it by eyeing him up and down.

"*Vad händer?*" Svea asked, walking back up to them, taking in the situation.

"*Ingenting,*" Antonia answered.

Brittany nervously stroked her hair. She needed to learn Swedish fast. Antonia unhooked her arm from Brittany's, gave her a weak smile, and took her leave, just as a large guy holding a stem of white Chardonnay strolled unhurriedly up to them. Jonny turned to the man, his face softening. He rushed over to Brittany, who took a step back when Jonny now planted himself in front of her. Then he pointed to the man who was standing a polite distance from them.

"Meet Ragnar. My best friend."

Brittany assessed his stoic friend. He and Jonny were about the same height, but this guy was broader, more muscular. While Jonny ran, this guy looked like he played a sport that required force. Hockey, maybe? He had deep dark-brown hair and regarded her with skeptical dark ocean blues she couldn't quite read.

"Welcome," Ragnar said.

"We've known each other since nursery school," Jonny said, smiling, looking at Ragnar, who nodded in acknowledgment as he wordlessly interrogated Brittany. She immediately recognized that if she was going to fully commit to growing her relationship with Jonny, this was one of the gatekeepers she had to go through. Right now, his face read "gate closed."

Ragnar had probably witnessed all the women who had barreled through his friend's life over the years. Brittany sensed his mistrust was tied to something deeper. As a Black woman, her radar never took a break. Because, besides uttering the word "Welcome," Ragnar avoided her for the rest of the evening and parked himself close to his petite wife, Pia, who looked like a gym bunny.

"How are you feeling?" Jonny inquired once they stole a moment alone, his palm instinctively moving over her stomach. She felt food at the back of her throat. Nausea. That seafood smell was all-consuming.

"Stop doing that!" she scolded between clenched teeth. His sisters had been observing her all night. That look of surprise was back on their faces. She had run to the bathroom twice that evening to puke. She'd already popped a couple of morning sickness pills as well. Whenever thoughts of an abortion surfaced, Jonny's elation dampened it. He couldn't wait to hold his child.

"I can't wait till they all find out," he whispered into her ear before giving it a little nip. She giggled. Her laughter quickly died when she caught Ragnar assessing them frigidly from a distance. She leaned into Jonny, needing to know more about his friend.

"Your friend Ragnar," she started while Jonny nibbled on her ear. "What's his story?"

"His story?"

"Yeah, I mean besides you going to the same kindergarten."

"Well," Jonny said, distracted by his current task, "we grew up together. Went to the same boarding schools. Even lived together in London for a bit." He grazed the ridge of her ear with his teeth. She didn't know how to bob and weave around what she wanted to say, so she was direct. Jonny only understood direct anyway.

"I don't think he likes me." She waited for Jonny's explanation, hoping it was all in her mind. He confirmed it.

"Ragnar never likes any of my girlfriends." He continued working on her ear. "He doesn't understand why I just won't be with a white girl." Brittany tensed beneath his caress and he stopped, concerned that he'd offended her. She turned to look at him.

"He's your best friend, you say?" She needed to be sure. If this man was going to hold a prominent role in their lives, she needed to be sure he wasn't a racist.

She had already gone through an ordeal with his parents that Jonny still hadn't fully explained. All she knew was that Astrid von Lundin had upset her son to the point of a public breakdown. Something she was rapidly learning was rather rare among this relatively reserved bunch.

"Yes, he's the one I trust most in this world. Besides you, of course."

Brittany took a deep breath. While she appreciated his frankness, this time, she would have liked it delivered less matter-of-factly. "So, he wants you to be with a Swede?" she confirmed. Jonny nodded.

"He thinks I have a fetish." He became serious.

She peered at him, and for the first time in a long time, she was transported right back to the clinic parking lot in Alexandria, Virginia, when he'd received stitches. When she'd looked in his eyes and was unsure of what to think. The cut had healed well, but a scar remained above his eyebrow as a whispered reminder. A few seconds of reticence passed between them.

"Do you?" she asked.

"Do I what?"

"I mean, is Ragnar right?"

When her words sunk in, wrinkles appeared on his forehead as he peered at her.

"I don't have a fetish," he said sternly. His fingers balled into fists at his sides. He didn't say anything, but Brittany felt him submerging into that space of anxiety.

"I was just..."

"I'm not crazy," he stated firmly.

"I'm sorry, Jonny. I didn't mean it that way," she said, but his eyes told her all she needed to know.

She needed to shut up.

———————

That night, Brittany lay quietly on her side, deep in thought as Jonny moved against her. She occasionally took a deep breath, gasping softly before returning to her wandering thoughts. The sound of Jonny's low moans was the only indication they were making love. He was lying on his side behind her, his left arm wrapped around her chest, crushing her back tightly into his own wildly heaving chest.

Something was bothering her. She wanted to know why his sisters had initially regarded her so suspiciously. And his friend Ragnar whose icy dark blues were filled with something like contempt.

Clearly he was prejudiced. Jonny had openly admitted this. Her presence was provoking to the person he trusted most besides her.

If Jonny knew Ragnar held such contempt, then why were they still close friends? How could she trust that Ragnar truly had his best interest at heart if he couldn't even accept who his friend fell in love with? Maybe Jonny also held deep-seated prejudices?

Or was Ragnar trying to protect his friend after witnessing a string of short-lived flings?

All these thoughts were swimming in her head as Jonny worked hard for her pleasure. She felt him moving against her softly. She closed her eyes, willing those wandering thoughts away so she could enjoy his love, but they latched on stubbornly, pulling her away from him.

His grip around her tightened as his heaves against her back became more hurried. He was struggling hard to be as hushed as humanly possible because Brittany was barely making any noise beyond tiny sighs. When he came, he muffled his cries into her shoulder, his grip squeezing the breath out of her.

The room became a noiseless cove once again as he shuddered behind her, trying to calm his racing heart. He pressed his lips to her shoulder while his left hand traveled the length of her side, dipping at her waist, scaling her hip, exploring.

She listened to his labored breathing begin to slow down. He let out the last traces of release as a loud gasp before his words made their way out in a low pitch.

"Marry me," he said breathlessly.

Brittany's body tensed up beneath his caress. He kissed her shoulder before panting out those words again.

"Marry me."

MUNA

"Why shouldn't I fire you?" Yagiz was furious. "*Uhnn*, Muna?"

Yagiz was back in their apartment an hour later, sitting in an armchair facing the gray sofa where Muna and Khadiija were parked with their hands on their laps. Khadiija was fiddling with her fingers, while Muna just stared at Yagiz, simmering with quiet anger. Yasmiin stood behind his chair, resting a hand on it, looking down at the floor.

The Turk was livid. He'd woken up with a throbbing head in the hallway when two Somali teenagers had kicked him awake and ran off cackling after pointing at his still-rigid penis. Realizing he was naked and finding his clothes out there with him, he'd quickly dressed himself and pounded his way back into their apartment. While fighting off both Khadiija and Muna, Yasmiin had managed to open the door and let him back in against their will.

Once back inside, he had recanted his embarrassment to them, trying to prod guilt out of the trio. The two seated women regarded him in silence. Then Muna broke it.

"What were you doing to Yasmiin?" she asked him.

"What we do is none of your business."

"She was screaming," Muna said, adamant for an answer.

"As women do when they're enjoying it!" he silenced her. "But you can't know, can you, right? Yasmiin told me you're a virgin." He cocked his head upward to look at Yasmiin, who was standing behind him. "Right, Yaz?" He tried garnering support from her. She glanced away, and he sniggered beneath his breath.

"I'm not stupid," Muna continued. "You were hurting Yasmiin. She's not talking because she's afraid of you." Yagiz scrutinized her through dark eyes. "I'm not afraid of you," Muna added. Yagiz laughed. A large smile spread over his handsome face, his handlebar moustache dancing.

"Maybe you should be afraid of me, Muna Saheed." His laugh died into a frown. "You should be afraid. You work for me."

Muna fell quiet. She needed this job. She needed to have a record of responsibility so she could become a citizen in a few years. She craved that security. Holding that small book would mean she finally belonged somewhere safe. A place where she could start rebuilding a family. Mr. Björn at Migrationsverket had intimated that it was unlikely she would become fully accepted as a Swede. At the time, she hadn't been sure if he meant before or after getting her citizenship in five years. After living in Tensta for a while, she began to realize what Mr. Björn had meant. She remembered him saying her culture was "too strong" for her to fully be accepted.

Dead air hung around the foursome. Yasmiin was shifting her weight nervously from foot to foot, while Khadiija had switched to examining her fingernails, not wanting to meet Yagiz's rage head on. Khadiija kept toying with her fingers, but Muna noticed her trying to hold back tears. She recognized that expression. Muna herself had worn a similar one for weeks after Ahmed died, shedding it in the safety of her room. The only time she'd cried publicly was on the first day she met these women, whom she now considered her sisters.

Muna turned to Yagiz once more. "Why do you bring it to our community?"

"Bring what?"

"Khat."

The sack of leaves, a chewable stimulant they'd found in Yasmiin's room. Many of the Somali communities in the suburbs had been marred by its effects. Even her Tensta wasn't spared. Whenever she followed Khadiija to the community center to hang with other Somalis, she watched some of the older men drowsily mill around.

Swedish media had focused heavily on the "khat epidemic" within their community because apparently, khat chewed by immigrants was less forgivable than cocaine sniffed by Östermalm's upper-class whites.

"Why are you selling this here? Why are you destroying my people?"

"It's always someone else's fault, isn't it?" Yagiz cackled. "Ask Yasmiin. She's my saleswoman."

Muna cut Yasmiin a look of disappointment. Yasmiin had so much more to explain. After she and Khadiija had dragged Yagiz's naked body out of their apartment, Yasmiin had broken down to them in her room. She told them she had been a prostitute in Rome since she was fifteen years old after fleeing the civil war. She'd roamed its streets, working for a pimp who financially strangled her and a couple of West African girls.

Her pimp had made it clear that Yasmiin was his biggest money-maker because she had an arse made for slapping and long "good hair." This meant she didn't have to wear a wig, which had the heightened chance of flying off during sessions with particularly aggressive customers. When Yasmiin fled Italy, it was through a customer who had smuggled her out of her pimp's claws and into a convoy of refugees making their way to Sweden.

"Be careful, Muna," Yagiz warned her. "A virgin is a rare specimen in this country. Do not play with things you don't understand, little girl. You might offend the wrong man."

He got to his feet, adjusted his pants, and straightened his shirt.

He ran his fingers through his black, rooster hair before turning to peer down at Yasmiin, who was still standing behind his chair. He slid his palm over her butt and gave one cheek an ample squeeze before making his exit.

Once the door slammed behind him, Khadiija, who had been quietly studying her fingers, sprang onto her feet and launched into a tirade in Somali, prefacing it by calling Yasmiin a whore.

"Why have you exposed us to this dangerous man?" Khadiija screamed. "Why are you doing this reckless thing with him?" Yasmiin's shoulders started shaking as she burst into tears.

"You selfish whore," Khadiija continued. "You have brought unnecessary evil into our home. Our home!"

"Khadiija!" Muna tried to pull her back to no avail. Khadiija tore into Yasmiin, dredging up all the unspeakable things she told them she'd done with strange men. Yasmiin crumbled to her knees while Khadiija hovered over her in a fit of rage. She asked her where she had truly met Yagiz. What hole she'd dragged him out of. When she had started selling khat on his behalf. What Yagiz had been doing to her when they burst in to save her.

Khadiija didn't wait for answers. She continued railing. Muna sprang up to grab Khadiija, but she screamed, "No!" and pushed the younger girl off her back.

Yasmiin's tears came heavily, and Muna sensed they weren't from Khadiija's tirade. What Yasmiin had told them in confidence, Khadiija had literally thrown back in her face less than an hour later. That was why they each kept their doors tightly shut. Letting people in came with unbearable judgment, Muna decided.

Above all, Khadiija kept stressing their exposure to the danger that was Yagiz until Khadiija finally broke.

"I ran away from a dangerous man!" Khadiija was letting them in now, her eggshell springing its first public crack. "I ran away..." She fell to her knees, her body rumbling with emotion. "I had to run away."

Khadiija's confession hung in the air. They couldn't ignore its presence, yet no one wanted to talk about it. While many men had forced Yasmiin to flee, a single man was responsible for Khadiija's run for her life. Muna wanted to know more, but right now, Khadiija imploded into herself, sobbing uncontrollably.

Muna recognized those cries of despair, when memories she'd tried to scrub from her mind slowly materialized like strokes of an invisible marker on special paper, clouding her mind with unexpected color. Khadiija must be experiencing her own Technicolor rush from the past.

Muna observed the others crying in separate heaps on the floor, away from each other. Who could she comfort first without the risk of offending the other? Muna was still reeling from everything that had been disclosed over the past few minutes. She was paralyzed.

Her mind cut to that statuesque couple she had seen outside work. How that white man who worked at von Lundin Marketing had grabbed that Black woman and kissed her, pinning her to that fancy car while people walking by kept turning around to look at them. Her mind raced back to Solsidan. How Ahmed had cradled her as he'd kissed her. How she'd run her fingers through his silken hair.

She had hope because that tall Swedish man and her Ahmed had shown her glimpses of true love. Yasmiin and Khadiija needed more hope too.

Muna stood rooted as she watched her greatest fear materialize— their already fragile sisterhood beginning to fracture.

KẸMI

Kemi tried to work, fingers typing furiously on her keyboard as she responded to an email, but her mind was elsewhere, replaying her morning encounter with Tobias instead.

Why hadn't she noticed him before? She had been going there for coffee every morning for several weeks now. He had to have been the world's greatest chameleon blending into his environment, because she hadn't spotted his fine self.

Tobias shared a similar coloring with Malcolm. A café au lait shade of brown. A fellow Afro-Swede like Malcolm often called himself, because he'd told her using "Afro-Viking" unwittingly tied him to a history of pillaging and raping he decided wasn't his to wear. "*No, thank you!*" was Malcolm's epilogue to that particular rant.

She wanted to see Tobias again. She made plans to go back to Espresso House for lunch. As she readied herself, packing up her bag, Jonny's unexpected voice cut through.

"Kemi."

He strolled into her small space, hands in his pockets.

"Jonny. What a surprise." Kemi turned to look at her boss. A man who became more of a phantom with each passing week. She often pondered what his actual work entailed.

"We've got an important potential client called Bachmann," he said, getting right down to business. "It's the largest German luxury shoe brand."

"Go on..."

"I want us to get this one right. They're launching a new range of luxury high-top sneakers, and I want us to show diversity. You know, people who are rich but like these types of shoes. Like rappers."

"Rappers?" Kemi let his words sink in.

"Yes. Rappers."

"Why rappers?" she asked.

"Because the shoes are expensive but also cool, urban, and funky. Plus this new line—B:GEM—has a lot of gemstones too. Bachmann is trying to tap into that market." Memories of conversations with Connor and his faux urban speak flooded her brain, and she shook them off with a shudder.

"So only rich rappers wear expensive high-top shoes?" Kemi questioned. Jonny's eyebrows arched awkwardly.

"Who else wears them?" he asked.

Kemi laughed, not sure of how to process his remarks. She knew Jonny spewed words from a deep well of ignorance. She had a difficult time reconciling his statements with the fact he carried on with Black and brown women. He should know better. There had been whispers around the office, mostly through his assistant Louise, that he was currently dating a Black sister and was now treading into serious territory. All Louise told her about the former model and flight attendant was, "*She is stunning!*" Kemi had craved more information, but Louise had been flighty with details. Around these parts, it seemed to Kemi that work and play were more like extended cousins than siblings.

"Do *you* see yourself wearing bedazzled high-top sneakers?" Kemi asked.

"No," he said, firmly.

She quickly scanned what he was wearing: a navy-blue dress shirt tucked into khaki trousers and tan Oxford shoes. His sleeves were slightly rolled at the wrists, revealing his watch and arms lightly brushed with golden hair.

"Then why do you want to represent them? A brand you don't see yourself ever wearing?"

He paused to think. She could see his mind furiously working behind those eyes, trying to digest her stance.

"If I liked every client we chased, then we would never have enough work," he answered.

"Maybe you should start thinking more like that," Kemi said. "You know...actually liking the people you chase." He pressed his lips tightly at her remark.

"How much do you want Bachmann?" Kemi quizzed, her tone getting serious.

"They are popular right now, especially in Asia. If we land them, they would be one of our biggest clients," Jonny explained. "I want them."

"Then let's take this to a new level, Jonny," Kemi said, getting excited.

"What are you thinking?"

"I'm going to help you hit this one out of the park. But you will have to trust me completely. Can you do that, Jonny?"

Jonny stared at her, dissecting her words.

"This means having my back in the pitch meeting when I present this idea to the team."

He was getting nervous, and his hands retreated into fists.

"Jonny...I want you to be the face of Bachmann's new collection."

———

Jonny invited her to lunch to discuss her reasoning around her idea. This meant trying to catch a glimpse of Tobias at Espresso House was out. She would have to try again another day.

"Think about it," Kemi said, propping some salmon on her chopsticks midsentence. "Everyone is expecting the cliché of some famous rapper in blinged-out shoes. No one would expect Jonny von Lundin in them. Especially not Bachmann." She popped the bite into her mouth. Her plan was to put him in the center of the campaign alongside a mix of races, religions, and sexual orientations all wearing Bachmanns.

As Jonny listened to her, Kemi noticed he occasionally seemed distracted by her chewing motion but then pulled himself back out in time to understand what she was saying and hang with their conversation. She was still getting used to his quirks and the characteristics that came with them. This one was new, and it disturbed her.

"Your idea is crazy," he began. "Me as a model for Bachmann shoes? I would never wear those shoes."

"But you want them badly, don't you?" She smiled mischievously. "Haven't you done anything crazy for something or someone you wanted so badly?"

Kemi watched a grin creep onto his lips and feared what he was thinking. Lord knows what crazy things he had done. She only had to remember her Google search on him to dig up images in her mind. But this childish grin spreading across his face right now? Kemi suspected it had to do with that sister whose name was being whispered among his staff.

"Maybe," he answered before biting his lower lip.

"Bachmann is no different. And I guarantee you: if you go back to them with this proposal, you will get a lot more money out of them. They will beg you to represent them."

Kemi pointed out that he had already stereotyped Black rappers as wearing bedazzled high-tops. By putting Jonny himself into those sneakers, she was branching out and broadening the appeal of those shoes to reach a larger audience.

"Diversity and inclusion are also about breaking stereotypes," she said. "Not only showing Black and brown faces in ads. Trust me."

Jonny still wasn't convinced. "This sets a dangerous precedent. If I model for Bachmann, then all our clients would want me to start representing them visually like a cheap salesman. I'm a very private man. I don't like gimmicks. That's too American."

"Jonny, this isn't a gimmick. This is von Lundin Marketing's chance at redemption," Kemi preached. "Picture yourself dressed as you normally would, doing things you'd normally be doing, like, I don't know, sailing or something. But then you've got the Bachmann shoes on. Everything else stays the same." She became more animated, turned on by all this creative babble. She loved this. She was finally in her element.

"And the slogan would be, 'Dare to be different'... Jonny, it's perfect!"

This was what von Lundin Marketing needed to shake themselves free from the IKON fiasco. Kemi observed him considering her energetic words. Something she said must have stirred something deep within him, because his gaze softened as he regarded her.

"I like it," he said. "Very much. I really do."

"Good!" She popped more raw fish into her mouth. He stared at her mouth, and she noticed him again mesmerized by the motion. It had drawn him like a sensor.

"Now, this could go both ways," Kemi said. "If critics attack us and say we're trying to appropriate a cultural icon, then our rebuttal is easy. We force them to reexamine their own prejudices and why they think only Black people would like bedazzled high-top sneakers."

Kemi continued talking as she ate, breaking down her idea,

considering all the different angles of attack it could draw and how they would prepare themselves. But above all, Kemi was professionally betting on the idea.

High on Kemi's vision, Jonny called an impromptu meeting back at the office. Ingrid, Greta, Espen, and a few more directors gathered into one of the conference rooms. Jonny was uncharacteristically excited. He launched into the Bachmann proposal, speaking in English for Kemi's benefit, explaining that they had a shot at landing the international account.

Then he handed the floor to Kemi to present her idea. The Swedes listened intently, unwaveringly focused on Kemi as she explained why she wanted to don their illustrious leader in bling for an advertising campaign.

When Kemi finished, it was dead silent. A stillness too uncomfortable even for the Swedes themselves. Greta seemed visibly agitated. She turned to Jonny and said something in Swedish.

"English, please," Kemi jumped into their argument, and Greta cut her a glare that burned tracks down her skin.

"You know we can't speak English forever, Kemi," she spat. "How is your Swedish coming?" Silence gripped the room once more, letting Greta's condescension settle like sediment.

Kemi didn't reply.

"You are trying to make Jonny a laughingstock," Greta continued. "Do you even understand his position within this firm? Within our society?"

"I think Kemi's idea is excellent, and I am on board with it," Jonny said in English.

"It feels too risky, Jonny," Ingrid jumped in. "I'm not comfortable with it."

"I am comfortable with it," he said. "I think it is a brilliant idea and will work."

"I'm worried about the negative press we will surely get," Maria from media relations postulated. "Will we be able to survive it? We barely made it out of IKON."

"That's *if* we get negative press at all." Jonny was persistent. "The media may love it."

"What *if* they don't love it?" Ingrid jumped back in. "What *if* this is the confirmation they need that Jonny von Lundin has indeed lost his mind?"

"Well, I think it's a bold idea," Espen offered. "I think it's a brave move, and we need to have more courage these days."

Ingrid shot Espen a hard look. "Of course, you do," she muttered to him in Swedish, and Espen matched her glare with an intense one of his own.

Kemi watched this new dynamic wash over the Swedes in the room, one that suggested she was now overreaching her bounds. That the full creative freedom she had been promised was in fact being checked by these gatekeepers of culture.

No, they weren't going to let her willingly make Jonny a joke, and they protectively banded around him. She witnessed that wordless solidarity in action, and it was quite remarkable. This was the super-glue that created impenetrable systems for people on the outside like her and protected men like him. But Jonny wanted Bachmann at all costs, and Kemi had convinced him how to get what he wanted.

"It's settled," Jonny said. "I've already made the decision. I called this meeting just to inform you."

That statement drew audible gasps from around the room. Kemi had lived in Sweden long enough to know what that collective gasp meant. How dare Jonny make a decision without consensus, especially considering how absent he had been? They were now treading in dangerous waters of dictatorship.

"Are you even allowed to do that?" It was Greta again. That he would make such an important decision without her input after she'd been running the entire company on his behalf was insulting. That much was obvious to Kemi.

"Björn," Jonny turned to Björn Fältström, head of business development. He was sitting quietly in a corner with his head resting on his right thumb and index finger, listening intently. "You, Kemi, and I will go to the pitch meeting."

With that brief statement, Jonny dismissed the room, leaving Kemi behind. Jonny gazed at her intently with a look that told Kemi he was praying she was right.

TWELVE

BRITTANY-RAE

There was nothing left besides bile. She had puked her stomach
clean and was now kneeling by the toilet bowl, crying. The whole
scene smacked of déjà vu—Brittany throwing up in London—as
Jonny stood by the doorjamb. She'd bolted straight out of bed to
vomit after he'd proposed. He probably wasn't sure if it was morning
sickness as usual or the thought of becoming his wife.

"Are you okay?"

She kept crying, her body shaking. This was spiraling faster than
Brittany could hang on to. They were barely six months in. He'd
already impregnated her and was now asking her to be his wife. It
was all too much to bear.

"You don't have to answer right now." Jonny was grasping at
straws, and she knew anxiety was building up within him. Brittany's
sobs slowed, and she got back on her feet, sniffing and wiping the
last few drops of tears away. She walked past him back to the bed,
sunk in, and pulled the covers up over her head, wishing they would
smother her.

The next morning, they awoke early to drive to the airport for her
flight back to Dulles. Jonny kept furling and unfurling his fingers
on the steering wheel, while Brittany stared out the window. Once

at Arlanda Airport, he helped her with the small carry-on she'd brought for the short trip. Before she went through security, he planted himself in his spot right in front of her.

"I'm going to miss you," he said before kissing her and placing both palms on her stomach. Brittany avoided his eyes and nodded. Then she bit her lower lip, suppressing tears.

"Please think about it," he pleaded, willing her to look at him, but she didn't want to. She nodded in response. He pressed a quick kiss to her forehead. "I'll come see you in two weeks. I have an important project I need to see to here."

She looked up at him and nodded again, silently.

"My God, Brittany." Tanesha was at a loss for words. "This is moving way too fast even for me!"

"I can't marry him," Brittany said over the speaker. She was sitting at her dining table, sorting through a few bills, unsure of any aspect of her life. A small part of her wished she'd gotten rid of the baby. Now she was sitting in limbo between two worlds. On one end, her job as a flight attendant, her rental town house, her life here in the States, and her parents in Atlanta—who thought she was still with Jamal.

On the other end was an unknown life in Sweden, living in style among its upper class. She'd be wrapped up in some precarious bubble made to float in their midst. This end also held a new life with a man who loved her and involved packing up her whole life, learning his language, trying to decipher social codes, and attempting to integrate herself in a country she wasn't sure wanted her. She wasn't sure she was ready for all that in addition to bringing their brown baby into a world hell-bent on making it a second-class citizen upon birth. Her baby deserved so much more.

As she kept sorting through bills, the singular factor making Sweden more attractive was privilege. Jonny's wealth and access would give her whatever resources she needed to make her move as smooth as possible. That thought made her feel like a gold digger. After all, he was already paying her rent here in Alexandria. But she wasn't after his money. She was lured in by his promise to take care of her and their baby.

"Brittany? Brittany?" Tanesha called her back from her musings. She'd forgotten her friend on the line and apologized.

"I mean, how did he propose?"

"In bed."

Tanesha puffed, not wanting to hear those details. "How was the meeting with his family?"

Brittany told her about the breakdown he had in front of his parents, the crayfish party where she'd met his sisters and best friend, Ragnar, and his assistant Louise, who whizzed around her like a pesky bee. Both sisters had looked at her like they'd seen her before. She wasn't sure how she felt about all of them yet.

Except for his mother. Brittany had decided she hated that woman. Now Jonny wanted her to be Astrid's daughter-in-law.

"I swear to you, Tee," she continued. "The only reason I'm considering this is because he loves me so much and I want our baby to be safe and taken care of. He's so excited about the baby."

"Can't he take care of you and the baby without tying you down into marriage?"

Brittany had been thinking the same thoughts.

"I don't know, Tee. I think marriage means a lot more, you know? Considering his family, they probably wouldn't think twice about cutting our child out of the picture. God, his mother was such a bitch!"

"And you want to marry into that?" Tanesha was helping her see reason. Brittany quieted down and reflected on her friend's words. Yes, she wanted security for her baby, and she knew Jonny would take care of them. But the thought of his parents as her in-laws was too much to bear.

"Why is he rushing into marriage anyway? That mentality feels so outdated."

"Marriage means legitimizing our child," Brittany said.

Legitimizing their child within the von Lundin dynasty. They wouldn't be expediting their relationship if the stakes were lower, but somehow, he was trying to make a statement, and Brittany feared she was a pawn in his plans. The child she was carrying took priority though.

"Hmm." Tanesha finally seemed to understand. This marriage was a strategic positioning.

"You know, Tee, I was waiting for Jamal to propose. I wanted that ring," Brittany said. "Four years, and he never once tried. All he talked about was building a family and how he wanted children."

Brittany shifted uncomfortably at her own half-truth. Jamal had treated her like a queen. Of course, he had wanted to marry her. Jamal was rich. He could take care of her the way she wanted. But that wasn't enough. It could never be enough because he didn't have access to the type of privilege Jonny had. One that said as long as she had him spellbound, no one on earth would ever touch her again against her will.

"Seriously, Brit. What took him so long?"

"He kept saying he was waiting for me to make up my damn mind. But he never said the words." Now Brittany felt she was parsing Jamal's actions to justify the fact that she was seriously considering marrying Jonny after knowing him for less than six months. Brittany wondered how long she would keep obfuscating to avoid the truth of what she'd chosen.

A fresh line of tears bubbled out, and Tanesha spent the next fifteen minutes consoling her. Once Brittany stopped sobbing enough to receive information, Tanesha suggested she bring Jonny down to Atlanta. She needed to meet this man herself. Brittany's parents needed to know as well.

Especially if Brittany, their only child, was considering leaving the country.

––––––––––––

"Tell Eva to route you to Atlanta instead. I'll meet you there," Brittany told Jonny over the phone while chopping carrots later that night. It was all she could stomach these days. She decided not to bid for a cabin crew schedule the following month. She needed time to digest her current trajectory.

"Why?"

"Some important people you need to meet live there."

"Who?"

"Are you kidding me?" she laughed. When he remained silent on the line, she continued, "My best friend, Tanesha, and my parents."

He went quiet again. Brittany began to worry. Was he nervous about meeting her people, or did he not want to meet them? Maybe meeting her extended network meant their relationship was actually being lived in the real world and not in their cozy bubble lined with bedsheets? Did he fully understand the weight the words "Marry me" carried?

As if reading her thoughts, he came back from his momentary hiatus.

"Have you considered it?" he asked. It was Brittany's turn to stay silent. "I want to marry you."

"Why?" she barked, startling even herself.

"Because I love you."

"Do you really?"

"Yes, I do."

"We've only known each other for a few months."

"Does it matter?"

"It does, Jonny. It does. You can't *know* a person in just a couple of months. Their lives, their struggles, their pain." Memories of Beaufount floated into her consciousness. "You can't know everything about them to decide you want to marry them so quickly."

"I don't care."

"But you have to care. You have to care about my past."

"Why?"

Brittany felt at a loss for words. Why did he seriously need to care about her past? That didn't define her. He wanted her now, just as she was. She remained quiet, lost in thought.

"I only care about our future together," he continued. "I don't want anyone else. I want you and our baby. I've even picked a name if it's a girl."

She sighed, exasperated. *He's already picked out a name!*

"Please marry me. I swear I will take care of you with everything I have."

This option couldn't be that bad, could it? A life wrapped in luxury beyond what she'd ever dreamed for herself. This was far from a foolish card to play.

"So, tell me, what name have you picked for our child?" she asked, derailing their conversation. Normally, Jonny would be agitated that his thoughts had been interrupted and their chat left unfinished, but she heard him giggle in excitement on the other end.

"Maya," he said. "I want it to be a girl..."

"Maya? Why Maya?" Brittany asked. She was met with silence from his end. "Jonny?"

"It's the most beautiful name I've ever heard." His voice came back stronger.

Brittany wasn't sure she liked that name. She had no emotional reaction to it. Not even an *awww*. She had been pondering Whitney if their baby was a girl or Whitfield for a boy. Then again, their baby was half Swedish. Maybe "Whitney von Lundin" wouldn't work as well in Sweden? Jonny chimed back in.

"Maya works in both English and Swedish. Please." His tone was pleading. "I think it's perfect for our baby."

Brittany told him she'd think about it.

———

Two weeks later, when Brittany picked Jonny up at Atlanta's Hartsfield-Jackson Airport on a Saturday morning, he launched into her arms and pulled her into a scorching kiss before she could utter his name.

"I've missed you so much," he breathed, resting his forehead on hers. "You..." He tore away to kiss her stomach. "And you...*Lilla*

Maya." Little Maya. Brittany laughed at his dramatic display of affection.

She decided they would spend the week in Atlanta, getting to know her parents, meeting her best friend, Tanesha, and giving each other one last chance to mull over their decision. Brittany was staying in her childhood room at her parents' place, but Eva had booked them at the Four Seasons so they could steal away to Jonny's hotel room during the week.

"Welcome to the ATL!" Brittany announced as they drove north along I-85 toward downtown Atlanta. She'd borrowed her mother's modest Hyundai for the airport pickup.

"I can't wait till you meet my parents. Hopefully they don't make me cry."

She stole a glance at him, just in time to see him lightly turn up his mouth before it turned into a serious line again. His own parents were sore spots for him—this she knew. This was her last-ditch effort at trying to jolt him back to reality to reassess their relationship.

She turned back to the road, thinking about the night before when she had prepped her parents for Jonny's arrival.

"What?" her mother had exclaimed with hands on cheeks and tear-filled eyes. "What are you saying, Brit?"

"Jamal and I are over."

"We love that boy!" her father had protested. "He had already asked our permission for your hand a year ago."

"But he never proposed to me."

"You were so busy, Brit," her mother had cried. "Jamal was finding the right time to ask you. He'd promised us."

Once the news of her breakup with Jamal had slowly sunk in, she told them she'd met someone else and was bringing him home to meet them...because it was serious.

"How serious?" Her father narrowed his eyes. "What is *so serious* you've thrown away four solid years with Jamal?"

"Please. Just keep an open mind when you meet him, okay?"

When Brittany and Jonny arrived at her parents' modest bungalow, it was to strong smells of curry wafting through the air. Brittany grabbed Jonny's hand and gave it a quick squeeze before pulling him along to the front door.

If Tyrone and Beatrice Johnson had been shocked by Brittany's breakup with Jamal, seeing Jonny at their table digging into their curried goat devastated them.

Jonny kept smiling at her parents after every bite. Beatrice watched him eat, a hand lying flat across her chest. Brittany knew what her mother was thinking. *What on earth had her baby girl dragged home?*

"So, *Yonny... Yonny*, right?" Her father attempted conversation.

"Yes," Brittany jumped in. "It's actually spelled J-O-N-N-Y but pronounced 'Yonny' in Swedish." Her father peered at her, accepting her explanation with a slow nod.

"How long have you known my daughter?" her father asked. Brittany rolled her eyes at this line of questioning reserved for teenage boys. Jonny turned to look at her, making love through his gaze, and her father cleared his throat to regain Jonny's attention.

"Since April. The second I saw her, I knew." He turned back to her.

"April?" Tyrone cut in. "And you want to marry her already?"

"I've never been more sure of anything in my life, Tyrone."

"Mr. Johnson," her father made a show of correcting him.

Jonny pinned her father with his glare typically reserved for business negotiations.

"Mr. Johnson... I love your daughter. I can't bear to be away from her."

Her father listened with a clenched jaw, taking in this foreigner. Then he turned to his daughter. There really was nothing he could do. She was nearing forty years old. She was no longer his "little" girl.

"Brit?"

She bit her lower lip and turned to her father. "Yes, Dad?"

"Do you want to marry him?"

She turned to look at Jonny, and for a split second, her parents' dining room turned into a quiet desert where only she and Jonny existed, and the howling wind churning through the sand was the sound of their beating hearts.

"I do."

MUNA

Malice was exhausting.

It hung in their apartment for months like an unrelenting Harmattan sun. Yasmiin became reclusive, retreating from the other girls, often staying out late. They knew she was probably hanging with Yagiz and hiding out in whatever cove they screamed together in. Soon enough, they rarely saw Yasmiin at all, and her room remained perpetually shut for days.

But Yagiz hadn't fired Muna. He had kept her on. He had let her keep her job as janitor at the Birger Jarlsgatan address where that pretty sister with the nice clothes worked. Just like Mr. Björn at Migrationsverket had told her, she had to be a good girl if she was ever going to get that book. Belonging and acceptance were curious siblings indeed, Muna often thought. These feelings made men grovel. One could try to belong for decades without ever fully being accepted.

Muna loved watching the sister with the important job. She always had an Espresso House coffee on her desk. Maybe one day, Muna would buy her a cup so they could *fika*—have coffee— together. Muna was slinking around as usual when the woman, who had introduced herself as Kemi, stopped her in the kitchen area.

"Muna, right?" She was trying out her Swedish. Muna nodded.

"You might be able to help me." Her Swedish seemed to be improving.

"Okay." Muna stopped wiping down the counter.

"I'm having a hard time finding an African store," Kemi said, piecing words together in passable Swedish. "Do you know any?"

"What are you looking for?" Muna asked, bunching the damp cloth in her hands.

Finding everything Kemi wanted in a single store was the holy grail of being an African in Stockholm. Their dietary needs were peripheral to salmon and potatoes. Kemi spewed frustration in the form of a list of food items she was currently craving, and Muna shared intel. Two good stores in Rinkeby. One she liked in Tensta. A grocery store and salon in one somewhere in Skärholmen. Muna helped her map out every African store within a ten-kilometer radius.

"Now I can add 'African food' as number two on my list. I already found a hairdresser," Kemi joked, switching to English. "Number three, finding good makeup for brown skin."

Kemi thanked her and left, leaving Muna staring after her, confused. Her English was weak, so she hadn't fully grasped the woman's meaning. Maybe getting her a coffee from Espresso House and trying to be friends was indeed a stretch. They could barely communicate as it was.

After waving goodbye to her cleaning crew, Muna zipped up her jacket over her black uniform and burst out of the office in darkness. The street was currently being dusted with flecks of snow, and it was already pitch-dark by four p.m. This had been the most difficult part of her two years at Solsidan—being locked up with nothing to do as inky darkness enveloped them. It filled some people with anxiety, while others turned to eating two or three extra plates at each meal. Ahmed had been the former.

Now free of Solsidan's walls, she could at least roam streets in the cold and dark. She could see other semblances of life milling around. Cozy-looking shops and cafés, stores decorated in twinkling lights for the season. Spending winter in the city and at Solsidan were very different experiences. One killed the soul quicker than the other.

She strolled toward T-Centralen in the biting cold, but instead of hopping on the blue line toward Tensta, she detoured to Hötorget and down into the basement where Yagiz's food stall was.

When he saw her, Yagiz froze his task of shearing thin slices of kebab meat.

Muna stood at the counter, regarding him.

He turned to a colleague and muttered Turkish at breakneck speed. Then he pulled out a cigarette and cocked his head to one side quickly, signaling to Muna to follow him. As soon as they reached the surface, Yagiz made a slow show of lighting his cigarette, taking a few puffs, and watching smoke condense in frigid air before turning to her.

"Muna Saheed." He half chuckled. "Is something wrong at work?"

"Where is Yasmiin?"

He fully laughed and took a few more drags of his cigarette. "You seem so interested in our relationship," he said. "Why so curious, Muna? *Uhnn?* You want to join us?"

"We haven't seen her in two weeks now," Muna replied, ignoring his insult. "We're worried about her. What have you done to her?"

He guffawed at her remark. "What a lovely way to talk to your boss, *huhn*?"

"Where is Yasmiin? Is she okay?"

She sensed she was provoking him, and her mind raced to the night when she and Khadiija had dragged him out of their apartment and left him naked in their hallway.

"Get out of my sight... NOW!" he yelled.

KẸMI

Before their Bachmann pitch team left for Germany, Kemi swung by Espresso House on her way home to grab a cinnamon bun, her nightly ritual.

No sign of Tobias though. Since he'd introduced himself, he'd vanished into thin air. She prayed he'd only taken several weeks of vacation as was common here, but she couldn't shake that deep sinking feeling that he was truly gone.

The rest of the week was spent preparing for their presentation in Germany amid a group of lethargic colleagues. No one else besides Jonny was on board with her idea. Even Björn Fältström, who led business development and was a member of the pitch team, walked around with the carriage of a man being forced into hard labor.

Kemi organized a photo shoot through a local design agency, which created sample poster boards with Jonny and two other models, a fuller Eritrean girl and a skinny Portuguese guy. Jonny had been out of his element, twitching nervously and fidgeting with his hands. But they had made it through the test shoot, and Kemi was satisfied with the spreads. This was what she did best.

Björn barely spoke to her on the entire flight down to Frankfurt. Frankly, she didn't care. She reviewed her notes and pitch angle, including rebuttals for potential questions that could arise. The last four months had been a blur of work meetings, lunches, several daily *fika* breaks, and more meetings as follow-ups to the previous meetings. She finally had a chance to prove why she'd won National Marketing Executive two years in a row back in the States.

The States...Andersen & Associates felt like a lifetime ago. Besides occasional emails from her former assistant, Nicole, no one else kept in touch. She missed having a personal assistant. Here in Sweden, she hadn't been assigned one, though some of the other directors, mostly the men on her team, all had assistants. She'd broached the subject with Ingrid, but Ingrid had brushed it aside, turning it into a feminist spiel.

"You know how guys need all the help they can get," Ingrid said, laughing it off.

After a chauffeured ride from the airport, they arrived in an austere conference room filled with six white men and one woman who looked mixed race, though by Kemi's estimation, she seemed to be passing as white in the room. She shared no covert smile or nod affirming sisterhood with Kemi. The team from von Lundin settled in. Kemi pulled out easels and placed the posters backward so their big reveal wasn't ruined.

Jonny introduced the team and then spent a few minutes stressing the importance of this account and why he was personally there. He handed it off to Björn, who discussed the business aspect of the campaign they were proposing, how inclusive it was, and how well it would go over in various Asian markets.

Then they turned to Kemi.

Taking a deep anchoring breath, she walked up to the easels and spun all three posters around to audible gasps and a *wow!*

In one of the samples, Jonny was dressed in a simple V-neck, wheat-colored sweater with a crisp white collar popping over its rim and tan trousers. He was holding a mug of coffee and sitting with his feet clad in high-top Bachmann B:GEMs, legs crossed on a table. Next to his legs was a plate bearing cinnamon buns. In the photo, Jonny was reaching for the lone chocolate muffin on the plate. DARE TO BE DIFFERENT was blazed beneath the imagery.

Kemi explained the multiple layers of the photo to the team. The cinnamon buns represented Sweden and homogeneity. His minimalist clothing paired with screaming shoes and him reaching for the muffin represented diversity and inclusion.

The room listened with bated breath as she deconstructed the idea behind her proposed marketing campaign. Each poster would depict stereotypes from a certain culture, while the model representing that culture would engage in an action that would break those stereotypes.

"Finally," Kemi was winding down her presentation. "Jonny is...*different*. Many people who know him know this, and there's nothing wrong with him," she continued. "Dare I say it, this may very well be his superpower."

Jonny stood like a frozen statue, hands balled at his sides, listening intently.

"His way of looking at the world hasn't limited him from running one of the largest marketing companies in the world. Having Jonny von Lundin as the face of this campaign, wearing shoes people would never associate with him, is a public statement. Dare to be different, and own it!"

When she was done, a round of applause roared from around the table, and two people stood up in ovation. One was the woman who now seemed to shed the distance she had walked in with.

The other was her teammate, Björn Fältström.

"How did it go?" Malcolm asked, hopping off the stage during intermission of his show a couple nights later. Earlier, she had been tapping her feet and bobbing her head to Malcolm's jazz band on stage, sometimes standing up and fully dancing, thrusting her hips side to side in sync with the jazz rhythm. Their beginning Swedish class was over, and she was now registered in the next level. Despite the antagonism between Malcolm and their teacher, José, he passed Malcolm with flying colors.

"Nailed it!" she sang. "*Nailed it, nailed it, nailed it!*" Malcolm gave her a hug. Then he reached for a mug of Carlsberg beer that the bartender had slid his way.

"I knew you would," he praised her after taking a swig. "With all that Black girl magic you got going ON!"

"You know I gotta represent." She took a sip of her mojito, laughing, just as José walked up to them with a fluorescent cocktail in hand. He stretched up on his toes to give Malcolm a light kiss on the lips, catching Kemi off guard.

"Oh wow. Wow! Wow! Wow!" Kemi was stunned. The couple laughed. The way they'd gone at it in class, Kemi should have known it was due to a simmering attraction between them. José sipped from his straw with raised eyebrows and pursed lips.

"Wanna grab a late bite with us after the gig?" Malcolm offered.

Of course she wanted to, she beamed back at them. She had so much to celebrate. Not only had Bachmann awarded them the contract, they had somehow managed to find an extra million kronor for them. They were also insisting on launching the campaign in the spring. Back at the office, von Lundin Marketing had celebrated with champagne when the team returned. Ingrid and Maria apologized for doubting her.

"You have to understand," Ingrid had explained. "It was too risky. It still is."

"Well, it hasn't launched yet," Maria said. "And we may get a strong backlash. But Kemi..." She toasted her. "I respect you so much more now." Kemi was left wondering how much respect Maria had initially had for her. The only director who had missed their celebrations was Greta. She had coughed lightly that morning and said she needed to take a sick day.

After Malcolm's gig, they found a small pizza place on Södermalm. They dug into greasy kebab pizzas topped with garlicky crème fraîche, celebrating the fact that she was a sister making it in Sweden.

Kemi's high didn't last long, though. She snuffed it out herself the next day.

———

The escalators at Östermalmstorg station were out of order, and Kemi was stuck behind a heavyset woman who was making her way up the stationary steps. One foot at a time, the woman was willing her body to do what it wasn't ready for. People overtook her impatiently. Kemi wanted to but feared using up all her own energy and becoming like this stranger who was stalling foot traffic. The helplessness of the woman's breathing stirred something deep within Kemi. When she got home that evening, she decided to step on her scale.

Seven kilos. She did mental calculations. Fifteen pounds. *Shit.* She'd gained fifteen pounds in five months. She peered down at the scale in shock and promptly declared cinnamon buns the work of the devil.

On a date later that night, she opted for a goat cheese, honey, and fig salad to start her carb-free campaign. Her investment banker date wore a dark suit with golden cuffs and a white shirt with the top two buttons unfastened.

He went on to order the priciest five-course dinner at Restaurang Kött. She watched the thick flow of burgundy red cascade into her wine glass as he poured her wine, more entranced by the swirling drink than the man in front of her.

Turned out, he'd picked the most expensive Michelin-starred restaurant in town as well.

Kemi knew this when the bill arrived and Cheap Bastard—her nickname for him—suggested they split the bill...evenly. In Stockholm, dates regularly split bills to drive home their egalitarian point, but leaving her with the Swedish equivalent of two hundred dollars to pay when she only had a salad and one glass of wine—well, two glasses?

"I mean, you did drink their most expensive wine in house," Cheap Bastard geared up his argument.

"I had two glasses...*you* finished the whole damn bottle!" Kemi's voice pitched higher. Other diners nearby cut them reprimanding looks. "I only had a salad too!" She lowered her voice.

"I guess that must have been some expensive goat cheese," he retorted.

She hated having to bear that burden of not "causing a scene" because she was Black, so she quietly paid half, grabbed her bag, and bolted out of the restaurant.

"Wait! Wait!" Cheap Bastard gave chase. Catching up to her on the sidewalk, he rounded her and blocked her path. Expecting an apology, Kemi got truffle-laced breath in her face instead.

"So...how about a kiss?"

She planted her palm, with fingers splayed, straight onto his face and shoved him out of her way.

"Are you *Shermmy*?" a blond barista asked Kemi the next morning during her Espresso House run.

"Yes?" She saw no point in correcting her.

"I think this is for you." The lady bent low to pull out an envelope from beneath the counter and handed it to Kemi. Thanking her, Kemi slipped the envelope into her large bag, heart pounding. She hoped it was what she thought it was.

Once at her desk, she carefully opened the envelope to find a small piece of paper with the word "Tobias" and a ten-digit phone number scribbled on it.

Kemi's heart soared with hope.

PART THREE

THIRTEEN

MUNA

"I hate this place."

When Khadiija said those words for the first time, she and Muna had been eating rice and lamb one evening in late January. Muna had listened quietly, waiting for Khadiija to continue. Since she and Yasmiin had fought, Khadiija had retracted back into her shell, only sharing what was necessary as she shuttled between her job, their apartment, and the Tensta community center.

Yasmiin, on the other hand, barely stayed at their place anymore, and they knew it was because of Yagiz.

When Khadiija dropped those words of hatred, Muna cherished them despite their gravity. It meant Khadiija was ready to start talking again.

"The boys at the center have been talking a lot," Khadiija added before turning back to her rice and lamb in silence once more.

"What are they saying?" Muna asked.

"You know." Khadiija shrugged.

"No, I don't." Muna's interest was piqued. "What are the boys saying?"

On the few occasions Muna had followed Khadiija there, their conversations in Somali had been rife with emotion. The atmosphere always felt charged.

"They won't even look at me," one boy named Ibraahin said before breaking down in tears. He had just turned sixteen. "Who doesn't look at another human being? Who doesn't?"

Muna thought of Gunhild, who listened to her, eyes warming as she did. When Muna mentioned this to the group, they fell into an uncomfortable silence until Khadiija broke it.

"One Gunhild is not enough. One Gunhild will never be enough. We need millions of Gunhilds."

Now Khadiija was telling her that the boys at the center had been talking...a lot.

"Is it Ibraahin?" Muna was grasping. "Is he the one talking?"

"They all are, and they are tired of staying silent, of not being accepted." Khadiija shoveled rice into her mouth. She chewed while Muna waited for her to swallow. "Silence is poison, Muna," Khadiija continued. "Silence is a slow, poisonous death."

"Then tell me about the man who made you run," Muna demanded, because her sister-friend's own silence was poisoning her too.

Khadiija stopped chewing and locked eyes with the younger woman. Muna stared back, barely blinking. She had caught Khadiija off guard, and Muna saw the armor beginning to form around her once more like a snail seeking protection in its shell.

"Please?"

"Why don't you mind your own business, *eh*?"

"What?"

"It's the same thing with you and Yasmiin. You are always in her business. Always sticking your nose where it doesn't belong," Khadiija said, her tone heated. Muna blinked back tears. "Let

Yagiz defile her body if she wants him to. It is none of your business!"

"But..." Muna stammered. "I care about you and Yasmiin. I am your sister."

"You're not my sister!"

This time, Muna lifted a hand to her chest, physically stunned by Khadiija's outburst. She tried to say something, but her mouth remained dry, the words stuck on her tongue.

"Look," Khadiija continued. "My family is back home in Somalia. I have many sisters and brothers. I didn't want to leave them behind, okay?"

Muna remained silent. She was now staring down at the plate of food in her lap, holding back tears. Khadiija pushed her own half-eaten plate away and got to her feet. She paused as if to say something to Muna but then shuffled off to her room.

Muna's shoulders bounced, startled by the slamming of Khadiija's door.

––––––––––––

"Johan von Lundin, CEO."

Muna mouthed the name and title, reading it off a tag attached to the glass wall of the corner office she was about to clean the next day. This space belonged to the top boss, and it was the only one in the entire building she'd never seen anyone enter or exit. By now, she knew everyone who milled around those gray spaces: the directors, designers, managers, interns. Not that she should care, because she was a janitor working in the background. But she had never met the owner of this glass room. She wasn't even sure it was in use. The desk was empty, the shelves were bare, and the cabinets remained locked. The sole pop of life was a vase of yellow and lilac tulips sitting on the desk, like they'd been freshly delivered.

That name sounded familiar. *Johan von Lundin. Johan...* She mulled it over and over again in her mind until recognition rushed in. It couldn't be the same man, could it? She remembered Mattias telling her about Solsidan's benefactor—a man with the same name. His last name didn't sound like a very common Swedish name. What if it really was him? What if this CEO was the one who had indirectly kept her and Ahmed and others safe in a paradise out in the middle of nowhere for two years?

If it really was him, then she needed to share her gratitude.

Muna pushed her cleaning cart into the echoing room and pulled out a damp cloth. She started wiping down the desk but then stopped, realizing how foolish it felt. She had already wiped it down earlier that morning. There had been no flowers then. She put the rag back and turned toward the tulips instead.

Their petals were large and vibrant, inviting her to caress them. She pulled out a yellow tulip, holding the bulb to her nose to sniff it. Flowers always reminded her of Ahmed and his exquisite gardening. She hoped Mattias was still tending to Ahmed's rose garden and keeping his memory alive through those roses. She took a deep breath, trying to tease out its fragrance. She delicately placed it back and bent low to sniff the entire bunch. Then she straightened back up and let out an exaggerated sigh.

Muna grabbed her cleaning cart and spun around to find a tall, foreboding figure blocking the doorframe. She yelped, one hand flying to her mouth, startled by the man's presence. She lowered her head, ashamed that she'd been caught. She wasn't sure how long he had been standing there and watching her touch his flowers.

She closed her eyes and squeezed out a formal apology. "*Jag ber om ursäkt.*"

The room remained silent, and she slowly opened her eyelids. Yes, he was still standing there, peering at her intensely. And she instantly recognized him. The tall, hungry man from the elevator. The one who had been kissing the Black model so fiercely in public. She shifted her weight under his burning glare. His brows began to dip inward, and she deduced that she should never have touched his tulips.

She remembered Ibraahin's words from the community center. "They won't even look at me," the boy had cried. But this Swede was looking at her. His clear eyes were burrowing into her as she stood in his office.

It couldn't be the same man, Muna decided. The statuesque man currently gazing down at her with such spite for touching his tulips couldn't be the same man donating thousands upon thousands of kronor every year to take care of refugees.

———————

When Muna arrived home that evening, it was to a tense scene. After weeks of absence following the Naked Yagiz incident, Yasmiin had returned with the man to pack up her room and move out of their apartment. Khadiija and Muna watched as Yasmiin, sporting a new hairdo with layers of makeup and lips dyed in a rich plum color, wordlessly dragged bags out of her room.

When Yasmiin was about to walk out the door, Muna launched herself toward her and threw her arms around Yasmiin, crying.

"Why are you going?" Muna asked between sniffs. "Why, Yasmiin?"

The older girl put an arm around the younger, trying to console her, while Yagiz looked on, chewing his gum loudly, arms crossed.

"I'm going to miss you the most, Muna," Yasmiin whispered into Muna's ear beneath her hijab.

Then Yasmiin peeled Muna off her, turned to Yagiz, and reached out a hand to him. He took in the other girls; then he grabbed Yasmiin's hand along with one of her suitcases and led her out of the apartment. Khadiija, who had been leaning against her bedroom door watching their grand departure, muttered "Good riddance" in Somali and retreated into her room, slamming the door.

Muna was left sobbing. She ran into her room, pulled out Ahmed's sack, and started looking at his photos again. She'd been doing this weekly since she'd moved to Tensta, memorizing every face and expression. Sorting through those passport photos and promising them final rest. Those Kurdish strangers immortalized in photos had now become her invisible family.

Her only family.

KẸMI

Kemi twiddled her thumbs, waiting for Tobias to arrive.

After she'd gotten his note, she had dug out her phone, dropping it in excitement. She picked it up, straightened her skirt, and resumed the task of eloquently crafting what she wanted to say to him.

The only words her fingers could type had been "Why did you disappear?" His response had been a smiley face emoji, followed by the words "I was fired."

They had arranged to meet over the weekend for a quick *fika* date, which had then morphed into a lunch date.

Kemi craned her neck to see if he was strolling up to the café she'd chosen close to Kungsträdgården, the most popular park in town. December had brought fluffy, white snow, twinkling Christmas lights, and a festiveness that enveloped Stockholmers in denial that true winter was around the corner.

She had missed spending Christmas with her sister in Richmond. Over the phone, she had told Kehinde everything was like a fairy tale. That she was living in a Nordic snow globe. That she had exciting Christmas plans. All Kehinde had done was let out an "*Umphf!*" sound before telling Kemi she loved her and disconnecting. In truth, she had spent Christmas and New Year's Eve alone and was too embarrassed to tell her sister she was failing at reinventing herself in Sweden.

January came with a vengeance, bearing deep darkness and miserable slush instead of powdery-white snow.

Kemi wondered why her heart was beating so hard. She'd met Tobias once, and they barely exchanged words besides introductions and him sharing that he had noticed her for weeks. She couldn't have scripted a more romantic approach than when he'd handed her that tall cup of coffee. She scratched that scene out, mentally editing her script as she spotted Tobias walking up to her now, bearing a small bouquet of wildflowers.

"Don't tell me you foraged for these yourself," she joked, getting to her feet, her dimples showing themselves. "Thank you!" Then she realized it was winter and not wildflower-foraging season, but her joke had washed over him. Something else distracted him.

"My God," Tobias said after hugging her and pulling out of their embrace. "You've got the cutest dimples." He grinned, showing that small sliver between his top front teeth, his brown eyes shining. She blushed at his flattery, her eyes wandering over him. He was wearing a brown aviator jacket with faux fur lining its collar. Once he pulled it off, underneath was a black long-sleeve sweater, which was stretched over his swimmer's chest. The fitted top disappeared into a narrow-waisted pair of dark jeans.

"You must have done something really bad to have been fired," Kemi started, once they'd settled in. "No one gets fired in Sweden." He chuckled.

"Well, nothing bad. Just indifference, I guess," he said, pulling the menu closer for a look.

"Indifference?"

"Yeah, I hated my job." He scanned the menu for something to order. "I've found something else anyway." He decided on the shrimp sandwich, dropped the menu, and turned his attention back to her. The thick sweater she was wearing had a plunging neckline, but his eyes didn't roam. They settled on her face, confusing her.

"So, Kemi. What brings you to Sweden?" He rested his cheek on his hand, readying himself for the full story. She giggled at his expression.

"Well, contrary to popular belief, it wasn't a man." She pulled the menu back from him. "Well...technically, it was a man, but he's my boss."

"You're having an affair with your boss?"

"God, no!" She shuddered at the idea of tossing in bed with Jonny. "No, he flew all the way to the States to recruit me."

"All the way, huh? You must have been worth flying over for." He let his words linger.

A waitress approached to take their order. After stepping on the scale recently and realizing she had gained fifteen pounds since moving to Sweden, Kemi had exorcised cinnamon buns from her life and sprinkled her apartment with fruit, as if it were holy water. So today, she opted for a salad. They chatted until their food arrived.

"I hope you're not one of those girls," Tobias said, before grabbing a fork and knife to start cutting into his open-faced sandwich.

"What?"

"You know, girls who must live by leaves alone; no bread." He took a big bite. She loved the way his mouth worked the food.

"Does my body suggest that?" she quipped. His eyes made an appreciative show of fully taking her in.

"I hadn't noticed before." He smirked before another bite. She slapped his forearm playfully.

Over lunch, she learned all about Tobias or, rather, all he was willing to dole out on a first date. He was Gambian-Swedish, but joint ethnic labels weren't really a thing here. He was expected to be one or the other, he told her. His mother had migrated from Banjul, Gambia, as an exchange student at Stockholm University. Within a year, she'd had an affair with one of her professors—a much older married man with children of his own. After Tobias was born, his mother went on to bear one more child for the man before he died of a stroke.

"So, you've got older siblings too?" Kemi chimed in, spearing a few leaves of romaine lettuce.

"Technically, yes." He chugged his water. "But we've never met."

"Don't you want to meet them?"

"Nah," Tobias said. "He was a good man, even though I didn't really know him. He took care of my mom in his will, which was a big deal. You don't incorporate mistresses into your will while still married. Especially if you're Swedish and your mistress is the blackest African woman you can find," Tobias explained.

Kemi couldn't wait to meet his mother.

Their conversation shifted to Kemi and how she had been caught by Jonny von Lundin and brought to Sweden.

"Yeah, I know him," Tobias casually threw out. "Who doesn't in Sweden? His family is this tight with the royal family." He crossed his fingers to demonstrate.

"Pretty reclusive guy though."

Kemi told him about her past life in the U.S. He impressed her with "*Ba wo ni?*" *How are you?* when she told him she was Yoruba. He just kept getting more perfect by the second. She then started dishing on her dating woes in Sweden, but Tobias quickly interjected.

"You don't have to worry about that anymore." Tobias locked eyes with hers, taking on a jovial tone. "We're closing that chapter right now!" She laughed loudly. He joined her, his eyes twinkling as he did.

"So, Tobias," Kemi asked him three hours later, "do you like jazz?"

BRITTANY-RAE

"I do."

Brittany repeated those words three months later on a frigid winter day at Stockholm's City Hall. White snow coated the sleepy city and its islands like icing on a cake. Ragnar stood stone-faced beside an elated Jonny, while Tanesha linked arms with Brittany, trying to contain floods of tears. Both their best friends signed their names as the only witnesses to their love.

Once the deed was done, the officiant must have leaked their secret wedding to various gossip outlets, because the next day, photos of Jonny and Brittany wearing her plum-colored summer dress as they roamed around Stockholm were plastered on several magazine covers. Antonia, Svea, and their parents read about the union for the first time on the front page of one such tabloid.

Sweden collectively mourned the loss of one of its golden sons.

Mrs. von Lundin.

That cape of a title took a while to fully settle perfectly around her shoulders. When they'd gotten married, Brittany hadn't expected a public unveiling of her life from the media vultures swarming around their relationship. Jonny had never engaged with the press. But they dug into her past anyway, interviewing former colleagues at the airline she worked for, and wondering if the model turned flight attendant was in fact a gold digger.

They even reached out to Jamal looking for commentary. He had called her to let her know he was being hounded, promising to protect her on his end. Then he asked her if she was truly happy, and if she was, then he wished her nothing but bliss with the man who had captured her heart.

But the backlash she received from Jonny's family had been much stronger, in the form of silence. A deep, laconic denial. She wasn't sure if they felt betrayed that they had had to read about their wedding on the front page of the tabloids instead of hearing it directly from Jonny's lips. His parents, Wilhelm and Astrid, had retreated to one of their cottages in the sleepy seaside village of Smögen in West Sweden. They needed time to fully digest the fact that the large society wedding they'd anticipated for their golden child once he found the "right girl," filled with glitter and guests, including members of the monarchy, was never going to happen.

His sister Svea had sent the newlyweds a bouquet of two dozen blush-pink roses along with her congratulations, saying she wished she'd been there to celebrate with them, but...*you know*...her invite must have gotten lost in the mail. She promised to throw a cocktail reception in their honor once she got back from the multiday book launch of a bestselling Swedish crime author she was currently promoting.

The only person who decided to physically reach out was Antonia. Scary Antonia, according to Jonny. Before Brittany and Tanesha returned to the States after the wedding so Brittany could continue her Swedish residency application process, Antonia invited the new couple over to her mansion in Elfvik for a lavish dinner and reception with a tightly knit group of friends including Ragnar and his wife, Pia.

Louise had booked a room at the vibrant boutique Hotel Rival on Södermalm for Tanesha, while the newlyweds had stolen away to Jonny's hobbit cottage. Now both ladies were in Tanesha's room, getting ready for Antonia's party. Tanesha was sitting on the edge of the lush hotel bed as Brittany got ready in the bathroom when someone knocked.

Brittany heard Tanesha push off the bed to open it.

"Jonny. Come on in." Tanesha closed the door behind him.

"Calm down, she hasn't run away. She's doing her makeup," she heard Tanesha say.

Brittany was applying mascara, her mouth open, when through the mirror she saw Jonny leaning against the door, watching her.

"You know, you don't have to creep around me anymore. You've put a ring on it." Brittany laughed as she caught him in the mirror. He didn't laugh though. When she turned to take him in, he stepped forward, grabbed her by the shoulders, and kissed her. She could feel him shake as his mouth moved over hers. He was nervous about something, and she pulled out of his embrace.

"Are you having second thoughts?" she whispered. His eyes pinned her. Then he shook his head.

"You're shaking, Jonny." She ran her hands down his sleeves toward his hands and fingers, which had started dancing.

"This is so new," he said.

"You didn't prepare yourself," she added.

"What do you mean?"

"Dating a Black woman for fun is one thing. Marrying her and fully owning your choice is another," she explained. "You weren't ready."

"I'm ready. I want to take care of you. I want to protect my child." He was getting agitated.

"From what?"

Her question hung between them like a knife trying to pry open his oyster of privilege so he would verbally admit it. What did Jonny think his child needed to be protected from by marrying her?

Jonny looked at her, wordlessly begging her to stop questioning him. She didn't want to stop, though. She loved her husband's most significant quirk: the fact that he couldn't lie and she could read everything so openly on his face. He was an aquarium with feelings swimming in clear view.

"I love you."

"I know you do, but that doesn't answer my question." He continued his intense stare until he was forced to piece a few words together.

"My name," Jonny dropped. "My name will protect our child. Brown kids have it harder here."

Of course they did. Brittany turned back to applying her mascara. They had to get ready for Antonia's reception.

"And what about Black women?" she asked as she moved on to her lipstick.

Jonny stood there...silent.

Still in the depths of winter, they arrived at Antonia's for dinner. She seemed in jolly spirits as she swept them into the vaulted lobby of her contemporary digs. There were already a handful of people warmly dressed in all forms of cashmere and Merino wool sweaters, stems of red wine in hand. They dropped off their coats and swapped their shoes for indoor slippers reserved for guests. Antonia then led the couple and their plus one, Tanesha, to a large living room where the rest of the guests, about twelve in total, were milling around and murmuring in low voices.

Once Jonny stepped in, his hand tensed up while holding Brittany's. The group stared at the couple for about two seconds in absolute quiet, ogling the now five-month bulge that Brittany could no longer hide. Jonny had gotten her pregnant and clearly married her in haste.

Someone, Ragnar, started tapping at his glass with a fork. His tapping was joined by more until it turned into a chorus.

"*Skål för brudparet!*" Ragnar led the group, who answered him with "*Skål!*" and finished it off with applause. Jonny's grip on her relaxed. People started stepping up to introduce themselves to both Brittany and Tanesha. She recognized many of them from the crayfish party in August when she'd barely been showing, her pregnancy still a secret. Jonny fetched her a glass of cranberry juice and a stem of Merlot for Tanesha, before disappearing into the midst of family and friends.

Ragnar walked up to them, assessing Brittany's bulge on approach. Jonny had told him about the baby before begging him to be his best man at their court wedding, so he'd already been privy to the news.

Ragnar reached for Brittany and gave her a kiss on each check before turning to Tanesha with an outstretched hand for a shake.

"Nice to see you again, Tanis."

"Tanesha," she corrected.

"I'm sorry. It's a difficult name for me to pronounce." He attempted humor, which didn't reach his eyes.

"I'm struggling with Ragn, Raggie, Raggedy, as well," she clapped back, which drew a small laugh out of him.

His wife, Pia, materialized from behind his broad frame with a wide smile on her lips. Pia was petite with straight blond hair and blue eyes. She was the physical manifestation of Swedish nostalgia.

"Congratulations, Brittany." She stood on her toes to hug the taller woman. "Wow, you finally got the bachelor to settle down. How did you do it?"

Brittany laughed at her comment, only to realize Pia was indeed waiting for an actual response to her question. *How did you do it? * Brittany peered down at Pia in disbelief. *What?*

"You know what they say in America," Tanesha offered. "Once you go Black..." She finished off with a sip of wine.

Ragnar bellowed. Both Brittany and Tanesha hadn't expected that deep, vibrating sound out of him. Pia's brows knitted uncomfortably as she looked from Tanesha to her laughing husband, trying to understand the joke. His chuckle died into a serious line before he turned to leave. Pia gave Brittany a weak smile and quick kiss before dashing off after her husband.

"Asshole," Tanesha muttered under her breath but still loud enough to elicit a snigger from Brittany.

FOURTEEN

MUNA

Muna watched Kemi, Johan, and another woman from behind the wall where she was hiding. It was a rare sight. She was witnessing signs of life in that corner office.

Kemi was talking to Johan in an animated fashion. He was sitting on the edge of his sparse desk, his arms folded across his chest, fully listening to what Kemi was saying. His eyes would occasionally follow Kemi's flailing arms as she described something, but then they would return to her face.

There was another woman—a petite brunette scribbling feverishly in a notepad.

Since her awkward run-in with Johan, Muna had felt guilty. She needed him to understand she was truly sorry for invading his space. He had probably bought those tulips for that Black model she'd seen him with.

As if propelled by a mysterious force, Muna slowly inched her way toward his office. By the time she got to his door, she changed her mind and spun around, but Kemi had already spotted her.

"Muna!" Kemi called out. Muna turned back and gave her a weak smile. The man and the brunette glanced toward her. Then he started speaking in Swedish to the brunette, who continued taking notes.

"*Hur mår du?*" Kemi asked as she walked out of the office. Muna simply nodded back in response to Kemi's question. Yes, she was doing well.

Then Muna gathered up the courage to face him.

"Johan," Muna called out softly. She wasn't sure how she powered her voice. He was clearly the owner of the company—von Lundin Marketing. He turned to Muna sharply as if the mere mention of "Johan" had burned his ears.

"Jonny," he corrected sternly. She swallowed nervously and then apologized once more for touching his tulips. "*Ingen fara,*" he accepted her remorse. *No worries.*

Muna wasn't done. "Solsidan..." She dropped the name of the center, hoping it jogged his memory. He stared at her blankly. "*Är det du?*" she asked. *Is it you?*

Was he the one whose generosity had fed her and Ahmed and hundreds of others who had passed through Solsidan's doors over the years? Was he the one who had created that oasis out in the countryside for them? Was he the one who had fanned their hope at the center through Mattias? Who never missed a monthly donation? Who kept their rooms warm during the winter, food on their plates, security guards patrolling the place for their safety? The one who deserved their gratitude for as long as they called Sweden home?

"*Vad pratar du om?*" Jonny asked. He sounded frustrated that he was being interrupted. *What are you talking about?* Then he turned to the brunette for guidance. "*Louise, vad handlar det här om?*" *Louise, what is this about?*

Louise held Muna's gaze before proceeding to remind Jonny that he was indeed Solsidan's benefactor.

Muna finally understood what Khadiija meant about the community center boys beginning to talk. Weeks after their conversation, Muna heard them loud and clear when she got off at Tensta station and breached its surface that evening after work.

She arrived to find her neighborhood up in flames.

Sirens blazed all over Tensta. Different pitches and tones differentiating police from ambulances from fire trucks. People pooled in groups outside various apartment blocks, trying to decipher what was going on. There were cars aflame and a few explosions as fire reached their fuel tanks.

And the screaming. It was the wailing more than anything else that stamped impressions on Muna. Many of these people had fled explosions in their home countries, and now they were reliving that trauma. Their terror was real. Women wearing billowing jilbabs ran amok, carrying small children who seemed shell-shocked. Teenagers, wearing scarves that covered half of their faces, were throwing Molotov cocktails indiscriminately in every direction.

Petrified, Muna started running toward her apartment, away from the commotion, trying to get herself to safety. Some of the youth ran toward her, and she recognized a handful of them. They were Khadiija's friends, including Ibraahin.

Then she spotted a vividly colored assailant wearing a pink hijab over a floral garb of fuchsia, lime green, and butter yellow, and her heart sank. Khadiija's favorite dress. The group ran past Muna, elbowing her out of the way. Muna stared after them. She spun around but was pushed aside by four police officers carrying shields and batons in hot pursuit. Khadiija never came home that night.

A few days later, Gunhild came to their apartment with a female police officer in tow. The officer searched Khadiija's room, and once she was done, Gunhild packed up all her belongings as Muna looked on.

"Where's Khadiija?" Muna managed to ask after a long moment of silence. The officer didn't respond, and Gunhild regarded Muna with heavy eyes.

"Is Khadiija dead?" Muna was desperate, wanting to know what had happened to her remaining sister. Yasmiin was already gone anyway. Gunhild shook her head. No, Khadiija wasn't dead.

"Khadiija will have to go to trial for violence toward the state and criminal activity for participating in the riots," Gunhild explained. "She is currently being held by them."

Muna narrowed her eyes in confusion. This couldn't be happening.

"Why, Gunhild?" Muna started to cry. "Why?"

Gunhild pulled her into a hug and held the younger woman as Muna shuddered in her embrace.

The riots had begun when a security guard had dragged a preteen Somali boy on the ground like a goat protesting its slaughter over a chocolate bar he had stolen from a kiosk. The aftermath of Tensta's riots had lured in a swarm of international media, quick to lap up a story spotlighting trouble in paradise.

Swedish media had used dramatic two-word headlines: *FÖRORTEN BRINNER. The suburbs are burning.*

For days after the riots, as she roamed around downtown Stockholm, strange eyes lingered on her for an extra second or two, washing over her hijab with suspicion.

Once the female officer had taken her leave, Gunhild walked into their kitchen to make coffee, while Muna took a seat on the sofa, trying to process what was going on. Khadiija. Arrested. Those words made no sense. But after witnessing Khadiija violently flare up at Yasmiin over the Naked Yagiz incident and seeing her participate in the riots, Muna wasn't so sure about her sister anymore.

"I am not supposed to tell you this. I can get in big trouble because I am bound by confidentiality, but Khadiija was married," Gunhild finally shared once she'd set down two mugs—tea for Muna, instant coffee for herself—on the table. "She still is." Muna studied the older woman's face. "Her husband has many wives, and she is the youngest." Gunhild lifted the hot coffee to her thin lips and set it back down.

"But she can't go home," Muna pleaded. "She ran away from that man. I think he did unspeakable things to her."

"I'm so sorry," Gunhild said, eyebrows crumpling with pity. "I don't know any more than you know right now, but try not to worry. It's very unlikely the authorities will send someone who has been granted asylum back to their country."

Muna cried over her own mug, settling into the realization that "very unlikely" meant there was a sliver of a chance Khadiija may be sent back to the dangerous man she'd run away from. A sentence much worse than death.

What if Khadiija had been her? Muna pondered. What if she was sent back? There was no one to claim her back in Mogadishu. Her mother and brother were in the sea, her father crushed beneath slabs of concrete. What was there to go back to?

This place was her only hope.

KẸMI

For their second date, Kemi dragged Tobias to one of Malcolm's gigs at Stampen in Gamla stan, after talking Malcolm up as the best jazz musician in town. The walls of the historic basement pub were plastered with aging posters of various soul, funk, and blues acts that had blown through its doors over the decades. From its roof hung an eclectic decor of old instruments: bass guitars, clarinets, saxophones.

"I had forgotten how cool this place is," Tobias said, lifting a glass of draft beer to his lips.

"You know this place?" Kemi asked. He cut her a questioning look, softening it with a smile.

"I grew up in this city."

They had come about thirty minutes before Malcolm was going to hop on stage. Kemi couldn't wait to show Tobias off. But Malcolm had already zeroed in on the handsome brother, his own boyfriend, José, hot on his heels.

"Okay..." Malcolm started once he reached the couple. "I don't want to be presumptuous, but can you please marry Kemi already?" He stretched out a hand and gave a laughing Tobias a firm handshake.

"I've heard only great things about you, Malcolm. I'm Tobias."

"José!" José introduced himself, reaching around Malcolm to shake Tobias's hand. "*Välkomna!*" *Welcome!*

"*Tack så mycket!*" *Thanks so much!* Tobias turned to smile at Kemi, whose cheeks were heating up with pride.

"Join us for dinner after the show," Malcolm said as he swung his sax over his shoulder. "We usually grab greasy kebab pizza afterward. It's our thing with Kemi." Beside him, José beamed, taking a sip of his scarlet-colored cocktail.

"I would love to," Tobias said. "Any chance to learn more about Kemi from her friends."

Malcolm and his band hopped on stage at eight p.m. Soon, the stuffy basement was rocking sounds of old-school funk and rhythms that even got the bartender gyrating and sidestepping as he poured drinks for the patrons. Kemi was swept up in the harmonies and beats, her hips swaying with each pounding drumbeat. She danced, throwing her hands up, clapping, and simply letting the music course through her.

Amid the overpowering boom of percussions and strumming of guitars, she caught Tobias watching her dance close to him.

"Are you enjoying the show?" she yelled over the music.

Tobias pulled her closer, his hand hooking her waist. His kiss was slow and gentle. Ample lips on ample lips. She reveled in his tenderness. This felt different. It felt right. Tobias's kiss was a warm, comforting blanket around her shoulders that winter day. He slowly deepened the kiss, and Kemi enjoyed this much-needed chicken soup.

It had been a long time since a man had taken his time kissing her.

———————

Around eleven p.m., the foursome walked over to Södermalm to the hole-in-the-wall pizza joint to tuck into delicious kebab pizzas.

"This always hits the spot," Tobias said before taking a large bite. Malcolm bobbed his head in agreement as he chewed while regarding his fellow Afro-Swede.

"So, bro...what's your story?" Malcolm asked.

Tobias laughed before responding, "You're definitely more American than Swedish."

Malcolm seemed puzzled. "Okayyy?"

"A true Swede would have asked what part of town I live in first," Tobias explained. José chuckled before nodding. "So, if you ask me where I live, you can quickly file me into a neat little box."

"It's true," José chimed in. "For example, if I told you I lived in Djursholm or on Lidingö, most people would assume I was filthy rich."

"Interesting." Malcolm lifted a can of Coca-Cola to his mouth. He took a contemplative swig then turned back to Tobias.

"So...Tobias, where do you live?"

"Norsborg."

"And what is that supposed to tell me about you?" Malcolm asked.

"It means my hood is filled with people who look like me. Most of the people there have no Swedish blood."

"Okay...so I'm gonna put my American hat back on and ask you what you do."

"I'm a security guard," Tobias replied, before taking another bite of pizza.

"I knew it had to be something physical...with that body of yours," José added. Malcolm laughed.

Kemi had been quietly observing Tobias as her friends chatted with him. The way he responded to their questions with a quiet confidence about him. Tobias probably grew up with no frills and only what his small family needed. He was so comfortable to be around. Effortless, it seemed. Technically, it was their second date, but she felt her body relaxing in a way it hadn't around potential suitors in a long time.

"NO WAY!" José's squeal cut through her thoughts, bringing her back to their pizza. "She's your sister?"

"Yup, the one and only Tina Wikström," Tobias dropped casually as he reached for his last slice.

"Oh my God!" José picked up a piece of paper and made a grand show of fanning himself.

"Okay, I clearly missed something," Kemi jumped in. "What's with your sister?"

"The most badass goddess in town," José said. "Besides you, of course." She rolled her eyes at him.

"And what does this badass goddess do?" she asked.

"She used to be a teen pop star before she quit that life and became an activist instead," Tobias said, punching his fist into the air in jest before taking the last swig of his soda.

"Pop star? Just pop star?" José screeched. Then he launched into impromptu karaoke of one of her hit songs while wiggling awkwardly in his seat in an attempt to dance. Kemi and Tobias burst out laughing while Malcolm shook his head.

By the time they spilled out onto the sidewalk, it was well past midnight, and José looked exhausted.

"I need to prep my notes for my Swedish classes next week, so I have to get some sleep."

Malcolm propped him up with a solid arm around his waist and bid Tobias and Kemi good night.

Tobias offered to walk Kemi over to Slussen, where she could catch the red line north, while he would catch the same line going south. They stood quietly on Kemi's side of the platform, Tobias clasping her hand.

"I like your friends," he said before turning to look at her.

"I think they like you too," she said. "You're easy to like." He gave her that gap-toothed smile before bending low to plant a soft kiss on her mouth.

"So, what are you doing next weekend?" Tobias asked against her lips.

BRITTANY-RAE

After Antonia's reception in honor of the newlyweds, Brittany and Tanesha returned to Atlanta, where Brittany wrapped up immigration paperwork she'd begun a few months prior. She had taken a temporary hiatus from her cabin crew job and had vacated her rental town house in Alexandria. A moving company had driven her possessions down to her parents' home in Atlanta for storage.

Eva had handled all the logistics, and Brittany began to realize she would never have to reach into her own piggy bank, or quite frankly lift a finger, as long as Jonny was in her life. In preparation, Jonny had already moved out of his bachelor pad and furnished a four-bedroom waterfront villa not far from Antonia's home in Elfvik.

Once her "specially expedited" residency came through, Jonny flew down to Atlanta to bring her home with him in March, at the beginning of her third trimester.

As Brittany said goodbye to her parents, Beatrice Johnson wouldn't let go of her daughter, her grip tightening around Brittany as they shared a goodbye hug. It had happened too fast for her, but she had to let Brittany go. She was almost thirty-nine, after all.

"Baby, I want to be there when that little angel comes," Beatrice said. "Promise me you'll let me come over to Sweden to be with you?"

"Mom, I'll let you know as soon as I'm all settled in. Of course I want you there." Brittany wiped her tears with the back of her hand before blowing her nose into a soggy napkin.

"Jonny, would you excuse us for a moment?" her father asked. Jonny nodded and glanced quickly at Brittany before leaving the room. Once the door shut behind him, her father turned back to her.

"Brit?" His brows were knitted with worry. "When are we going to meet his parents?"

"It's complicated, Dad."

"Complicated? Baby, you're moving to live with people we've never met, in a country we know nothing about." He was shifting on his feet. "This marriage, your baby... Do you know what you're doing?"

"He loves me. And he's going to take care of me and my baby. That's all that matters."

"Really? So screw everyone else?"

"Tyrone!" her mother reprimanded. Then she turned to Brittany. "Will you two plan a real wedding later on? We wanted to be a part of this. We still want to."

"What about his parents?" her father asked. "They haven't reached out to us yet."

"They're not going to."

"What do you mean? Aren't they behind you guys? The baby?" Her father seemed confused.

Brittany looked down at the damp napkin and lifted it back up to her nose, trying to push back sobs. Her mother pulled her into another embrace, and she heard her father sigh loudly.

———————

Jonny had parked his car at Stockholm Arlanda Airport. After loading her two suitcases—Eva was responsible for shipping the rest of Brittany's belongings to her new life in Sweden—and his leather carry-on bag into the car, they were quickly zooming down E4 toward Stockholm.

When she walked into their new home in Elfvik, it was as though she was walking into a replica of his watchtower in Canary Wharf. A sparsely furnished modern showroom with gray monotones, the same furniture, and a mix of yellow and lilac tulips.

It startled her.

"What's this?" she asked once she'd kicked off her shoes by the door and padded into the space. "Are you serious?"

"What do you mean?" Jonny seemed confused. "I wanted to make it comfortable for you."

"It looks exactly like your apartment in London. Except it's a house."

"I used the same interior designer."

She peered at him as he stood nervously with his balled fists by his sides. "Don't you like it?"

"I do... I just...*whoa*, yellow and purple." She walked up to one of several large vases of tulips dotting the space. "Why yellow and purple? The same colors from London."

"They are special." She saw color rush to his cheeks but dared not ask him why.

"That dress you wore on our first date...was yellow." He paused to swallow. She remembered her buttercup-yellow spring dress. "And purple... Purple is from Alexandria."

"From Alexandria?" Brittany couldn't make the connection right away. She pondered for a second or two until her purple silk night slip from the first night they were together floated into her mind.

"I thought you would like it."

"Thank you, they're beautiful. This place is really beautiful," she said. "But I just want it to be *our* place. Not just a place Eva, Louise, or your interior designer creates for us."

She continued strolling around their house, with its grandiose vaulted ceilings and waterfront views. Trees were slowly springing back to life with green leaves and flower buds. The glass walls were pretty thick and soundproof. She could see waves flowing into one another in the bay through the glass, but all around them was an unnerving stillness.

Out in this wooded piece of luxury, her first friend in Sweden became silence.

She looked all around her, moving in a surreal daze that this exquisite piece of property was hers because she was his wife. Jonny's wife. This strange man she was still getting to know. She turned to look at him as he stood across the room, brows arched.

The intensity with which Jonny regarded her from that distance began to suck the air out of her lungs, slowly asphyxiating her.

———

Brittany's late-term pregnancy kept her holed up for her first few months in Sweden as spring pushed winter out of the way. She hadn't been to any public engagements with Jonny. There had been no photo opportunities to stand proudly by his side as his wife in those months.

While her pregnancy had been relatively smooth, almost unnaturally effortless, she spent most of it in Elfvik, feet raised and mindlessly surfing television channels. Jonny's Stockholm assistant, Louise, ensured her ultimate comfort by getting her everything her heart desired.

That was only when Jonny wasn't available to do it himself.

He crisscrossed town in search of a particular brand of chocolate truffles she wanted. He made sure chefs customized anything she ordered from menus when they went out to dinner, taking out vomit-inducing ingredients. He bought what she was craving and made sure the fridge was always filled with carrots.

Through Louise, Jonny had registered her for private, late-term prenatal care. He'd organized for a yoga teacher to come work out with her at home three times a week along with a private language instructor so she could start learning Swedish. Her first three months in Sweden, Brittany von Lundin lacked for nothing.

FIFTEEN

"Muna!"

The sound of someone calling her name startled her as she was refilling paper towels in the kitchen at the von Lundin offices. She turned to see Kemi trotting up to her.

"Tack så mycket!" Kemi stopped in front of Muna, breathless with excitement.

"Why are you saying thank you?" Muna asked in Swedish, unsure of what was causing Kemi to thank her so cheerfully.

"De afrikansk affärer!" Kemi said, struggling in Swedish. *The African stores.* "The ones you recommended to me. Thank you! I went to two of them and found goat meat and spices I have been looking for," Kemi finished in English, her Swedish still weak.

Then she began to ramble. "I did find some fermented melon. We call it *egusi* in my language. You know I'm from Nigeria, right? You're from Somalia, not Sudan, aren't you? Anyways, it ended up being rotten when I brought it home," Kemi continued. "It made me sad though. Maybe there just aren't enough Africans to meet the supply. So sad. That something fermented to actually last for months rotted due to lack of demand."

Muna could barely follow Kemi's stream. She only picked out

"Nigeria, Somalia, Sudan, home, Africans," and the word "sad" twice.

"Sorry, my English no good," Muna apologized.

"Oh no, please. I am the one who should be better by now in Swedish," Kemi noted. "Can I practice my Swedish with you? *Får jag träna svenska med dig?*"

Muna looked at her, not knowing what to say. She would love to help Kemi with her Swedish, but her mind wasn't at von Lundin right now. Tensta and the aftermath of its riots had swallowed her whole. She was unsure of what remnants of herself it would spit out once done. Her apartment felt like a graveyard. The daily silence was unnerving. No wafts of spices coming from Khadiija, who had loved to cook. No random banter coming from Yasmiin, who had talked incessantly.

All she was left with were photos of ghosts in her room.

"*Är du okej, Muna?*" Kemi asked. *Are you okay, Muna?* It was when Muna felt Kemi's hand on her arm that she realized she had been staring absentmindedly for a couple of seconds.

"*Ja. Tack,*" Muna said softly before turning back to her task of refilling paper towels. She felt Kemi still looming around.

"*Vill du prata?*" Kemi was offering her ears if Muna needed to talk to someone. Albeit in painfully grating Swedish that made Muna look like a native speaker. Muna turned to Kemi and nodded. Kemi gave her a lopsided smile, one mixed with concern and empathy.

"*Har du familj?*" Muna asked. *Do you have a family?*

"*Familj?*" Kemi repeated. Muna nodded. "Well...*jag har en pojkvän!*" Kemi trailed off with a giggle, telling Muna she had a boyfriend.

"*Ingen pappa? Mamma? Syskon?*" *No father, mother, siblings?*

Kemi's face took on a more serious look when she realized Muna wanted depth beyond her love life.

"*Ja, jag har en mellanstor familj,*" Kemi said, describing her medium-sized family to Muna. Not to mention extended family, too many to count on both sides.

"*Pratar ni ofta med varandra?*" Muna asked. *Do you speak often with each other?*

"*Inte ofta,*" Kemi said. *Not so much.* Everyone was so busy, she explained. Muna glared at Kemi as if she had cursed.

"*Varför inte?*" Muna asked, her voice terse. *Why not?*

Muna saw Kemi's face tense up, her brows bunching, and Muna felt maybe she had upset her. But it made no sense to Muna that Kemi had a family she wasn't talking to every day. Was there a reason Kemi didn't talk to her family? It didn't sound like it because her face had lit up when she'd mentioned her twin, parents, and other relatives.

A second of silence passed between them before Kemi broke it.

"You're right, Muna," she switched to English. "I have no excuses."

Kemi gave her a deep smile that showed dimples in her cheeks, then a nod of acknowledgment before saying, "*Tack, Muna! Vi ses snart.*" *Thanks, Muna! See you soon.*

Muna pushed her cleaning cart out of the kitchen area toward the large elevator. When the double doors pulled apart, Jonny was standing in there with a smartphone to his ear. Muna swallowed and tried pushing her cart into the elevator, expecting him to take a few steps aside, but the look on his face seemed terrified. His normal intensity had been replaced by fright, and his petrified gaze fastened on her cleaning cart.

Jonny quickly lifted a palm up to stop her advance. No, his raised hand seemed to say to her. He didn't want to share his space with that dirty thing she was pushing.

Muna quickly apologized and watched the elevator doors consume him once more.

Three slow raps on her door. Gunhild's signature knock. Muna opened the door without peeking in the peephole to find Gunhild standing there holding a greasy paper bag that looked like Chinese takeout. She was also carrying a smaller bag that Muna guessed had some buns for *fika*.

"*Kära Muna*," Gunhild greeted, handing both bags to the younger woman. Muna ferried them to the kitchen and unpacked their contents: Thai curries with jasmine rice and two vanilla buns. Gunhild had picked up a vegetarian curry for Muna and chicken for herself.

"Thank you so much," Muna said as she started setting the small dining table. Gunhild slowly took a seat, looking more fragile than the last time Muna had seen her.

"How are you?" Muna asked. The older woman simply waved delicate fingers at Muna, telling her wordlessly not to bother. *Toppen!* She felt great. Despite what had happened to Khadiija, which was sad, she added.

"Have you heard anything more about Khadiija?" Muna asked. Gunhild shook her head, finishing off with a sigh.

"Nothing. But I will let you know." She made a show of clasping her hands together. "Now, let's get some food in you!"

The women ate with large appetites and filled the long pauses with updates. Muna told her about her days at von Lundin as a janitor. About Kemi and their scant interactions. About the boss Jonny and the beautiful Black model she'd seen waiting for him outside. Gunhild listened, fully trained on Muna. Gunhild filled her in on some of the new residents she was meeting that week as well as some who had left their subsidized housing and moved on, carving manageable chunks of life in Sweden.

"You would have been a wonderful mother," Muna randomly added before scooping another forkful of rice. She noticed Gunhild wince.

"It's not from lack of trying," Gunhild said with a strained laugh. "I love children and wanted so many of them."

"What happened?" Muna asked. "What happened when you tried?"

Muna knew she was treading that line of being too personal. Over time, she had learned that many Swedes kept concentric circles of privacy around them, like onions. One could keep peeling back layers upon layers and still never reach their core, even after decades of friendship. She had already peeled so many layers off Gunhild, but the older woman was holding back so much more.

"I made a mistake a long time ago," Gunhild said. "In my early twenties, I fell in love with a man... My parents thought he was the *wrong* man for me." Muna sat up straighter in her chair, hanging on to every word Gunhild was sharing with her.

"I became pregnant. I was scared and got rid of our baby without asking him." Gunhild paused to take a sip of water. "He never forgave me."

KẸMI

"I think I've met someone serious," Kemi confessed to Kehinde over the phone in a hushed voice. Tobias was still sleeping off their lovemaking in her bed after they'd gorged on cardamom buns and made it halfway through a movie.

"Is that your voice?" her sister teased. "I've forgotten how you sound. *Abeg*, please call your mother o!" Kehinde pleaded. Kemi chuckled before apologizing for how bad she'd been about staying in touch. She filled Kehinde in on the mundane details of her life, but her mind kept going back to Tobias.

"This guy..." Kemi paused, savoring the thought of him. "We just click. He makes me feel beautiful. He really does. I don't have to be extra."

"Hmm." Kehinde listened intently.

"We've been casually seeing each other for weeks, but I think we just made it official."

"Too much info. Get to the point. Is he husband material?"

"Does that matter right now?"

"Well, if it doesn't matter now, when will it matter?"

"I just want to enjoy getting to know Tobias better. I don't want to rush things."

"Tobias? Can I call him Tobi? Oluwatobi?" Kehinde joked.

"Stop it!" Kemi said, trailing off with a laugh. "Seriously, though, you will love him. He's so down-to-earth. So real."

"Tobias. Is that Swedish?"

"His mother is Gambian."

"Gambia *l'oun l'oun*?" *All the way there?* Kehinde was dramatic. "Who haven't Nigerians married, *ehn*?!" They chatted for a few more minutes with Kemi asking when Kehinde planned on coming to visit.

"Very soon," Kehinde said. "It's expensive with three kids. Well, four kids if you count Lanre," she joked about her husband. Kemi promised to send them a package soon filled with all things Swedish, from chocolates to marshmallow fish.

"Anyway, I'm happy for you," Kehinde wrapped up. "Sounds like this guy's head is correct. As long as you're not leaving electricians in America to go find electricians in Sweden." Kemi pondered her sister's words. They were back to that point again.

"What do you mean?"

"You know what I mean. Anyway, love you and please...call your mom!"

The line went dead before Kemi could respond. She stared at the phone. With that one parting statement, her sister had planted a needless seed of doubt in her.

"Hope she approved?" Tobias's voice startled Kemi.

She wasn't sure how long he'd been standing there and listening to her chat. He clearly hadn't heard Kehinde's own side of the conversation. When she turned around, he was pulling on his security guard shirt and adjusting the collar. Kemi ogled Tobias as he got ready for his job, one she knew Kehinde was never going to approve of as worthy enough for her.

With the shirt settled correctly on his torso, Tobias gave her a quick peck and left for his night shift.

The next few weeks were an intense rush to get the Bachmann

campaign ready for its spring launch. It stole most of her waking hours—from directing the design company to choosing a diverse mix of models representing different cultures to finding printers, preparing press releases, and planning launch events. They even got to reserve Stockholm's glitziest billboard right in the heart of Stureplan, reserving it for Jonny's own cover.

Kemi buried herself in Bachmann while the other directors hovered around her like bumblebees, not quite landing to check in, but making sure they kept abreast of her flurry. Espen often lingered in her office longer than necessary, but she always shooed him away. If confident women attracted men like ants to sugar, then in hindsight she should have learned to siphon that work confidence into her love life years ago.

Because right then, working on the Bachmann account with fervor and determination and exuding confidence, she was the most attractive woman at von Lundin Marketing.

When Kemi's campaign launched that May, it was to a global conversation on race, stereotypes, and stigmas. Swedish media could not get enough of one of their golden boys as the face of a worldwide discussion.

While Kemi knew Jonny silently bore the weight of this publicity, he still eschewed all media interviews. Culture critics hopped on the dismantling of stereotypes. Some even cited cultural appropriation as Kemi had anticipated, but those arbiters had been quickly shut down by rebuttal articles citing their own biases in associating blinged-out high-tops with urbanites of color and hip-hop socialites.

But the love for Kemi's vision trumped its few dissidents.

"I mean..." one pundit had marveled on CNN Style, "that strategically placed plate of cinnamon buns was ingenious."

Tabloids jumped on Jonny reaching for a chocolate muffin as publicly owning his sexual preferences at last.

When the media wanted to know who the brains behind the campaign had been, von Lundin Marketing had put out a blanket press release saying that it had been a team effort with too many players to list, much to Kemi's disdain. She wanted the glory and the recognition. She felt she deserved it all.

But Kemi quickly learned that putting the team first was the unspoken rule in Sweden. Teamwork and consensus ruled over individuality. After all, hadn't other people been attending those Bachmann meetings too? Of course, she couldn't hoard all the glory to herself. She had to share it equally across her team.

So while they all celebrated and reveled internally, externally, Bachmann was relegated to a simple project update on her LinkedIn profile.

After that grand showing, Bachmann renewed its contract with von Lundin Marketing for five more years, and at last, Kemi thought she was part of the team.

BRITTANY-RAE

"Breathe in... Breathe out... *whoosh*..." Brittany's yoga instructor was helping her stretch her limbs as they sat cross-legged on mats. They were out on the patio that spring morning, listening to birds with the bay as their backdrop.

Brittany was heavy, uncomfortable, and irritable. Baby Maya was due any day now. They'd finally found out they were having a girl.

"I'm tired," Brittany interrupted the instructor, whose eyes were closed.

"That is absolutely fine," the yogi started. "You have to listen to your body, learn its wavelengths, and..."

"Yes, yes, yes, I'm tired," Brittany cut in. "Can we skip the next class as well?"

Once her yogi was packed and out the door, their Bulgarian housekeeper, Sylvia, burst onto the patio as if on cue with a spinach-based shake she'd whipped up for Brittany. Brittany accepted the drink, thanking her. Sylvia waited next to her until she had downed the entire glass and handed the empty tumbler back to her.

"Where is Jonny?" Brittany asked once Sylvia turned around to go. The older lady spun back around with a quizzical look on her face, as if questioning Brittany in return. *How the hell would I know?*

"Maybe you should give him a call?" Sylvia offered instead. Brittany had already tried calling Jonny multiple times. Information she didn't think their help needed to be privy to. Even Louise, who knew his every move, had been elusive about his whereabouts.

"I'm sorry, Brittany," Louise apologized. "He has turned his phone off. He does this once in a while when he doesn't want to be disturbed."

"But what if I go into labor and can't reach him?" Brittany was frustrated.

"Oh, you don't have to worry. You're in good hands here in Sweden. We can always get you an ambulance right away."

Brittany hadn't been comforted by those words.

She rolled onto her side and then onto her feet, her stomach feeling heavier by the second. She stopped to collect her breath. Once on her feet, she waddled back into the main hall, her bare feet on polished wood echoing into the silence. Why would he turn his phone off when he knew she needed him now more than ever?

That evening, after Sylvia had fed Brittany poached salmon and avocado salad, the housekeeper prepared to take her leave for the night. She helped Brittany tuck in amid mountains of goose-feather pillows, propping her feet and head.

"I know it's my weekly night off, but give me a call if you need anything, and I'll take a taxi back here," the woman offered.

"Thank you, Sylvia."

"It is very safe, so you don't have to worry."

Jonny had cocooned her out here, so safety was the least of her worries. For someone who worked with so many people and saw so many faces every single day as a flight attendant, isolation was far worse.

By midnight, Jonny still hadn't turned up, and Brittany was wide awake, binge-watching episodes of *Real Housewives of Atlanta*, all alone in their mansion. Suddenly warm water began to pool around Brittany's lower half, and she realized baby Maya was done marinating.

Her greatest fear had come true.

———————

"Stop making those sounds and answer me with actual words!" Brittany screamed right before another contraction seized her, and she writhed in agony.

When her water broke, she had dialed 112 for an ambulance to the hospital. Jonny had materialized after the paramedics were able to track him down. Now he was confessing to her that he had spent the entire day barely a mile away at his sister's, while Brittany lay in a sterile hospital bed hooked up to monitors.

"I was alone all day, and you were practically next door with Antonia?"

Jonny made that air-gulping sound again, and Brittany screamed again.

Fifteen hours later, Baby Maya made her arrival, screaming her lungs out in the delivery room. Jonny had been in there holding Brittany's hand as tightly as she had squeezed his. He wiped sweat off her forehead and tears from her face. When the doctor tried handing Maya to her father, Jonny froze solid, fingers dancing by his sides, staring intensely at the brown baby he was being handed.

The doctor and maternity ward staff in the room exchanged looks. Brittany couldn't tell them why Jonny was refusing to take his baby, that this was what happened when he got overstimulated. He wasn't frozen because he was surprised by the shade of his baby. He was overwhelmed, and his brain couldn't catch up with what his heart was feeling.

Brittany requested her baby instead and grabbed her beautiful girl with the dark-brown eyes. Maya looked up at her mother, as if trying to make out the blur that was Brittany's face, before latching on to her breast hungrily.

If Jonny thought their baby needed "protecting" with his wealth and privilege because she was going to be brown, then Maya needed maximum security upon her arrival. Besides taking Jonny's nose and thin lips, she had tight, brown curls, the most intense brown eyes, and was barely two shades lighter than Brittany.

When Brittany was discharged a few days later, they arrived home to Jonny's sisters and Ragnar waiting for them with a *fika* spread of freshly baked buns, chocolate truffles, and a custom-made cake with the words, *"Välkommen hem, finaste Maya!"*

Both Svea and Antonia cooed over the baby. Ragnar also peered at Maya, mesmerized, before turning to Brittany and commenting on just how strong Brittany's genes were.

Brittany cut Ragnar a wordless glare that told him to fuck off.

SIXTEEN

Swedes were excellent at recycling, Muna noted.

So excellent that they ate the same food at every celebration. Christmas, Easter, Midsummer, it didn't matter. She was staring, once again, at meatballs, cured salmon, pickled herring, and *prinskorv*—prince sausages. Except, under the meatballs and *prinskorv* were small, handwritten notes with the word "HALAL."

Spånga-Tensta municipality had organized a Swedish Midsummer buffet at the community center as well as set up a maypole on a nearby football field.

"Muna!" It was Gunhild wearing a handmade wreath of wildflowers. "Here." She handed Muna another wreath she was holding. "This is yours. I made it for you."

In the corner of the large meeting hall was a table where volunteers were teaching residents how to make their own flower wreaths. Girls and women milled around the table in excitement, grabbing various blooms to personalize their floral crowns and giggling when they put them on to assess their creations in mirrors. Muna observed them, noting how just wearing flowers on their heads instantly made them feel more beautiful.

"Thank you." Muna took the accessory and placed it atop the

hijab she was wearing over a green summer frock. "How does it look?" Gunhild reached up to help her adjust it until it was sitting just right.

"Perfect!" Gunhild said before turning toward the buffet. "Now let's go eat something. I think there are more activities planned for later today." Gunhild shuffled slower than the last time Muna had seen her. "Plus, we're going to sing '*Små grodorna.*' It's my favorite part!"

They both padded over to the Midsummer spread and joined a line of people holding paper plates in anticipation, many wearing flower wreaths over covered heads.

Muna's eyes swept across the room. She knew it well, having spent hours here with Khadiija, Ibraahin, and other Somali youth before the riots. Gunhild had broken the news to her that Khadiija was on trial. Muna had quietly absorbed the information, nodding with the same helplessness she felt when Ahmed's residency had been denied.

Ahmed... She saw his face every day, pinned to her magnetic board. In the boredom of her apartment, she often daydreamed about what life with Ahmed would have looked like. A Somali-Kurdish relationship? Would they have been happy? How would he have taken care of her? Would he love her and only her? Or would he have taken another wife, which their faith permitted?

She remembered the times when his eyes washed over her after telling her she was beautiful and she had turned away shyly. He often laughed at her bashfulness. She seemed to amuse him in a way she hadn't fully understood. But whenever his full-bodied laugh dropped, his face was hooded in pain again.

"My dear Muna... I love your spirit. But I would rather go back home and die fighting for something than die here in paradise doing nothing and listening to birdsong."

The very birds he could name just by hearing their chirping. Right now, his voice still filled her heart. Its cadence and tone whenever he complained about something, mocked his enemies at the center, or flattered her in vain.

Muna's deepest fear was forgetting the sound of Ahmed's voice.

Her eyes wandered toward the entrance of the community center, and she froze when she saw a familiar handsome profile with that black rooster hairdo step in...*Yagiz*.

He was wearing a fitted black T-shirt and jeans, and his black handlebar moustache looked recently groomed. He swaggered in, looking around before landing on an acquaintance who walked over to give him a hug.

Muna's eyes darted around. Where was Yasmiin?

She stared at Yagiz again, who was talking animatedly. He was momentarily distracted by another Eritrean, this time a woman, who sashayed past both men before he continued gesticulating. Her eyes roamed over him as he talked with passion, a laugh breaking out sometimes.

"Your turn." Gunhild gently poked her to get her moving. Muna turned back to the buffet. She placed three meatballs on her paper plate, balancing it carefully once the meatballs started rolling around like pinballs. She added a few links of halal *prinskorv* made from lamb and slivers of cured salmon. She scanned the room for Yagiz once more. She saw him shake hands and pull the man into a half hug before continuing into the crowd, milling around and looking for more acquaintances.

"Is he someone you know?" Gunhild startled her. Muna turned to find her turquoise eyes twinkling, her crow's-feet bunching up.

"No, no," Muna shook her head, almost too violently. Gunhild had never met Yagiz, and Yasmiin had never shared him with the older woman either. Muna realized Gunhild didn't know who he was.

"Well, he's a very handsome man," Gunhild said. "I don't blame you for having a crush on him."

"What?" Muna's eyes widened at Gunhild. "No, I don't like that man." Gunhild smiled as she speared boiled potatoes with a fork and placed them on her own plate.

"My dear. I've been around a long time... I know a crush when I see it."

Muna turned away from Gunhild. She was wrong. Gunhild had to be wrong. She did not fancy Yagiz. Not in the way she was implying. She would never betray Ahmed that way. Never.

Despite all that had happened between them, she still had her job. Yagiz was a good boss who paid her once her team leader, Azeez, turned in his weekly report.

But he was a bad man who sold khat. He had been very aggressive with Yasmiin, and Muna wanted to know what he had done with her sister-friend she hadn't seen in months.

Muna looked over her shoulder, searching for him once more in the crowd.

KEMI

"Good God."

Malcolm stood, taking in the Midsummer maypole decorated with rings of wildflowers and blue and yellow ribbons flapping in a gentle breeze. Around the pole were about a hundred people jumping in circles, singing "*Små grodorna.*" *The small frogs.*

"I swear...white people. They've got Black folk hopping around that pole like frogs too," Malcolm continued. The crowd dancing before them was a mix of dashikis, turbans, hijabs, and jilbabs alongside traditional Swedish costumes and various levels of undress to match the summer heat.

"What? Do you want them to crip walk around the damn pole instead?" Tobias retorted. José and Kemi burst out laughing while Malcolm shrugged off his dig.

"Seriously, bro. Just relax and enjoy Midsummer, okay?" Tobias added.

Tobias had brought them to Farsta strand south of town to enjoy one of Sweden's most cherished festivities. Afterward, he was taking them over to Norsborg where his mother, Nancy, had invited them all for a true Gambian Midsummer. "Because you know Africans always have to be extra," Tobias said, laughing it off.

He was carrying a small cooler with drinks while Kemi cradled a bag of cardamom buns Tobias had baked the day before. José had a wicker basket lined with red-and-white gingham cloth packed with crackers, brie and blue cheeses, red grapes, and charcuterie. Nancy had promised to feed them properly after the festivities and had banned them from filling up on pickled herring beforehand.

Spread out across picnic blankets on grass were about two hundred more people. After navigating the human minefield, they found a patch of grass they could squeeze on to spread out their picnic. Kemi turned to the dancing crowd once more as voices jubilantly singing off-key filled the warm air. Her eyes roamed over them, zeroing in on seemingly odd couples, watching people hold hands and dance, wondering who were friends, or strangers, or just friends for two hours before returning to being strangers after the day's festivities.

"What are you looking at?" Tobias nipped at her ear. She leaned back into him, savoring his touch.

"Hmm, nothing. I wish I could freeze this frame of happy people and file it away for those days when I feel like saying screw this all."

"Yet, there's no place I would rather live right now," he whispered. She turned to him, and he planted a quick kiss on her lips.

"Really?"

"This is my home."

"Yes, I know," Kemi said. "But do you truly feel like you belong? What was it like for you as a kid?"

Tobias let out a sigh of frustration, and she knew this was a topic that required hours. He wasn't going to get into it now. He'd only skim the surface. In that regard, Tobias was very Swedish. In fact, she'd yet to see semblances of his African side, and she hoped Nancy would give her a glimpse later that day. Kemi needed a more complete picture of the man she had now nested in so comfortably.

"I belong in many ways," Tobias said, glancing over bodies milling around them. "Growing up, though, I was definitely made to feel different. And the weird thing is, I don't think it was intentional."

"Exclusion is always intentional," Kemi said, her hand moving up to stroke his cheek.

"I'm not so sure. Especially if everyone else looks the same— blond hair and blue-eyed—and you already look different," Tobias said. "I think it's a lot more nuanced than that."

"And what does your sister, Tina, think?" she asked. Tobias smirked, pulling a grape from the bunch and popping it into his mouth.

"You'll find out when you meet her" was all he offered before reaching for another grape.

"Please don't embarrass me... Please don't embarrass me," Malcolm begged José under his breath.

The couple and Kemi were waiting behind Tobias, who was fumbling for keys to the apartment he shared with his mother. José knew his musical idol, Tina, was going to be there. He shifted on his feet. He rested his hands on his hips. He took deep breaths. He twirled back and forth. José was a bag of nerves that simply unraveled when Tina opened the door instead.

"TINA WIKSTRÖM!" he screamed before biting his knuckles to contain himself.

Tobias quickly introduced José to his sister in Swedish. Kemi watched Tina step forward and pull a jittery José into a hug. She shared the same coloring as Tobias, with brown freckles dotting her face. Thick, reddish-brown locks twisted into a circular beehive crown sat on her head. A golden ring looped through her left nostril was the only jewelry she wore to accentuate the long, green batik gown she donned. Her amber-brown eyes were several shades lighter than Tobias's.

"Oh my," Malcolm said as he stepped in for his own hug. "I chose the wrong lifetime to be gay."

Tina giggled before turning to Kemi.

"Finally." Her thick lips curved into a smile, revealing one gold tooth. "Lovely to meet you, Kemi." She stepped in for a hug, leaving Kemi with the lingering smell of incense and coconut. "Please, everyone, come in." They all walked in to the sounds of old-school Youssou N'Dour filling the air.

The three-bedroom apartment Tobias had grown up in and still shared with his mother was modest. From its eleventh-floor perch, it looked over similar sand-toned apartment blocks in their complex.

As a single mom, Nancy had raised both Tobias and Tina with some financial support from the now-deceased Lars Wikström, the state, and not much else. The space was lined with photos of all three of them at different ages. There were a few music awards from the Swedish equivalent of the Grammys—*Grammis*—which belonged to Tina. Photos of a younger Tobias at various swimming meets over the years. A couple from trips to Gambia. Kemi learned more about the family scanning those family photos than she had from Tobias telling her himself.

"Look at you!"

Nancy's voice cut through as she came rolling out of the kitchen. She had shimmering, dark-cocoa skin and was wearing low-cropped hair with the same gap between her top teeth Tobias had inherited. She gathered Kemi into an embrace and then held her at arm's length, assessing her.

"A proper African girl with a solid body!"

"Mamma!" Tobias scolded her. Nancy simply shrugged and pulled Kemi along with her toward the kitchen. Tobias followed them as if to chaperone their conversation.

"Tobias and all his white girlfriends. Finally, he brings a Black one home." She was the only Black woman Tobias had ever dated? Kemi pondered. She asked Nancy how so, and his mother simply laughed before answering, "Look, Tobias also had two loooong *sambos*— long-term partners—for many years before he met you. Two blond Swedish girls. The type that just wake up, shake their hair, and go."

"Thank you, Nancy...but why are you telling me this?" Kemi asked defensively.

"Because he has been waiting for you all his life," Nancy exclaimed. "A strong African woman like me!"

"Mamma!" Tobias chided her once more before shaking his head, embarrassed by his mother.

Kemi let Nancy's words settle into a pile at her feet. She wasn't sure what to do or how to parse them. Did she represent that hidden part of Tobias he so wanted to wear with pride but was being forced to choose between both cultures? To be fully Swedish, did he have to give up a part of himself that felt at odds with the culture he'd known all his life?

Nancy immediately put Kemi to work. She helped Tobias and Tina set the table, with Tobias stealing kisses whenever they crossed paths during their tasks. They helped Nancy adorn the table with bowls of a heavy rice dish Tobias explained was *benachin*, grilled chicken thighs, fried fish, corn on the cob, and a spring salad loaded with tomatoes, cucumbers, and avocado. She had also boiled potatoes and laid out a jar of pickled herring, some meatballs, and *prinskorv*—prince sausages.

"In case you miss your Swedish food." Nancy specifically turned to look at José, the fairest of them all, who could pass for white. José wore a questioning look at her statement. Malcolm shook his head and laughed. Kemi could see Tobias's concerned look, and she moved to his side. Censoring his mother wasn't needed, her touch told him. Tina finished off the table setting by placing a Swedish flag as its centerpiece.

"Okay!" Nancy announced. "Everybody, sit."

"Do you have any special spots where you'd like each of us to sit?" Kemi asked. Nancy glanced at her, laughing before repeating, "*Everybody sit!*" with extra emphasis. Soon it was a cacophony of people passing dishes, cutlery clinking plates, and drinks being poured.

"This is excellent, Nancy," Kemi announced after a few bites of her *benachin*, which had pieces of roasted lamb in it. She tasted nutmeg and cumin in the mix.

"I know it is." Nancy revealed her gap-toothed grin. "Now, you Nigerians and Ghanaians can finally shut up about which *jollof* rice is better. Our Gambian *benachin* is the original."

"Mamma!" It was Tobias again.

"Well, Gambians need to publicly defend that title then," Kemi challenged.

"We have better things to do with our time than fighting over rice." Nancy grabbed a chicken thigh and lifted it for a bite. Kemi chuckled, catching Nancy's smiling eyes, before turning to Tina.

"Tina..." Kemi started. "If José's reaction was any indication, I'm sitting before pop star greatness."

Tina took a sip of apple cider, amused. "That was in the past."

"Huge all over Scandinavia!" José chimed in before taking a bite of corn, his eyes never leaving Tina. "She even won *Melodifestivalen* once and represented Sweden at Eurovision!"

"Yeah, but I do much more important work now," Tina said, turning her attention to Kemi. "I run an organization for people who identify as Afro-Swedish. A way of centering both our cultures."

"I see," Kemi said. "Is identifying as Afro-Swedish an issue? Tobias told me Sweden tries to make you one or the other, not necessarily both."

"Yeah," Malcolm added. "I mean, back in the States, I'm African American. I've got friends who are Italian American, Jewish American, Iraqi American. Why can't you be both? Here, I just call myself Afro-Swedish because my mom is Swedish, but I am African American. Now it's sounding complicated even for me," he trailed off with a laugh.

"That's what my organization is working on." Tina smiled.

Kemi turned to study Tobias, who sat quietly.

"It's so intriguing. There's still so much I'm trying to figure out here in Sweden...especially at work. How my colleagues perceive me as an independent Black woman. What my future career prospects are."

"Tobias told me all about you," Tina said. "I think you're a rarity here in Sweden."

"How so?" Kemi asked.

"A Black woman who is a top-level director at one of the most influential companies? Especially one who doesn't speak fluent Swedish yet?"

"And why is that rare?" Kemi asked defensively.

"Sweden tackles one social problem at a time," Tina said. "Right now, the priority seems to be gender equality for white women. We're still waiting in line for our issues to be properly addressed."

"But that feels absurd," Kemi said.

"Look, don't get me wrong, Kemi—we Swedes are way ahead of the world in terms of feminism, with dads pushing strollers, but that was why I quit my music career." Tina took a bite of chicken. "I was done performing for society in every way."

"Maybe you would have been Sweden's own Beyoncé if you hadn't quit?" Kemi asked. She saw Tina shift in her seat and knew she was broaching a sensitive topic. The silence was broken by Nancy's laugh.

Tobias's mother laughed and laughed before settling herself down.

"Kemi, my dear," Nancy started. "You are the only one trying to be like Oprah where they don't want you."

BRITTANY-RAE

The von Lundin estate in Sandhamn, on the island of Sandön, was a sprawling beast even by modest Swedish wealth-flashing standards. A twelve-room rectangle of a manor that took up as much water-front real estate as it could.

A month after Maya was born, the family had gathered for Midsummer at this communal retreat on the island—one of over thirty thousand islands, islets, and skerries—in Stockholm's archipelago. Antonia's family had arrived two days prior with their own housekeeper to stock up and start preparing for the rest of the guests, including Brittany's parents.

Jonny had offered to fly them out to Sweden, but they had refused. They thanked him for the offer before digging into their meager savings and buying economy tickets to Stockholm. Jonny had already flown Tanesha in days before to spend time with Brittany, lift her spirits, and coo over Maya.

Brittany saw her parents gape as they took in her lavish digs in Elfvik. Her father had turned to give her a look she knew too well—one that wanted her to start explaining herself.

The next day, they were shuttled by boat from their private jetty to Sandhamn along with Sylvia—their housekeeper—and Maya's au pair.

Now everyone was gathered around a large mahogany breakfast table with floor-to-ceiling views of the bay, digging into poached eggs on toast, smoked salmon and avocado with organic yogurt, fresh berries, and homemade granola. Everyone except Wilhelm and Astrid von Lundin.

"I hope you've been able to rest?" Antonia asked Brittany's

parents, passing a jug of freshly squeezed orange juice to her husband, Stig.

"Yes, thank you," Tyrone said, before turning to his wife. "This is our first time in Scandinavia, and we hear summer is the best time to visit."

"Yes," Antonia said. "Especially during Midsummer. It's such a special celebration for us Swedes."

"I've heard," he continued before cutting into his breakfast. Maya began to whimper, and Brittany adjusted her in her arms to breast-feed. The baby coiled tiny fingers around Brittany's index finger, a move that blotted out everyone around them and wrapped mother and daughter in a cocoon of love. Brittany tugged lightly at her firm grip, her baby brightening her world.

"Maya is such a sweet addition to our family," Antonia added. "I wish I had a girl of my own. I've always wanted one too."

"Maya is our first grandchild, so you can imagine how blessed we feel," Brittany's mother said.

Brittany silently fed Maya beneath her feeding blanket, listening to the conversation. Her hair was pulled into a bun, her face makeup-free. Next to her was Tanesha, who kept shifting uncomfortably with each bite. Brittany turned to look at Jonny, who was quietly twirling a butter knife, entranced by its flipping.

Besides a bouquet of lilies from his parents to congratulate them on Maya's arrival, Wilhelm and Astrid had maintained radio silence. Now that Brittany's parents were in town, they sent a welcome message along with a note saying they were indisposed and unfortunately couldn't be there to celebrate Midsummer with them.

A celebration Jonny had told her they hadn't missed for as long as he could remember.

"So, your parents," Tyrone started, clearing his throat. "What are their names again?"

"Wilhelm and Astrid," Antonia replied icily.

"Wilhelm and Astrid," Tyrone repeated with a slow nod. "And where are they again?"

"Unfortunately, they couldn't make it, and they send their sincerest apologies."

"Hmmm." Tyrone let out air. "And are they in Sweden or out of the country?"

"They have a place in a village called Smögen on the west coast. Very lovely place by the sea."

"Hmm," Tyrone hummed again. "Do they have a number we can call?"

Brittany saw Antonia rapidly blink at his request before glancing toward Jonny, who was still cartwheeling the knife in his left hand. She needed to end the misery of the chilled exchange between Antonia and her parents.

"Dad," Brittany jumped in, "they know where we are, and they should be the ones to call." Her father studied her intently before nodding in acceptance. The conversation died once more. The silence was so uncomfortable for Tanesha that she sprang to her feet.

"Excuse me," Tanesha said. "If it's okay, I would love to go explore the grounds. This place is exquisite."

Antonia nodded.

"I should join you, Tanesha." Tyrone slowly pushed to his feet. "This old man needs to stretch his legs." Tanesha waited and escorted him out of the breakfast room.

"You know, Brittany," her mother started to say, "maybe we

should go feed Maya in private. I need to catch up with you anyway and spend some time with that sweet little angel." She got to her feet as well. "Brittany?"

"I'm coming right behind you, Mom." Brittany motioned over to the au pair to come get Maya. "I need a quick word with Jonny." Beatrice nodded and then trailed the au pair, who was now carrying and burping the baby as she went.

Left at the table were Jonny, Antonia, and Svea, who had been uncharacteristically silent throughout. Antonia's husband, Stig, promptly grabbed the jug of orange juice and retreated to the study.

The foursome sat in silence. Brittany broke it when Jonny tried to touch her. "I will not tolerate your parents disrespecting my parents this way!"

Jonny remained quiet.

"I completely understand, Brittany," Antonia started. "But we don't control Wilhelm and Astrid. They are adults and responsible for their own actions."

"They are pretentious snobs. That's what they are!" Brittany raised her voice. "From the moment they saw me, they judged me. I don't expect them to like me, but I expect them to respect me. I am Jonny's wife!"

"Brittany, you're upset."

"The hell I am! My parents flew all the way here, and they can't even acknowledge their presence? How heartless and cold are they?"

"Brittany." It was Svea jumping in this time. "Calm down. My parents aren't heartless."

"They have yet to prove me wrong!"

"Please give them time," Svea pleaded. "I think the shock of finding out you were pregnant before marriage still hasn't left them."

"Really?" Brittany was frustrated. "Not the fact that their only son, their golden boy, is married to a Black woman and now has a brown kid?"

"They are not racist." Antonia's voice was terse. Brittany chuckled before getting to her feet. Jonny got to his as well and reached for her waist, trying to pull her into an embrace.

"Jonny, can you just stop?" Brittany was livid. "Don't touch me. Just don't. The doctor said no sex for six weeks, okay?"

She saw his cheeks warm up and flush red, his fingers balling into fists. She had embarrassed him in front of his sisters.

"Leave me alone!" she shrieked before storming away from the siblings.

SEVENTEEN

MUNA

"Fy fan! You are pestilence, Muna Saheed!" Yagiz was furious. "Pure pestilence!"

She found him and his Turkish colleague cleaning up and getting ready to close early for the evening. Yagiz was always angry whenever she came around, but this time, he seemed to have been having a bad day, with her appearance being the final trigger.

She had come to ask about Yasmiin again.

"Do you need a man to fuck you so you can leave me alone?" He was exasperated. "Should I find someone for you, *eh*?" Yagiz turned to his colleague. "Nusret? Do you want to do it?" The man shook his head nonchalantly as he kept wiping down the counter with a damp cloth.

"Don't talk to me like that!" Muna found her voice, and Yagiz sneered.

"Why are you here?"

She became quiet once more.

"Muna! Stop wasting my time!" Yagiz yelled. "What do you want? Why are you here?"

"Have you seen Yasmiin?"

"So, Yasmiin is the only reason you're here? Just Yasmiin?"

He peered down at her as if reading her innermost thoughts. Muna turned away shyly and shifted on her feet. Yagiz always made her uncomfortable. Right now, though, being in his presence was unbearable.

"I thought you cared about me too, Muna." He laughed, elbowing Nusret, who was standing close by. Nusret dropped the damp cloth he was holding and padded off, uninterested.

"I care about Yasmiin. She is my sister."

His gaze turned dark once more. "Don't worry about Yasmiin." His voice was threatening. "You, Muna...you need to go find a man to fuck away your own sorrow!"

Muna's eyebrows furrowed at his harsh words. She glared at him, not blinking, and he matched her stare. She wasn't going to cry. She wasn't going to give Yagiz any more power over her feelings.

"You are a nasty man!" Muna spat back at him, and she saw a look of surprise wash over his face. Then one of realization. Something within Yagiz snapped. As if he finally just figured out the best way to get rid of her forever.

"Give me your keycard," Yagiz said, holding out his hand.

"What? Why?"

"Give me your fucking keycard!" he cursed. His words startled Muna, and she jumped. "Yasmiin begged me not to fire you. This is how you repay, *hmm*?!"

Yasmiin? Was Yasmiin still pleading on her behalf? That meant she was fine?

Muna began to search the depths of her tote bag. Once she found it, she handed it over. Yagiz snatched it with enough force to pull her forward with his jerking motion.

"Get out!"

As Muna rode the train home, she cried silently, constantly wiping any tear that dared break through. Her sporadic sniffs were the only clue she was emotionally processing her fresh unemployment. The train was quiet as usual. The creaking and bobbing of the train as it shredded down the tracks filled the otherwise noiseless air. People either buried themselves in their phones or looked past each other completely.

This was her least favorite part of the day, when she had to ride the train to and from work under the glare of curious passengers. She could feel eyes on her whenever her head was bent. Except they would avert themselves back into nothingness the instant she looked up at them.

Never smiling. Never acknowledging her presence.

BRITTANY-RAE

Midsummer hadn't panned out the way they had planned. Though Antonia had organized an expensive spread of traditional Swedish food and activities to entertain Brittany's parents, an archipelago storm descended upon Sandhamn with such fury that everyone remained holed up inside. Singing and dancing around the maypole were canceled. The storm mercilessly brought down their pole and destroyed its ring of wildflowers, as if spitting in their faces.

When Jonny had called Louise to inquire about Stockholm's weather, she had beamed back in excitement. "Glorious!" Jonny and Brittany's father barely exchanged full sentences, adding a layer of icy awkwardness to the day.

"Brit," Tanesha said, sitting on Brittany and Jonny's bed, staring at the raging storm outside that made the bright summer night uncharacteristically dark. "*Girl*, I don't know."

"It's so hard." Brittany was lying on the bed next to Tanesha, staring straight at the ceiling. "I have everything I could ever want, and I'm not sure I want it."

"I would have lost my damn mind a long time ago," Tanesha said.

"It's the isolation that's killing me, you know?" Brittany said. "But I can't be friends with just anyone."

"Why not?"

"Because of his family's name and position. People are hungry for scandal and inside information. Jonny never talks to the press. People want access to his resources. Heck, his parents think I'm one of those people. I can't trust anyone."

"The bastards," Tanesha muttered under her breath. "I can't believe they haven't seen that sweet baby yet." Brittany closed her eyes as tears trickled down the side of her face, dampening the sheets.

"Am I ungrateful, Tanesha?"

"*Girl*, don't play. Of course not."

"He has given me so much. And yet, I feel so trapped."

"But he loves you, right?"

"Yes, and he loves our Maya with everything in him," Brittany added. "I mean, sometimes he makes me jealous. Maya is the one person he seems to love more than me."

They spent a few more days in Sandhamn before their private boat ferried Brittany's parents and Tanesha back into Stockholm for their return trip home. It had taken Jonny physically peeling Brittany off her father before she let him go. They eventually left, but not without Tyrone first requesting a moment alone with his daughter.

"I'm gonna miss you, Daddy," she cried into his neck, shaking and turning into his little girl once more.

"I know, baby," he whispered to her. "I don't like this at all, and I'm going to get you out of it." She pulled back to study his face.

"I love him."

"His family disrespects you," Tyrone whispered back angrily. "I can't be at peace back in Atlanta when I know my baby is suffering in another man's country."

"Dad, he gives me everything I need. He takes care of me."

"And yet his parents still can't get past your skin color. Never forget that, baby."

Brittany's sobs became desperate, and Tyrone pulled her closer, fighting tears of his own.

"Privilege comes in levels, Brit," he continued. "You have the privilege he has given you. But you will never have the privilege he has just because he breathes." Brittany kept crying against his neck. Then he cradled her face between his palms, regarding her with glassy eyes.

"I know you've seen wealth beyond your dreams," he said. "But he ain't worth it. Never forget who you are, baby. Never forget."

"Six weeks," Jonny repeated calmly.

They had stayed behind in Sandhamn an extra week after Antonia's family and Svea had left. Jonny wanted the privacy before they returned to Stockholm's mad dash. He sat on the edge of their bed, legs apart, palms resting motionlessly on either leg. He watched her change for the night, following every stroke of her hands. The way they rubbed lotion down her long legs. The way they pulled her silk nightdress down over her head. The way they settled its thin straps in place.

Outside, another summer storm raged, pelting their windows with rain. The wind howled and occasional flashes of lightning illuminated the waters of the bay, dark, murky waves churning.

"Yup." She took off her diamond stud earrings. They could get creative regarding sex, but Brittany didn't want him touching her. She knew he was going to suggest workarounds. Brittany planned on staying adamant.

She caught him staring at her through her vanity mirror. He kept peering intensely through his reflection, his eyes dark and brooding in the low light of their room. Enough for Brittany to avert her gaze in discomfort. She wasn't sure how her husband was going to survive six weeks of abstinence.

Those thoughts that had been milling within her since she met him—now paired with this leering look as he watched her undress for the night—pointed to one conclusion:

Her husband had a fetish.

KEMI

"Hmm," Kemi murmured against Tobias's full lips. "That feels so good."

He smiled against hers before nipping them again.

She had loved spending Midsummer with his family, and Saturday mornings in her new Nacka apartment were her favorites when they lounged in bed for hours before Tobias rolled out to make them pancakes. Tobias kissed her thoroughly, and she wrapped her arms around his broad back, pulling him closer, sinking them deeper into her soft mattress.

Those months with Tobias had moved like chili beans simmering in a Crock-Pot. Her love for him had grown as a slow burn. Comfort on low heat. He made her laugh and wasn't demanding. He never commented on her hair unless she was fishing for compliments. He regularly baked her cinnamon buns and begged her to forgive them since she had exorcised them from her diet.

But that kernel of doubt Kehinde had planted in her months ago had been watered by her sister's words: *As long as you're not leaving electricians in America to go find electricians in Sweden.*

For Kemi, her sister's words smacked of irony in hindsight. God's time was right, but God's electricians were not right for her. Tobias worked the night shift as a security guard. Her perfect Tobias suddenly didn't seem so perfect anymore, and she started pulling at the seams of their exquisitely tailored relationship.

"What are you thinking about?" Tobias cut into her thoughts as they lay in bed that Saturday morning.

After a few moments of silence, she spoke up.

"Do you like your job, Tobias?"

"Why are you asking?"

"I don't know." Kemi shrugged. "I mean, don't you want something more challenging?"

"I have a job I enjoy," Tobias replied. "The benefits are great. I get five weeks of vacation. I have what I need."

He turned, his eyes locking on hers. "I am content, Kemi. I don't need to be an entrepreneur or CEO of someone else's company to validate my worth."

Kemi furrowed her brows. She wasn't trying to change him. She wasn't sure she could even if she tried.

"Of course not." Kemi closed her eyes and shook her head. "I was just wondering."

"Okay, I'll go make us pancakes then."

He marked his exit with a kiss, and those lips that had once warmed her core felt heavier.

"You shouldn't have come here."

That unsolicited advice was offered up by Godwin, half of a Nigerian pair of Igbo men she had randomly struck up a conversation with at Slussen while waiting for her bus home to Nacka. The younger was Benjamin. When she'd slid up next to both men at the bus stop, Godwin had turned to her with taut, dark skin that belied his true age. She knew he was much older. Salt-and-pepper stubble along with slight wrinkles in his face suggested he was in his early sixties. She hadn't spoken with her own father in weeks. Maybe that was why she struck up a conversation with him. Godwin's eloquence made her miss her family more.

Kemi was on her way home from another useless day at work. Besides the Bachmann project, she twiddled her thumbs daily. Autumn was back again, and Kemi's second winter in Sweden was on its way. Her work attire had drawn the men's admiration in a nonsexual way.

"Our sister," Godwin had greeted her. "You're doing big things here o!" Benjamin, about half Godwin's age, nodded in agreement.

"Thank you o! I'm trying." She smiled.

"What do you do?" Godwin interrogated like a nosy uncle.

"I'm a director at the biggest marketing firm in town," she said. In other circles, she would have been branded a braggart. Among their trio, it was a perfectly subdued response.

"*Chai!!*" Benjamin punched his right hand into the air in pride over her. "Big madam!" She laughed at his theatrics and basked in its familiarity.

"But the most important question we're missing..." Godwin stuck an index finger in the air instead. "Is there a clear path to becoming CEO of that company?" Kemi giggled at his musing.

"Ha, I am serious *o*," he answered her chuckles, both palms opened toward her. "How long have you been here?"

"Almost a year and a half. I used to live in the U.S."

"Ha? America!" Benjamin pumped his fist again in salute.

"And in all that time you have been here, have you seen anybody like Oprah?" Godwin wasn't really asking her a question, but she thought about his statement anyway. She really hadn't. Besides a rotation of Black entertainers hopping from sing-along music shows to dance shows on TV, she hadn't seen any Black woman with the level of authority and power Oprah wielded in America. Godwin was pointing out her dead end in Sweden.

"You shouldn't have come here," Godwin concluded. "At least in America, you're fighting your enemy in broad daylight." The grin that had been resting on Kemi's face throughout their conversation began to lose its gleeful curve.

"Is your family still there?" he asked. Kemi nodded. She told him she had a twin, to which he bellowed "*Ibeji!*" Twins! Godwin's wife and four kids were living in Italy at the moment, he told her. Sweden was the quickest way for him to earn higher pay for the same nursing aide job Italy would have paid him a fraction to do, despite the fact that he'd been a practicing public health doctor for decades in Nigeria. Insulting compensation had forced him to seek better opportunities abroad.

"How often do you speak to your family?" she asked Godwin.

"Every day," Godwin responded with a tone that questioned her judgment for asking him such an obvious question. "I'm actually considering moving my wife and children to England for better opportunities." Kemi felt ashamed for letting weeks pass between her own calls back to her family.

"Maybe living in England would be better for them in the long run?"

"They will see people who look like them in prominent positions," Godwin added just as their bus rolled up. "So, my sister, become their CEO, or go back to America."

Godwin's words lingered like a bee sting after they boarded their bus. They waved goodbye before shuffling toward the back of the bus, while Kemi parked herself closer to the driver.

Had she really moved here to flatline professionally? Was Sweden giving her Tobias in exchange for her career?

PART FOUR

EIGHTEEN

KĘMI

Kemi felt a charge the minute she walked into the office that Monday morning. Something hung in the air. Heavy, mysterious, heady.

Through Jonny's glass office, she saw a dark-haired white man sitting with his back to the door. Jonny was standing, explaining something passionately, without flailing his arms. He caught sight of her and waved her over. She hurried to her desk to drop off her bag and swap her sneakers for heels.

Since she'd moved to her own apartment in Nacka, which was southeast of town, she'd started taking the bus to Slussen then walking across the bridge toward work. She still hadn't bought a car because walking was how she got her daily exercise in to counteract those cinnamon buns that had crawled their way back into her life through Tobias. Especially since he knew how to bake them like a damn pro.

She smoothed her dress before walking up to his cubicle door.

"Ha, Kemi!" Jonny called out as she peeked in. "Come meet Ragnar."

At close range, the color of Ragnar's hair morphed into 70 percent dark, Colombian chocolate she wanted to reach for. He turned toward her, getting up in tandem. His rise slowed down as he got to his feet. Dark ocean blues, a cross between sapphire and ultramarine, pinned her in place. Then they sucked her in with the gale-force intensity of a raging sea. Churning because something had thrown them off-kilter.

They stared at each other in silence.

"Kemi, meet my best friend, Ragnar Pettersen. Ragnar will be helping us with the Bachmann account." Her mouth went dry, and no elegant words formed beyond a weak "*hej*." Ragnar remained silent. "And Ragnar, Kemi is director of global diversity. You'll be working together."

Ragnar coughed in the back of his throat before stretching out his hand to her.

"Nice to meet you, Kemi," he croaked out in a distinct lilt that told her he was born, raised, and schooled here in Sweden.

She took his large hand and found it warm, comfortable, and a little sweaty.

"Likewise." She found her voice, powered by the heat he shared through their handshake.

There was nothing particularly special about Ragnar Pettersen. One could say Ragnar was rather ordinary while her Tobias turned heads. Her love for Tobias was a simmer that had grown over time.

Ragnar had just incinerated her with one look.

"Ragnar officially starts next week, but we're going over some paperwork. Maybe you can join us for lunch?"

She saw Ragnar stiffen, his jaw clenched.

"I wish I could." She prepared an excuse. "But I already have lunch plans." His hands relaxed out of their fists.

"Welcome to von Lundin," she added before turning to go under his wordless glare.

Her brain was useless, and she couldn't work. She tried answering emails, typing up some copy, but nothing gelled. Ragnar was still in the building, and she couldn't think straight.

Who on earth was he, and how were they going to work together?

She had seen his reaction. Surprise mixed with confusion and then a shedding of face that made him vulnerable. She had seen his pupils dilate after he turned to face her. In the few seconds they had studied each other, she had outlined his square face framed by an angular jaw. Dark-brown hair fell around his neck and was pushed off his face, revealing a wide forehead. A clean-cut, dark-gray shirt was tucked into his lighter-gray pants. His shirt was unbuttoned just enough to reveal his toned chest.

And muscle. Lots of solid muscle. The build of a jock compared to Jonny's lean runner's frame or Tobias's broad-shouldered swimmer's build. She wanted—no, *needed*—to know everything about Ragnar.

She pushed out of her chair and grabbed her bag, shoving items into it: advertising copy she was reviewing, her laptop, water bottle. She saw Ragnar leave Jonny's office after exchanging a few words. Then he seemed to be scanning, looking around him for something until glancing in her direction. She averted him, burying herself back into her task of fleeing. She had to leave the office immediately. Away from this potent energy, maybe she could continue working from home.

She felt his presence hovering by her desk and looked up from her bag. They drank each other in for what felt like everlasting time until he broke it.

"Jonny speaks so highly of you," Ragnar started. "You helped him win Bachmann."

"Indeed. Now you have a job," she joked. He smirked, eyes trained on her, before his lips returned to their straight line.

"Well, I'll definitely be bringing some changes to the creative direction."

"Changes?" That got her attention.

"Yes. We can't rely on American-style gimmicks for every campaign."

"American-style gimmicks?" She was stunned. Who the hell was this guy?

"You know, something fresh, modern, more subtle, more Nordic," Ragnar continued. His statement was met with a laugh from Kemi.

"You're joking. You've got to be," she reeled him down. "Look, Ragnar. This is my account to manage. Jonny casually mentioned we will be working together. He hasn't outlined responsibilities—"

"How's your Swedish?" He cut into her statement. She wrinkled her brows.

"It's coming along... What has that got to do with anything? Bachmann is a German company."

"Jonny feels you need more reinforcement in that area when it comes to negotiating and working with local companies to support the account," Ragnar said directly. "That's why I'm here."

"That hasn't stopped me so far. Everyone in town speaks English." Kemi felt her voice getting louder. Enough to turn three other heads in nearby corners. She checked herself, adding quietly, "I'll be scheduling a meeting soon to discuss this. Once you start next week." She lifted her bag onto her shoulder, not bothering to change back into her sneakers.

He stretched out a hand to her. She felt it instinctively. He wanted to *touch* her, not shake her hand. She held on firmly to her oversize bag with both hands.

"Nice meeting you, Ragnar. I'm sure we'll work well together since we have no problem speaking our minds." She smiled at him, dimples surfacing, and caught his nostrils flaring. Kemi bid him farewell before taking a large curve around him to leave, making sure not an inch of her surface area touched him.

She stormed over to Östermalmstorg station and cursed out loud when she found out the train was delayed again. If the world knew just how often the trains were delayed here, they wouldn't put Sweden on such an efficiency pedestal, she fumed. An announcement in Swedish came over the intercom that an accident had occurred on one of the blue line tracks heading into town from Akalla. She had now lived in Sweden long enough to know that an "accident" meant someone had jumped in front of a train.

She wasn't going to walk all the way back to Slussen in heels, so she waited twenty minutes until a train came chugging by, people packed in like sardines. The accident had spurred subsequent delays. This was now affecting the other train lines, including the red line she was currently waiting for. By the time the third train had arrived, she could barely squeeze onto it, and her irritation level had reached its peak.

As the train hurtled south, Kemi gawked at a poster. She couldn't look away. An interracial couple kissing, lips locked. A white man kissing a Black woman with locs. The positioning of their mouths hanging open was paused provocatively, drawing one's eyes every few seconds. Underneath their photo were words promoting some family planning institute: "*Älskling, jag vill ha barn.*" *Darling, I want to have a child.*

Fiery emotions coursed through Kemi—seeds of doubt that were now sprouting little leaves; a primal reaction to Ragnar, which had shocked her; provocation she felt from the couple in the train advertisement, who seemed to be mocking her.

When Tobias swung by for his usual dinner before heading off to work, she pinned him to the wall, kissing him aggressively, sucking up his breath, not giving him time to react.

They never made it past the lacquered wooden floor by her front door.

BRITTANY-RAE

Nearing her first two years in Sweden, Brittany von Lundin had now organically wrapped herself in luxury. A cloak so steeped in privilege that she flew in special hairdressers from London to properly fix her hair—her crown—as she sat like a queen in Jonny's kingdom.

Albeit, a bored queen.

She went looking for Jonny and found father and child playing on a plush faux fur rug in the middle of Maya's room, which had been decked out in a pastel pink and turquoise unicorn theme. When Maya saw her mother, she scrambled onto chubby, unsteady feet and wobbled toward her, shouting, "*Mamma! Mamma!*"

Brittany scooped Maya up into her arms, planting kisses on her cheeks with emphasized *muahs*. Strolling in behind Brittany was the British au pair that his assistant Eva had sourced for them over a year ago. Brittany handed the baby off to her au pair as Jonny got to his feet.

She turned her gaze back to her husband.

"Have you got a few minutes?" He simply stared at her, so she turned to go, and he quietly followed her out. They walked to his study, a sparse, functionally decorated room with a large, sturdy desk, an ergonomically fitted swiveling chair, a bookcase with over a hundred books he had arranged by color, and a chaise longue in his favorite color—gray.

The only personal touches were photos of his girls: Brittany and Maya. Their wedding day at Stadshuset. A black-and-white one taken in bed, selfie-style. One family photo with all three of them. Two additional photos of Maya: one where she was dressed up in a yellow dress and another taken when she was still crawling. A few casual shots of Brittany around his hobbit cottage or out in the archipelago. Brittany on his family's yacht. Brittany on his speedboat. Brittany laughing. Brittany eating. Brittany... Brittany... Brittany...

"I've been thinking," Brittany started once she closed the door behind them. She walked over to his desk, sitting on the edge. "I've been at home for a while now. And I'm bored, Jonny—I want to work again. I want to do something I love."

"Besides me?" he said. She smiled at his attempt at humor. He returned her grin childishly.

"Seriously, I want to work." Her life had been filled with pampering and jet-setting, her every whim and desire fulfilled. Maybe it was time to finally pursue her lifelong dream now that she had boundless resources.

"You know I've always wanted to be a fashion designer," she said. "But I'm turning forty soon. It feels late to start pursuing that right now. I mean, I don't even know where to start. I studied fashion in school. Maybe I could go back to school. Maybe take a course. Intern with a fashion house here in Stockholm," she babbled, her hands gesturing wildly.

Jonny walked up to her sitting on his desk and planted himself in front of her.

"Is that what you want?"

She looked up at him as he peered down at her. This was a position she was now struggling with. Symbolically always looking up to him as he looked down at her. She hated it. The thought launched her off his desk as if it were a hot stove but right into his arms instead.

"Is that what you want?" he asked again. She hadn't answered him.

"Yes, I want—" His tongue swept into her mouth, cutting her off before she finished her sentence. His lips moved over hers, prying them apart for his invasion. He kissed her exactly the way she liked. Ran fingertips along her skin at just the right pace, teasing goose bumps to the surface. He knew when to deepen his kiss to possess her. When to pull back out, leaving her begging with those brown eyes. He reached for the cashmere sweater she was wearing and slid it off a shoulder before sinking his mouth and grazing his teeth along her exposed skin.

"Jonny—" She tried pulling him back to their conversation, but he covered her mouth once more with his, silencing her.

Brittany was realizing Jonny didn't like her thinking too much. She made him nervous whenever she came asking questions he couldn't answer or wasn't ready to. He often responded with silence. She had unwittingly given him ammunition throughout their relationship, prodding him along to learn every inch of her. How to bend her to his will because he had memorized her body and knew all her weak spots and points of touch.

His imperfections were a superpower he wielded over her.

When she called his name again, his grip tightened around her, crushing her into his chest. He waddled over to the chaise longue, carrying her along, her arms wrapped around his neck. They made love in haste, fully clothed. Five minutes later, Jonny got to his feet, zipped up, and turned to Brittany, who was still on her back.

"I'll give Svea a call about your fashion thing."

Then he spun around and left her lying there.

MUNA

Muna was back to where she started.

Sitting in her empty apartment, which now felt like an echo chamber with the other two girls gone. Khadiija's and Yasmiin's rooms had been permanently closed. Muna had to vacate it within the week.

Those months had tortured Muna. Yasmiin's and Khadiija's rooms had been rotated among new temporary roommates—an Eritrean couple, a Syrian family of four, another Somali woman for a couple of months—before emptying out again for the last few weeks.

Befriending them would have exhausted her. Muna knew they would leave anyway. She hadn't bothered, and her room remained her dwelling place.

The only positive was that she did have a new job after Yagiz had fired her. Muna had walked over to the Lebanese restaurant where Khadiija once worked and had asked for Khadiija's old dishwashing job. She had no reason to venture downtown, as her entire life was within a mile-and-a-half radius of her apartment: from her dishwashing job to the community center—which had become more somber since the riots—to Swedish class and to the local African and Middle Eastern shops for supplies.

Muna's mind wandered to thoughts of Kemi, who always seemed so happy when she mentioned her boyfriend. She wondered if Kemi had a group of girlfriends who met for fancy cocktails, ate expensive dinners, and went clubbing. Friendships that would help Kemi crisscross town and enjoy everything Stockholm had to offer her.

That tall Black model also crossed her mind. Her beautiful clothes. How she had been standing by that expensive-looking car like a Barbie doll. How Jonny had grabbed and kissed her, and if they were also driving around Stockholm in that fancy car.

In comparison, Muna felt her life had retracted down to a small, postage-stamp-sized area, making her feel trapped and isolated.

Now, Muna sat in her apartment waiting for her friend Gunhild. Three raps on the door announced her arrival. She was carrying a small sponge cake and wearing a smile.

"Happy birthday, Muna!" she greeted, pulling her into a hug with her free hand. Muna accepted it and muttered a low thank-you.

The last time she had celebrated her birthday, it had been with Khadiija, Yasmiin, and Gunhild. Khadiija had roasted some chunks of lamb in the oven, and Yasmiin had dolled her up with makeup and blown out her natural curls for her. They had celebrated at home together, dancing to some Afrobeats Yasmiin had been blasting from her phone. Gunhild had also shown up with a green *Prinsesstårta*. The older woman had wowed the girls into a clapping frenzy when she started gyrating to the rhythmic drumming too.

Today was Muna's birthday, and she had already lost the will to live another day.

"Thank you for remembering," Muna managed to say.

"Of course. May I come in?"

Muna opened the door wider for Gunhild. The older woman kicked off her walking shoes and floated into the quiet apartment.

"I will prepare this for us and make some tea," Muna said, taking the cake from Gunhild and walking into the kitchen to heat water and pull out dishes and cutlery for the cake.

She carefully carried everything into the living room, where Gunhild was sitting on the loveseat.

"Thank you," she said.

Gunhild grabbed a mug and dunked a tea bag into it. She kept dunking, watching hot water slowly turn caramel brown. Muna sliced a piece of cake and handed it to her.

"Did you bake this?" Muna asked after a bite. Gunhild nodded proudly. "Then you must open your own bakery."

Gunhild laughed, ending it with a pained cough. Muna looked concerned, which Gunhild waved off before turning back to her task. She was still dunking her tea bag, and Muna's eyebrows arched as she studied the older woman, who seemed distracted. Something was wrong. It was written all over Gunhild's face.

"Muna..." She started, still focused on her tea, which had now turned the color of weak coffee. "I have something to tell you."

She looked up at Muna through turquoise eyes filling fast with tears, and Muna's heart sank.

NINETEEN

Jonny and Ragnar were already in the conference room when she arrived on time. *Dammit, those punctual Swedes.*

She was carrying her closed laptop, her Espresso House cup balancing on it. Both men sat at an empty table. Jonny was twiddling his thumbs nervously. Ragnar was leaning back in his chair, arms folded across his chest. No laptops. No notebooks and pens. Kemi realized she was walking into a meeting they could have easily conducted in passing in the hallway.

"*Hej!*" she greeted into the air between them and made a show of setting down her coffee, settling her laptop, and flipping it open before sinking into her own chair.

"*God morgon!*" Jonny greeted her, adjusting in his seat. Ragnar's "*hej*" was weak, but she heard it anyway.

"How was your weekend?" Jonny asked. She knew he didn't have good news for her, because he was making small talk. He never made small talk.

"Good. Let's jump right in. I've got a phone call with Bachmann at ten," she announced.

"Of course." He darted a quick look at Ragnar and his crossed arms. "You guys have already met." It wasn't a question, though

Kemi and Ragnar used the opportunity to exchange loaded glances before she turned back to her boss.

"Ragnar is here to help us with the Bachmann account in Sweden. Ragnar has a strong local network of advertising and design agencies in the Nordics as creative director of his own company." She listened to Jonny sell his friend, her whole person turned in Jonny's direction.

She could feel Ragnar's eyes warming her back.

"I'm sure we could use as many resources as possible on this," Kemi said. "We only need to clarify Ragnar's role since I'm both project manager and creative dir—" *Ha*, there it was. Ragnar hadn't been bluffing about taking over as creative director when they'd briefly met in her office.

"I don't want to be used in any more advertising." Jonny's voice turned stern. "What you said about me being *different* at Bachmann... I'm a very private man."

"But the campaign was successful. What's the problem now?" Kemi felt blindsided. Was he punishing her in hindsight for outing his quirks?

"You can still manage the project, but we're thinking about bringing a Nordic style to creatively market more of Bachmann's products." Jonny laid out his plan. "The way you marketed B:GEM was successful because of your bold, American approach. We need something subtler and more nuanced for its new line of hiking shoes."

"No one knows nature and the outdoors better than us," Ragnar chimed in, uttering his first sentence of their meeting.

"Us?" She recoiled. He shrugged, arms still crossed defensively. That was when she noticed movement from down below. His trousers ruffling. He was tapping his right foot rapidly under the table. Was he nervous? She turned back to Jonny.

"If I don't have any creative control, it doesn't make sense for me to stay on this project."

"I agree. You're director of diversity and inclusion and you report to Ingrid, who is HR." He was rewriting her fate again. "We need you to help us hire more diverse talent."

She hadn't expected Jonny to agree with her bold statement so quickly. She had been bluffing.

"I'm a marketing executive. That's why you hired me. Frankly, I was surprised when I found out I would be reporting to Ingrid, but I let it slide because I thought I would have some creative direction when it came to bringing diversity into von Lundin Marketing's work." She took a deep breath after the words streamed out of her.

"Yes, and we will bring your expertise into projects when we need it."

Kemi felt betrayed. After digging them out of the IKON disaster and placing them on a Bachmann pedestal, this was how she was being repaid? Rage began brewing within her. This was not what she signed up for.

"What exactly is my job, Jonny?"

Silence hung over their heads. Jonny had snatched Bachmann—her baby—out of her hands. Now he had to find a way to appease her without fully handing it over.

"Do you want to stay on as project manager?" A peace offering.

"Does that mean I have the final say?"

"It means Jonny has the final say," Ragnar interrupted. She didn't turn to acknowledge him.

"Very well." She started packing up her unused laptop and undrunk coffee. "I want to stay on as project manager. I hate to admit it, but I'm emotionally invested in this account."

Jonny's phone rang, and he grabbed for it immediately, ignoring the fact he was in a meeting with two other people. He hummed and *jaha*-ed in response to the person on the other end.

Kemi sat, lips pursed, irritated that she had to wait this out. Ragnar swiveled his chair away from them, looking out the low windows, arms still crossed. She gave his back a quick look and saw it heaving beneath his shirt.

Jonny disconnected the call abruptly without a *hejdå* and turned back to Kemi and Ragnar. Other people must be used to him getting easily distracted, but it still grated on Kemi.

"While I have you both here," he said, switching lanes, "I'm throwing a small dinner party for Brittany. She's turning forty this weekend." Ragnar was his best friend, so Kemi assumed Jonny was speaking to him. But Jonny turned to her instead.

"I would be so grateful if you can make it. Brittany doesn't have a lot of friends here, and I think she would really appreciate having another...*you know*."

"Black woman?"

"Yes, that. She feels alone sometimes, and I think having you there might lift her spirit. I'm flying her best friend, Tanesha, over to celebrate too," he continued.

For all Kemi knew, Jonny's wife was a myth. She'd never met the woman and had heard through office rumors that she was tall, a former model turned flight attendant, and was stunning. Now Jonny was soliciting her to entertain his wife simply because she was also Black.

"You can bring someone too, if you want. Will you consider it?"

"Of course." Kemi nodded. Then she realized she was back to going along with whatever Jonny proposed.

"Good." And with that, Jonny sprang to his feet and bolted out the door to his next quest, ending their meeting on an abrupt note. Kemi was left absorbing Jonny's exit, Ragnar absorbing her from behind. She dared not turn around.

When she did, it was to his intense glare. He was giving her a glimpse into his battlefront. She got to her feet, grabbing her laptop en route.

"Kemi…"

She left before letting him finish. Once out of the conference room, Kemi leaned against the wall, eyes closed, letting air rush into her lungs. Her heart was racing, and she tried calming it down with deep breaths.

"Are you okay?" Ragnar's bass vibrated through her, leaving the tiny hairs on her arms standing. Her eyelids flew open, only to peer right into his as he hovered close. Heat rushed to her cheeks. He had left the room and come after her.

"Yes…yes." Kemi was flustered. "I probably need coffee, that's all." She took an exaggerated gulp from the cup.

"So, are we good?" He studied her intently.

"Good on what?" She pushed off the wall, standing tall.

"Me helping out with the account?"

"What do you want me to say? It's out of my hands." Kemi watched him shrug. "You call the creative shots now."

"Well." Ragnar stretched out his hand toward her. "I'm looking forward to working on this with you." He waited for her hand. Kemi hesitated then adjusted her laptop and coffee before slipping her hand into his firm grip.

Rather than shaking it, Ragnar simply held her hand in his, his eyes hooking hers intensely, and Kemi knew she never should have let him touch her.

Those tiny, green leaves of doubt were now sprouting into large, dark fronds she wanted to rip out of her soul as savagely as she could. Years of struggling to be enough and she'd finally found a man—Tobias—who wanted nothing from her beyond basking in her presence. She thought she knew what she wanted, yet those roots were extending into her brain and grabbing deep into her psyche, trying to convince her that Tobias was unworthy. That he, a mere security guard, didn't deserve her.

"How does this look?" Tobias asked, adjusting a silver silk tie over a gray dress shirt, while Kemi sat on her bed—more like their bed, since he'd essentially moved in months ago. She wore a burgundy wrap dress that followed her curves while dipping into a deep V at her bust and silver drop earrings that framed her face. She left her hair falling in curls around her shoulders.

"Perfect" was all she muttered as she fastened her jewelry before getting to her feet. Tobias turned toward her then swallowed up the gap between them.

"God, you're beautiful," he murmured, his hands moving to her hips. "What time do we have to be there again?" He gave her that squinty-eyed, gap-toothed grin that always melted her. This time, she resisted it, unsure of why but knowing it was tied to those green buds growing in her brain. She tentatively received his kiss but pushed him back once he tried to deepen it, telling him they had to leave for Brittany's birthday party and she didn't want him smudging her makeup.

Jonny's house wasn't easy to get to. Kemi still hadn't bought a car because her social life orbited around downtown Stockholm and

Malcolm's jazz gigs. She usually flitted around town using the subway, trying to feel like a true Stockholmer, but that night, she ordered a taxi because they were also carrying an oversize bouquet of red tulips.

As their taxi sped toward the island of Lidingö, their driver—a Nigerian man in his forties with a phone to his ear—kept speaking loudly into the device at a decibel that drowned out the car's engine. He kept stealing glances at Kemi through his rearview mirror as he spoke in Yoruba, her native tongue.

Hearing those familiar intonations was enough to excite Kemi and conjure up memories of her own family. She eavesdropped, soaking up the cultural source that was her lifeline. A space where she could exist without explanation. She didn't have to strain to hear, because his words floated right back to her in a boisterous ring.

"*E kpele, Mommy.*" *I'm sorry, Mommy.*

"*Ehn...ehn... e ma bi nu... Mo gba gbe ni.*" *Ehn... Ehn... Please don't be angry... I forgot.*

His free hand would occasionally leave the steering wheel and motion shapes to the woman on the phone, who clearly couldn't see what he was doing. Then his eyes traveled back to Kemi once more. The look was one of awareness. He had recognized her as one of his sisters, dressed in a way that suggested money, alongside a brother, albeit one who looked like he had blood from this country. Kemi tried averting her eyes, unsure of how to read his look. Whether it was one of pride, disappointment, or simply a brazen willingness to take Tobias's spot by her side.

"*Herregud,*" Tobias muttered under his breath, flashing her animated Yoruba brother a look of irritation. She turned to look at him. He stared back at her. "Does he need to speak that loudly? I mean, seriously?"

Tobias didn't drop it. "Seriously, why all the theatrics?" Tobias's judgment didn't sit properly with her.

"He's just speaking to his mother. It's urgent," she said in a low voice in the man's defense. Was Tobias embarrassed by his darker counterparts who spoke too loudly? She hadn't noticed Tobias for weeks because he had been a wallflower at Espresso House before he approached her. She wished Tobias also spoke as loudly as this man who—*damn it!*—was still occasionally leering at her through the rearview mirror.

"Yes, but he has to be considerate. A little more *lagom*." Tobias seemed exasperated. "He's going to get us killed!"

Kemi studied Tobias, eyebrows bunching. While he did have a point, she needed reasons to keep that cerebral weed growing. She added this exchange with Tobias to her sparse list of reasons.

When they got to Jonny's house forty-five minutes later, it was exactly what Kemi envisioned it would be. A minimalist waterfront abode with sharp architectural lines and a view reserved for Stockholm's elite. Jonny answered the door with Merlot in hand and received the couple with a nod, before leading them into a room framed by high ceilings and glass walls on three sides.

It was an intimate party. She counted ten guests including herself and Tobias. There was Jonny, Brittany, Ingrid and her husband, Oskar, Espen and his Cape Verdean wife, Rosa, and Ragnar with a strong arm around the narrow waist of his fair-haired wife, Pia. Suddenly, Kemi felt self-conscious, the fabric of her burgundy dress now constricting her like a snake.

Tanesha, Brittany's best friend, had been delayed and was overnighting in Jonny's London pad before heading to Stockholm the next morning.

"So great to finally meet you." Brittany bent low to give Kemi a hug, before stretching back to her full height to give Tobias one too. Kemi handed her the bouquet of red tulips, so large she had to carry them with both hands. Brittany thanked them for their thoughtfulness. She was wearing a sleeveless black dress that Kemi was sure had Armani or Dolce & Gabbana sewn into its tag. She wore her hair straight and parted down the middle like a statuesque Nia Long.

"Likewise! You actually exist," Kemi joked. Brittany laughed, and both women were left wondering why they hadn't connected sooner. Maybe they could have been friends all this time.

They took their seats around a large dining table that had been decorated with white linens, brass napkin holders, polished silverware, and small bouquets of white daisies horizontally cutting through the rectangular table. Dinner was a five-course extravaganza of scallops, salmon tartare, pork belly, braised lamb, and a blackberry pavlova birthday dessert. The catering staff of three ran in and out of the kitchen all night.

Over the clicking and clacking of expensive cutlery, they learned more about the various significant others. Everyone was clearly putting their best feet forward. Espen's wife, Rosa, had been a dentist in Cape Verde and was now going through the motions of recertification here in Stockholm. Ingrid's husband, Oskar, was into the burgeoning startup scene here in town. His gaming company had recently secured another thirty-eight million kronor in funding.

Everyone toasted his success with "*Skål!*" The group broke intermittently to salute the birthday girl, who looked every bit the queen sitting at one end of the table, her king at the other. Only ten people at her fortieth birthday. It felt like an injustice to Kemi. Such a milestone party would shut down a street in Lagos, Nigeria, or fill up a hall in the U.S. within her own circles.

As Ragnar's wife talked about her job in PR promoting Nordic luxury brands and her dedication to working out and yoga, Kemi couldn't help but notice Ragnar's muscled arm possessively resting on the back of his wife's chair. Ragnar drank often, assessing the party between sips of wine but never saying a word. Kemi wondered if his usual snark seemed to have been snuffed out by Tobias's presence.

The only words Ragnar exchanged with Tobias were to ask him if he was a Swede and which part of town he lived in. All Tobias told the group was that he was half Gambian and worked in security. Tobias didn't give any more details, leaving them wondering if it was stock securities or IT security.

As person of the hour, Brittany went last. She skipped the part about being a flight attendant and dove right into her past as a model and how she was slowly looking to crack into Stockholm's fashion scene as a budding designer.

"How's your Swedish?" Ragnar's question was directed at Brittany, cutting through the buoyant chatter. Brittany peered at him before laughing.

"I can't even say hello properly," she joked. "I find it so hard. I mean, when I go to stores, some attendants are rather rude when I use my sorry Swedish until I switch to my American accent. I figure, why learn Swedish if everyone speaks English anyway and customer service improves tenfold?" She laughed again before lifting a glass of Cabernet to her cherry-red lips.

"If I had all that time doing nothing, my Swedish would be a whole lot better by now," Kemi casually said before reaching for her third glass of red wine. She turned to look around when the table fell into a hush.

It was at that moment Kemi knew that warm feeling of sisterhood she had felt with Brittany earlier died an instant death.

"Being a mother is the hardest job in the world." Brittany's tone was stern. "I don't count that as doing nothing."

"Oh, no, I didn't mean to discredit you. I mean, I know you do have help. I mean, just that, if you wanted to learn, you could find time." Kemi was digging herself into a deeper hole. Tobias placed a hand on her thigh underneath the table to stop her. Brittany was clearly upset.

"How is *your* Swedish?" Brittany clapped back, and Kemi had to apologize, saying it wasn't her intent to upset and disparage her. It was unfortunately too late. It seemed Brittany wasn't one to forgive easily.

The rest of dinner was filled with an underlying tension. Kemi reached for her phone to bring up a taxi app and request a ride. A notification beeped indicating her taxi was ten minutes away. In the meantime, she exchanged hugs with the birthday crew then found herself in front of Brittany, tail between her legs.

"I'm so sorry," Kemi apologized wholeheartedly. Brittany nodded, but her goodbye hug felt cold. The noncommittal grasp Kemi sensed in that embrace said everything. They would remain cordial, nothing more.

While she waited for Tobias, who had gone off in search of a toilet, Ragnar sauntered over to where she was standing by the front door, his eyes reaching her first, a wine glass in hand. She'd lost count of how many he'd downed.

"It was good to see you outside of work." His words were hushed, a little slurred from the wine. "I'm sorry we got off on the wrong foot." She held Ragnar's gaze, watching his pupils dilate under the low light, his eyes getting darker. They roamed over her dress and back to her face. "That is your color," he remarked, his blues locking hers in place. She bit her lower lip.

"*Klar, älskling?*" Tobias cut through Ragnar's flirting, sliding his arm around Kemi's waist, ready to leave. She turned to Tobias, and he planted a possessive kiss on her lips. Ragnar didn't backtrack or turn to go. She caught him watching them, his oceans churning. Ragnar stood rooted in place, sipping from his glass and drinking them in as they kissed.

As the taxi ferreted them across the Lidingö bridge toward Stockholm proper, way past midnight, Tobias finally spoke words into the void.

"Is that your kind of crowd?"

"What do you mean?" Kemi asked, her head lying drowsily on his shoulder.

"You know, guys who make a shitload of money? Who run the world standing shoulder to shoulder so no one else can break through?"

"If I wanted to be with *that* crowd, I wouldn't be with you, would I?" She tried allaying his fears. It did quite the opposite, because Tobias frowned back at her, trying to parse her words.

"Oh, I'm sorry. That came out wrong," she began to apologize. "I mean, I chose you instead of them."

"Well, there's certainly one person there who wants you in his crowd," Tobias muttered, looking out the window, twinkling city lights turning into horizontal streaks as they traveled.

"Don't be silly," Kemi said nervously. "Who?"

Tobias turned to look at her, but he didn't have to say the name.

BRITTANY-RAE

The day Brittany decided to perpetually use English in Sweden had started as any ordinary day.

Away from Lidingö's protective bubble, she often felt bare and vulnerable when navigating town, and when she had to speak Swedish, she retreated with insecurity like a snail into its shell once touched. Maya was with her au pair as usual, while Brittany had taken a taxi from Lidingö island to Östermalm to pick up the Armani dress she had ordered for her birthday—a birthday she wasn't looking forward to.

She was turning forty and had no one to invite.

Besides promising to fly Tanesha in for her big day, Jonny had also rounded up a measly number of people in his current Stockholm circle, including some work colleagues who were Black or had brown spouses, thinking that these strangers' mere presence would make her feel more at home. She understood his intent, but it wasn't enough to make up for the fact that after all this time in Stockholm, she had buried herself in a cushy maternal bubble with no friends of her own.

Her meager social life in Sweden revolved around Jonny's oldest sister. She often spent Sundays at Antonia's, pushing Maya's stroller more than half a mile over to her place, while her au pair walked behind them carrying a hefty diaper bag overflowing with supplies. Antonia had grown fonder of her niece with each passing month, grieving the fact that she'd never had a girl herself.

But even his sisters couldn't make her birthday party due to prior commitments.

Picking up her dress had gone without incident, but when she decided to duck into the nearby luxury shopping center MOOD, she met an adversary. She'd casually strolled into a women's apparel store behind a heavyset Black African woman sporting red braids, when a svelte attendant clad in black with severe eyebrows and nude lips blocked the woman's advance.

"Can I help you?" The attendant asked the woman in English before she had fully stepped into the store, inadvertently blocking Brittany's entrance and stalling her behind their conversation. The woman launched into fluent Swedish, which Brittany didn't understand a word of. It seemed those words hadn't been enough for the attendant, who shook her head and pointed to the mannequins in the window display.

The African woman seemed distressed, taken aback by what the attendant seemed to be saying. Her pitch, fringed with frustration, got louder, and then she turned to go, visibly shaken. Brittany watched her shuffle away, shoulders hunched, before turning back to the attendant. She knew this wasn't the right time to practice her nonexistent Swedish.

"What was wrong with that lady?" Brittany spoke in English, her American accent sailing through. She saw the attendant relax into a disposition enveloped with awe.

"Hiiii!" the attendant greeted. "Oh, I just told her we didn't carry her size, that was all," she said in a forced American English accent.

"She seemed upset, though. Was she shopping for herself or someone else?" Brittany was curious.

The attendant went silent for a moment before confessing that she hadn't asked.

A topless Jonny reached wide palms around Brittany to cup her breasts, but she elbowed him off. She was standing in front of their bathroom mirror, applying her signature cherry-red lipstick—the same shade she'd been wearing the day they'd met in business class en route to DC.

"Stop," she reprimanded as she pressed her lips together to even out and seal in the color. She caught his eyes through the mirror and read his face completely. Yeah, he would gladly skip the party too. He grabbed his black shirt and buttoned it over gray pants, matching his wife's chosen look for the evening.

Tanesha's flight had been delayed, which meant she wasn't going to make their dinner, though Brittany was looking forward to meeting Kemi, a fellow American. Well, a Nigerian-born, naturalized American, who had essentially helped Jonny land a major campaign. She wondered why they hadn't connected before in person. After all, they'd both moved to Sweden because Jonny had brought them here.

Jonny's phone beeped, and Brittany saw Ragnar's name flash across it. She promptly rolled her eyes. Their feeling of disdain for each other was mutual. Jonny's best friend had arrived early with Pia, and they'd made themselves at home downstairs while the caterers worked to prepare the five-course dinner in the kitchen.

Jonny jogged down the winding staircase, Brittany following five minutes later as the guests began coming in. Kemi and her plus one were the last to arrive.

There she was. The woman for whom her husband had flown all the way to the U.S. to personally recruit. Something burned within Brittany along the lines of jealousy. She pored over the curvy lady, who had deep dimples and was carrying an impressive bouquet of tulips in her favorite color. Kemi walked up to her, and Brittany couldn't help but take in her curves—from bounteous breasts to broad hips. Enough to elicit envy from any man wishing to replace her dress with his body wrapped around hers.

As the night went on, Brittany was visibly shocked when she realized that Ragnar was that man.

Brittany watched as his eyes followed Kemi across the room, trailing her every movement. They stealthily danced over her curves. He hid behind several glasses of wine or behind Pia as they worked the room. If Kemi was aware that she was the object of his fascination, she did an impeccable job of hiding it.

Their conversation ebbed and flowed, with Brittany growing to like Kemi with each passing topic, until Ragnar questioned Brittany's lack of Swedish in front of everyone. Her vulnerable spot. She wanted to recoil snail-style, but she couldn't. All eyes were trained on her, and her hatred for Ragnar reached new depths.

She tried to defend herself, her mind conjuring up her experience at that apparel store earlier that afternoon, and the difference in treatment the African with the red braids had received. She never wanted to feel that exposed again in Sweden, so she wrapped her Americanness around her like a protective cape.

She half expected Kemi to jump in with reinforcement and an anecdote about how pulling out her American card had been worthwhile on occasion. So Brittany was stunned when Kemi didn't. Brittany wanted to scream at her. *How dare you judge me for not speaking Swedish?*

But visions of her Maya bubbled up instead. She wasn't sure what she was feeling in addition to anger. If it was hurt, betrayal, or disappointment that Kemi had chosen to inadvertently belittle her in front of their group where white skin outnumbered theirs.

Kemi began to apologize, digging herself deeper. Brittany noticed Tobias, *bless his heart*, trying to reel his woman in by leaning closer, moving his arm toward her, his hand clearly doing something under the table. The verbal knife had already broken skin because Kemi thought she was better than her. Any flickers of sisterhood shattered that evening. Kemi had decided to judge her because Jonny took care of her while Kemi took care of herself.

Brittany excused herself from the table for a quick bathroom break.

"I'm sorry she upset you," Jonny apologized as he watched Brittany undress for the night. He was already naked and buried under the plush sheets, eagerly waiting for her to hop in and thank him for the party.

"Don't worry about it." Brittany pulled off her earrings.

"Did you like it?" Jonny asked.

"The party?"

He nodded. She hadn't. The only person she loved besides Jonny, Maya, and her parents was Tanesha, and she hadn't been there. Instead, she had been stuck between Ragnar's sanctimony and Kemi's self-righteousness.

In hindsight, maybe they were made for each other, the way Ragnar's eyes had ravaged her. For Brittany, her sweetest revenge would be to witness Ragnar lose a sleepless battle against lust over a woman he could never publicly carry on his arm. Ragnar had yet to convince her he wasn't prejudiced against Black women.

"Did you see how Ragnar was acting tonight?" Brittany changed the topic. Jonny wasn't having it. He couldn't give a damn what Ragnar had been doing that night. He wanted to know if she had liked the party. He asked her again once she climbed in beside him.

"Thank you, Jonny," she said to placate him and gave him a scant kiss before turning away and pulling the sheets over her shoulder.

Silence filled their room once more. She heard his soft breaths behind her and knew he was still propped up on an elbow, staring at her back.

And for the first time since she started sharing his bed, Jonny didn't reach for her.

MUNA

Gunhild and Muna strolled around the block side by side, Muna slowing her pace to match Gunhild's laborious steps. Gunhild was giving Muna time to process the news. How could a perfectly healthy woman who walked more miles per day than Muna walked in a month get this sick so quickly?

"This type of cancer runs in my family," Gunhild had explained before sipping her tea when they'd been in the apartment and she had initially shared the news. "Unfortunately, there's nothing more my doctors can do if the next set of treatments don't work."

Muna had quietly digested Gunhild's news, not knowing what to say, what questions to ask, or how to console her. Everyone she'd loved—her father, her mother, her brother, her Ahmed—had died right in front of her. Khadiija was on trial with her residency in jeopardy. Yasmiin was long gone. Now she was going to witness the only person she had left to care about die a slow, painful death.

Muna was finding it more and more difficult to see the point of living anymore. Gunhild had suggested they go for a brisk walk around the block to shake off the bad news.

"Have you made new friends?" Gunhild cut into Muna's thoughts.

"No," she told Gunhild. The older woman bobbed her head in thought.

"Do you have anywhere to go?"

She shook her head. She had to leave the subsidized apartment for the next wave of refugees, making space for the others to land on their feet when she hadn't even found her footing. Even though she'd managed to save about seventy thousand kronor, she still felt like a failure. Maybe once she was eligible to apply for citizenship in three years, it would all be better. Being a Swedish citizen would open up more doors that were currently closed to her.

Gunhild took a deep breath as they continued walking down Muna's street.

"Do you still want to be an accountant?" Gunhild asked. Muna looked at her, surprised that she was dredging it up again.

"Yes... Yes, of course, but I also need to work. I need to have a good job and show I can support myself and not just take money." Muna wasn't sure who she was proving this to, but thoughts of Mr. Björn and his flat voice telling her to be good swam in her mind. She had three more years. She could see them hovering at the horizon of her life.

"Good!" Gunhild seemed excited. "Then I have a proposal for you." Muna's interest was now piqued. What was Gunhild thinking about?

"I want you to become an accountant too. I know you can. You're so smart."

"Thank you."

"You can move into my spare bedroom for free on one condition." Gunhild turned to look at Muna, whose face had begun to light up. "You go to school to become an accountant."

Muna was relieved. With one week to go in her apartment, Gunhild was redirecting her trajectory and giving her newfound hope in her future.

"Thank you, Gunhild! Thank you!" Muna wrapped her arms around the older lady as tightly as she could until Gunhild had to cough for air.

"It's the least I can do for you, Muna. I have no children of my own, and you've come to be like a daughter to me. Plus, I need help around the house. I'm getting much weaker these days." Gunhild paused.

Muna's eyes filled with tears, letting the gravity of Gunhild's words fully sink in. Gunhild had just called her "daughter." She had parsed out that single word from Gunhild's stream of speech. Muna sniffed back her tears, halting them. She couldn't sob in front of Gunhild. Not now.

"I will help you clean and take care of the house," Muna said proudly. She explained her chores as a janitor at both Solsidans Asylcenter and von Lundin Marketing. She was good at cleaning. She thought about her dishwashing job at the Lebanese restaurant and asked Gunhild if she could keep it.

"Dream bigger than those dishes, Muna," Gunhild said before launching into another coughing fit.

After exchanging hugs, Gunhild left, and Muna took a deep breath, feeling lighter. One weight off her chest, and she didn't feel like she was sinking as fast as she initially had thought.

Muna ran into her bedroom to pore over the photos tacked

on her magnetic board. She beelined over to smiling Ahmed with the black-faced sheep on his shoulders and pressed her lips to it, which she often did when she was happy. She loved sharing her small wins with Ahmed. When she'd first met Khadiija and Yasmiin. When she'd landed her job as a janitor. She also shared her sorrows with him. How she missed his quiet presence around her. How she missed their chats on the verandah. She had kissed that photo multiple times with more tears than smiles on her face.

Muna wasn't sure what had possessed her to hop on the train and go downtown after her shift at the Lebanese restaurant, but she suddenly found herself in Kungshallen, where she took those familiar escalators down to the basement. The last few customers of the day were finishing up their meals from the food kiosks. Muna padded over to Yagiz's kebab shop, hoping he was there.

She hadn't seen him in a long time, and the man who stood in front of her was a tired one, aging quickly. He was still sporting his stylish rooster hairdo, but a black goatee had joined his handlebar moustache, framing his still-handsome face. His normally trim frame was sporting small love-handles, and his cheeks seemed a bit fuller.

When Yagiz saw her, he let out a groan of exasperation and looked up at the ceiling, begging Allah in an exaggerated stance. "Why won't the witch leave me alone?" he said loudly before letting out air again, his small potbelly popping out with the motion.

Muna stepped up to his counter and planted herself there as if she was his eternal haunting. To Yagiz, she was probably a ghost now following him who may never set him free.

"What have I done to vex Allah, *uhnn*? Why are you back here?" Yagiz was embittered.

"Where is Yasmiin?" Muna quizzed him. "I just want to know that she is all right."

Yagiz's black eyebrows, which had been raised in frustration, lowered into a slight frown.

"Yasmiin is an adult. Leave her alone. Why do you keep looking for her?" he asked. At least she was still alive, Muna deduced. But why the radio silence all this time? Hadn't her sister cared about her too? Unless Yasmiin had only considered her a roommate, nothing more.

"So she's okay?" Muna's pitch rose in excitement. "Where is she?"

Yagiz studied her, his stance relaxing. He turned to a colleague and muttered something rapidly in Turkish. The man waved him off midsentence, uninterested. "*Whatever...,*" the man's disposition seemed to say as he flapped his hand at Yagiz, not looking at him. Yagiz wiped his hands on a kitchen cloth, pulled off his apron, and walked out from behind the kiosk. He cocked his head, signaling Muna to follow him to sit in a corner of the hall.

They settled into small wooden chairs and parked their knees beneath impossibly narrow tables.

"What do you want, Muna?" he asked a few seconds later.

"I am worried about Yasmiin."

"But she is not your family. Why are you latching on to her? Go find new friends!"

Muna clasped her hands tightly on the table, trying to hold back tears. Yagiz didn't understand she was tired of being alone. She looked down at the fingers she was toying with under his gaze. Yagiz remained quiet, observing her. When she pulled away from her fingers to look at him, his eyes had warmed with pity.

He adjusted himself, sitting taller and reached into the back pocket of his lean jeans. He pulled out his wallet. After sifting through its contents, he produced a card-sized photo and gently flicked it with two fingers toward Muna. Muna grabbed it and peered into the face of a small baby. The little boy couldn't be more than six months old. He seemed alert, his wide, dark eyes soaking up the world around him. He was perched in his mother's lap, a wide grin across her pretty face with protruding cheeks... Yasmiin.

"Yasmiin is my wife." Yagiz let the words float over Muna as she scanned every inch of that photo. "That is Mehmet... The reason I haven't been sleeping for months."

"You should have heard my friends," Yagiz continued. "They laughed at me for months when I told them I was in love with an African woman and wanted to marry her." He chuckled. Then his laugh died down into a wince of pain, Muna noticed.

The photo seemed frozen in her hands. She was glued to mother and child. She was trying to understand how all this could have unfolded. She and Khadiija had burst into Yasmiin's room to save her from this man who seemed to have hurt her because of their screaming. She didn't understand why Yasmiin would choose to go with this man, marry him, and bear his child.

Yasmiin was never her sister, simply a roommate. She realized that now as she peered at little Mehmet and his smiling mother, who seemed to have found where she wanted to be. Yagiz reached for the picture from her paralyzed fingers and secured it safely back in his wallet.

"Now you know," he said. "So...please stop coming here and looking for Yasmiin." He prepared to get to his feet.

"Why?" Muna paused his ascent. "Why did she not tell us she was fine?"

"Because you're her past," Yagiz explained. "Yasmiin wants to move on from her past. I take good care of her. I know what she likes, and I give it to her." Muna absorbed his words.

"Look," he said, beating his chest lightly. "Yasmiin is here, okay?" He patted right above his heart. "So don't worry, Muna Saheed. Move on. Go find new friends."

A text message notification interrupted him, and he pulled out his phone to read it, cursing under his breath.

"Azeez just texted me," he said, turning back to her. "You remember Azeez?" Of course she did. "Huda is sick, and he needs someone to cover next week..." His gaze lingered on her once more.

"I can do it! Please, let me do it," Muna pleaded, surprising even herself by her own desperation.

"Are you sure?" Yagiz regarded her skeptically.

"Yes, I need it," she begged. He let out air of exasperation and then texted Azeez back.

"Okay, just this once," he stressed. "You're still fired, understand?" She nodded and thanked him. She was to bring the keycard immediately back to him once her fill-in shift was done.

Yagiz got to his feet, pulled out a cigarette, and balanced it between his lips. Staring Muna down one last time, he cocked his head quickly to the side, motioning for her to get out.

Instead of the quicker option of Hötorget station, Muna decided to walk a few blocks down to T-Centralen so she could process her thoughts. She strolled along, aware of curt glances from other pedestrians taking in her full-length jilbab.

Yasmiin wanted to move on. She'd cut both Muna and Khadiija

out of her life to do so. She pondered Yagiz's words. *"Move on. Go find new friends."* As Muna ambled down the street in no hurry, Gunhild's words floated up to her. *"I want you to become an accountant too. I know you can. You're so smart."*

By the time she reached T-Centralen, Muna had decided she would dream bigger than dishes.

TWENTY

KẸMI

"I'm so sorry," Kemi apologized, rushing up to the table in the restaurant, around which sat Jonny, Maria, Espen, and Ragnar.

While at the office, their group had been talking about press releases and media announcements when Jonny had suddenly started craving a burger. On a whim, he relocated their meeting to a nearby hamburger joint three blocks away from the office. Kemi was running ten minutes late after being delayed by an important call with a design agency.

"It's all right," Jonny said. "We haven't ordered yet. Ragnar saved you a seat." He pointed toward his friend. Ragnar pulled his jacket off a metal chair between himself and Maria. They were all cramped tightly around a small table in a packed restaurant. She made her way over to his side, pulling out the chair, and muttering a quick thank-you. When she settled herself in, her left thigh brushed his. Ragnar made no effort to adjust for her. Kemi absorbed his apparently strategic move.

"So," Jonny announced, "let's order, shall we?"

At the flick of his hand, a waiter came running up to take their orders. While they waited for their food, the Swedes exchanged quick words before Maria broke into English.

"Kemi," she started, "how comfortable would you be giving an interview in Swedish?"

"In Swedish?" Kemi asked, uneasy.

Maria nodded in response.

"Uhmm, no," Kemi said firmly. "I've barely been here two years. How do you expect me to free-flow fluently in Swedish? It's a difficult language."

"I've heard you speak. Your Swedish is really improving," Espen chimed in.

Kemi turned to him. "Really? Enough to give a full interview in Swedish?" she chided him for patronizing her. He lifted his hands up in defeat.

"What's this all about anyway?"

Maria looked at Ragnar before turning back to Kemi. "We've been invited to talk on the most popular business television show, *Dagens Affärer*, and were just wondering how comfortable your Swedish is."

"I've been taking classes but..." Kemi adjusted in her seat. Ragnar was manspreading underneath the table, stealing into her space. His leg found hers again. Kemi was astonished to feel herself wanting to lean into him, reach under their table, and run her fingers along his toned thigh.

"I'm sorry," she said. "What did you say?" She pulled her leg away.

"It's okay," Jonny said. "You can take the interview in English when it's your turn. As creative director for the Bachmann account, Ragnar will be on the show as well, and as project manager, you can take your own questions in English."

"Do I really need to be on this show?" Kemi didn't want to look incompetent. But her heart couldn't take thousands of people judging her for not mastering their language in less than two years.

"Maybe not." Ragnar spoke up. Then he trained his eyes on her, studying her face. "We can discuss this later?" She felt his heat again under the table, and it snuffed out her voice. She nodded instead.

When their food arrived, Kemi was quickly distracted by Ragnar chewing next to her. While both Espen and Jonny used forks and knives to eat their burgers, Ragnar cradled his between his large hands and tore into it. Kemi watched his strong jaw work his meal, veins bulging on his thick neck, a frown resting on his face, as if perpetually etched in suspicion.

Ragnar was uncomfortable, she could tell. He seemed to be eating faster than the others. He licked the back of his thumb, and Kemi made a tiny sound. He must have heard that low whimper because he cut her a quick look, his thumb still at his lips. He turned back to his meal.

Then she felt his heat once more through the fabric of her tailored pants. She let it stay there. Her thigh leaned closer, and she watched him stop chewing. Ragnar seemed to be contemplating something for a second or two before turning toward her. His heavy eyes held hers intensely. They made a slow trek down to her full lips, which had stopped chewing. Then they washed over her bust before trekking back up to her face. He drank her in so fully that the weed growing within her instantly sprouted new leaves.

Kemi averted her gaze and turned back to the table only to find Jonny staring at them, his eyebrows dipping inward in confusion. Once they had finished and Jonny paid the bill, the group made their way back toward the office, led by Ragnar and Jonny. Kemi hung back, trying to clear her confusing thoughts. All she could think about was Ragnar running his thumb across her lips. She watched Ragnar's wide swagger, both hands in his pockets, head slightly bent while listening to Jonny intently.

This was dangerous. He clearly felt what she was beginning to feel. The heat that burned brighter when they orbited around each other. They needed to stay away from temptation.

When the group got to the office lobby, Brittany was there. She was wearing a red jacket over a black catsuit and sunglasses indoors. Jonny dashed over to her and pulled her in for a quick kiss. Espen and Maria took their leave, giving them privacy.

"Fashion Week came early," Ragnar muttered as they both approached the couple. Brittany pulled off her shades and glared at Ragnar. He stopped in front of her, smirking, while Kemi stood close by.

"I didn't know you worked here," Brittany said. "Who dragged you in?"

"There's a lot you don't know about me. Or von Lundin." Ragnar turned to Jonny, who was now holding Brittany's hand tightly. "Good seeing you, *Fru von Lundin.*" Then he left.

"Thank you so much for accepting my invitation," Kemi said as she moved closer to the couple. "I'm so grateful you could make time to meet with me." Kemi watched Brittany purse her lips, trying to decipher if she was insulting her or not. Kemi knew she spent most of her days at home, surrounded by a full team of staff to help her take care of their daughter and fulfill her every desire.

"Of course," Brittany said. "It's my first time inside the office anyway, so it was a good opportunity too." Kemi blinked at her words. Brittany had never come here in close to two years?

"Come." Jonny tugged on Brittany's hand. "I want you to meet everyone!" He morphed in front of Kemi into a giddy teenager anxiously waiting to show off a shiny new gadget. Once on their floor, Jonny paraded Brittany around the office. Hands in pocket, his gait slow, he walked behind his wife as she introduced herself to colleagues. Kemi quietly strolled behind the couple, her mind racing.

Didn't Brittany see what Jonny was doing? Didn't she see it? Jonny was showing her off like a trophy and nothing beyond arm candy.

They strolled past the kitchen area, where Muna was refilling the coffee machine.

"*Hej*, Muna!" Kemi called out. The younger woman turned toward her voice, her eyes immediately widening as she glanced from Kemi to both Jonny and Brittany, who had stopped alongside Kemi. Muna lingered on Brittany in admiration.

"*Hej*," Muna greeted weakly.

"How are you?" Kemi asked in Swedish. Muna nodded and smiled back. Kemi turned to Brittany.

"Muna's from Somalia and has been helping me with my Swedish."

Brittany made a sound, a slight chuckle in the back of her throat, and Kemi frowned at her condescension. Was Brittany actually laughing at Muna because she didn't think she was Swedish enough to help Kemi's command of the language? The very same Brittany who had a private Swedish instructor but still refused to learn the language after two years?

In their scant interactions, Kemi felt Brittany was an irritatingly entitled creature, but Brittany's patronizing smirk at Muna had solidified her opinion of her. She was nothing more than a shallow gold digger, and Jonny would soon tire of her. Kemi was sure of it.

"Nice to meet you, Muna," Brittany greeted in English.

"Muna speaks Swedish," Kemi stressed sternly before turning to give Muna a wink.

Jonny, who had been quietly standing there, suddenly decided he was done and marched off, forcing both Brittany and Kemi to trail him. Jonny led them into a private room then took his leave—but not without kissing Brittany passionately in front of her. It seemed out of character for him. Kemi had witnessed the way Jonny had doted over his wife at her birthday party. That had been a special occasion. But this... Brittany broke off their kiss and wiped red lipstick off his mouth.

"Let me know if you need anything," Jonny whispered before turning to go, Kemi's presence long forgotten.

"Finally." Kemi laughed. "We get some time alone." Brittany gave her a half smile and Kemi cleared her throat.

"Listen, Brittany. I invited you here because I wanted to apologize," Kemi started to say, but after witnessing Brittany's flippant display at Muna, Kemi wasn't sure she even wanted to apologize anymore.

"You could have done that over the phone."

"No, I wanted us to meet face-to-face," Kemi said. Brittany shifted in her seat. "I came off harsh and judgmental at your birthday party. That wasn't my place. I know it's not easy for us here, and I should have supported you instead."

Brittany nodded. Kemi was unsure if her apology had been accepted.

"It's okay," Brittany said. "I mean, I guess I should be much better at Swedish by now. I do have a private tutor. It's such a difficult language to learn, you know."

"Oh, I do," Kemi said. "How are you liking it here so far? In Sweden, I mean?"

"Some days are better than others." Brittany shrugged. "I used to be a flight attendant, and I worked with so many people every day. This..." She swept a hand around the room. "This can be so isolating."

Kemi nodded. Besides Malcolm, José, Tobias, and his family, she still hadn't built a solid network of friends. Despite not speaking with Zizi for close to two years, she often missed their chemistry and raw banter. Malcolm had told her about the club for American expats. Kemi still hadn't been to any of their events. Maybe this was an opportunity to ask Brittany?

"You know, if you're looking for things to do, a friend of mine is in a band. Maybe we could go watch him play sometime?" Kemi wasn't even sure why she was offering. "And he also told me about the American club. Maybe we could check it out together?" Kemi saw Brittany shift uncomfortably in her seat.

"Thanks for the offer, Kemi. I have to think about it," Brittany said. "The last few months have been hectic with Maya, and... *I don't know...*"

Kemi peered at her, blinking in disbelief.

"The thing is," Brittany said in explanation, "I can't just be friends with anyone. Jonny's family is too influential for me to expose them like that."

BRITTANY-RAE

Brittany didn't want to be in Jonny's office.

She was already tired of eyes on her whenever she was out and about with him in public. The last thing she needed was his employees assessing her with suspicion and intrigue.

The only other time Brittany had been close to that building was when she'd waited outside his office for him. Jonny had quickly rushed in to sign a document that needed his approval. This had been before they'd gotten married. Before Maya came into their lives. She and Jonny had been on their way to that dreadful lunch meeting with his parents. Since then, she'd had no reason to go into the offices of von Lundin Marketing. Jonny was rarely there anyway.

But Kemi had summoned her, touting the importance of a face-to-face meeting. Now she glared at Kemi, who seemed to be looking at her in confusion.

"Thanks for the offer to hang out, truly," Brittany said again. Yes, of course she wanted to check out new bands and meet other expats, but right now, she had a lot on her mind.

"Look, I know how hard it is to make friends and force yourself to get out there. To be vulnerable," Kemi said. "Sometimes, this all feels like quicksand. Pulling us into spaces where we get so complacent, we lose our edge."

"Tell me about it," Brittany muttered. She hadn't washed her own clothes since she moved to Sweden. She hadn't shopped for groceries herself, and she could count on both hands how many times she had cooked a meal. She had become a trophy, constantly being polished by Jonny and his staff to do nothing but shine. She couldn't go out to the American club and have a bunch of fellow citizens judge her because a wealthy man had swept into her world.

"So, why did you come here?"

"You mean besides for your husband?" Kemi said.

Brittany laughed. *Sister got jokes.*

"Jonny isn't that convincing."

It was Kemi's turn to laugh and nod. "Well, he convinced you to marry him and have his baby, so..." Kemi attempted humor. Brittany didn't laugh, and Kemi cleared her throat to change the subject. "I wanted to explore something different. Shake up my life a little," Kemi said.

"And has Sweden shaken up your life?" she asked.

"Oh, I'm definitely shook for sure!" Kemi said. Brittany watched a smile spread across her face. "Tobias remained standing once the dust settled."

"And Ragnar?" She saw the grin quickly leave Kemi's face.

"What about Ragnar?" Kemi asked.

"Oh, I don't know. Just wondering if you guys work together a lot or what," Brittany said. "He's Jonny's best friend and always acts suspicious of me." She shrugged. "Didn't you witness that display in the lobby? Is he like that with you too? I'm still trying to figure him out."

"Ragnar and I have a respectful relationship here at work," Kemi said, though her voice sounded weak.

"Really?"

"Yes, we're managing a project together."

"And he respects you on his team? Actually sees you as an equal?"

"Why wouldn't he?"

Brittany smirked. "If you ask me, I think he's low-key racist."

"Low-key racist? What does that even mean? You're either racist, or you're not," Kemi said defensively.

"You know what I mean," Brittany said, irritated. "He's obviously prejudiced. He always looks at me with such spite." Brittany remembered the way Ragnar had visually ravaged Kemi at her birthday party. Clearly, Kemi seemed to be witnessing a different side of him. Not the mucky, self-important bits that Brittany knew made him a complete asshole to her.

"From what I gather," Kemi started, "Jonny and Ragnar have been friends since they were toddlers. Knowing Jonny's wealth and history with women of color, I'm not surprised Ragnar is super protective of his friend."

Brittany peered at Kemi, her face heating up. That judgmental bitchiness had surfaced again. She saw Kemi close her eyes, as if realizing what she had said.

"Well, I'm not a gold digger, if that's what you're implying."

"I'm so sorry." She was apologizing again. "Of course not. I didn't mean it like that." Brittany got to her feet, and Kemi hopped to hers as well.

"Thanks for the invitation," Brittany said, pulling her bag over her shoulder. "Nice seeing you again."

"I swear I didn't mean it like that."

"I get those looks every single day. Especially from his family and friends," Brittany said. "I just wasn't expecting it from a sister too. If you will excuse me…"

She left Kemi standing behind in the room, all alone.

Jonny drove them home from his office in silence, bypassing the tunnel toward Lidingö, opting instead for a scenic ride through town. Brittany looked out the window, still mulling over her conversation with Kemi.

"How much do you need Kemi?" Brittany turned to him.

"What do you mean?" Jonny frowned, still focused on the road.

"I mean, how crucial is she to your team?"

"She landed us one of our biggest clients. I can't afford to lose her."

"Even if she keeps disrespecting your wife?" She saw his jaw tense.

"What are you saying?" Jonny seemed confused. She turned back toward the window. "I'm not firing her for you." Jonny's tone was terse. Brittany remained tight-lipped. Jonny had promised her he would do whatever she wanted. Now Kemi seemed to be off-limits for him.

"You know I would do anything for you, right?" Jonny looked for confirmation from her. She didn't answer him. "Right?" She knew she was provoking him.

When she still didn't answer, Jonny made an abrupt U-turn and started driving them back in the direction they'd come.

"Where are you going?"

Jonny didn't answer but kept driving until he made a left instead of a right back onto Strandvägen, and Brittany recognized the route. He was taking them to his hobbit cottage. His solace in the city.

When Jonny opened the door, the place looked lived-in. There was a half-drunk glass of wine on the dining table. A few books on the floor by the sofa. Had he been hiding out here often behind her back? Was Sylvia, their housekeeper, regularly swinging by and keeping this place clean for him?

"Jonny..." She turned to find him pulling his shirt out of his trousers, unfastening buttons, his eyes heavy on her. "What are you doing?" He tossed his shirt aside. "Jonny?" He slid up to her, grabbing her hand in one fluid motion and leading her up the staircase.

Once up in the loft space, Brittany was struck by his unmade bed, the duvet in disarray, and she yanked out of his grip.

"What is this? Are you having an affair?"

"What? Never!"

"What's going on here?" She padded around the room, pulling at misplaced items: a pillow on the floor, pieces of torn paper dotting the room. She picked up a piece with the words, "*Förlåt mig, Maya...*" "*Forgive me, Maya...*" written and then crossed out over and over again.

Before she could fully decipher its contents, Jonny was upon her, grabbing the note from her hand and spinning her around to face him.

"I swear to you." He looked crazed. "I'm not having an affair." His fingers dug into her upper arms. "I would never lie to you."

"Then what is all this?" She bent low to pick up another piece of paper with her daughter's name crossed out multiple times. "Why are you writing Maya's name like this?"

"I need a break from it all sometimes." Jonny began to cry. "It's so overwhelming. All this." His fingers boring into her arms started dancing.

"Us?"

"Yes."

Brittany stepped back, her heart pounding faster. Was he regretting their life together? She backed away, and he sank onto the bed, cradling his head in his hands. She let him cry until she noticed him rocking from side to side. He was slipping into that dark space his mind created whenever he got overwhelmed, and she needed to pry him back out. She settled in front of him, and his arms circled her waist, pulling her to stand between his legs. He rested his head on her belly, crying. She let him sob.

Jonny had only cried three times in their relationship. He'd been devastated when his parents had rejected her. He'd cried at their court wedding. And when Baby Maya had come, he'd sobbed as he cradled his child.

Brittany threaded her fingers through his hair, soothing him, letting him weep against her until his breathing evened out.

Then Jonny's grip around her waist tightened.

The sound of silence hung in the room along with the scent of them. They were lying in bed, facing each other. Jonny wasn't asleep but his eyelids were pulled shut.

"*Maya...*" she whispered into the space between them. Jonny's eyes bolted open, and he peered into hers with that gaze, but he stayed quiet. Brittany studied him, looking for signs. He simply stared back. "The most beautiful name you've ever heard, huh?"

Jonny remained taciturn. He ran his hand down her shoulder, following her arm, and then dipped by her waist. Before moving on to her hip, he paused at a small rise of fat along her waistline. The little love handle she was still working off with her personal trainer after birthing Maya. He gave it a pinch before leaning in to silence her with a kiss.

"*There's a lot you don't know about...von Lundin.*"

Ragnar's words floated in between them. The heaviness of those words sat on her chest, pushing her deeper into the plush bed.

Something didn't feel quite right, and it was all connected to that name she'd seen scribbled on pieces of shredded paper.

Her daughter's name.

MUNA

Muna's move to Gunhild's apartment the following week had been relatively smooth. Not only was she getting new lodgings, it was also with someone she deeply cared about. Besides Ahmed's sack of memories and photos of her deceased kin, Gunhild was her only family.

She didn't have a lot of possessions, choosing instead to save as much as she could over the years. Before moving, she'd bought a small, wooden box from a secondhand shop and transferred all the contents from the dirty sack with the precision of a brain surgeon. She had poured the brown, cinnamon-colored sand into a fist-sized plastic Tupperware bowl and had carefully placed it into the box as well, preserving Ahmed's memory the best way she could.

In due time, she would find the perfect moment to share him with Gunhild.

"Muna!" Gunhild lit up when she saw the girl at her door.

Muna pressed the keys of her former apartment into Gunhild's delicate hand before receiving the older woman's hug. Gunhild turned to lead Muna into the airy apartment, her graying blond hair framing her small head like a helmet. Muna kicked off her sandals by the door and followed her in. They walked right into a living room that seemed stuck in the sixties with vintage-looking cabinets, floral Victorian lamps with fringes, dark-red velvet couches, and a wooden piano in the corner with the word *Bösendorfer* etched into it.

Every available surface area seemed to be holding knickknacks from all over the world. Wooden elephants, babushka dolls, and many other items Muna couldn't recognize, like a bronze sculpture of what looked like a wall and many stairs, and a wooden pole with scary-looking faces carved into it.

The only photo in the place was of a young Gunhild with long, blond hair wearing shorts. The background looked tropical. Africa maybe. She was leaning against a large canoe, and sitting inside the canoe was a Black man with an uneven Afro, a thick beard, and an unbuttoned shirt.

Muna had found it odd that there were no photos of Gunhild's late husband. She had told Muna that she had been married for thirty years to a Swedish man from the north. Norrland. Even when they had found out she was barren, the man had stuck around, Gunhild had said.

Sixty-three. Muna had found out a week after they'd initially met that Gunhild was sixty-three years old—*well, sixty-five now*—and had no children of her own.

"What are all these things?" Muna swept a hand over the souvenirs and memorabilia Gunhild had amassed over decades as a traveler. Gunhild met her question with a smile that pronounced her crow's-feet.

"Don't worry, we have time to discuss all that," she said as they continued toward one of the rooms. Gunhild pushed open the door to a room that had a double bed hidden under a large knitted blanket with fringes around its edges. There was a white dressing table with a large mirror and a chair with a lace doily hanging over its arm, parked beneath the table. A distressed armoire made from mahogany stood in a corner as her wardrobe.

The whole setup looked like an oversize dollhouse to Muna.

"This is your room." Gunhild paused by the door, knob still in one hand. "It's my guest room for when family comes over...if they come over." She finished with a chuckle that felt pained to Muna.

"It is so pretty." Muna beamed. "Thank you." She turned to give her a subdued hug. Gunhild was looking more tired than usual.

"Good! Settle in. I'll get some *fika* ready." She turned to go, shutting the door behind her.

Muna took in her room. This was all hers, and it was so pretty. She dropped her bags in a corner and removed her hijab. She went over to her dressing table, pulled out the chair, and settled into it. She assessed her dark-brown face and arched eyebrows. Now she had a table where she could properly apply makeup like those dainty ladies in movies. She turned her face to the right, then the left, caressing her profile. She started giggling until it bubbled into a laugh of joy.

Gunhild had prepared sandwiches for them. Four slices of generously buttered sourdough bread topped with a single slice of cheese each, thinly sliced cucumbers, and slivers of red bell peppers.

She had brewed green tea for Muna and a cup of black coffee for herself. A sponge cake baked in the oven for later.

Quietude washed over them again as they ate and sipped.

"I want you to be happy," Gunhild said.

"I know. I promise I will be an accountant," she said.

"Promise it to yourself, Muna. Not to me," Gunhild stressed before sipping more coffee.

"Are you happy?" Muna saw shock spread over the older woman before her eyes softened again behind large, thinly rimmed glasses.

"Yes, of course. I was happily married for many years until he died," she said. "I told you this."

Muna wanted to know all about the Black man with the uneven Afro in the photo and why he was the only one left in this house and not her dead husband, who had stayed by her barren side. Muna wanted to understand.

"Were you married to the man in the photo?"

Gunhild paused mid-drink. "What photo?"

Muna got to her feet, scurried out of the kitchen where they'd been eating, and out into the living room. She carefully pulled the frame off its shelf and came back to the kitchen with it, setting it down between them. Gunhild took in the photo, warming over memories it held. She looked up at Muna.

"That was a dear friend from a long time ago. I spent a lot of time in West Africa as a young student," she said. "Ghana, Benin." She placed her coffee down. "Togo..." She lingered on that country.

"This was not your husband?"

"I already told you it was a friend and my husband was from the north of Sweden." Gunhild's tone turned terse. Before Muna could utter another inquiry, Gunhild grabbed the frame, slowly pushed off her feet, and moved toward the living room. She didn't set it on the shelf. Instead, she shuffled slowly toward her own room with the photo in hand.

Guilt bubbled up in Muna. She hadn't wanted to upset Gunhild. It seemed asking about that photo and her husband had poked at wounds that were still healing. She had so much more to ask, including why Gunhild was working so hard to help refugees like her.

Maybe it had to do with the man in that photo she grabbed and ran off with. Or the baby she had gotten rid of.

Maybe if she shared Ahmed with Gunhild, then the older lady would open up fully to her. If she showed her everything he'd handed her, maybe Gunhild would learn to trust her and realize she wasn't alone. Because the apartment Muna had just moved into belonged to a lonely woman. One who didn't want to die a slow death alone and had moved Muna in as company.

Muna reached for another meager slice of open-faced sandwich with her plan solidified.

TWENTY-ONE

The weeks following Brittany's uncomfortable birthday dinner and Kemi's equally uncomfortable apology meeting had been filled with tension at work. Between Greta, who barely engaged with her, and Ragnar, who was now pacing their halls frequently, she was finding herself in a space feeling more constrictive with each passing week. Everything at work was being made more potent by Ragnar's presence.

Meetings were the worst time of her workday. Besides the fact they were called often for the most mundane reasons to reach consensus for a decision that one person could have easily made, she always felt on the periphery of their conversations. She was still at basic conversational Swedish, and it wasn't enough. It would never be enough, and she could sense restraint among the directors. They wanted to speak freely in Swedish but were being forced to speak halting English.

With Bachmann firmly in Ragnar's hands creatively and Greta back at the helm, Jonny had gallivanted off again, muttering something about yachting with his family along the Dalmatian Coast. Kemi pictured Brittany lying on a stupendously expensive yacht, probably donning an expensive white bathing suit, wearing an oversize brimmed sun hat with oversize sunglasses. She wondered what Brittany had run away from to get onto that yacht.

The weed growing within Kemi had begun to twine around her sanity, strengthening with each convolution. A new leaf popped out whenever Ragnar was near, protected in the greenhouse of their attraction.

Until one day, after an infuriating meeting, Ingrid got a peek into its nursery.

Ingrid had called an impromptu meeting after an anonymous employee had leaked to the press that Jonny was never around and didn't really run the company. The real hero was Greta, Anonymous had complained. Jonny was basking in glory that was rightfully hers. That insider had gone on to leak about how sexist their working environment was. The male directors had assistants, while—besides Greta—none of the other female directors had one.

Maria read the most damning bits out loud from an article in a Swedish business journal. Kemi pulled out the easiest Swedish words from Maria's speech to follow context.

"*Jaha,*" Ingrid calmly exhaled once Maria was done. Everyone else who needed to be in the room was present, including Ragnar. As Jonny's best friend, he was the closest thing to the man himself. Ingrid linked her fingers then turned to Kemi.

"What should we do about this, since you lead diversity and inclusion?" she asked. All eyes focused on Kemi, waiting for guidance. Except she had none to offer. She was a marketing executive, not a human resource specialist.

"I don't know what to tell you, Ingrid," she replied. "I don't handle employee issues."

"But you're in charge of diversity and inclusion," Ingrid fought back.

"On marketing and advertising campaigns, yes. Not filling diversity quotas in HR." Kemi was agitated. Why were they looking to her to fix this? The room remained quiet as the Swedes threw looks at each other.

Maria jumped in. "Maybe you can work with me to put out a press release?"

"I'm sorry, but that's not my job. That's Ingrid's. You know, as head of human resources?"

"Yes, but you report to Ingrid and are in charge of diversity and inclusion."

"On marketing campaigns," Kemi repeated. "Look, I didn't come here to be the fall gal for every single blunder you made before my tenure, so I suggest Louise call Jonny and he get his ass back to Sweden to fix his own mess!"

"But, Kemi," Ingrid argued.

"With all due respect, we have nothing more to discuss. You built this, you dismantle it." She got up to leave. Her deep fear of being stripped of creative control and pushed into a quota-filling corner was materializing. They had lured her here under false pretenses and were now trying to park her in a corner in which she had no expertise.

Being a Black woman didn't automatically mean she was professionally qualified to handle race relations and gender issues on a corporate level.

She gathered her laptop in silence. The others waited eagerly for her exit. Kemi had been around them long enough to know they would burst into Swedish chatter once she left the room. Kemi walked out of the conference room and started down the hallway when Ragnar grabbed her arm. The heat he transferred was enough to boil her already simmering blood. His thumb stroked her skin. She let it linger there for a few seconds. Then she spun around to face him, inching out of his touch. They stole with their eyes what their bodies couldn't.

"Are you okay?"

She was surprised by his concern. She had half expected a backhanded compliment drenched in condescension. That had been his style months ago when they first met. Nowadays, he had become a quiet observer who barely spoke unless absolutely necessary.

"I'm fine; thanks for your concern." He inched closer, and she retreated, stopping his advance.

"How is Pia feeling these days?" She knew his wife was expecting their second child. She summoned up the woman's name like a shield, hoping it would kill the weed or at least stunt its growth.

"She's fine," Ragnar said flatly. "Thanks for your concern. And Tobias?"

"He's fine, thank you."

Ragnar moved closer, and this time, she didn't retreat. He ran his hand up her forearm, his thumb stroking her skin through the light-blue chiffon blouse she wore.

"Did Ingrid upset you?" His eyes held hers, raging with emotion. She knew that look. One that was working hard not to pin her against the wall. She had seen something similar in Connor for years. But this felt different. Darker. Exhilarating.

"It takes a lot to upset me." Kemi tried to focus, his caressing thumb rendering her daft by the second. He took one step closer, his chest heaving, his hand still on her.

"Ragnar..." She swallowed. "I'm fine. Thank you."

They stood in silence, basking in lingering looks. They were so wrapped up in each other's heat that they didn't hear Ingrid noiselessly slide up next to Ragnar. Kemi turned to acknowledge her presence, catching the intrigue Ingrid wore on her face.

"And the Bachmann account?" Ingrid asked. "I hope it's fine too?"

Startled, Ragnar's hand fell to his side and curled into a fist. He turned to regard Ingrid with a churning stare before pushing past Kemi.

Over the following weeks, Kemi skillfully avoided Ragnar, distancing herself as much as she could, considering they worked closely on the same project.

The weed was now fully grown, spilling green twines and offshoots out of her ears and nostrils, threatening to consume her. Late summer made way for autumn, which was slowly pushed out by winter.

By December, their attraction had turned lethal.

BRITTANY-RAE

The only time Brittany had talked to Jonny's mother had been at their botched lunch at Berns two years ago. Jonny's parents still hadn't seen their grandchild in person, only in photos Louise sent to them on Jonny's behalf, a task Brittany refused to do herself.

When Jonny, Brittany, Maya, and her au pair returned from two weeks sailing the Adriatic Sea along the Dalmatian Coast, Astrid von Lundin materialized. But it wasn't to seek forgiveness.

"What's that spice again?" Brittany was trying to guess the nutty flavor her tongue was picking up in Antonia's seafood casserole. Antonia didn't answer. She stared at Brittany with a resignation indicating weight on her mind. "What's wrong?"

"My mother sent a letter... I need to discuss it with you privately."
Brittany pursed her lips. There was nothing Astrid could do or say
at this point that could thaw her indifference. That Astrid couldn't
love her grandchild was a cut that refused to heal.

"Now?" Brittany asked. Antonia nodded then motioned for her to
follow. Brittany wiped her lips, tossed her napkin, and got to her feet.
Maya was napping in one of Antonia's guest bedrooms upstairs, her
au pair recovering in an armchair by the bed. Antonia moved slowly,
and Brittany matched her pace, concern filling her pores. Antonia
walked them over to her glass-walled sunroom, which overlooked
the bay now coated with fresh winter snow. She pointed to a sturdy
wicker chair padded with sheep fur, motioning for Brittany to
take a seat. The normally demure room had been decked out with
sparkling red, green, and silver touches of Christmas.

If Brittany had been nervous before, a quiet Antonia exponen-
tially incited anxiety.

"You're scaring me." Brittany crossed her long legs. "What is
going on?"

"This arrived from Astrid." Antonia reached into her pocket and
pulled out a white envelope with etchings in gold—von Lundin
stationery—and handed it to Brittany.

It was a letter handwritten in Swedish with a photo inside.
Brittany found herself looking into the eyes of a teenage Jonny
with that grin of a thousand teeth. An arm was thrown possessively
around a teenage girl, her own hand resting on his stomach.

Brittany inhaled sharply as she gawked at a dead ringer for her
teenage self. Dark, cappuccino-brown skin, narrow face, arched
brows, and thick lashes over small eyes, her own hair straightened
with relaxers. The resemblance left Brittany breathless, and she

touched her throat, gasping for air. He couldn't have been more than fifteen or sixteen with wind-tousled hair as they embraced in the photo taken in front of Big Ben in London.

"What is this? Who is this?" Brittany wanted answers immediately. Why was Antonia showing her this? Why was Antonia showing her that her dear husband, who couldn't lie, did in fact have a fetish with her very image?

"Maya Daniels."

"Maya... *Oh God.*" A hand flew up to her forehead as she connected her child to his obsession. "Who is Maya?" Brittany peered down at the photo once more, her world collapsing into it. "Did you know about her?"

They all did.

The name Maya Daniels had long been tied to an iron anchor over two decades ago and sunk to the bottom of von Lundin history. Antonia, by way of Astrid, had just dredged her up from the depths, bloated with secrets.

At sixteen, Jonny had been an exchange student at an international school in London for a semester. He had mailed them this picture with a hastily scribbled note saying he had met the love of his life, a Black Brit named Maya Daniels. The beginning embers of his proclivity.

"*Hon älskar mig för den jag är,*" he had gone on to explain in his letter. *She loves me for who I am.*

He had detailed how much Maya loved him despite his eccentricities, Antonia told Brittany. Maya had had a brother who had officially been diagnosed as being on the spectrum, and she was the only person who had looked him in the eye with love when everyone else had bullied him. Jonny had refused to return home after his single semester, begging his parents to extend his term because he couldn't live without this person.

Brittany watched as Antonia contemplated her next words, her chest heaving as she gulped for air.

"He got her pregnant," Antonia explained to Brittany, whose hand had now moved from her neck to cover her slightly parted lips. "Astrid paid for her abortion," Antonia confessed, lingering on those words. "She didn't make it. She was quite young, and something went wrong."

Brittany gasped, hand still over her open mouth. Then her tears fell. They gushed relentlessly as Brittany realized she was living the life of Jonny's first love, Maya. He had meticulously crafted the life he'd always dreamed of living with Maya around Brittany instead.

"You all knew this? You? Svea?" Antonia's betrayal tasted foul on Brittany's tongue.

"I'm so sorry." Antonia's voice shook. "We all swore never to mention her name for Jonny's sake. So, when Svea and I saw you at the *kräftskiva*, we couldn't believe it." Brittany's wails punctuated her confession.

"As far as we are all concerned, Maya and Jonny never existed," Antonia continued. "Jonny never recovered from her death."

The room was closing in on Brittany, smothering her, cutting air from her lungs, her breaths deep and loud.

"Jonny never gets over things," Antonia explained. "He doesn't like loose ends. We all know this."

"Loose ends?"

"Jonny is...different."

"Tell me something I don't know!"

"Yes, but my parents never accepted this. He was the boy they longed for. But..." Antonia collected her breath.

"But what?"

"Jonny didn't start talking until he was five years old. He was always collecting and hoarding small things like insects, especially snails. He loved snails. But then he would crush them with his feet when others tried to take those snails away from him. If he couldn't have them, no one else could." Antonia paused for air. "When he got angry, he never screamed, but he was always pounding and punching at anything and anyone in his way. He was a very angry child."

"Why didn't anyone help him?"

Antonia sighed. "That would have meant admitting he was different. Our parents didn't want him to feel different. He was already perfect the way he was."

"This makes no sense!" Brittany screamed. "Being different doesn't mean there's something wrong with you or that you aren't perfect as you are. It simply means getting special support so you can live your best life."

"I know all this."

"Then why didn't you give him what he needed?"

"There are a lot of other people in the world like Jonny..." Antonia started, but Brittany cut her off.

"No! The difference is, *they* have people supporting them and admitting they have extra needs. *You* have built a privileged palace of lies around *your* brother!"

Antonia regarded Brittany, quietly contemplating her next words. "But..."

Brittany cut her off again.

"Jonny has special needs!"

"But no one has ever said that to my brother," Antonia said. "No one has ever said he was different. No one has ever told him no."

Two years later, and Jonny's words from that clinic parking lot in Alexandria slowly slipped back into her mind, clearing up her fog and finally devastating her.

"Nothing is wrong with me."

"You didn't tell me to stop."

"I would have if you'd told me to."

"If you had said no."

"Why are you telling me all this? Why now?" Antonia could have simply ignored her mother's request to *"Berätta för henne! Tell her!"* which was written on the back of the photo. Astrid's letter had wrapped Maya and Jonny's photo like a birthday gift.

Why did Antonia willingly want to be the proxy for Astrid's damnation of Brittany? Were they trying to save their brother from himself?

"I had no choice. Astrid forced my hand."

"Forced? Did she threaten you? How can she force you to do this to me?"

Antonia remained quiet with a look Brittany interpreted as guilt spreading across her face.

"I see." Realization hit Brittany. "It's about your kingdom, isn't it?"

"Kingdom?" Antonia seemed confused.

"All this." Brittany swept a hand around the room. "All this! Astrid threatened you, didn't she? To take it all away?"

When Brittany was met with silence from Antonia, her palms moved to cover her face, shoulders trembling. Jonny had been pining for a ghost all these years. It all made sense now. London was his hideaway. His glass watchtower in Canary Wharf was where his spirit wailed like a banshee for Maya's over London's twinkling lights. The realization Jonny may never have loved Brittany at all grabbed her beating heart and squeezed it of life.

"Please forgive me. Astrid forced me to tell you," Antonia said.

Brittany held up a splayed hand to stop her from talking. Antonia pressed on.

"He was obsessed with Maya. He still is." Antonia peered at her. "That's why he married you. Her face is all he sees when he looks at you. That was why he was at my house when you were in the hospital. He couldn't look at you. He was afraid you were going to die like her."

"Why are you saying these things to me?" Brittany's chest was heaving, its rhythm, wild and frantic.

"Would you rather keep living a lie?" Antonia's voice was stern.

YES! Brittany wanted to scream. Living this lavish lie was spades better than the opposite. The peculiar man she simply thought couldn't lie now seemed diabolical. What else had he lied about to her face? Staring down that possibility was much worse. Antonia's sunroom became stuffier, and Brittany launched to her feet.

"Brittany, I'm doing this for you."

She pushed past Antonia and ran across the great hall and up the stairs in search of her Maya. She burst into the guest room, startling her au pair and inadvertently waking the child. Maya began to cry, and Brittany rushed to scoop her up.

"Quick, pack up her things! We're going to Rival!" she ordered the au pair before whirling out of the room, child in hand. The von Lundin bubble was closing in on her. She couldn't breathe. She had to flee to survive.

She had rushed into Jonny's kingdom to be taken care of only to find it tailor-made for Maya Daniels, the loose end Jonny was still trying to tie up. She had given up everything to be with him and was now left with a shell of her former self. Jonny had stripped her bare while his archangels—Eva and Louise—hovered around her. She had been primed and primped for Jonny's pleasure while he remained lord of his universe.

Brittany had simply become a ghost.

MUNA

Muna planned it all out.

First, she would complete the bachelor's program in business and economics at Stockholm School of Economics then move on to a master's degree in accounting and financial management. She surfed the school's website, pride swelling within her as she looked at stock images of people with purpose. They were smiling at one another, pointing at whiteboards, beaming with confidence, ready to change the world, one ledger at a time.

She scrolled through the program description, soaking it all in with possibility, and then looked at what was needed of her to be a part of their smiling world. The application deadline had passed weeks ago, but this news didn't deter Muna. She was a woman on a mission. She could easily wait a couple of months until new waves of applications were being accepted. What was a couple of months in a lifetime?

But dread gushed up through her, her mouth resting between her fingers as she glanced at the screen. She had nothing to show. No high school transcripts or proof that she had indeed been a student in Mogadishu before she had been forced to flee with her family. This meant starting from scratch and going back to high school. Even if she tried taking the exam to test out, she couldn't properly write in Swedish. Her SFI classes weren't enough to help her. SFI got her to an elementary level of comprehension.

At twenty years old, she wasn't sure she could handle sitting through lectures with fifteen-year-olds.

She logged out of the computer at Tensta Library and got up in a daze, trying to process this roadblock. That sliver of hope that had slid into her life had escaped like air from a popped balloon. She was now back to the drawing board. After all, Gunhild had told her to dream beyond her dishwashing job. She had strutted into the Lebanese restaurant like a peacock, announced that she was going to be an accountant, told them she wasn't coming back, and had strutted out in similar fashion. Beyond covering once for Huda on short notice when she fell sick, Muna hadn't been back to von Lundin Marketing.

Naturally, she couldn't show her face there anymore, so she had only one place to go.

"Muna Saheed," Yagiz stressed her name as he continued slicing kebab meat. He didn't seem annoyed to see her like he usually was. This time around, it was a casual indifference, which she much preferred. He served two customers before turning back to her. "What do you want?"

"It's not about Yasmiin, I promise."

He eyed her suspiciously. "So, what is it, then?" he asked before turning to a new customer. He carved lamb, piled it high into pita bread, and stuffed it with iceberg lettuce, red onions, and tomatoes before drenching it in a garlicky sauce. Muna watched him roll up the bread, which seemed ready to burst at its seams. Like a magician, he created the perfect shape then sealed it in aluminum foil and handed over to a customer.

"Yes, Muna. You can see I'm busy. What do you want?"

She shuffled nervously on her feet. Yagiz hissed and turned his back to her, forcing her to cry out, "I need my job back."

Yagiz turned to face her, peering down from behind his kiosk.

"Please. It is the only thing I'm good at right now."

He twisted his lips in thought while examining her.

"Let me think about it," he offered. "If I think it's a good idea, Azeez will text you, okay? Now leave me in peace."

Muna smiled at him before dashing off.

Gunhild was asleep when Muna arrived back at their apartment later that afternoon. She had recently undergone a bout of radiation, was currently *sjukskriven*, on sick leave from work, and was constantly tired. Now wasn't the time to unload her disappointment on Gunhild about not being eligible to apply for university, so she decided to prepare dinner for them.

As she was working in the kitchen, she heard the shuffling sound of Gunhild approaching her.

"What are you making? It smells so good." She arrived in the kitchen wearing her frayed pale-pink bathrobe. Muna was sad, but she couldn't bring her concerns to Gunhild. She would broach the conversation tomorrow, hoping to get advice about her options and, maybe, possibly enrolling in high school all over again.

Right now, Muna desperately wanted Gunhild to share more with her. She was used to waiting for intimacy. Ahmed had waited years before divulging his life to her. Yasmiin and Khadiija had offered themselves in bits and pieces. She was tired of breadcrumbs. She wanted to be fully invited into the bakery.

"*Oj vad gott!*" *Oh, how good!* Gunhild punctuated every other bite of salmon with approval. Muna smiled and thanked her again and again after every exclamation.

Once they'd cleaned their plates of fish, rice, and greens, Muna rushed the carnage to the sink. She put on the kettle for her tea and the coffee machine for Gunhild's coffee.

"I want to show you something," Muna said. The older woman sat up in her chair, concern wrinkling her face.

"Is everything all right?"

Muna ran to her room and returned bearing a box.

"What is this? Is it a gift?"

Muna carefully pried open the box and pulled out its contents: silver chains, several misbaha prayer beads, pewter rings, burnished jewelry, a small flag striped red, white, and green, sheared sheep wool, and a plastic container full of sand.

Gunhild immediately reached for the flag before Muna was done emptying the box.

"Peshmerga." Gunhild's eyes widened. "Kurdistan." Then she looked at Muna, probably wondering how a Somali had amassed so many personal effects from that region. "Where did you get all this?"

Muna didn't answer. She pulled out photos of Ahmed and his family and then the stack of one hundred and four passport photos. She took her time laying out each photo one by one until the dining table was covered. Then she unfolded the browned piece of paper that read:

Al Zawr village, 2013,

Kurdistan. North Syria.

When she looked up at Gunhild, tears had already drowned those kind blues. Muna pulled out her favorite photo—of Ahmed with his sheep—and positioned it in front of the older woman.

"Gunhild," Muna began, almost matter-of-factly. Frankly, she had no more tears to shed. "I want to tell you about the man I loved. His name was Ahmed Tofiq Rahim."

Muna started from the first time she'd met Ahmed. When they'd boarded that bus from the border. When he'd turned around to reach for her sack with his beguiling smile. How they often sat in silence together.

She paused to grab their tea and coffee, while Gunhild kept blowing her nose into a kitchen napkin that smelled of lemon and dill.

Muna continued to tell Gunhild how a group of his countrymen hated him. How he'd starved himself. How despair ultimately had driven him to burn himself alive. How he'd handed his sack to her before committing the act, trusting her with his memories.

"His hair was like silk in my fingers." Muna motioned with her hands while Gunhild sobbed.

"These things could have brought him peace, but Migrationsverket kept denying him because they didn't know his whole village had been destroyed." Muna swept a hand over the memorabilia she'd laid out. "Ahmed trusted no one. Only me."

Reverence filled their solemn apartment for the next ten minutes as Gunhild wept and Muna held her hands.

"Gunhild," Muna called softly to the weeping woman. "Please tell me about that man from Togo you once loved."

Gunhild's eyes shot up at Muna, questioningly. Muna didn't buy her story about him being just a friend from long ago. Muna waited patiently until Gunhild hatched out of her own shell.

"I spent a lifetime learning to love someone else," Gunhild shared. "I wasn't allowed to love him back then."

Muna had shared the most precious gift she was given, and she wanted Gunhild to reciprocate her offering. Gunhild peered at Muna behind glassy, turquoise eyes, and the semblance of a smile crept onto her lips.

"He was the only man I ever fell in love with," Gunhild said. "He was my baby's father."

They spent the rest of the afternoon and evening reminiscing. Muna had never seen Gunhild so animated before. The older woman seemed ecstatic to be able to share what had been sitting on her chest for decades. To Muna, it felt like Gunhild could breathe again.

Gunhild had traveled the world. She had spent years in Togo working with an international health organization as a photojournalist. That man had been the love of her life. They had lived together in the capital city of Lomé until her parents had summoned her back to Sweden, threatening to disown her. They'd done so anyway when they discovered she was pregnant.

Gunhild pulled out more photos, some sepia-toned, others fading, to show Muna her past, her delicate fingers carefully tracing over them. Muna observed as the older woman's face lit up with memories flooding behind them. Muna wished she had met Gunhild as a young woman. They would have become fast friends if they had been age-mates. She was grateful now anyway, because Gunhild had told her she was like a daughter to her.

By eleven p.m., both women were visibly exhausted, and Muna shuffled to her feet.

"Aren't you tired?" Muna asked before yawning.

"Go to bed, Muna," She smiled. "I want to look through these photos one more time. *Sov gott!*" *Sleep well!*

TWENTY-TWO

KẸMI

Kemi glanced down at her phone to check the time. Eleven fifty-
three p.m.

She hadn't anticipated staying at the office Christmas party this
late, but the killer DJ had pulled out old favorites, and she dragged
herself off the dance floor two hours later in a sweaty stupor. She
grabbed a few paper napkins and furiously dabbed at old sweat as
she walked over to the coat check desk.

Digging into her purse for a mint, she felt him before she saw
him. That potent energy that seemed to choke her of any breath
from across the room. He lightly brushed her bare arm to get her
attention, instinctively aware of the burn marks his fingers left
behind.

"*Hej*." Ragnar inched closer to her, forcing her to straighten up.
"Leaving so soon?"

The girl with pink hair manning the coat check handed over her
black winter coat. Kemi smiled a thank-you and turned back to him.
His eyes were darker beneath the hallway's low light, and she caught
a slight whiff of red wine lingering on his breath.

"Yes, I have a flight to catch tomorrow." She busied herself with
putting on her coat.

"Please," he offered, reaching out to help her into it. Taking in a deep breath as anchor, she let him. His fingers lingered over her shoulders before slowly smoothing themselves down her arms.

"Thanks, I need to run." She turned and walked down the hallway toward the shiny elevators.

"Early morning, right?" He trailed her.

"Yes." She didn't break stride. He followed her casually. Sooner or later, she would have to stop for an elevator. He didn't need to chase her.

"Where are you going?"

"Girona for a long weekend with Tobias. Have you been?"

"Not yet."

"You would like it." She reached the elevators and pushed the call button. She wanted to flee. She couldn't trust her body anymore.

"I'm sure," Ragnar started, "but there are other places I'd rather be."

She turned to look at him, and they drank each other in fully. She had never physically desired a man as much as she wanted Ragnar. As if she were reeling him in with her thoughts, he slid up to her, inches from her face. What was he doing? They were feet away from drunk colleagues and guaranteed gossip.

"What other places?" Her voice was low.

His response was lower. "You."

Ragnar's brazen declaration killed her breath. Stunned, she looked at him with a frown, hating him for making her weak. He returned her look with a puzzled one of his own, unsure whether he had aroused her, gone too far, or completely misread her all these months.

When the first elevator opened, she fled in and pushed frantically for the ground floor. He rushed in after her, and his wild look told her he hadn't come in to apologize.

Ragnar backed her up against the elevator wall with one quick advance. His mouth hungrily parted hers, and she melted into him, savoring him, wrapping her arms under his to pull him closer. Fervent kisses they knew might never happen again so they selfishly took as much as they could in the moment. They consumed each other carelessly as the elevator inched from the nineteenth floor of the downtown hotel rooftop to the first floor in a building crawling with colleagues. He pressed one hand against the wall behind her, bracing himself, his other hand pulling her closer to feel him, before sliding lower for a handful of her derriere.

"Jag vill ha dig." I want you. He groaned the words against her lips.

Pulling apart for air, they looked at each other wordlessly, chests heaving wildly. As the elevator fell past the third floor, pure greed pushed them back together once more. Ragnar crushed her to his chest. His tongue sought hers, reveling in the warmth tinged with champagne.

They were so engrossed that they missed the elevator door open. They felt a looming presence. Kemi pulled out of Ragnar's heavy kiss and lowered her head quickly, while he spun around to take in the intruder.

Ingrid.

He dropped his arms, which had been wrapped tightly around Kemi. Shame cloaked in silence surrounded the trio, and Kemi knew Ingrid had seen enough.

"Kemi...Ragnar." Ingrid's pitch was higher than usual, clearly tipsy. She leaned against the elevator doors, keeping them open, glancing from Kemi to Ragnar, her eyes twinkling with amusement. "I forgot my scarf," Ingrid said in Swedish.

Ragnar cleared his throat, which drew Ingrid's attention back to him. Ingrid's index finger then made a circular motion over her own face.

"*Du har brunt smink i ansiktet,*" she said to Ragnar. *You've got brown makeup on your face.*

Kemi pushed past both of them and rushed out of the elevator, pulling her coat tighter like armor, clutching her last shreds of dignity.

BRITTANY-RAE

Brittany was resting on the edge of the desk in Jonny's study when he arrived close to one a.m. from his company's Christmas party. She watched him pull clumsily at his tie as he approached her, his eyes heavily drinking her in.

"*Hejjj.*" Jonny planted himself in front of her, resting his hands on either side of Brittany on his desk. "I'm glad you didn't come to the party. There was an ambulance and lots of noise."

He leaned in for a kiss, but his lips brushed her cheek instead when she turned away sharply. "*Hmm...*" He reached to cup her face, turning her forcefully back for his kiss. She knew him well enough to know he had been interrupted. He hadn't finished the task at hand. Loose ends. Brittany thudded his chest and followed it with a slap across his face. He staggered backward, stunned by her assault.

"What's going on?" he asked, reaching a hand up to his cheek.

She crossed her arms over her chest, a long leg dangling over the other in a rhythmic pulsing motion, derailing his concentration.

"I can't do this anymore."

"Do what?"

"Be your wife. I can't."

He squinted at her, trying to process her words. He staggered toward her once more, crushing a kiss against her lips. She struggled under his weight as his tongue forced its way into her mouth. He grabbed a fistful of her hair, tilting her head backward for deeper access. She pushed him off and burst into tears.

She got off the desk, backing away, her face distorted with tears.

"What's going on?" he asked once more. She shook her head, trying to collect her breath in order to power her voice once more.

"DON'T TOUCH ME!" she screamed. "I can't do this." Jonny stood in front of her, hands balled into fists by his side.

"Please tell me why you're crying," he said desperately. "What's going on? I want to understand."

"This is not real. This was never real. You've lied to me all along."

"What are you talking about? I have never lied to you." Jonny's fingers escaped those clenched fists. They began dancing, powered by agitation. "Please tell me what's going on."

"Do you love me?"

"Of course I do. I've given you the world!" he said in a terse tone. "I've given you everything!" Anger brewed within him.

"It's ME who has given YOU everything!" Brittany countered. "I have given you my whole life. It has always been all about what you want, hasn't it?"

"Everything you ever wanted, all you had to do was ask me, and I gave it to you," he said.

"No... Archangels do your work for you!" she cried. "Eva... Louise..."

"What do you mean?" he asked, confused.

"You're not God, Jonny!" Brittany screamed.

She shuddered as he kept glaring at her. He had a crazed look, and it scared her. He stormed up to her, and she pushed him away once more. He tried grabbing her, but she fought him off. Jonny's forceful kiss had been salt scrubbed into an old wound that was never going to heal. Alcohol had recalibrated his pressure on her.

"What the FUCK do you want from me, Brittany?" He stunned her. "I've given you the world. I've given you everything!"

Brittany.

Her name sounded foreign on his lips. Brittany realized she hadn't heard him say her name in weeks, maybe months. It couldn't be years, could it? She couldn't remember the last time Jonny had uttered her name out loud, and she sobbed in despair.

"The world was never yours to give me," she wailed. "The world let you believe it was all yours and no one else's!" She threaded fingers through her hair in despair.

"Your whole life is a lie, Jonny," Brittany cried. "Astrid, Wilhelm, Antonia, Svea... They've been lying to you since the day you were born. You've built this delusional universe around us. It was never real."

She watched him tense, gritting his jaw as her words settled like iron weights on him. He peered at her, apparently realizing that she was flinging the keys to his kingdom back at him.

You're not God, Jonny!

"Maya Daniels." Brittany dropped the name. She saw Jonny freeze at the mention of that name, and his fingers stopped fidgeting. "Who is Maya Daniels?" she asked painfully between sobs.

"Maya Daniels?" Jonny repeated.

"Who is she?" Brittany asked again.

He glared at her, pinning her with the same raw look he'd given his mother when she had met Astrid for the first time. His unblinking, piercing focus that had wanted Astrid dead, and it had terrified Brittany.

"I have never heard that name before in my life," Jonny answered her calmly. "Never."

Brittany's hands flew to her chest. She let out a piercing wail as she pulled her eyes shut at Jonny's lie.

MUNA

Azeez's text woke Muna up at close to eight a.m.

Yagiz had agreed to let her come back to work, the message said. But, unfortunately, she would have to work evening shifts starting that very day. Muna texted him back right away. She would take it, she told Azeez, who then proceeded to tell her to go pick up her keycard from Yagiz before coming into von Lundin Marketing later on.

"Tusen tack!!!!" she texted back before bolting out of bed.

She hadn't anticipated this level of excitement about going back to her janitorial duties, but this time, things felt different. Gunhild had completely opened up to her. This meant she had fully earned Gunhild's trust. Muna also remembered Kemi and how she had stuck up for her when that tall Black model had sneered at her, as though Muna was beneath her. Muna decided she would try to get to know Kemi better. And dare she think it—maybe they could become good friends. But Muna wondered how it would be possible with her now working evening shifts. Maybe she would go in earlier before Kemi left for the day. Then maybe they could have *fika* together in the kitchen area.

"Gunhild," Muna called out as she left her room and padded

toward the living room. Gunhild had fallen asleep in her armchair, old photos spread all over the place, and a smile crept onto Muna's face. "Gunhild?"

As Muna inched closer, she realized Gunhild seemed to be sleeping with her eyes open, her neck propped at an odd angle on her shoulder. "Gunhild?" she called her again. Those turquoise blues seemed dull, but her face had relaxed the way it often did when she was laughing or in a jovial mood. Her mouth was hanging slightly open with a smirk. Her fragile hands were cradling a single photo in her lap. Her Togolese lover.

"*No, no, no, no...*" The words flew out of Muna like bullets, the same way they had rushed out when she'd witnessed Ahmed set himself ablaze.

"Why?" she cried out to Allah. "Why did it have to be her?" Muna wailed. Why had everyone she had ever loved been yanked so suddenly away from her?

Was love this painful? Was she so difficult to love that it cost other people their lives? Conflicting thoughts raced through Muna's mind as she tried processing her feelings.

"*Hooyo!*" she screamed. "*Hooyo!*" She wasn't sure whether her cries for "Mother" were for Caaliyah or Gunhild, but they echoed through the modest apartment.

Devastation and fear ripped through her. She was all alone in the world once more. She had no one.

Gunhild had been recovering from her radiation treatments. Her body had been too weak. Had Muna conjured up too many memories out of curiosity, flooding Gunhild so her heart could no longer take it all? Had Gunhild finally become happy?

If only she had minded her own business, Muna cried. If only she hadn't dug into Gunhild's past. Khadiija had always called her nosy. Yasmiin had always likened her to a curious goat. Both Khadiija and Yasmiin were no longer in her life. This was what happened when she tried to get too close to people, to learn to love, to build a family. They either went away or died.

Muna fell to the floor as her screams pierced the room. She kept gasping for air, fearing she was never going to get enough oxygen to keep her breathing.

Visions of Ahmed flashed across her mind. Of his disarming smile and golden glare. Of the way he fully took her in as they sat silently in each other's company without needing words to express their love.

And Muna wailed "*Habib Albi*" over and over again as she lay on the floor crushed by her memories. *The love of my heart.*

When the paramedics arrived to move the body later that morning, Muna was sitting on the floor, her back against a wall, her eyes blank. They spoke to her in Swedish, trying to prod answers out of her to their "what, when, how" questions—when she had found the body, what her relationship with Gunhild was like, how long they'd known each other, how her condition was when they'd been laughing together into the previous night.

They suspected complications relating to her cancer and radiation treatments but needed to take the body in for an official autopsy. Their words simply buzzed around Muna inaudibly because none of it was making any sense.

From the corner of her eyes, she saw a team of two work around Gunhild's body, before heaving it onto a stretcher and covering it with a white sheet. Muna didn't turn to look. She kept staring into a void, wondering if she was indeed dreaming. Dreaming that Azeez had actually texted her that Yagiz had given her back her job. Then she could rewind back to the morning and wake up once the alarm clock on her phone actually shrilled.

"We will call you as soon as we have more information," one of the paramedics informed her, worry etched across his olive-colored face as he glanced down at her. Muna didn't turn to look up at him. She simply nodded her response.

"Do you have any family to call?"

Muna shook her head, biting hard on her lower lip. Her tear ducts were dry.

"What about friends?" the man asked. He didn't want her to be alone in the apartment at the moment, he stressed.

Muna shook her head once more.

"Do you have anywhere else to go?" he continued to prod.

Muna remained quiet for a few moments. Yes, there was still one more place where she could go. A place that added purpose to her very existence at the moment.

Muna slowly nodded before mouthing, "Work."

TWENTY-THREE

KẸMI

Kemi burst out of the revolving doors and gasped for air, the cool winter chill rushing into her lungs. She paused to regain control.

Don't panic. Don't panic, she kept telling herself, trying to calm her racing heart. A futile task. She pulled out her phone and booked a taxi through an app. The nearest one was six minutes away. She waited out there in the cold, not risking going back in there when colleagues roamed around like zombies. Ingrid had probably started spreading the news, which would have reached Louise by now. And she knew Louise wasn't one to hold on to secrets, since strategically leaking information was her pastime.

The sounds of a man screaming, "Jocke!" alongside the distant wails of an ambulance's sirens caught her attention. Right across the street from the hotel, something was going on. A man was lying on the ground unmoving, a small crowd was gathering, and a handful of people seemed to be yelling and chasing after someone who had just ducked into the subway.

She had debated taking the train home but knew she couldn't. Besides the commotion unfolding in front of her, she couldn't sit and bear strangers judging her in expensive black lace, out way past midnight. She couldn't let them see trails of mascara running down her cheeks once the tears came.

And she knew they would come because she was disgusted at herself.

The private, nonjudgmental bubble of a taxi was what she needed right now until she could get back home to Nacka and into Tobias's arms. He was probably up waiting for her, watching a crappy movie, curious to hear how her evening went.

She gently rocked herself warm with her back turned against the doors, waiting for her taxi to hurry the fuck up. She needed to get out of there.

"*Hej då, Kemi!*" a familiar voice called out, wishing her good night. A few more "*hej då*"s were thrown her way as groups came out, making their way home or to a nearby joint for more drinks. A clutch of male voices floated into the air, and she closed her eyes when she heard Ragnar's pitch among them.

"Kemi!" Jonny called out. She was forced to turn around. Jonny rushed up to give her a hug, followed by an exaggerated peck on the cheek. "*Tusen tack!* Thank you for another amazing year with us!"

Jonny was clearly drunk. He never touched anyone when sober. She had already deduced this while working with him.

The sirens got louder. The ambulance's blinking lights flashed all around upon its approach, but over Jonny's shoulder, Kemi caught Ragnar's cloudy eyes. They only saw each other.

Jonny was momentarily distracted by the flashing lights as the motion drew him like a sensor. Then he snapped out of his daze.

"*God Jul!*" Merry Christmas! Jonny turned around and patted his friend on the back to prod him along. Ragnar hesitated. He exchanged words in Swedish with his boss-friend, and Jonny waved him off.

Kemi turned away, still waiting for her taxi. One minute, the app assured her. God, please let him go away, she prayed. *Please*. She felt a leather-gloved finger hook one of hers resting by her side. It tugged lightly to get her attention. She didn't oblige him, so he stepped in closer, threading all five fingers with hers. She felt his breath trail her neck, his fresh-forest scent soothing her, and she shut her eyelids. They stood in silence waiting for her taxi.

Right on time, the black cab pulled up in front of them. Ragnar opened the door to let her in. Once inside, she tried pulling it shut, but he slid in right next to her, settling in and taking off his gloves.

"Nacka, *ja*?" The taxi driver double-checked her destination in accented Swedish.

"*Ja, tack,*" she confirmed, strapping herself in. "*Till...*" Ragnar swallowed her words with a swift kiss. Not the frantic desperation they had shared in the elevator. This was calculated, slow-burn lust, dripping into her in bits and pieces. He didn't need to make love to her. He was already coursing through every vein.

The button signaling an unfastened seat belt started beeping, and the driver just watched them kiss in his back seat, unsure of when to jump in to interrupt. The beeping grated as he pulled out of parking mode. His voice rose, urging Ragnar to fasten up.

"*KÖR!*" DRIVE!

Ragnar's voice was terse. It surprised their driver and jolted him into action with a foot on the accelerator. As they sped away, Ragnar unlatched her belt and pulled her toward him, intensifying their kiss, his tongue claiming every inch of her mouth. His hands reached into her coat to find her butt and pinned her firmly to him.

"Ragnar..."

"I know somewhere we can go," he whispered against her mouth before tugging her with another kiss.

"Go home to your wife," Kemi whispered back against his lips, out of earshot of the driver, who kept stealing glances at them. Ragnar pulled back to study her with darkened eyes.

"We can't do this," she continued.

"I know you want me." He was breathless, his hands tightening on her rear, locking her against him so she felt his want too. She reached up to stroke his square jaw, tracing his lower lip with her thumb, and shook her head.

"This is reckless. You're married," Kemi cried. "And Tobias makes me happy."

"Happy enough to be here?" Not waiting for her rebuttal, Ragnar pulled her head down for another scorching kiss while reaching to push the heavy coat off her shoulders.

"Go home to Pia," she whispered uselessly, letting him deepen the kiss anyway, his tongue twisting hers into submission. What else could that tongue do?

"Ssshhh," he hushed, kissing her to stop her from saying his wife's name.

"Nooo, go home. Okay? Go home," she murmured. Her body surrendered, at odds with her words. She let him touch her as she'd dreamed. His hands stroked her arms speckled with goose bumps. They moved down to her thighs, over her long, black, lace ball gown, in search of hems to grab and pull up.

"Please," he pleaded, his voice hoarse. The low rumble of despair and desire. A planet afraid its light source was slipping away. "Let me take you there."

"*Ursäkta!*" the taxi driver called out. "*URSÄKTA!*" *EXCUSE ME!* He raised his voice before proceeding to tell them having sex in his car was forbidden.

Kemi began to quiver against Ragnar's lips. He pulled back, taking in Kemi's crumbling face. He tried thumbing away her tears, but they kept falling faster than he could reach them.

She felt herself begin to shake. Why was she doing this all over again? She thought she'd left this mucky, self-destructive side of herself behind in the States. That soft, self-sacrificing part that drew men who only wanted to empty themselves into her because she truly believed she couldn't have it all. A high-powered executive with the perfect partner who would truly love every imperfect inch of her too.

"What's wrong? What happened?" Ragnar asked, his voice tinged with frustration.

Kemi kept sobbing, and he gathered her into his arms, cradling her. They watched Gamla stan's sparkling lights fade into the distance as the taxi crossed over to Södermalm and made its U-turn toward Nacka.

Ragnar let her cry against his shoulder, lust slowly fizzling out of her body as she became limper with each passing mile. She was silently letting him go. She had fought the turmoil she'd had for months and had won.

Kemi looked up and caught his face flush red. She wasn't sure if it was from shame or anger.

Their attraction felt primordial. If they got together, they'd forever be colliding without enough reprieve or pause to see if they were actually meant to love each other. This wasn't what she needed. She needed something else that Ragnar couldn't give her beyond this ephemeral intensity.

"I have to hand over Bachmann," he said. "I can't work with you."

She didn't protest his decision. He *should* resign for both their sakes. Ragnar was privileged enough to be able to find another client within the week. She wasn't worried about him. Sweden hadn't given her that privilege.

The taxi was a few hundred feet from her apartment when she turned back to Ragnar. He bent low to kiss her. She received his tender kiss, his tongue stroking hers slowly.

Then he murmured words against her lips. "What a waste."

She pulled back sharply and caught his smirk.

When the taxi stopped in front of her building, Ragnar grabbed her right hand before she climbed out and lifted her hand to his mouth.

"Too bad," he said, giving the back of her palm a quick kiss. "You would have been one sweet fuck." He peered at her, and shame washed over Kemi anew.

Ragnar didn't care about her. He was married to his first choice. He was just another Connor who wanted to sample her like cheese handed out on toothpicks.

She was never going to escape herself, Kemi realized now. Running didn't help. She needed balance. Her own moon that would rise and fall with her, keeping her equilibrium, loving her unconditionally. That was true love. Not this. That was how the universe worked. A perpetual state of balance. Ragnar was a sun to her sun. They'd burn each other up within a year. To stay alive, she had to set herself free. What she needed all along was waiting for her in Nacka.

She needed a moon instead.

Kemi yanked her hand out of Ragnar's grip and swept it hard

across his face. He received her hit then turned back to her, his sapphire eyes blazing with spite, his jaw clenched.

Kemi climbed out of the taxi and didn't look back.

She walked to the front door, her head light and shoulders heavy. Calmly punching in the key code, she waited for the familiar opening buzz. Their apartment was pitch-black when she stepped in, save for flickering light coming from the living room. She found a tired Tobias sitting in the dark with a bag of pretzels, watching a movie.

"*Hej!*" he called out, trailing off with a yawn. "How did it go?"

She glanced down at her watch. Twelve thirty-three a.m. He'd waited up for her.

Sliding out of her coat and letting it fall to the wooden floor, she kicked off her black heels then joined him on the sofa. She reached into his bag and grabbed a pretzel in silence. A few moments later, the weed in her brain fell out, uprooting itself completely and transforming into words once it reached her lips.

"Tobias," she called out softly.

"Hmm?" he murmured on the brink of surrendering to sleep.

"Move back to the States with me. Please."

BRITTANY-RAE

Brittany's phone rang and rang, dancing on the nightstand. The tenth time in just fifteen minutes. Then silence once more. She glanced at her phone. Three thirty-five a.m.

Brittany was relieved that Maya was safely hidden away at the hotel and out of Jonny's grasp. She needed space to think. To fully process the fact that Jonny had lied to her face. The one thing she'd convinced herself he couldn't do with conviction, the one thing their entire relationship was built upon.

As depraved as she'd felt when she first thought it, she had basked in the fact that Jonny was obsessed with her and lavished her with attention. That her husband loved her with everything he had. Until she realized she was just a warm, flesh-and-blood stand-in for a ghost.

She had left a good man for him.

Brittany had barricaded herself in one of their guest rooms. At first Jonny had tried pounding his way in. She knew he was scared that he had broken something he could never fix. Not with his money anyway. He kept yelling her name over and over again. Out in their secluded piece of woodland, it might as well have been whispers. He clawed and clawed at the door.

And then he stopped banging.

Now he was ringing from outside that bedroom door. She contemplated calling the police, but she wasn't sure what she would say. *I'd like to report an emergency... My husband is a liar?*

The ringing eventually stopped and then came a low rapping on the door before a female voice came through.

"Mrs. von Lundin?" The soft-spoken British accent of her au pair floated through the door. "Mrs. von Lundin?"

Brittany rushed to the door and leaned against it.

She bit her lower lip, fighting back tears.

"Vicky?"

"It's me, Mrs. von Lundin," she said. "Maya is fine. She's with Mr. von Lundin." Brittany stifled a gasp with a quick palm over her mouth.

"How...how did you get here?" But she already knew. Stockholm didn't belong to her. It belonged to Jonny.

"Louise came to get us from the hotel. She said it was urgent. I had no choice, Mrs. von Lundin."

"It's okay, it's okay." Brittany calmed her breathing. "It's not your fault." Then she gently opened the door to find her au pair standing wide-eyed with remorse. "It's okay."

"They're in Maya's room."

Brittany made her way to the world of unicorns that was their daughter's kingdom. The door was ajar, and she heard giggling. Maya was wide awake as Jonny carried her around the room, still wearing his clothes from the office Christmas party. His hair was disheveled, and he looked tired.

Brittany leaned in through the door and heard him singing. Chanting Maya's favorite nursery rhyme in Swedish as he carried her, rocking from foot to foot, his voice hovering just above a whisper.

Lilla snigel akta dig,
akta dig, akta dig
lilla snigel akta dig
annars tar jag dig.

He turned toward the door and saw Brittany. His exhausted eyes locked on hers, but he kept singing and rocking Maya. She cooed in his arms, basking in her father's love. She was the only one who could bring Jonny to his knees. This sweet little girl called Maya.

He stopped and pierced Brittany with that intensity that often asphyxiated her. He slowly walked up to her, landing in his favorite spot, inches from her face. Then he repeated the last line as he peered at her, singing in a whisper.

Lilla snigel akta dig...annars tar jag dig.
Little snail, be careful... Otherwise, I'll get you.

And at that moment, Brittany knew Johan von Lundin was never going to let her go.

MUNA

"I bet you're fuckable under that bedsheet!"

Those words, delivered in Swedish, were carried on the drunken waft from a stranger's lips. They floated from behind Muna as a whisper, albeit a loud one, into her ear. The man's foul words were followed by a strange hand grabbing her butt and giving it a hard squeeze.

This was why she hadn't wanted the night shift from the very start.

It was past midnight, and Muna stood at a bus station opposite a vibrant hotel emitting loud, booming music with some sort of Christmas party going on inside.

Earlier that Friday, she had popped into Kungshallen to grab her keycard from Yagiz. He had pored over her face, sensing something was deeply wrong with her. He'd asked her if she was okay before handing her a brown paper bag holding a complimentary doner kebab dinner he'd wrapped himself for her. Muna had simply stared blankly back at him. Working that late shift was going to take her mind off what she'd witnessed that morning. Gunhild's eyes glazed over and hanging wide open. Her thin mouth cocked into a small smile. A sad woman who was finally happy. Her substitute mother who had left her all alone. Another member of her family gone.

She spun around to face the offender—the kind of man who would never offer her his seat on the train while sober. He was young. Early twenties maybe. He was wearing a well-fitted, lean-cut jacket with hidden seams that suggested it wasn't cheap. He sported skinny jeans over sleek, black boots. His blond hair was gelled back under layers of grease, and his blue eyes were laughing at her, pupils doubled from intoxication. Typical upper-class *stekare*—brat— from Östermalm, she deduced. The wealthy part of town.

He wasn't alone. Cackling beside him was an identically dressed man, except this replica had darker hair.

"So, are you, *uhn?*" he taunted her in Swedish, trying to grab at her again. "Are you *hooot* under that?"

She slapped him before he could follow those words with another laugh. She kept slapping him again and again as he struggled to peel her off him, while his friend tugged at her jilbab to yank her away. They both succeeded in pulling her from him. Her original oppressor swaggered on his feet, swaying from side to side.

"*Jävla idiot!*" he cursed at her, spittle flying before screaming at her to go the hell back to where she came from.

Back to where she came from. Those words developed prehistoric claws. They slashed her skin, ripping flesh, spilling blood, reaching bone. She had already been to hell.

As he stood shouting, arms flailing and failing to balance him, all Muna saw was his mouth moving, no more recognizable words following. Her hands flew at his chest with the strength and confidence of a woman on a mission. She was tired of feeling helpless every day. She thudded him with such brutal force, it caught him off guard because beer had turned his arms into jelly.

As she felled him like a log rotted by termites, she saw his eyes widen in shock for a split second. He hit the concrete pavement cleanly, the back of his skull breaking his fall instead. She heard a crushing sound and froze, watching as his friend dove down to assess his condition.

"Jocke! JOCKE!" his friend howled, trying to shake life into a man whose eyes were still open while blood pooled around his head like a red Afro.

Muna stood there stunned, trying to figure out what had just happened, what was happening. She saw people approach as if in slow motion as the guy continued pulling and shaking his friend, willing him to respond.

Once her brain thawed, the first signal it fired off to her body was flight. "*Run for your life, Muna!*" Those nerve endings delivered in Morse code.

Muna turned and ran as screams of "*Ta fast henne!*" Catch her! filled the air. Her gown billowed around her, giving her the weightlessness of jellyfish floating in the Mediterranean.

She had to get out of downtown. She ducked into the nearby subway station as people chased her, hot on her heels, but she dared not look back. They would grab her and lock her in that dark space of isolation she had crawled out of.

She ran at such speed, it propelled her through the ticket control gates, pushing a commuter pressing his card to enter in front of her. Muna fell to the ground on the other side to screams from people jumping aside. She quickly scrambled back onto her feet, possessed by her mission to hop on the first train out. The pounding of feet behind her suggested more people had joined the pursuit. She took the stairs three steps at a time, her gown parachuting her down toward the tracks.

She made it just in time as the green line toward Farsta strand was pulling out from the tunnel. She ran toward it, willing its doors to open midmotion but knowing full well they wouldn't until the train had pulled to a complete stop.

Images floated into Muna's mind as she ran. Caaliyah's floating gown. Aaden's boyish grin. Mohammed's hoarse cough. Ahmed's honey eyes glowing with love. Gunhild's turquoise ones filled with warmth. Everyone she ever loved was on the other side. Muna knew that was where she needed to be.

So she pushed her fellow passengers aside and jumped.

———

Minutes later, a female voice came on over the intercom in Swedish. It apologized to passengers for the delay.

There had been an accident on the green line.

YOU ARE NEVER ALONE

While you may feel isolated, there are support systems you can reach out to who truly care about you and deeply understand what you may be going through.

Please reach out if you need someone or know someone who needs extra love and a listening ear.

Samaritans—Call 116 123—www.samaritans.org

CALM—Call 0800 58 58 58—www.thecalmzone.net

Shout Crisis Text Line—Text "SHOUT" to 85258—giveusashout.org

Always choose hope.

AUTHOR'S NOTE

On autism and being on the spectrum...

I wanted to create a very complex character in Jonny. One with multiple layers of discomfort caked on by a lack of transparency and full acknowledgment. Coupled with his immense privilege, this level of denial within his family can create opaque worlds around people with special needs.

Many of you dear readers might have deduced that Jonny has an undiagnosed condition. My intent is not to link any speculations of autism or being on the spectrum to his fetishism.

Far from it.

After all, I truly believe being on the spectrum comes with its own superpowers.

Rather, I wanted to show how important speaking openly about issues is and how giving one another the special support we need is essential to living our best lives.

While having an undiagnosed condition does not justify bad behavior and Jonny remains fully accountable for his actions, I often imagine what he would have been like if his family had used their privilege to give him the tools and resources he needed to fully wear his skin.

What if Astrid, Wilhelm, Antonia, and Svea had looked Jonny in the eye as a child, told him he was different, helped him embrace his superpowers, and let him know it was okay?

One of the things I appreciate about living in a society built on balance and homogeneity is the fact that it tries to make everyone feel like they aren't different, but therein lies its downfall. This unflinching need to not recognize and amplify what makes each of us uniquely beautiful means some very deep issues are often skimmed.

We are in fact all perfectly different, and what makes us different needs to be fully celebrated within society.

READING GROUP GUIDE

1. We see three very different Black women in this novel. How do you think each of their backgrounds informed the choices they made?

2. The themes of tokenism and fetishization are prominent in this book. Discuss how they each played out with the women and what impact that had on them in the book.

3. There are many comparisons between Swedish and American societies. What did you find different about how the two countries handled issues of racism and sexism? Was there something about the setting in Stockholm that changed your perspective about the social issues tackled in this book?

4. Kemi seems to make a spur-of-the-moment choice to move to Sweden. Why do you think she did this? How did her sister's opinion factor into her decision?

5. Jonny's infatuation with Brittany borders on unhealthy, and yet there is a part of her that is drawn to him in the beginning. What about him do you think she found appealing? How did her past relationships factor in?

6. At Brittany's birthday party, Kemi awkwardly stumbles during their conversation and insults Brittany. Why do you think the author chose *not* to have these two Black women become friends?

7. Muna experiences a tremendous amount of loss in the novel. What do her experiences show of the struggles refugees go through when displaced from their homes?

8. Kemi's relationship with Ragnar is unhealthy almost from the start. What does her final interaction with him show about her own growth and what she's learned about herself in Sweden?

9. Throughout the novel, Muna develops many short-lived relationships, with the longest being her uncomfortable acquaintance with Yagiz. Why do you think these relationships are transient, and what do you think the author is trying to convey in her relationship with Yagiz?

10. Jonny's privilege and the protection his money affords him ultimately become problematic for Brittany and her child. What do you think the author was trying to say about wealth, choice, and accountability at the end of Brittany's story?

11. Kemi, Brittany, and Muna only have one small interaction with all three of them on the page together. Why do you think the author chose for them not to interact more?

A CONVERSATION WITH THE AUTHOR

What was the inspiration for *In Every Mirror She's Black*? What did you draw on as you developed the story?

In Every Mirror She's Black was a story that organically developed after years of living in Sweden and observing how the voices of Black women resonate within society, which spaces we are invited to occupy or not, and if those spaces allow us to thrive or simply survive. Having lived in both Nigeria and the U.S. for extended periods of time before moving to Sweden, I wanted to pull out the nuances of navigating the world in my skin against the backdrop of very different cultures.

You took on some very serious social issues in this novel: racism, classicism, sexism, fetishization of Black bodies. Why did you feel it was important to tackle each of them in this book?

They often say debut novelists are quite ambitious because we want to tackle every single societal problem in a single book. With *In Every Mirror She's Black*, I wanted to address them in a seamless way while spotlighting all these issues because they aren't mutually exclusive.

At what point does racism become tokenism as one moves into a certain economic class, and isn't tokenism a form of racism? Can one have sexism without some form of fetishization?

So simply picking one issue to focus on didn't make sense to me. In reality, they all blend into one another because life is frustratingly complex and multilayered.

You're a Nigerian American woman living in Sweden. How did your own experiences inform each of the three main characters' stories?

Right away, I want readers to know that I am not Kemi, nor is her life based on mine. With that out of the way, making her Nigerian American meant I could pull from cultural references to root her. Brittany is a physical metaphor for the "acceptable" Black woman in society, one who is meant to be perfect in every way, including physically. With Muna, I spent time as a photographer regularly visiting an asylum center in Sweden, getting to know newly arrived refugees like Ahmed and Muna, and vowed to help give space to their individual voices.

I wanted each of the women—Kemi, Brittany, Muna—to be free of having to carry the weight of society simply because they are Black. Even though they are strong, I wanted to give them space to make mistakes and to humanize them deeply. The world asks so much of us Black women, and we're tired of being held to triple standards.

What are you hoping readers will walk away from your book thinking about or talking about?

To me, the power of *In Every Mirror She's Black* is that everyone will walk away with something different. It could be anything from fully understanding that Black women are not monoliths to the effects of denial on not confronting issues, and how isolating and excluding even the strongest among us can end in tragic loss. There is no one specific "Black culture." The same privilege of treating White people as individuals is long overdue for Black people.

Ultimately, each of these women has a sort of tragic ending. Why did you make that choice?

It is extremely important for us as Black authors to write stories that keep uplifting Black joy and Black hope. That would have been the cliched ending many people would have expected me to write, to tie everything up neatly because we're tired of reading about Black pain. However, for me, based here in Sweden, the soil isn't even fertile enough to allow Black women to thrive and grow. So, how could I transparently address Black joy when we're still not confronting the problems that prevent Black women from thriving here?

The three women don't interact very much at all in the book. Why did you opt to keep them isolated and disconnected from one another?

This harkens back to my goal of presenting each of them as individuals and not the bearers of a nonexistent homogenous Black culture. I wanted Muna to be fully seen as her bright-eyed innocent self and not have to bear the burden of carrying the entire Somali community on her very young shoulders. I wanted Brittany to be fully seen as herself, a woman who wants the finer things in life without being judged as being Black bourgeoisie. And I wanted Kemi to be seen as her imperfect ambitious self, who shouldn't be afraid to fail when many African parents pressure their kids to always succeed.

I also wanted to show that not all Black women are automatically friends or have much in common. One of the most insulting things a White person can say to their sole Black friend is, "Oh, I met another Black person today! Do you know them? Maybe you should meet and become friends?"

I wanted to reflect all this in the book in a nuanced way.

Muna's life seems to be filled with so much tragedy for someone so young. Was there something that inspired you to tell the story of a refugee?

Many years ago, while writing my book *LAGOM*, I came across a Swedish proverb that says "The deepest well can also be drained," and it arrested me. That even the strongest, most resilient among us can eventually break too because we are human.

I loved Muna's character so deeply and often cried when I wrote her life out on the page, because I connected with her deep isolation the most. As someone who has been isolated and sidelined so many times, personally and professionally, I could feel Muna's pain in trying to create connection and understanding of who she truly is as an individual.

As previously mentioned, I often visited an asylum center deep within the Swedish countryside, and it was simply to spend time with asylees and set up photo shoots for them so they fully see themselves without the labels of being "refugees" as they awaited news about their migration status. Even the name of the fictional center in *In Every Mirror She's Black* called "Solsidan" is named after one of Sweden's most affluent neighborhoods as tongue-in-cheek.

Many of us who live in Sweden have heard those announcements about train accidents. I wanted to put a name and face that we've grown to love on one of those nameless announcements.

This is your first adult novel. What advice would you give to young writers out there?

The very same advice I gave in the opening credits of the book: Your voice is more powerful than you think. You are allowed to exist without explanation even if you feel uninvited, unappreciated, and invisible. Never, ever let the world convince you that your struggles are invalid.

And I'll end with my absolute favorite quote from E. E. Cummings: "To be nobody-but-yourself—in a world which is doing its best, night and day, to make you everybody else—means to fight the hardest battle which any human being can fight; and never stop fighting."

ACKNOWLEDGMENTS

These beautiful characters wouldn't have come to life without my family and an entire community of friends and champions propping me up all along the way.

I am deeply thankful to my agent, Jessica Craig, who realized she had signed a crazy person with unearthly perseverance and a strong resolve that just never quits.

To my wonderful Head of Zeus family, including Clare Gordon, Kate Appleton, Lizz Burrell, Jessie Sullivan, Jade Gwilliam, and everyone who has championed IEMSB. Thank you for amplifying Kemi's, Brittany-Rae's, and Muna's voices.

To my dear friend Leigh Shulman and my sister, Dami Ákínmádé, for turning my first draft into something worthy. To my special beta readers and friends for all your invaluable feedback, which steered the initial manuscript along in the right direction: Andrea Pippins, Astrid & Bengt Sundgren, Anja Mutic, Kimberly Golden, Kristin Lohse, Merci Olsson, Gerry R. Bjallerstedt, Lily Girma, Maddy Savage, Irene Nalubega, Kendra Valentine, Lizzie Harwood, Pamela MacNaughtan, and Dr. Alia Amir.

Thank you for listening to me incessantly talk about this book, especially Janicke Hansen, Yomi Abiola, Lyota Swainson, Par Johansson, the late Sandra Carpenter, Germaine Thomas, Meryem Aichi, and everyone at our ladies' dinners.

To my beautiful family near and far who continue to keep me grounded and loved. Thank you, Urban, for this wild ride and for your steadfast support.

And to God for graciously challenging me to fully trust His timing and my journey.

ABOUT THE AUTHOR

LỌLÁ ÁKÍNMÁDÉ ÅKERSTRÖM, Nigerian-American and based in Sweden, is an award-winning author, speaker, and photographer. Her work has appeared in *National Geographic Traveller*, the *Guardian*, *Sunday Times Travel*, the *Telegraph*, the *New York Times*, *Travel + Leisure*, *Slate*, and *Adventure Magazine*, and on BBC, CNN, Travel Channel, and Lonely Planet TV, among others. In addition to contributing to several books, she is the author of *Due North*, the 2018 Lowell Thomas Award winner for best travel book, and the bestselling *LAGOM: the Swedish Secret of Living Well*, available in over seventeen foreign language editions. She has been recognized with multiple awards for her work, including the 2018 Travel Photographer of the Year Bill Muster Award, and she was honored with a MIPAD (Most Influential People of African Descent) 100 Award within media and culture in 2018. Her photography is represented by the *National Geographic* Image Collection. She is based in Stockholm and tweets at @LolaAkinmade.